NORTHERN TWILIGHT

THE HIGHLANDS SERIES

BOOK FIVE

SAMANTHA YOUNG

Northern Twilight

A Highlands Series Novel

By Samantha Young
Copyright © 2024 Samantha Young

Cover Design By Hang Le
Couple Photography by Regina Wamba
Edited by Jennifer Sommersby Young
Proofread by Julie Deaton

Also by Samantha Young

ABOUT THE AUTHOR

Samantha is a *New York Times*, *USA Today*, and *Wall Street Journal* bestselling author and a Goodreads Choice Awards Nominee. Samantha has written over 60 books and is published in 31 countries. She writes emotional and angsty romance, often set where she resides—in her beloved home country Scotland. Samantha splits her time between her family, writing and chasing after two very mischievous cavapoos.

ACKNOWLEDGMENTS

Thank you to my friends and family who had to listen to me agonize over Callie and Lewis's story and whether I was doing justice to their epic romance. A special thank you to Catherine Cowles who had to hear it on a daily basis, lol, and read an early version of their story just to reassure me! You're an awesome friend, Catherine, and I'm so grateful to you.

I have to thank my amazing editor Jennifer Sommersby Young who is always tremendous and encouraging and wise and smart and kind. Thank you, my friend.

Thank you to Julie Deaton for proofreading *Northern Twilight* and catching all the things.

And thank you to my bestie and PA extraordinaire Ashleen Walker for helping to lighten the load and supporting me more than ever these past few years. I really couldn't do this without you.

The life of a writer doesn't stop with the book. Our job expands beyond the written word to marketing, advertising, graphic design, social media management, and more. Help from those in the know goes a long way. A huge thank-you to Nina Grinstead, Kim, Kelley, Sarah, Josette, Meagan and all the team at Valentine PR for your encouragement, support, insight and advice. You all are amazing!

A huge thank you to Sydney Thisdelle for doing all your techy ad magic to deliver my stories into the hands of new readers. You make my life infinitely easier and I'm so grateful!

Thank you to every single blogger, Instagrammer, and book lover who has helped spread the word about my books.

You all are appreciated so much! On that note, a massive thank-you to the fantastic readers in my private Facebook group, Samantha Young's Clan McBookish. You're truly special. You're a safe space of love and support on the internet and I couldn't be more grateful for you.

A massive thank-you to Hang Le for creating another stunning cover in this series. You are a tremendous talent! And thank you to Regina Wamba for the beautiful couple photography that brings grown up Lewis and Callie to life.

As always, thank you to my agent Lauren Abramo for making it possible for readers all over the world to find my words. You're phenomenal, and I'm so lucky to have you.

A huge thank-you to my family and friends for always supporting and encouraging me.

Finally, to you, thank you for reading. It means more than I can ever say.

For my cousin Clare.
Love you lots.

PROLOGUE
CALLIE

EIGHT YEARS AGO

Caelmore, Scottish Highlands

"Are you okay?" Lewis asked as I lay wrapped up tight in his arms.

A thrill of giddiness thrummed through me at the feel of his strong, naked body. Lewis's striking blue-gray eyes were filled with tenderness and awe. Sometimes I couldn't believe he was mine. Not just because he was the most beautiful boy I'd ever seen in my life, but because that beauty ran deep. Lewis was kind, attentive, smart, and funny.

And he belonged to me now, as I belonged to him.

That night we'd given each other our virginity.

No one else would ever have *that* from either of us.

The very thought of Lewis with another girl sent a bolt of panic through me, and I crushed it by kissing him fiercely.

"I'm more than okay," I answered breathlessly when we finally broke the kiss.

He slid a hand around my nape and brushed his lips across my mouth. "I love you so much, Callie Ironside."

"I love you too." Feeling him pulse against my stomach, I giggled. "Again?"

He grinned, dropping his forehead to mine. "Ignore it. You'll be sore."

A twinge throbbed between my legs. "We can do other stuff."

Lewis groaned. "I want to ... but we need to get you home before my dad or yours finds us."

We'd taken to sneaking into Lewis's parents' guest annex at the side of his house. So far we hadn't been caught, but Lewis was sure our luck was going to run out. A glance at the alarm clock on the nightstand told me it was nearly midnight. Usually, I told little white lies to my parents that I was at a friend's house sleeping over, but I hadn't tonight because I hadn't expected to have sex with my boyfriend.

If anyone had been leading the physical side of things, it was me. Lewis was a perfect gentleman. I'd told him weeks ago I was ready to have sex, but he said he didn't want to rush me. Tonight we'd snuck into the annex to fool around, but things escalated quickly, and I wasn't sorry for it.

Lewis wasn't merely my boyfriend. He was my best friend. Since I'd moved to Scotland with my mum when I was ten years old, Lewis had been an important part of my life. He'd taken me under his wing because he sensed I'd been through something. And when I went through something even more traumatic, he was right there at my side. Ever my protector.

As we got older, we shared our pasts with each other. I knew that Lewis and his wee sister Eilidh had lost their mum and had been through a terrifying home invasion experience a few years before my arrival. We, unfortunately, had trauma in common. But fortunately, having my best friend understand a horrific moment in my life had made me feel less alone and not as scared.

Lewis was protective and affectionate, and he always had my back.

I'd known since I was thirteen that I wanted him to be the kind of best friend I kissed every day. It had taken him a little longer to catch up. He'd been afraid of ruining our friendship. But when I'd started dating our classmate and Lewis's friend, Michael Barr, everything changed. Lewis was jealous and hurt and finally admitted he wanted me to be his girlfriend. Poor Michael got caught in the crossfire, and when I broke up with him to date Lewis, he stopped talking to both of us.

However, I was happy to report that he and Lewis had gotten their friendship back on track this past year. Michael was dating Lana, a girl in our year who lived in Golspie. All was well again. In fact, we had a nice friendship group that made school fun. Lewis's best friend since first year, Fyfe Moray, was now one of my close friends, too, and even more so since he'd started dating my friend Carianne.

Maybe we'd end up all getting married at the same time and raising our kids together. The thought filled me with excitement for the future. I wanted to work at my mum's bakery in Ardnoch, maybe take over running it when she was ready to retire, and live there for the rest of my days. After living my first ten years in LA, I could, hand on heart, say I never wanted to live anywhere but my wee village in the Scottish Highlands.

Lewis wanted to be an architect like his dad, so I imagined him working for his dad's firm in Inverness and us building our house here in Caelmore on the edge of Ardnoch where the rest of his family had built their homes.

A perfect, simple, happy life.

I smiled dreamily at the thought and felt Lewis's chest vibrate with his laughter.

"What's that look for?"

I grinned harder. "Just really happy."

His expression softened. "I'm glad. Me too."

Spotting the twinge of worry in his eyes, I laughed. "But we need to get me home, I know."

The truth was, I didn't blame Lewis for being a little nervous. My stepdad, whom I thought of as my *dad* dad, was a former Royal Marine and built like a brick shithouse. He probably knew how to kill a man and get away with it. Lewis might be a newly minted black belt in tae kwon do (as was I), but there were very few people who could go up against Walker Ironside and win.

With one last kiss, I rolled out of Lewis's arms and got up to get dressed. In the end, we helped each other dress, copping a feel here and there, kissing and laughing, and taking twice as long to do it.

Eventually, we snuck out of the annex and got onto our bikes. Lewis never let me cycle home alone, even though it was only a six-or seven-minute bike ride. It was the height of summer, so it wasn't fully dark. This far north, between May and August, there was no true nighttime. And between the end of May and the end of July, there was no astronomical twilight. Tonight, the sky was the dusky dark blue of nautical twilight.

We'd switched on our bike headlamps, anyway, in case we passed a vehicle, which we did. But soon we were cycling into the quiet street that housed my parents' bungalow. Slowing a few houses down, I hopped off and curled my fingers into Lewis's shirt to bring him down for a kiss. He was six foot three and still growing. My boyfriend bent his head and kissed me voraciously. Skin flushed hot, I reluctantly broke the contact.

I couldn't wait to have sex with him again, and I could see the same thought in his eyes.

"Mum and Dad are going to Inverness tomorrow to buy a new car, and your mum is taking Harry and Morwenna to the petting zoo," I whispered, referring to our respective younger siblings. "We'll have the house to ourselves."

"What time?" Lewis asked gruffly.

"I'll text you when they're getting ready to leave."

He nodded and bent down for another kiss. "I can't wait. I love you."

I smiled against his mouth. "I love you too."

Lewis waited until I'd settled my bike against the side of the house and slipped into the front door before he left.

I could still feel the throb of him between my legs as I toed off my shoes and crept quietly down the hall toward my bedroom. My brother, Harry, slept in the room across the hall from me, but that boy could sleep through a rave.

Mum had texted me earlier to ask when I was coming home, and I'd lied and said we were watching a late movie with Lewis's parents. Hopefully, that lie wouldn't come back to bite me in the arse.

The tiptoeing was pointless, because when I walked into my bedroom, it was flooded with light and my mum sat on the bed, her back against my headboard.

Guilt flushed through me as she stared like she could see right down to my soul.

For a long time, it had been us against the world. And then we'd moved here, and a shit ton of bad stuff happened that I didn't like to think on too long before Mum and Walker fell in love. Walker quickly made me fall in love with him, too, and he'd been Dad ever since.

He'd legally adopted me after he married Mum because they both wanted peace of mind that if something were ever to happen to Mum, I couldn't be taken away from Walker. And when Mum fell pregnant with Harry, I was even more glad to legally be my dad's. I wanted us all to have the same name and feel like a real family, without any half-sibling labels or feeling like I maybe didn't belong to him the same way Harry and Mum did.

Mum and I were still as close as two peas in a pod. When she'd first told me she was pregnant with Harry, I was excited but also a bit afraid that it would change our special bond. It hadn't. Not even a little. And only for my love of Lewis Adair would I lie to her.

"You didn't need to stay up," I whispered as I crossed the room to open my chest of drawers. Pulling out my pajamas, I couldn't quite meet her eyes.

"I wanted to make sure you got home all right." She still had a strong American accent. There was a slight inflection of Scottishness on the ends of her words, but that was about it.

"Lewis made sure of it." I sat down on the bed, waiting for her to get up.

I was practically my mum's spitting image. She fell pregnant with me when she was sixteen years old and had me at seventeen, so she looked way too young to be mother to a seventeen-year-old. We had the same long blond, wavy hair, same eye shape, and the same nose and apple cheekbones. The only differences were my mouth, which was slightly fuller, and my eyes were light blue while hers were brown.

Silence stretched between us, and my gut churned. I disliked keeping things from Mum. I usually told her absolutely everything. But I knew she feared I'd follow in her footsteps and get pregnant as a teen, too, so I couldn't tell her about my night. Lewis and I had been safe, and I was happy, and I didn't want her parental concerns to ruin it.

Finally, Mum sat up and nudged me with her elbow. "Everything okay? Was the movie good?"

Feeling terrible, I nodded.

Her gentle touch on my chin brought my head around. Our eyes met.

Mum's drifted over my face, searching. Knowing seemed to settle in her expression. "I thought you'd look different, but you look the same. My beautiful Callie."

"Mum?"

She sighed heavily. "Please tell me you were safe."

It shouldn't surprise me that she knew. Mum always seemed to have a sixth sense when it came to me. "Mum ..."

"We've never kept things from each other before, so let's not start now."

"Even ... this stuff?"

"It terrifies me you're growing up so fast ... but even this stuff."

I licked my lips nervously and finally admitted, "We were safe."

The breath whooshed out of Mum and she leaned into me. "Did he look after you? Are you okay?"

I reached for Mum's hand. "He loves me, Mum. He loves me so much and I love him. Sometimes I feel like I might explode with it. Like ... as happy as loving him makes me, it hurts too."

Mum covered our hands with her other. "That sounds like real love to me."

"I'm not going to do anything stupid," I promised her.

She met my gaze. "Callie, you are the best thing that ever happened to me, and I wouldn't change having you for the world. But I want you to have your entire childhood, and mistakes happen. So ... on Monday, I'm making you an appointment. I'd like you to go on birth control."

Relief flooded me. I'd been so scared she was going to ask me to stay away from Lewis. "I can do that."

Her lips pinched together. "And unless he asks me outright, we're not telling your father."

The thought of Dad learning about Lewis and me having sex sent a nervous chill down my back. "That's probably for the best."

Mum patted my hand again. "No more lying to me, though."

"I'm sorry. I didn't ... I'm sorry."

"I know you are. I know you love him."

Mum began to stand, but I grabbed her hand to stop her from leaving. She looked down at me expectantly. "He's my Walker Ironside, Mum. I'm going to marry him and make a family with him, and we're going to raise them right here. I don't want to have a kid as a teenager, but I want you to know that whatever happens, as long as I have Lewis and I have you and Dad and Harry, I'll be the happiest person in the world."

Her eyes shimmered with unspent emotion as she reached out to caress my cheek. "I believe you, baby girl. I'm happy for you. It's scary for me seeing you grow up ... but all I want is your happiness. And if you've found yourself your own Walker Ironside, I'm the happiest mom in the world. But you will *not* be a teen mom. Ever."

I nodded because I truly didn't want that either. "I love you."

"Love you more than life." She tapped my nose. "Now get some sleep, Juliet. I'm sure you want to see your Romeo in the morning."

I wrinkled my nose. "Love that play, Mum. But bad comparison. That ended tragically. Lewis and I won't."

She smiled. "I know. Night, baby girl."

"Night, Mum."

I waited for her to leave the room and then sank into my

bed. Another silly, dreamy smile lit my face as I stared at the ceiling. I couldn't wait to grow up and buy a house with Lewis and share a bed every night. To wake up to him and then, after a morning of sweet lovemaking, I'd head off to work with Mum at the bakery.

It seemed like a dream that I could be this happy. I knew not everyone was given this kind of bliss or found the love I'd found as a teen. However, my start in life hadn't been great. Mum had tried her hardest to make it good, and I'd always felt her love ... but my real dad was a nightmare, and he'd attempted to make our lives a nightmare.

First Walker and then Lewis had felt like the universe's way of paying me back for my rocky start.

Now I couldn't wait to start living the next part. Mrs. Adair. I giggled into my pillow. One day, I'd be Mrs. Callie Adair.

I'd miss Ironside as a surname because it was bloody sick, but I'd give up practically anything to make Lewis mine forever.

Mine forever.

I couldn't wait for forever to start.

ONE
LEWIS

PRESENT DAY

London, UK

There were people here I didn't even know.

The hotel's roof terrace was packed with familiar and not-so-familiar faces. I'd put the latter down to my wee sister Eilidh, who'd gained a number of so-called friends since she'd had success acting in a popular British dramedy. We'd both ended up in London, and in an effort to prove she wasn't being sucked into the world of celebrity—that family was still the most important thing to her—Eilidh had insisted on throwing me a graduation party.

After seven long years, I was finally a qualified architect. Just like my dad.

I turned my head and locked eyes with the man I'd probably always hero-worship. I didn't think that was a bad thing.

To respect and admire my father. If my future kids felt the same way about me as I felt about Thane Adair, I'd die a happy man.

Dad stood drinking a glass of champagne with my step-mum, Regan. They'd been married for so long and had given me and Eilidh our wee sister, Morwenna, that Regan would always be Mum to me.

A hard hand clapped my shoulder, and my fellow graduates Gary and Sean suddenly appeared in front of me. "Mate, your sister knows how to throw a party," Gary said, stuffing a canapé into his mouth. "She said after the free food and champagne, we're all hitting the nightclub in the basement of the hotel. Is she single, your sister?"

I gave him a flat smile before replying blandly, "Touch my sister, and I'll fucking end you before you've ever truly gotten a chance to begin."

Gary raised an eyebrow. "What is it with you Scotsmen and your bloodlust?"

"I think it's more he doesn't want a lecherous bastard like you near Eilidh," Sean offered dryly.

In answer, Gary's searching gaze moved through the crowd toward my parents. "So, I take it that means I'm also not allowed to say that Lewis's mother is a smoke show? Seriously, Lew ... if the phrase *MILF* had a spokesperson, your mum would be it."

An old irritation sizzled in my gut. For years back home, kids had teased me about my mum. She was younger than Dad. So they teased me about that, about how attractive she was. In high school, they'd said some repulsive things, and Callie had often talked me down from retaliating. I soon learned she was right. The more I reacted, the more they did it. Gary, unfortunately, was one of those.

I took a sip of my beer. "I dare you to say that in front of my dad."

"Protective is he?" Gary's attention flickered to Dad.

"Understatement."

"Yes, well, I'd be protective of that prime piece—"

Sean smacked our mutual acquaintance across the back of the head. "Where are your fucking manners, man?"

Gary winced. "Bloody hell, I was joking."

I sighed wearily. For most of my life, I'd been impatient with guys like Gary. I think I came out of my mother's womb as a forty-year-old. My birth mum, Francine, died not long after Eilidh was born, so I wasn't even three yet. I couldn't remember a thing about her. All I knew of her were photographs that revealed a woman who had given me and Eilidh dark hair in a sea of blond Adairs. And the stories Dad had told us whenever we asked. Even from those, I couldn't discern what else I'd gotten from Francine.

I knew for a fact I'd gotten my seriousness from my dad.

It wasn't that I didn't know how to have fun or laugh.

But the things most lads my age found funny, I found stupid and immature. It had made me feel like an outsider most of the time. The only people I'd never felt that way with were my best friend Fyfe ... and Callie. And my family, of course.

Yet I was truly considering staying in London and joining the same architectural firm as Gary? We'd both done our last two years of practical experience at Wyatt, Johnson, and Baird, a prestigious firm that had won two RIBA (Royal Institute for British Architects) awards last year. They'd offered us both a position, which we hadn't expected. We'd been in low-key competition for what we thought was one spot.

The thought of seeing Gary day in and day out irritated me.

But it was more than that.

Unbelievably ... I was homesick.

And I had been for a long time.

As if he sensed I needed a rescue, my dad led Mum over to us.

Sean tapped Gary on the arm. "Let's grab another drink."

I thanked my friend with a nod. Sean I *would* miss because he was taking a position at a firm in Manchester.

My dad was only a few inches shorter than me, and he wrapped his arm around my shoulders. "So proud of you, Lew."

"Thanks." I patted him on the back and then leaned down to kiss my mum's proffered cheek. "Where's Morwenna?"

My youngest sister was thirteen years old this year and the complete opposite of Eilidh. While Eils had always been outgoing, outspoken, and social, Morwenna was quieter and preferred her own company most of the time. According to Dad, she'd found a group of friends at high school that she spent a lot of time with, but on the few occasions I'd ventured home or when my family had visited me, Mor usually had her nose in a book. The age gap between us meant we weren't as close as Eilidh and I were, but I hoped she knew she always had me.

"She opted to stay in the hotel and read," Mum said in her only slightly diluted Boston accent before she nibbled her bottom lip. She and her sister, my aunt Robyn (married to my dad's brother Lachlan), were transplants from the US, and neither of them had entirely lost their accents the way Callie had. "Your father assured me she was safe to do so."

"The door is locked, she has her phone, and she will call us if she needs us." Dad slid an arm around her waist.

I frowned. "I'm not sure I'm keen on Mor being left alone. You should go be with her."

"But it's your graduation party."

Snorting, I gestured around. "I barely know half the people here. It's an Eilidh party."

"Your sister means well," Dad reminded me.

"I know that. But honestly, if you need to get back to Mor, go. I'm good."

Mum reached out to take my hand. "Are you sure?"

"Of course. Thank you for coming all this way."

She gave me a quizzical smile, the dimples in her cheeks flashing. "Sweetheart, my son just graduated. Where else would I be?"

Longing for my family scored through me. It seemed foolish and childish to still need them like this. I pulled Mum into a hug, her familiar perfume cascading over me and filling me with nostalgia.

"Your dad wants to talk to you. Please hear him out," Mum whispered in my ear before pulling back to press a kiss to my cheek. "We'll see you tomorrow for breakfast."

I nodded, bemused, and waited for her to kiss Dad good night before she strode through the crowd toward Eilidh.

Dad's attention lingered on her, and I recognized the love in his expression. He was lucky. He'd found the love of his life and managed to keep her.

Some of us could not say the same.

Finally, Dad turned to me and gestured to a quiet corner of the terrace that overlooked the city. "Let's talk."

I followed him out of the crowd and into that small space of privacy. London stretched before us like a dark blanket sewn with a thousand golden lights. A cascade of neon stood out across the Thames as the London Eye lights reflected in its waters.

"What's up?"

Dad leaned against the balcony. "I want you to consider coming to work for my firm in Inverness."

There was that pang of longing again, this time fiercer, more painful. "Dad ..."

"I'm a partner now. My name is on the building. I get to hire who I want. And this isn't nepotism, Lewis. The work you've done is incredible, and it fits our firm to a tee. You could create some special sustainable buildings in the Highlands. And we could use a fresh eye."

"I've already said yes to Adam Wyatt." I referred to one of the partners of the firm who'd offered me and Gary positions.

"So?" Dad shrugged. "You're allowed to change your mind, Lew."

I stared out at London and as much as it had been the place I'd lain my head every night for the past seven years ... it had never felt like home.

"If this is about Callie ..."

"Don't."

Dad exhaled slowly. "After all this time?"

I couldn't talk about her. And I knew my family probably thought I was crazy and obsessive, and as far from the mature man I professed to be, but seven years later ... no, I was not over Callie Ironside.

I probably never would be.

Which was why I couldn't go home. Too many memories. It hurt too much. I had to hope that someday, I would move on. I just didn't think I could do that in Ardnoch where every street was laced with the memory of her.

"The offer stands, son." Dad squeezed my shoulder. "There's a place for you no matter what, no matter when."

Emotion thickened my throat. "Thanks, Dad."

"At least if you're here, you can look out for Eilidh." Dad glanced over his shoulder, back toward the party. "There's not a day that goes by I don't worry about her. That she chose this life, following in her uncles' footsteps ..."

"For now." I followed his gaze to where Eilidh was holding a small group of men's attention, gesturing wildly as she told them one of her many stories. They laughed at all the right parts, their eyes devouring her in a way that made my skin crawl. Sometimes I wished she were more like Morwenna. Easier to protect her that way. But Eilidh was Eilidh, and honestly, I wouldn't change her for the world.

"She misses Ardnoch. I know she does. I reckon one day she'll follow her uncles' footsteps all the way home," Dad said gruffly.

Both of my uncles—my dad's eldest brother Lachlan and younger brother Brodan—had made names for themselves in Hollywood. Uncle Brodan had been an acclaimed actor until he'd returned home to Ardnoch to marry his childhood sweetheart, my aunt Monroe. Uncle Lachlan had returned long before that to turn our family's ancestral castle and estate into a members-only club for film and TV professionals.

Now he and Uncle Brodan also ran a whisky distillery. With their fame and money and coastal smoky whisky that was actually bloody good, the brand was a success. It had taken a few years, but Ardnoch Whisky was becoming a household name. It was even more popular in Japan than it was here.

"Do you think so?"

"I do."

"I suppose the allure of Ardnoch *is* strong," I said without thinking.

"I can only hope so," my dad answered. At my silence, he leaned forward. "Lewis."

His tone forced me to look at him.

"For the longest time after your mother passed away, I was afraid to live for anything but you and Eilidh. When Regan came into our lives, she terrified me. And I pushed her away."

I frowned because I was seven when Regan first started working as our nanny. To me, it seemed like my parents quickly fell in love, got married, and she became my mum. "I didn't know that."

He nodded. "You've probably forgotten. But I was unkind to Regan. You even gave me a telling off for pushing her away."

I didn't remember that. There were some things about that time I'd never forget, but I didn't remember that.

"I'm ashamed of how I treated your mum."

That didn't seem right at all. My dad treated Mum like she walked on water.

"But fear can do strange things to us. It was only when I realized that I couldn't live without her that I decided to fight my fears and win her back."

"What fears?"

"Of being hurt again. Of losing her. She was younger, and I was afraid that one day she'd wake up and want something different."

"But you loved her enough to fight your fears?"

"I did." Dad gave me a sympathetic smile. "I think I knew when you were fifteen that what you felt for Callie was deeper than puppy love."

An emotional sting burned across my chest. "Dad—"

"And it fucking kills me that after all this time, you're still in pain." His voice was gruff now. "But, Lewis, you cannot live your life making choices because you're afraid of that pain."

His words ricocheted through me, freezing me to the spot.

"You will regret it, son, and I don't want any of my children to live with regrets." He cupped my nape, giving it a firm squeeze, and suddenly I was a boy all over again. "If you want to come home, you come home ... don't let anything or anyone stop you. You get me?"

I nodded, too overcome with emotion to speak.

Dad pressed a kiss to my forehead. "Proud of you, Lew."

"Proud of you," I forced out.

"I'll see you in the morning."

I nodded again as he released me and strode away to say good night to Eilidh. For a moment, I watched my sister and father embrace.

Maybe Dad was right. Maybe I was letting fear stop me from being back with my family.

Turning to stare out at the city again, I contemplated what life in Ardnoch would look like now, if I was remembering it through rose-tinted glasses and I'd miss the hustle and bustle of the city. Or if that longing for a quieter pace of life, for golden beaches and rugged mountains and wild weather, was more than nostalgia.

For years, I'd longed for something beyond Ardnoch, and it seemed impossible and almost cruel that I could miss it as much as I did. Considering it was my desire for something *more* that had lost me Callie.

I pulled my phone from my pocket and swiped the screen. Tapping the social media icon, I opened the app and searched her name.

Her feed was a collection of photos of her, the baked goods she'd created, France, and the people she'd met there.

One of her latest photos glared up at me. Like the masochist I was, I tapped on it for the hundredth time.

Callie's beautiful face was wreathed in smiles as she beamed into the camera while *he* pressed a tender kiss to the corner of her mouth. The caption said: "Another day in Paris with him." The lips and heart emojis followed.

She'd tagged the Frenchman in a clutter of photos throughout her feed for the past year. His name was Gabriel Dumont. The year before him, there had been Remy. She'd dated that Frenchman for a few months. Both were good-looking bastards, and I hated them with the fire of a thousand suns.

A part of me hated Callie too.

Because she said she'd never leave Ardnoch.

But there she was in Paris at a baking and pastry school. Dating French men. I clicked on another photo of them. Callie had clearly taken the selfie of them kissing beneath the Eiffel Tower. My gut twisted.

"What are you doing?"

I jumped, almost dropping my phone. Glaring at my sister, I ignored her knowing look. "Where is your harem of men?"

Eilidh nudged me. "They're boring. All they do is talk about how much money they want to earn, what car they want to buy, what TV shows they've booked."

"You invited them."

"No, I invited my castmates, who invited everyone else in London." She leaned her elbows against the balcony, facing me. "You still look at her social media?"

Glowering, I stared straight ahead. "You're too nosy for your own good."

"Maybe. But I'm worried my big brother is pining his life away."

I'd already had this discussion with our dad and I wasn't in the mood to have it again. "Eils—"

"It's been seven years, Lew."

"So everyone keeps telling me."

"Well, I'm not telling you to move on."

That drew my gaze to hers.

Eilidh stared back, expression fierce. "I'm telling you to go find her."

My heart rate increased at the thought. "What?"

"Go find Callie. See if what you had is still there. Because if what you feel for her isn't true love, big brother, I'm not sure I know what is."

A sudden deluge of grief crashed down on me. "It's not. I

was just ... tonight made me nostalgic. Anyway, even if I did feel that way, and I'm not saying I do, she's moved on. With a Frenchman."

"Gabriel."

I raised an eyebrow.

Eilidh licked her lips nervously. "Callie and I still talk. We're still friends."

"Oh."

"I'm sorry. I should have told you. I ... I never know if I should mention her or not."

I smiled wryly. "Hasn't stopped you before."

"I didn't want to hurt you."

"You being friends with Callie doesn't hurt me." Though it filled me with a million questions. How was she? How had the last seven years of her life been? Did she even want to live in Ardnoch anymore? Why did she leave when she said she never wanted to? Why ... why did she leave when she couldn't leave for me?

"Well ... her boyfriend's name is Gabriel. He's a police officer. They've been dating for nine months and—"

"Eilidh, I don't want to know about him." I cut her off. "It's none of my business."

My sister fell silent, and I refused to look at her. Sometimes all she had to do was stare into my eyes and she'd know exactly how I was feeling.

"Come to my wrap party next week."

I was unsurprised by her abrupt subject change. The show Eilidh was on had finished filming its third season. She played a pessimistic, world-weary young Londoner who couldn't be further from the real Eilidh if she tried. To be honest, I was blown away by her performance. She'd been given some tough scenes to depict, and I was in awe of her talent.

Eilidh started showing an interest in acting at the end of

primary school. She'd been accepted into Glasgow's Royal Conservatoire junior summer school throughout her high career. She'd wanted to attend full time, but our parents weren't happy with her living alone in Glasgow. Eilidh had gotten accepted into the conservatoire as a full-time student at seventeen. Between that and our uncles' connections, she'd booked several jobs throughout as a teenager and during her time as a university student. Then she landed this part three years ago, and her life changed dramatically.

While it had never been strange for me that people recognized Lachlan and Brodan when we were out and about, it was weird when people recognized Eilidh and acted like they knew her.

She had nearly five *million* followers on social media.

"What?" she asked, frowning.

"Nothing."

"So, is that a no to my wrap party?"

I didn't particularly feel like going. I'd been to the last one and felt like a fish out of water. "I'll be there. Just let me know where and when."

"Thanks, big brother." She pushed away from the balcony to hug me. I wrapped my arms around her, and the years seemed to melt away and she was my wee sister who needed a hug every day from everyone she loved. Eilidh had always craved affection. Sometimes I longed for that simpler time. Tenderness filled me, and I kissed the top of her head.

"Your audience awaits," I teased.

Eilidh pulled back. Her eyes were the exact shade as mine, and I could still see the concern in them. "Love you, Lew."

"Love you." I shoved her gently toward the crowd. "Now, go enjoy."

"You too." She grabbed my arm, pulling me with her. "This is your graduation party, and I won't let you mope the night away."

I grumbled under my breath, but I didn't really mean it. In fact, I grabbed a beer as soon as we hit the bar. Because I *was* a broody bastard tonight. It was probably graduation stirring up all those old ghosts. However, I was done with them.

I wanted to drown the memories that had risen up to plague me.

TWO
LEWIS

TEN YEARS AGO

My gut churned.

Pushing away from my computer, I practically jumped to my feet and started pacing. It felt like there was this energy inside me that had no place to go. Between that and the gut churning, I was agitated beyond belief.

Fyfe spun in his chair and pulled off his headphones and mic. My best friend's eyebrows were practically in his hairline. "What's going on?"

We'd been in the middle of playing *League of Legends* with two lads from Glasgow when I'd made my abrupt departure. But I couldn't think. Couldn't concentrate.

What was going on?

I was an idiot. That was what was going on. "I ... uh ... I don't feel so great."

"Aye?" Fyfe put the headphones back on and told the lads

we needed to finish up for the evening. He turned back to me. "Should I head home?"

Considering I was the worst company ever right now, I nodded. "I'll see you out."

We were halfway down the stairs when Fyfe asked quietly, "It doesn't have anything to do with Callie going out with Michael tonight?"

He'd heard, then.

"I don't know," I answered truthfully.

Fyfe gave me a look. When we reached the bottom of the stairs, Eilidh, who was sitting at the island chatting with Mum, jumped off her stool. Her big eyes were locked on my best friend.

"You're not leaving, are you? We're making pepperoni pizza, just for you." Eils batted her eyelashes at him.

My sister had made it clear this past year that Fyfe Moray was her latest crush. It annoyed the hell out of me, which only made her flirt with him more.

Fyfe smirked and nudged his glasses higher up his nose. "Thanks, but I've gotta go."

Eilidh pouted. "Are you coming around tomorrow?"

My friend looked at me. I nodded. He nodded in turn to Eils, who practically bounced on the balls of her feet. "We'll make you pizza then too. Bye, Fyfe." She blew him a kiss and hurried back up onto the stool.

I glowered at Mum as if to say *Do something about that*, but Mum merely chuckled and shook her head.

Once outside, I waited as Fyfe got on his bike and said, "Sorry if Eils is making you uncomfortable."

Fyfe grinned. "It's fine. She's kind of hilarious."

"She has 'Eilidh loves Fyfe' scrawled all over her sketch-pads. I think these drama lessons are making her worse."

"She's just a kid," he said with the sage wisdom of a fifteen-year-old. "It's fine. Text me later."

I waved as he cycled down the drive onto the single track that led out onto the main road back to Ardnoch.

As soon as he was gone, I saw Callie in my mind, her chin tilted back in defiance as I confronted her about Michael Barr. Michael at least had the decency to tell me he and Callie were going to the movies in Inverness. Callie's mum was dropping them off, and Michael's stepmum Kenna was picking them up.

I knew Michael had always liked Callie. She'd told me he'd asked her out a year ago and she'd said no. But ... she'd changed her mind. Because of me.

In a foul mood, I stormed back into the house.

"Pizza's almost ready," Mum called to me.

"Eat it yourselves," I huffed and took the stairs two at a time. Slamming my bedroom door behind me, I prayed my mum and sister left me alone as I dove onto the bed and slipped my headphones on. Biffy Clyro filled my ears, and I tried to ignore the panic that gripped my chest.

———

It wasn't Mum or Eilidh who walked into my room later that evening.

Dad popped his head in a few hours later, and I reluctantly slipped off my headphones. "May I come in?" he asked.

I nodded and scooted up against my headboard, waiting as Dad sat down on the end of the bed. He gestured to my headphones. "Who are you listening to now?"

"Biffy Clyro." I'd only gotten into them because my dad and uncles liked the older band.

He grinned. "Good taste."

I stared down at my lap, unable to engage in small talk.

"Your mum says something's up."

Callie's face flashed before me again. The hurt in her eyes.

Then the determination. I should have known what that determination meant.

If Michael kissed her tonight, I'd lose my fucking mind.

My hands unconsciously clenched into fists.

Dad noticed. "Talk to me, Lew."

"I'm fine."

"You're not fine."

He waited patiently. Then, "Does it have something to do with Callie going on a date with Michael tonight?"

My head whipped up. "How do you know about that?"

Dad's expression was neutral as he replied, "You know Kenna helps out at your mum's daycare now and then. She told her about the date."

"Right." I'd forgotten that Michael's stepmum filled in whenever one of Mum's full-time staff was on leave.

"So ... is it a problem for you? I know you and Callie are best friends and you and Michael are friends ..."

"It can't be a problem for me." I shrugged. "I told Callie I just wanted to be friends, so she can do what she wants."

Dad frowned. "Do you mean Callie told you she wanted to be more than friends with you?"

Months ago. And I'd wanted to kiss her and tell her I felt the same way. But ... "She's my best friend, Dad. And I know I'm not supposed to say shit like that—" I winced at the curse that slipped out. "Sorry."

Dad waved off the apology and gestured for me to continue.

I sat forward, running a hand through my long hair. "Callie is one of the most important people in my life. If we started going out and then something happened and we broke up ... I'd lose her. And I can't lose her."

"So ... you have those feelings for her? Romantic feelings?"

My heart rate picked up and I huffed. "Who wouldn't? She's amazing. I know how amazing she is. Michael only wants to go out with her because she's the prettiest girl at school. Wanker." This time I didn't wince at cursing in front of my father.

Dad smirked. "I thought Michael was your friend?"

"Until he went after Callie. He knows what she means to me."

"Does he?" His question was asked quietly, but it still made me flinch. "Lewis ..." He reached out and patted my knee. "I wish it wasn't true, but you've been through so much already, losing your mum a big part of that. You hold on to people so fiercely, and I admire that about you. But I don't want your fear of losing people to stop you from living. You're fifteen. If you want Callie to be your first girlfriend, you should not let the fear of losing her friendship get in the way. Life is too short, son."

Guilt suffused me. "What if ... what if she doesn't want me now, anyway? What if I did something?"

"Like what?"

I saw Callie's hurt face over and over in my mind. "We were all at Fyfe's birthday party last weekend." Fyfe lived with his mum, and she wasn't around a lot. Whenever we wanted to hang out without parental supervision, we went to Fyfe's, even though his place was small. His eighteen-year-old neighbor and her friends dropped by with some beer. I got a bit drunk and got talking to her. We were in the back garden, talking one minute, and the next she was kissing me. "I got off with this older girl who was there."

Dad raised an eyebrow. "Got off as in ..."

"Just kissing, Dad."

"Right. And Callie found out?"

She'd interrupted us. I nodded, swallowing hard against the guilt. The hurt on her face had killed me. I felt like I'd cheated on her, and we weren't even dating.

"But you don't like this other girl?"

I shook my head vehemently. "*She* kissed me, and I didn't ... stop it. But I don't like her. I love—" I cut off.

Dad was good enough not to give me a patronizing smile. "You love Callie?" he asked seriously.

That panic in my chest flared.

I nodded.

"Not dating her isn't going to change that, Lew. You either give it a chance and risk losing her ... or it seems like you lose her for definite if you don't. You're at that age where her boyfriend will become the person she spends all of her time with."

"What if she's too mad at me to give me a chance?"

Dad grinned. "Callie Ironside thinks the sun rises and sets with you, son. That doesn't go away because of one moment of hurt. You can apologize and tell her the truth."

"You really think so?"

"I know so."

That nervous agitation thrummed through me again. "Will you give me a lift to her place?"

"Now?"

I nodded. "I want to be there when she gets back from ... her date."

Dad sighed but stood up. "Okay. But what about Michael?"

The thought of hurting my pal didn't sit right with me either, but he'd gone out with Callie, knowing what it might do to our friendship ... so fair play and all that. "We'll figure it out later. Callie's more important."

"Get your shoes on, then."

———

Callie's mum, Sloane Ironside, could very well pass for Callie's big sister. In more ways than physical appearance. They both had this optimism and goodness that radiated from them, which was amazing, considering everything they'd been through.

When she opened the door to find me on her doorstep, Mrs. Ironside gave me a sympathetic, knowing smile. I was also sure I saw relief in her eyes as she stepped aside to let me in.

Mr. Ironside was a different story. Callie's dad never said much because he didn't need to. He could terrify a bloke just by looking at them.

We sat in awkward silence as I waited for Callie to come home.

Then Mr. Ironside broke the silence. "Better you than Barr, I suppose."

For Ironside, that was almost a blessing. Mrs. Ironside seemed to think so because she gave me an encouraging smile.

I cleared my throat. "Where's Harry?" I referred to Callie's brother.

"Sleeping."

Right.

Because it was like ten o'clock at night and I was severely intruding.

Guilt filled me. And discomfort.

"Can I get you a drink?" Callie's mum offered for the hundredth time.

"No thanks, Mrs. Ironside."

"Lewis, please call me Sloane," she pleaded for the hundredth time too.

The sound of a car pulling up outside made my heart leap into my throat. At least I knew with Michael's stepmum in the car, there would be no good-night kiss. Although that didn't mean there hadn't been kisses at the cinema.

My hands clenched at my sides. Feeling someone's eyes on me, I turned and saw Mr. Ironside looking at my fists.

I unclenched them.

He looked me in the eye, but his expression didn't give away his thoughts. The man was a big affectionate giant with Callie and Sloane. I'd seen it. With everyone else, he was slightly scary and a lot intimidating.

My palms turned clammy at the sound of Callie letting herself into the house. She walked into the sitting room, lips parted as if about to speak, and then froze at the sight of me.

I drank her in.

Jealousy burned in my chest.

Her long blond hair was styled in waves, she wore a bit of makeup, and her legs went on forever in the long-sleeved mini dress she wore with ankle boots. She was so bloody gorgeous, it made everything inside me ache.

But it was more than those big blue eyes or the full lips I'd fantasized about kissing a million times ... it was her. Callie. The person who knew me inside out and not only accepted everything that was me but liked it all. She'd made it clear that she was never going anywhere.

Until I'd hurt her.

I stood abruptly.

Her eyes flared. "What are you doing here?"

Her mum winced at the high-pitched question. "Why don't you two talk outside so you don't wake your brother?"

Callie glowered at me. "You're unbelievable."

I gave her an apologetic look, which only seemed to make her angrier, but she gestured for me to follow her into the kitchen and out of the sliding doors.

As soon as she'd closed them behind her, she crossed her arms defensively over her chest. "What the hell are you doing here, Lewis?"

Before I'd been nervous as anything, but now with her in front of me, I felt nothing but determination. "I made a mistake. Months ago, when you told me you wanted us to date, and then last weekend."

Hurt flashed across her face. "What? You accidentally tripped into her mouth?"

I blanched. "Callie ... it was stupid. I'd had too much beer, and I ... I regretted it immediately. She's not the one I want to kiss."

"So, someone else asks me out, and all of a sudden, you have a change of heart?"

"No. I realized today that I could lose you for real. And the only reason I said no to dating was because I didn't want to lose you. I didn't want something to happen, for us to break up and I'd lose you for good. I can't lose you, Callie. You're the most important person in my life. I ..." I let out a shuddering breath. "I love you."

Her expression slackened. "What?"

I swallowed against my nerves and stated more boldly, "I love you, Callie Ironside."

Doubt and fear crept in as she stared at me for a few seconds. Then she crossed the distance between us, grabbed my hand, and tugged me to follow her around the side of the house.

"What—"

She whirled and pulled me into her before she threw her arms around my neck. Her warm, soft body flushed against mine, and my skin was instantly on fire. "I love you too."

And then her lips touched mine.

Utter relief flooded me, and I wrapped my arms tight around her, lifting her off her feet to meet my mouth more fully. I pressed her up against the side of the house for leverage and kissed her like she was fucking oxygen.

It felt right.

Perfect.

And I was an idiot for waiting so long to make this girl mine.

But I'd never be an idiot with Callie again. I'd never, ever let her slip through my fingers. How could I?

It would be like losing a part of myself.

THREE
CALLIE

PRESENT DAY

Ardnoch, Scottish Highlands

Stepping back from the plate of patisserie cakes I'd created for my mum, I eyed her, feeling almost as nervous as when I'd baked anything for my teachers. I'd spent the better part of the last three years in Paris at a top culinary school, earning my bachelor's degree in French pastry arts. Between classes and internships at some of the busiest restaurants in the city, I'd not only grown in experience but in confidence.

And yet, I was still nervous to make the pastries I wanted to sell in Callie's Wee Cakery. My mother named her bakery after me, not knowing that I'd grow up to want to follow in her footsteps. I loved every hour I'd spent here as a child, baking with Mum. Some of my fondest memories, both while we were in LA and here in Scotland, include the days spent in the kitchen with her.

By the time I was fifteen, I'd known with certainty that I wanted to stay in Ardnoch and help Mum run the bakery. That never changed. But after a few years in the village doing just that, I'd yearned to learn more than what Mum could teach me. She understood that. So I applied to the school in Paris because I was lucky enough to have a parent who not only believed in me but could afford the fees.

I missed my family. I missed Scotland. But I was glad I left the Highlands to experience a bit of the world, to earn my degree, and to learn through missing it that our wee village was exactly where I wanted to be.

However, every time I talked about coming home and bringing all I'd learned back with me, my mum either got quiet or changed the subject. I'd begun to wonder if she didn't want me working at the bakery and taking it over one day.

She'd been strange with me ever since I returned home a few days ago. I'd begun to worry that maybe I assumed too much when I announced all those years ago that I wanted to work with her. And now that I was back, she didn't *want* me back. While I was gone, she trained a young lad called Phil from Golspie, and he was now her assistant baker. I tried not to get nervous or jealous about that. But now I had to wonder … maybe she didn't need me anymore.

"These look too beautiful to eat, Callie." Mum stared at the pastries in awe. "Ardnoch won't know what's hit them. But are you sure you have time to bake such complicated pastries for the store? Are you sure we can charge what we need to charge to cover the cost of the ingredients?"

I nodded. I'd worked all of that out already when coming up with my creations.

I'd taken classic French pastries such as the Saint Honoré and modified them, made them smaller. They were somewhere between the size of an entremets and a petit four. My specialty was choux pastry. Two of my teachers had claimed I had the best choux in my year.

Mum finally cut her fork into the dessert. It was six profiteroles filled with salted caramel diplomat cream, glazed in chocolate hazelnut, with diplomat cream piped between them in the shape of a star. A seventh glazed profiterole topped the star. I watched in glee as Mum's eyes rolled with pleasure.

"Ohmagawd ..." The mouthful muffled her words.

"You like?" I beamed in delight. There was nothing that brought me more joy than when someone enjoyed my desserts. Especially Mum, because she was such a fantastic baker.

However, Mum finished chewing and got worryingly quiet.

"Mum?"

Her eyes flew to mine. And I saw guilt there. "You should be a pastry chef in one of the finest restaurants in Paris. Not here in Ardnoch."

Understanding dawned, and with it a humongous wave of relief. "Oh, Mum ..." I rounded the large island in the bakery's kitchen. "Is that why you've been weird since I got home?"

She chewed her lower lip. "I don't mean to be. But I'm so worried that you've left behind *everything* in Paris because you feel obligated to be here."

Hearing the emphasis on *everything*, I winced before drawing her into a tight hug. We were the same height—five seven—and since my return home, I'd been mistaken for Mum several times by villagers. As I'd gotten older, we'd only grown more alike. When I posted photos on socials of the two of us, I got so many comments from friends about how young Mum looked and how similar we were. I considered it a huge compliment.

She hugged me so hard it was almost painful.

I squeezed her back. "I'm home because I want to be home."

When Mum released me, I looked deep into her eyes. "Home is where you are, where Dad is, where Harry is. And I'm grateful that Ardnoch is where you are because it's home to me. It has been since we arrived fifteen years ago. Paris was a wonderful experience, and I'm so glad I did it. But I don't regret leaving it behind. Any of it. Including Gabriel."

She searched my eyes for the truth. "You didn't love him, then?"

I shook my head. I'd met Gabriel through a classmate. He'd been a sexy, charming, hardworking police officer. He worked in a tough arrondissement in the north of the city. Out of the nine months we'd been dating, I'd say we'd spent the equivalent of four of them together. He was exactly what I'd needed after Remy, my first boyfriend in Paris. Remy was a fellow student and arrogantly confident in a way that was sexy at first. But he'd needed to feel superior to me, and when I started excelling in class, moving past him, he resorted to insults and belittling comments, so I kicked him to the curb.

Gabriel had been complimentary and sweet and our relationship had been wonderfully shallow. However, his evasiveness not only became annoying but raised alarm bells. I never met any of his colleagues, didn't know anything about his family, and in the last few months of our relationship, he'd grown even more distant, cagey, and he'd started drinking more. I knew his job was difficult, but I also didn't feel like he'd ever let me in long enough to be a safe place for him to come home to. The fact was I didn't have the energy to find out. I didn't *want* to find out. It hadn't hurt a bit to break up with him, and honestly Gabriel had seemed relieved when I broke it off. We'd both known I would be leaving Paris once I graduated.

Mum sighed. "Your social media posts were very deceiving, then. You two ... you looked in love."

I raised an eyebrow. "We did?"

"Very much so."

"Well, we weren't, I assure you." I could never love someone as closed off as Gabriel. "I know absolutely nothing about him beyond the obvious stuff. He wouldn't tell me about his family, if he was originally from Paris or not ... it was all superficial. He was always working, so I barely saw him."

My mum seemed to deflate before me. "Oh, thank God. I've been so worried that you were giving up this amazing life in Paris because of a promise to me."

"Don't you think I would have told you if I was in love?" I'd told her every detail of my life. She was my best friend. Shaking my head at her silliness, I pulled her in for another hug. "I am exactly where I want to be, Mum."

"I'm so glad," she whispered, sounding a little teary.

When we finally released each other, Mum picked up her fork and dug into the Saint Honoré again. She shook her head in wonder as she moaned around the bite. "These are going to sell out fast," she said once she'd finished. "Let's take the others home to your dad and brother."

"Sure." I watched as she boxed up the selection of pastries, feeling nervous again as I considered broaching another topic I wanted to discuss. As Mum grabbed the keys to lock up, I finally blurted out, "How would you feel if I opened the bakery an extra day? You wouldn't have to be here," I hurried to say.

Mum only opened the bakery three days a week. It was one of the reasons that made it so successful because people, including tourists, clambered to get to the bakery first thing on the days it opened. We were usually sold out by one o'clock in the afternoon, sometimes by ten a.m. during the summer months.

She considered this. "I only open three days a week because of the early hours. Do you really want to be up at three in the morning four days a week?"

"I was thinking I could do a lot of the prep work the night before. In fact, I was thinking of introducing that idea to the bakery in general. If we make the right things, we could do that."

"Not bread." Mum shrugged. "The bread has to be freshly baked."

"So, I don't make bread on day four."

Mum shook her head. "You'll get nothing but complaints from our regulars."

"Not if we market it as patisserie day. And I was thinking, maybe I could handle the running of the bakery so you can concentrate on the cake-making side of things." Mum specialized in celebration cakes, like weddings and birthdays. Her cakes were to die for, and she had a strong following on social media for her creations. But she was extremely exclusive and difficult to book because she only had time to do so many, what with the running of the bakery.

"Actually, I was going to run that idea by you, so I'm happy to do that. But I think we still need to discuss this day-four idea." She opened the back door, gesturing me out. "Why don't you settle into things first and we'll see how it goes?"

I nodded, knowing I couldn't throw all my ideas at her at once. "Sounds like a plan."

Once we were settled in the car, we chatted a bit about recipes. Anytime I'd returned home from Paris over the last three years, I'd shown Mum the things I'd learned, and she soaked it all up like a sponge. She wanted more lessons, and I was more than happy to oblige. We never had so much fun than when we were baking together.

As we drove down Castle Street, the village's main thoroughfare, my chest filled with a happy ache. It was almost summer, so the days were longer this far north. The Victorian streetlamps that lined the village were only beginning to glow, and the car park out front of the Gloaming was filled. The

historical architecture and design of the village appealed to
tourists as much as the celebrities staying on the village
outskirts. Everything predated the mid-twentieth century, and
dominating it all, near to the Gloaming, sat a medieval
cathedral.

Shops, restaurants, and bed-and-breakfasts were scattered
throughout the village on quaint row streets. Castle Street was
the main road off the square that led out of Ardnoch toward
Ardnoch Castle and Estate. It was an avenue of identical nine-
teenth-century terraced houses with dormer windows. Many
of the homes had been converted into boutiques, cafés, and
inns. There was Morag's, a small grocery store and deli that
did great sandwiches, and Flora's, the most popular café in
Ardnoch, and, of course, Callie's Wee Cakery.

Some of the row cottages, however, remained residential.

"Oh, there's Ery and the twins." Mum slowed to a stop,
and I gaped at the sight of the two tall beings at Ery's side as
they strolled from the Gloaming to an SUV. "Ery!"

Eredine Adair was the willowy, elegant wife of Arran
Adair.

One of Lewis's uncles.

I wanted to sink a little deeper into the passenger side as
Lewis's Aunt Ery and cousins looked our way. The twins were
Kia and Keely. The girls were the spitting image of their
mother. And tall. They had to be teenagers now. How had
that happened? It didn't seem that long ago when I'd been
allowed to hold them in my arms as babies. Back when ... well,
when I'd been as much a part of the Adair family as I was of
my own.

A different kind of ache spread across my chest. A less
than pleasant one.

"Is that Callie?" Keely, the more outgoing of the twins,
yelled before loping toward the car. She was all long limbs and
awkwardness, in that in-between stage where you haven't

quite grown into your body. Her pretty, light hazel eyes lit up as she stopped by the driver's window, grinned at Mum, and then ducked her head to greet me. "You're back!"

Mum flinched slightly at the loud yell by her ear but shot me a grin.

"Look at the size of you two," I huffed, forgetting my awkwardness in Keely's bubbly presence. "How many inches have you grown since I was last here?"

"Three!" Keely hopped onto the balls of her feet. The twins had taken up dance at a young age and did ballet, tap, and all the things. They'd constantly been on the move as kids, and it didn't look like much had changed. "Are you really back, then?"

Before I could answer, Ery and Kia approached. "I am," I said to them all.

Ery gave me a soft smile. "It's good to have you home." Her gaze turned to Mum. "You must be so happy."

"Unbelievably."

"Hi, Kia." I waved at Keely's twin sister. The girls were identical, but Kia had her father's blue eyes instead of her mother's hazel. It was the one thing that made it easy to identify each girl.

She gave me a soft smile much like her mum's. "Hi, Callie."

"We were just grabbing dinner with Arran." Ery, like me and Mum, was originally from the US. Unlike me, but much like Mum, she'd hung onto her accent. "He's working the late shift because a bartender quit suddenly. He's there all week, so we're taking the chance to spend time with him when we can. Aren't we, girls?"

Arran Adair owned and ran the Gloaming, the local pub and hotel that had been a vital part of Ardnoch for centuries.

"We're heading home from the bakery. You guys need to

stop by soon. Callie is introducing the most delicious pastries known to man," Mum said proudly.

"All that hard work in Paris has paid off?" Ery asked.

I nodded. "Definitely. I'm excited to share what I've learned."

"Well, we're all very proud of you, Callie."

My cheeks flushed at her kindness. No matter what had transpired between me and Lewis, I was grateful that his family hadn't allowed it to affect our interactions. "Thank you. That means a lot."

"We better get going. See you soon." Ery stepped back from the car.

"Callie, do you want to go hiking sometime soon?" Keely asked as her mum led her away.

"I'd love that."

"I'll call you!"

I grinned as we waved and drove off.

"She's desperate to be older," Mum explained. "Keely. She'll latch on to you like you're her new best friend."

"I'll take all the friends I can get," I joked. Even though it wasn't really a joke.

All my friends from school had left Ardnoch, scattered across the country and parts of the world. We commented on one another's posts on social media, but that was the extent of the friendship. My best friend here had always been Lewis, and his sister Eilidh was also one of my closest friends. Eils and I still talked, but she was living her life in London.

And so was Lewis.

He didn't have social media, so I couldn't check in with him. But sometimes Eils would post a photo of Lewis. And I'd find myself staring at it for hours.

He'd only gotten more handsome, and his hair was even longer now. At least it was when she'd posted a photo of him last week. He'd worn it in a man bun, and he had enough scruff on his face for it to qualify as a short beard.

My heart physically hurt as I took in the streets of Ardnoch. On every single one, I saw the ghosts of me and Lewis. As kids riding our bikes through the streets. Then as teens, ducking down quiet lanes to make out beyond the eyes of the local gossips. His arms around me, his hand in mine, our laughter ringing in the air.

I didn't believe happiness was a constant. I believed we had moments of happiness that made life worthwhile.

But I didn't use to think that. Back then, with him, I was happy almost all the time.

Pain long buried thickened my throat as those memories hit me in wave after wave.

This was the drawback to coming home.

Lewis was everywhere.

And nowhere.

Because he was gone.

And I hated him for it.

I wished, after all these years, I could be over it.

But I despised Lewis Adair for not loving me enough.

For tainting my home with memories so sweet, they stung like razor cuts.

"You okay over there?" Mum asked as we pulled into our cul-de-sac.

"I'm fine," I lied. But it wouldn't be a lie forever. Just because Lewis Adair had shattered my heart seven years ago didn't mean I was ready to give up on love.

In fact, now that I was home, I was determined to be open to a deep, meaningful relationship. I'd plant new memories with a new guy here, and I'd erase every single ghost of Lewis from the streets of Ardnoch.

As if I'd conjured thoughts of them, my phone buzzed in

my purse, and when I pulled it out, I tensed at the name on the screen. Eilidh.

> Come to my wrap party next weekend. Not an invite, but a command. You haven't been to any of my TV stuff, and I'm prepared to guilt you into it.

"Who is it?" Mum asked as she parked on our drive behind Dad's Volvo.

"Eilidh. She wants me to go to her wrap party next weekend. She's practically demanding I go."

"Then you should go."

"It's in London."

"It's a quick flight."

I nodded, my thumbs poised over the screen. Then, "Do you think *he'll* be there?"

Mum hesitated a second. "I don't know. I do know he graduated last week and has a permanent position at a firm in London—"

"How do you know that?"

She gave me a strained smile. "You know Regan and I are friends, and we made a pact not to let what happened between you and Lewis come between us. She was excited and proud and wanted to share her news about her son."

That was fair. Even if it was the one part of small-town life that had proven to be a pain in the arse. "So, he might be there."

"Who knows? He might be too busy for a party. Are you really going to let him stop you from doing what you want? You haven't before."

True. I wanted to go to Eilidh's wrap party. It sounded fun. And I missed her. Although we spoke every week, I hadn't seen her in over a year. She came to Paris for a few days at the beginning of last year, but that was the last time we'd seen each other in person.

> I'll be there. Just tell me where and when.

Mum chuckled as she got out of the car. "I take it you said yes."

"I did."

"Good. Guess you need to book some flights."

My phone buzzed.

> Ahhhhhhhh! I can't wait to hug you and squeeze your gorgeous fucking face!!!

I burst into laughter. Eilidh was worth the risk of seeing Lewis, I promised myself. Even as my gut suddenly felt like an entire kaleidoscope of butterflies had taken up residence in it.

FOUR
CALLIE

NINE YEARS AGO

"I can't believe your parents are trusting you two to camp together," Michael said with a knowing smirk.

"Uh, correction, they're trusting us all to camp together ... and they're trusting Lewis. Not me."

Our friends laughed as Lewis shook his head with a wry smile. He knew it was true. While my boyfriend had been a total gentleman the past year we'd been dating, I was the one leading the way with the physical part of our relationship. Lewis was all about taking it slow because he didn't want me to feel rushed or to regret anything we did together.

"*Our* parents are cool with *us*," Michael's girlfriend, Lana, reminded him.

"And ours are trusting me and Fyfe," Eilidh threw in as she helped Lewis's best friend build his tent.

Fyfe looked up in panic. "Eh, what?"

I bit my lip against a smile as Lewis huffed, "You and Fyfe aren't dating, Eils."

"Only because Fyfe is stubborn." She stood up, hand on her hip. Tumbles of black curls fell down her back, the dark hair and olive skin only making the blue of her eyes more striking. Even at fourteen, Eilidh Adair was a beauty. But still too young.

"And completely uninterested in you," Lewis informed her gently.

"Let *him* say that."

Fyfe's expression said he wanted to melt into the soil beneath our feet.

"He's dating Carianne." I gave Eilidh a chiding look because Carianne was my friend.

"And where is Carianne?" Eilidh asked, all sass.

"*Her* parents don't trust *me*." Fyfe scowled as he put the last peg in his tent. "I'm going to get firewood."

"I'll come with." Eilidh followed him.

"Eilidh—"

I grabbed Lewis's arm, stopping him. "Leave her. She really doesn't bother Fyfe."

"Until the day she really doesn't bother him." Michael waggled his brows.

Lewis scowled. "What does that mean?"

Lana smacked Michael across the shoulder. "Hush, you."

"What?" He shrugged. "I'm just saying. Eils is cute. And in a few years' time, a couple of years won't matter."

"She's my wee sister." Lewis had gone worryingly blank-faced. "The first bloke who tries to go there dies."

Michael nodded. "I get it, bro."

And he did. Michael's wee sister, Willow, was a lot younger than us, but the sentiment was the same.

"What do you think she sees in Fyfe?" Lana whispered. "He's kind of a geek, no?"

Irritation thrummed through me. "Eh, he's smart, he's nice, he's good-looking ... need I go on?"

Lewis nudged me. "Should I be worried?"

I rolled my eyes at his teasing. "Never."

"Sorry. I didn't mean to insult him." Lana shrugged. "I just don't get why she's so obsessed with him. I'd get it if it was Michael."

"Of course you would." Michael winked, and I rolled my eyes at his cheesiness.

Lewis, however, stared off into the woods where Eilidh and Fyfe had disappeared. "She's had a crush on him since she was eleven. We'd taken off on our bikes and I told her she couldn't come with us. She followed us, anyway, and I got really pissed off and shouted at her like I never had before." Guilt flashed across his face. "She burst into tears and ran away. Fyfe told me I was a dick, and he went after her. Two wee shits in Eilidh's year had found her and were pushing her around. Fyfe knocked them on their arses, and they took off just as I got there. Fyfe was her hero that day, and she hasn't stopped flirting with him since."

I laughed because it was so Eilidh.

"Well, maybe when she's rich and famous, he'll fancy her back." Lana grinned, and I assumed she referred to the fact that Eilidh had started summer courses at a prestigious conservatoire in Glasgow and had also gotten a minor role on a Scottish TV show. It worried Lewis that Eilidh wanted to act, but she was headstrong and determined, even at fourteen.

"Fyfe isn't about that stuff." Lewis dismissed. "And he isn't about Eilidh. She's just a kid to him. So can we drop it?"

"Back to the last subject," I said, trying to lighten the mood. "The only reason Lewis and I were allowed to go camping together is because our parents knew we'd never get up to anything with Eilidh around."

"Well, that was naive." Eilidh suddenly appeared out of the woods with Fyfe. "Because I brought earplugs."

Laughter exploded around the campsite, and just like that, Lewis's big brother protectiveness was forgotten.

———

Despite Eilidh's joking, there was no way I intended to lose my virginity in a tent surrounded by our friends and Lewis's sister. Eilidh had finagled her way into Fyfe's tent because she decided last minute she didn't want to sleep alone. Fyfe was so unbothered by this, as if she was *his* little sister, that Lewis "allowed" it. I'd been about to suggest she sleep with us, when, as if she had a sixth sense, Eilidh had shot me a half-pleading, half-murderous look.

She lived in vain if she thought Fyfe was going to see her as anything but a kid, but I kept my mouth shut.

By the time we went to bed, my eyelids were heavy and Lewis's words had grown rough and slow, which was always a good indicator he was tired. It was no surprise that the last thing I remembered was drifting to sleep, sprawled across his chest, within seconds of getting into our sleeping bags. Even though the days had been warm this summer, the nights could still get chilly. But Lewis was like a furnace, and he kept me toasty.

The nightmare came out of nowhere. Or at least that's how it seemed. I was lost in it, the bad dream made up of memories mixed with fear. Suddenly cutting through it was Lewis. He was calling for me.

Saying my name over and over.

Then the feeling of being shaken finally yanked me from the sharp claws of my dreams.

I blinked, terrified and confused, as the nightmare faded and I found myself staring into Lewis's face.

"Callie?" He was holding me, his expression creased with concern.

Light flooded our tent and my eyes dropped to the battery-operated lamp we'd charged earlier. Lewis must have switched it on.

"What ..." I pushed up from the ground, and Lewis's arm slid around me, helping me. My hair clung to the back of my neck, and I realized I was clammy with sweat.

At once, the nightmare came rushing back, and disbelief and horror filled me. Tears burned my eyes.

"Shit." Lewis saw and pressed his forehead to my temple. "Talk to me, *mo chridhe*."

I leaned into him at the Gaelic endearment. We'd learned it in our Gaelic language class at school. One day, a few months ago, I got insecure by how he kept pulling back every time our kisses got a bit hot and heavy. I'd started to think he wasn't into me romantically after all. Lewis couldn't believe I'd think such a thing and had kissed my tears away. The endearment had slipped out.

I wondered later if it was because his dad called his mum by a Gaelic endearment. If he liked the sound of it. I knew I did. He never called me mo chridhe in front of anyone else, though. His friends would never let him hear the end of it.

But those two words made me feel safe and loved in Lewis Adair's arms. Even as the memories continued to make me shiver.

"You were whimpering in your sleep," he whispered hoarsely. "You sounded so scared."

Hearing the question in his words, I pulled away but only to look him in the eyes. I knew confusion colored my tone. "It was about the day my birth father kidnapped me."

Lewis tightened his embrace.

"I don't know why. I haven't thought about it in forever."

"Michael and Lana were talking about that documentary they watched. About the kidnapped girls."

My lips formed an *O*. And then frustration filled me that something so simple and meaningless could still trigger nightmares after all this time ...

"In the grand scheme of things, Callie ... six years isn't a long time. It was only six years ago."

"I know."

"Do you want to talk about it? I ... I still have bad dreams about the night Mum's ex broke into the house ..."

I knew that his stepmum's deranged ex-boyfriend had not only come after Regan, but had broken into the house, assaulted Eredine who was watching Lewis and Eilidh at the time, and then tied Eilidh and Lewis up in the guest annex. The man had gone after Regan then, and she'd fought him off. Her ex had slipped off a cliff's edge, never to be seen again. They were assured he'd drowned.

As awful as it sounded, I wished my birth father were dead so I never had to worry about him coming back.

"He took me from school," I told Lewis. "Do you remember?"

Lewis pursed his lips. "I felt guilty. I'd been too busy watching the fight that broke out in the playground, and I didn't see Andros approach you."

Nathan Andros. My father. The psycho drug dealer. What a legacy. For a long time after he'd kidnapped me, attempted to kill Mum, I'd worried I was tainted by him. That by merely being his daughter, I didn't deserve good things. Didn't deserve Walker. Didn't deserve Lewis. Lewis's constancy as my friend had helped me shake off those fears.

Walker adopting me finally made me realize that who my birth father was wasn't my fault. Walker was my real dad, in all the ways that mattered. And if he found me worthy of love, then surely, I must be. Now and then, however, that old inse-curity would whisper insidiously in my ear.

"It wasn't your fault he took me," I reassured Lew.

Lewis didn't look like he believed me. My boyfriend could be frustratingly overprotective sometimes. He took on too much responsibility for things. We were alike in that way.

"I mean it. You couldn't have stopped it, anyway." *Make a scene and I'll shoot your mother in the fucking head, kid.* "He threatened my mum. I was going with him no matter what." *Say "Yes, Daddy."* My lip curled in disgust. "He made me call him *daddy*, like his sperm donation to my existence meant any-fucking-thing to me."

My boyfriend's arms squeezed around me at my uncharac-teristic cursing.

"He ... he took me to this motorhome in the middle of nowhere. And he ... he said the most awful things about Mum." Nausea roiled in my gut. "I didn't understand some of it then, but I understand it now." I looked at Lewis. "That man is my flesh and blood, and he threatened to rape Mum with his gun. He said that to me. His ten-year-old kid."

Lewis looked sick for me. "Callie ..."

"He called Mum all the names under the sun. Tried to turn me against her, like he ever could. Kept telling me I was going home with him to the States. And I was so afraid it would happen. When Mum showed up, he threatened to kill me. My own father threatened to kill me. And then Mum had to leave with him to protect me ... I ... I was terrified. Because she went with him to save me, and if something had happened to her—"

"But it didn't. Your mum is alive. And Andros is in prison."

"I ... two years ago, I asked Mum to find out more about him." I hadn't told Lewis or anyone that. Only Mum and Dad knew. "He's still in the same prison in California. He's been diagnosed by a psychologist. Andros has an antisocial personality disorder. He's a sociopath, Lewis. My birth father is a diagnosed sociopath. That's what I'm made of."

"No." Lewis turned me fully toward him, his expression fierce. "The only thing he gave you was the color of your eyes. That's it. You are good and kind and strong."

"Like my mum?"

"Aye, but more than that, you're you because of what you've experienced. You've been through so much, Callie. And you moved to an entirely different country and took it all in stride. Everything you've been through makes you more compassionate. You don't judge, you see the best in people despite all the bad you've witnessed, and you're the fiercest friend anyone could ask for."

Love was an ache in my chest. "I like the way you see me."

"Good, because I see you the way you are."

Embarrassed, I apologized. "I'm sorry for waking you."

"Don't apologize." He snuggled me close. "I still have nightmares too sometimes. Out of the blue. I can't remember much about them other than the leftover feelings they cause."

I hated that he still had nightmares, but it was comforting to know he understood. "What feelings?"

"The fear I felt when Mum's ex attacked Aunt Ery and dragged us into the annex. I thought we were going to die. Then he left us there and Eilidh was terrified, and I felt like shit because I didn't know how to help her."

"Oh, Lewis, you were only a wee boy." I smoothed a hand over his chest. "If I had one wish, it would be that you stopped trying to carry the weight of the whole world on your shoulders. Not everything and everyone is your responsibility."

"I know that." He flashed me a boyish grin that made my belly flutter. "Just the people I love." His smile died, and he clasped my face in his hand, his thumb brushing my cheek. "I'd do anything for you."

It was official. I was ruined. Lewis Adair made all other boys my age pale in comparison. They were emotionally immature and self-absorbed. Lewis was the complete opposite. Part naturally older than his years, part molded by his experiences, Lewis was mature, open, caring, loving. He made me feel safe ... and no one else would ever do.

"I love you," I whispered.

He sighed and leaned his forehead against mine. "Never stop," he pleaded hoarsely. "Because I'll never stop loving you."

FIVE
LEWIS

PRESENT DAY

"Aren't you going to be late?" Fyfe asked.

I glanced over at my laptop, open on a video call with my friend. He was dressed in a button-down shirt because he'd come from a meeting with my uncles. It was no exaggeration to say that Fyfe was a computer genius. While at Edinburgh Uni studying computer science, he'd created an online game in his spare time that grew so popular, he sold it for millions. By the time he graduated, he already had more money in the bank than he knew what to do with, and had been recruited by one of his professors to join his cybersecurity team after helping him with several jobs during his education.

Now Fyfe was back in Ardnoch, ran a small cybersecurity team, and had taken over the management of protecting my families' businesses. He ran all the tech security at Ardnoch Estate and the whisky distillery and also managed the cybersecurity of some of the estate's celebrity members.

He'd come a long way from the grungy teenager with a chip on his shoulder he only ever let me see.

"You know I don't want to go."

"It's Eilidh," Fyfe reminded me. "And she might pretend like she doesn't need anyone, but she needs you. More than ever, probably."

"She's changed since you knew her, Fyfe. She's ... she's all in my business and everyone else's, but whenever anyone tries to dig deeper into hers, she evades like a champ."

"More reason for you to go to her wrap party. Make sure she's behaving."

I snorted at that. "What are you up to this fine Friday night?"

Fyfe glanced at his phone. "I actually have a date."

"Finally."

"Says the bloke on the longest dry spell known to man."

"Fuck you," I replied without rancor.

He chuckled. "I'm just saying ... maybe tonight's the night."

I gave him a look because he knew me.

My friend nodded. "Well, some of us are less discerning. I, for one, intend to get laid this evening."

"Enjoy." I walked over to the laptop, envious of his ability to take his feelings out of sex. "Talk to you later?"

"Aye. I've got a meeting in London in a couple weeks, so maybe we can grab a beer?"

"Definitely. Talk to you later, bud."

"Later." Fyfe tapped on the screen and was gone.

I blew out a beleaguered breath and snatched my keys off the kitchen counter of my small, one-bedroom flat in Hammersmith. The club Eilidh and her castmates had rented out for their wrap party was in Holborn. But I'd get there in no time on my bike because I wasn't planning to drink.

The green Kawasaki was the best investment I'd ever made.

Getting around London was less stressful with it. My precious Harley-Davidson was parked in my parents' garage back in Ardnoch because the Kawasaki was the better bike for the city, in my opinion. I longed to get back to the Harley, though. Another reason to miss Ardnoch.

When I first took an interest in motorbikes, it was for the sole purpose of making my way around London more easily. But I soon fell in love with how it felt to ride. Journeys before were contained by vehicles that encased me, walls of metal and glass between me and the outside world. On a bike, the concrete was beneath my feet, the wind against my body. I was part of that outside, connected to it in a way I couldn't be in a car or a truck or a train or plane. There was something almost therapeutic and invigorating, as if I were part of the wind. Like flying.

I had to be extra switched on, more aware of every turn, every bend, every curve. I'd come off the bike once. Luckily, I was mostly bruised and beaten. Nothing fractured. It was enough to scare the shit out of my mum who begged me to stop riding, but I think my dad knew motorbikes had become integral to me. And I couldn't stop being me.

He must have convinced her to let it go because she'd not made me feel bad about riding since.

The city was a blur of traffic and lights on a Friday night. People were out in their best clothes, suits and shirts and jeans, heels and skirts and cleavage. I could practically smell the perfume and aftershave already.

Thankfully, there was off-street motorcycle parking near the club. I had an app that told me exactly where I could safely leave my ride.

I pulled off my helmet and secured it beside a passenger helmet I kept in the lockable hard case on the back. Seeing the extra helmet, I couldn't remember the last time I'd taken someone out on my bike. It was probably Sean. The last woman on my bike was Charlotte. I threw off the thought of her, my cheeks hot with embarrassment.

I tightened the tie that held my hair up off my neck and reluctantly strode down the back lane toward the club entrance. They asked for my name at the door, and as soon as I stepped inside, a wall of heat and music and the cloying mix of multiple designer fragrances, and alcohol hit me.

The wrap party had clearly grown out of hand because there had to be more than a hundred people here. It was a large space, so it wasn't jam-packed, but it was crowded enough I couldn't immediately see Eilidh.

A flash of bright green against dark hair at the bar caught my eye. I moved in that direction, recognizing my sister's profile as she gestured animatedly with her hands. My gaze flicked to her companion, half expecting some panting moron drooling over her—

I froze on the dance floor, bodies jostling into me at my sudden halt.

Their complaints barely registered as I stared at the woman smiling at my sister.

Callie Ironside.

Callie was here.

The last time I'd seen Callie in real life was in passing. I'd come home for Christmas my second year of university, determined after being away for sixteen months that I could be in Ardnoch. I could see my ex. I'd be fine.

But when she'd seen me across the street from her mum's bakery, she'd looked right through me. As if I were a stranger.

And it killed me.

So I didn't go back. Not until I knew she was in France and there was no chance of bumping into her.

Now here she was. In the flesh.

Was her Frenchman here with her?

Panic lit through me at the thought.

In fact, I was seconds from turning and walking back out when Callie suddenly stiffened and snapped her head toward me. As if she'd felt me there.

A sensation, like an electric buzz, flared up my spine. The nape of my neck prickled.

Then I was shoved forward, jerking me out of the feeling.

"Oh my God, I'm so sorry!"

I turned toward the apology and found an attractive redhead smoothing down her skirt in a flustered manner. She blinked rapidly as she looked up at me. It was hard to tell under the club's lighting, but she might have been blushing. "I'm sorry," she repeated. "I, uh, don't know what happened." Her voice hardened as she shot a dirty look to her left.

A quick glance revealed two young women who were snort-laughing into their drinks as they peered at us.

"I'm Amy." The redhead held out her hand, her expression filled with interest. "I've seen you around. You're Eilidh's big brother, right? I'm a PA. Production assistant."

Realization dawned.

They'd pushed her into me.

"Nice to meet you." I gave her a toothless smile because I could feel Callie at my back, and while I'd been seconds from walking out, I found now I couldn't. She was here. And I hadn't heard her voice in so long. "I have to get to my sister. Have a good night."

The redhead's face fell with disappointment as I swiftly turned and marched toward the bar. Now both Eilidh and Callie were watching me, but I only had eyes for my ex. Her long blond hair curled over her shoulders, and she wore a figure-hugging black dress that stopped above the knee. It had a modest neckline, but it didn't matter. The dress was so tight it did little to hide the fact that Callie was curvier than she'd been when we were teenagers. And she still had the best pair of legs I'd ever seen. Right now, every strong curve of her long legs was enhanced by the sky-high heels she wore.

Heat tightened in my gut.

And when I dragged my eyes back up her body as I arrived at the bar, I saw Callie swallow hard. It suggested she was just as nervous to see me.

Good.

"Lewis!" Eilidh reached out, tucking her arm in mine. "You remember Callie, right?"

I shot her a look before returning my attention to my ex. "It's been a long time."

Callie straightened to her full height, her expression uncharacteristically blank. "I didn't know you'd be here."

Meaning ... she wouldn't have come otherwise?

Irritation gnawed at me. "Well, I'm Eilidh's brother. What are you doing here?" I cursed inwardly at how accusatory that sounded.

"Oh, Callie's home now," Eilidh answered for her. "Back in Ardnoch, running the bakery with her mum."

Shock thrummed through me. "No more France?"

"That was always the plan," Callie answered politely but emotionlessly. "School in Paris and then bring what I learned back to the bakery."

It was always the plan? She hadn't ... she hadn't left Ardnoch for good after telling me she never planned to leave? She hadn't lied.

Something in me eased.

"Isn't that great?" Eilidh nudged me mischievously. "And she left the Frenchman behind."

I watched as Callie narrowed her eyes suspiciously at Eilidh, all the while feeling a relief like I hadn't experienced in a long time.

"He was a French fling after all," Eilidh continued.

They weren't serious? She wasn't in love with him? My pulse raced and the room swayed a bit.

Fuck.

"It looks like Amy fancies you." Eilidh suddenly released my arm to stand between me and Callie. But I couldn't take my eyes off my ex. It took extreme willpower to drag my attention to my sister.

"What? Who?"

Eilidh chuckled. "Oh, poor Amy."

Oh right. The redhead.

I looked at Callie again. She was leaning against the bar now, her back almost turned to me as she played with the straw in her drink.

"Beer, brother?"

"Do they have NA? I'm riding tonight."

"Of course they do." She gently pushed me toward Callie. "You two catch up. There's a castmate out there I can finally hook up with now the show's over."

"Eilidh," I warned.

She grinned unrepentantly and sauntered off in pursuit of another conquest.

Heart thumping so hard I could hear the blood whooshing in my ears, I stepped up to the bar beside Callie.

Her perfume was different.

When we were sixteen, I'd bought her a bottle of perfume for Christmas, and she'd worn the same scent for the next two years.

This new scent was more intense—something fruity, floral, and spicy all at once. Sexier.

She refused to look at me, staring into her drink.

I knew her profile like I knew the back of my hand. And yet there was something different about her that I couldn't quite put my finger on. Perhaps because the last time I stood this close to her, we were eighteen. All at once seven years felt like forever and no time at all.

We said nothing as I waved down a bartender and ordered an NA beer.

Callie was tense beside me but made no move to leave, so I was encouraged by that.

By the time the beer arrived, someone had pumped up the music to an obnoxious level. So, I leaned my elbows on the bar, close enough to almost touch her, and sipped my drink.

Glancing at her out of the corner of my eye, I was satisfied to see her chest rising and falling a bit too quickly.

She was as affected by my proximity as I was hers.

"I thought maybe you'd moved to France permanently," I called over the music.

I felt her look at me and turned to meet her gaze.

"No." She shook her head. "I never lied about wanting to stay in Ardnoch." She gestured around us. "Just as you never lied about wanting to get out." With an abrupt shrug, she threw back the rest of her cocktail and then strode away from the bar.

I followed her movements with the hungry determination of a starving lion stalking his next juicy meal. And there was no fucking way, now that I'd found her again, I was letting her out of my sight.

SIX
CALLIE

SEVEN YEARS AGO

My stomach was in knots as I watched Lewis chat with Tyra West. Carianne's cousin had come up for the weekend from Glasgow, and Lewis had been paying her more attention than I felt comfortable with. I wasn't a jealous girl. Our friendship group included other girls, and Lewis talked to them all the time. Of course that didn't bother me. But between Lewis avoiding me and now monopolizing Tyra's attention at the impromptu party at Fyfe's ... I was getting seriously pissed off.

And seriously worried.

For the last few weeks, Lewis had been so distant. At first, I thought he was stressed about school and final exams so that's why he always had an excuse not to spend so much time with me. But then he'd taken to being evasive when I attempted to talk about our future.

"You all right?" Carianne suddenly appeared in front of me with a fresh bottle of beer.

"Fine. Thanks." I took the beer and gulped a huge swig.

Carianne looked over at Lewis standing by the fireplace with Tyra. She was a pretty brunette only a year younger than us. I scowled as she laughed at something Lewis said and playfully shoved him. "Need me to bitch-slap my cousin?"

"She's flirting with him, right?"

My friend grimaced. "Looks it. Also looks like Lewis isn't doing much to stop it. What's going on there, then?"

Fear thickened my throat, and I took another swallow of beer to stem the emotion bubbling within me. "I think he wants to break up."

Carianne's eyes widened. "No way."

I nodded, trying to feel numb about it. I couldn't. I was terrified of losing my best friend, and I was raging at him for making me feel like this when I never thought he'd ever make me feel uncertain of him. "I am invisible at the moment."

"How do you mean?"

"He avoids me. When we do spend time together, he's quiet and distant, like he's somewhere else or wants to be somewhere else." I looked back at him, grinning down at something Tyra was saying. As I turned away, hurt, Fyfe caught my expression. He was chatting up Emma Andrews, who was in our year. Whatever he saw on my face made him glare over at Lewis.

I yanked my attention away and stared into the crowd of friends packed into the kitchen. "Maybe *I* should find someone to flirt with."

"That's the hurt talking. Tell Lewis he's being a prick. Or I will."

"He shouldn't need to be told." I threw back the rest of the beer and slammed the empty down on the kitchen table.

Carianne followed me out into the narrow hallway. "Where are you going?"

"Home. I'm not sticking around to watch my so-called boyfriend flirt with someone else." I stormed out the front door before she could say a word.

Fury and hurt lengthened my strides, so I was halfway down the street before I heard him shout my name.

I ignored him.

Fuck him!

Then his footsteps grew faster and louder until he was at my side, grabbing my arm to draw me around. "Callie, what the hell?"

I yanked free of Lewis's hold. "Piss off. I'm going home."

"I was only talking to her." He reached for me again, but I shoved him away. Lewis's eyes widened and he swallowed hard. "Callie, I was just talking."

"Aye? So ... who told you I left then?"

He blanched. "Carianne. Fyfe said something and when I went to look for you, Carianne said you'd left. I wasn't flirting."

I searched his face, not recognizing the boy in front of me. The last few weeks had been the worst in ages as he grew more and more distant. I felt like I was waiting for the ax to fall. "You know, I wish you'd just get it over with. You're hurting me over and over again this way." My lips trembled, but I was determined not to cry. "It's sadistic."

Lewis took hold of my arms and this time held tight as he pulled me to him. "What are you talking about?"

"Breaking up with me."

He had the audacity to look confused and shocked by the suggestion. "Because I was talking to another girl?"

"Don't." I shoved him away, and he stumbled back.

"Callie—"

"You have been cold and distant to me for weeks. And

then Carianne's cousin shows up from Glasgow, and you're all over her like a bad rash. Who the hell are you?" I yelled tearfully.

"I wasn't all over her. I didn't mean to be cold and distant. I've been stressed." He reached for me again.

"Lewis, I swear to God, if you touch me right now, I will deck you."

Something like panic flickered in his eyes. "Callie, I swear I wasn't flirting with her. I was asking about Glasgow and what it was like living there."

"Why?"

He shrugged. "I was interested. I've lived in a tiny village my whole life."

"She was flirting with you."

"I wasn't flirting back."

Anger was still hot in my blood. "I'm going home."

"Callie, don't go home like this. Please."

I cut him a dirty look. "I don't know. I think I'll give you the cold shoulder for a few weeks and then let Ollie drool all over me in front of you." I referred to a guy in our year who'd asked me out three times, even though he knew I was dating Lewis. He drove Lewis nuts. "See how you like it."

"If you let Ollie come anywhere near you, I'll kill him," Lewis said calmly, but I saw the fury flash in his eyes.

"Why would you care?"

He scoffed. "Really, Callie?"

"It doesn't feel like you care very much lately, Lewis. Do you ..." I looked away, frantically blinking back tears. "Do you not love me anymore?"

Suddenly, I was yanked against Lewis's body, his mouth on mine, his kisses bruising and desperate. I didn't kiss him back. I was too confused.

He pulled away, eyes bright. "Of course I love you. I love you so much." He leaned his forehead against mine. "Shit,

Callie, I'm sorry. I'm sorry if I made you feel like I didn't. I'm sorry if I hurt you."

Hearing the sincerity in his voice, I nodded. "Okay."

"Aye?"

I nodded again but stepped out of his hold. "I'm going home. We'll talk later."

"Don't." He tugged on my hand. "Please, let's go back to the annex. Don't go home like this."

"No, I want to go home." It had been an awful few weeks and he couldn't erase it with an *I love you*.

Worry furrowed Lewis's brow. "Then let me walk you home."

That I could do. I nodded and turned to walk in the direction of the bungalow.

Lewis fell into step beside me and took my hand in his. I let him. But I didn't speak.

When we reached the bungalow, he stopped and kissed me again. "I'm sorry. I'm so sorry. Please don't be mad at me. I can't stand it." He kissed me again, and it was needy, yearning. "I love you so much."

A little of my hurt and anger dissipated. "I love you too."

Lewis groaned and wrapped his arms around me so my cheek rested against his chest. "I'm going to make it up to you, all right? I'll never make you feel that way again. I'm an arsehole. I don't deserve you. I'm so sorry."

I locked my arms around his waist and shoved the fear I'd been feeling down deep. Lewis was here, he loved me, he'd merely been stressed. We were okay. "I forgive you."

His relief was obvious. "Please come back to the annex with me."

A flicker of movement at the front window told me it was too late. "Dad just saw us. I better go in."

"Come to mine tomorrow?" Lewis pleaded.

"Okay."

He kissed me again, hard, deep, apparently uncaring if my dad was watching. "I love you," he repeated.

"Love you too. I'll see you tomorrow."

"I'm going home." He added, "Not going back to the party."

Where Tyra was.

Relieved, I smiled and gave him a wee wave.

As I walked into the house, I shoved my hurt and doubts way down deep, so I wouldn't have to deal with them. So they wouldn't get in the way of what I had with Lewis. He was stressed. That was it. Nothing else.

We were fine.

We were going to be fine.

SEVEN
CALLIE

PRESENT DAY

I didn't expect it to hurt like this. To chafe. To feel uncomfortable and a bit raw.

But this was still bloody agony, and I hated him for it.

Lewis Adair.

The bane of my existence.

My legs shook as they carried me away from my ex.

The image of him walking through the club was burned on my brain.

He was different, but in a way that made sense.

He didn't look like a professional architect striding through the room. Lewis looked like a biker. With his messy man bun, short beard, and tattoos.

Lewis had tattoos.

They were revealed in the short-sleeve tee that molded to his strong biceps. I knew from Eilidh that, like me, Lewis still regularly attended tae kwon do classes. But he also had to work out to be *that* in shape. He was as tall as his uncles, and his strong, athletic frame had filled out to something bulkier, more intimidating.

No wonder the redhead had literally thrown herself at him.

When he'd approached us, I thought I might not be able to speak. It felt like my heart had lodged itself in my throat. And the way he'd stared at me, dragging his gaze insolently up my body.

Heat flushed my skin as I pushed into the ladies' restroom.

With it being a private event, it wasn't too crowded. But unfortunately, the redhead and her friends were in there too. If they recognized me, they didn't acknowledge it.

I fumbled with my clutch, pulling out my lipstick and reapplying it. My reflection revealed flushed cheeks and wide eyes. I almost looked like I'd had a shock.

Then the redhead's conversation started to register.

"I don't want anyone else. I want to go home with Lewis Adair. I've had my eye on him for months."

"Do you think he's gay?" one of her friends asked. "I've never seen him with a woman at any of these parties."

"Not according to Eilidh." The redhead shrugged. "Maybe he likes his women to be more obvious. Maybe I need to go up to him and say 'Let's fuck.'"

Her friends laughed; my stomach pitched.

People must throw themselves at Lewis all the time.

There were guys dressed to the nines in three-piece suits at this party, and they'd all paled in comparison to Lewis who had strode through the room in jeans and a tee, looking as lickable as a cold ice-cream cone on a muggy hot day. He had a commanding presence he'd very much inherited from his father and uncles. The kind of charisma a lot of these actors would kill for.

And I hated him for it.

How many women had he slept with since we broke up?

My fingers trembled as I finished with my lipstick.

Why did the thought of it hurt so much?

I'd moved on.

I'd slept with other men.

The sex had even been fantastic.

With Lewis it had been romantic and sweet and loving and great. But we'd been kids who were just discovering sex with each other. The first bloke I'd slept with after Lewis had been a disaster, so much so I couldn't even think about it. Then there had been Remy. The sex was okay (Remy was a selfish lover), but with Gabriel, it had been adventurous, sometimes rough, and exciting. Grown-up sex.

The thought of Lewis with other women shouldn't bother me at all. It was hypocritical.

Shoving away from the sink, unable to bear listening to the redhead's conversation as she planned her next approach on my ex, I hurried out of the bathroom.

Only to smack right into the object of my current distress.

Lewis reached out as if to steady me and suddenly afraid of what his touch might do, I jerked away.

Coming here was a mistake.

"Callie—"

"It's too loud in here, so I'm heading out. Will you tell Eilidh? Thanks!" I didn't wait for a response, hightailing it to the exit as fast as I could.

Bursting out of the club, I sucked in a lungful of shoddy air and shakily exhaled. Laughter and traffic filled my ears, and the air was thick with smog. So much so, I longed for Ardnoch. There was nothing like a fresh gulp of Highland air. Clean and crisp.

I stumbled away from the club, suddenly hating this city

for being something Ardnoch could never be. Its pull so strong that it had torn me and Lewis apart.

It was a mistake to come here.

I hated London and all it stood for in my life.

"Callie!"

No.

Halting, I briefly closed my eyes before turning to face him.

Lewis's concerned gaze met mine as he reached up to tuck a strand of hair behind his ear. A few chunky silver rings glinted on his big-knuckled fingers. It was difficult in the glare of a million streetlights to make out the images on the full-sleeve tattoo of his left arm.

Where had he gotten the tattoo? When? Why?

All these things I would have known seven years ago. I probably would have sat in the chair next to him while he took the ink. But I knew nothing about the last seven years of his life, and I was knocked on my arse to realize how much that still hurt.

I despised him for that too.

He searched my eyes. "Can we ... can we go somewhere?"

Surprised by the request, I shrugged. "Why?"

Lewis made a sound of disbelief. "Because we haven't seen each other in years."

"That was your decision."

Anger flashed in his eyes. "Callie—"

"I need to get back to my hotel."

"Please," he bit out, voice rough. "You never have to speak to me ever again after it."

The curious part of me, the part of me that would always, unfortunately, be drawn to him, nodded reluctantly. "Okay."

Lewis seemed to sag with relief. "Great. Follow me."

Falling into step beside him, I didn't feel even a shred of uncertainty as he led me down a dimly lit lane between the club and the next building. No matter what had occurred between us, I'd always feel physically safe with Lewis.

Emotionally, not so much.

"Where are we going?"

He gestured to a green motorbike sitting beneath a lamppost.

It shouldn't have surprised me.

I already thought he looked more like a biker than an architect.

Yet it was one more thing in the evolution of Lewis Adair I'd missed when once upon a time, I thought I'd be around to see it all.

"You want me to get on that?" My bitterness seethed in the question.

And I blamed him for that too. I didn't want to be a bitter person!

"Scared?" Lewis unlocked the hard case box on the back of the bike, flashing me a teasing grin I knew all too well before he pulled out helmets.

"No. My ex had a bike." It was true. I'd ridden on the back of Gabriel's bike often.

Lewis's smile dropped. "So, what's the problem?"

I gestured down to my clothing. "Not exactly dressed for a ride."

His eyes dragged down my body in a way that made my pulse flutter. When our gazes locked, he wore an expression I'd never seen on Lewis's face before. Pure, unadulterated lust. "I adamantly disagree."

It took a second for his hoarse words and their meaning to register. I gaped at him. "You did not just say that."

His mouth kicked up at the corner. "I didn't mean it that way."

I could tell by the devil in his eyes, he absolutely meant it that way.

Lewis held out a hand. "Give me your purse. I'll put it in the box."

Still a bit stunned by his overt flirting, I held out the clutch and watched as he locked it away. With one more wicked smirk in my direction, he swung his leg over the bike with ease. "You coming or not?"

So this was who he was now?

Flirty and cocky, and probably a total manwhore to boot.

Fine. If he wanted to play it that way ... I marched over to the bike, tugged the hem of my dress up indecently high, and swung my leg over. Then I scooted as close to Lewis as possible to protect what little modesty I could. My heels rested on the passenger footpegs, bringing my thighs closer to him.

He was tense against me, staring over his shoulder at my bare legs.

"Well?"

Lewis looked forward and pulled his helmet down. I followed suit.

Then I slid my arms around his waist. His heat hit my palms through the thin fabric of his shirt. I could feel the hard ridges of his abs and noted how much broader his shoulders were now.

He was Lewis ... but he wasn't.

He wasn't *my* Lewis anymore.

"Ready?" His question was slightly muffled by his helmet.

I tapped his stomach to let him know I was.

With that, the engine purred to life and Lewis kicked up the stand to take off. I loved being on the back of a bike, but it was different with him. Whereas before I got lost in the sensation of riding—it was almost like flying, taking in the scenery passing by at speed—now I felt nothing but him.

His heat, his hardness.

The vibrations of the bike between my thighs while I pressed my breasts against his strong back.

Memories flooded me.

Random moments. Like searching for him in a room, only to find him watching me with such tenderness on his expression, I could die with happiness. His hungry kisses. His loving touch. How perfect and right it felt to be naked in his arms.

The way it broke me in half to realize that for him, none of it was enough to stay with me in Ardnoch.

———

Less than twenty minutes later, Lewis halted the bike on a well-lit, well-maintained, tree-lined street occupied by pretty townhouses.

As soon as the engine stopped, I released my hold on him and pulled off the helmet. "Where are we?"

Lewis took off his helmet. "My place."

Annoyance and anticipation were my friction-filled companions as I swung my leg off the bike and smoothed my dress down. When I looked up, it was to find Lewis staring hotly at my body. "Stop ogling me," I huffed.

He smirked as he got off the bike. "If you didn't want me to ogle you, you shouldn't have worn that dress. Or those shoes."

"Does that kind of talk work for you with other women? Because it seriously does nothing for me." I slammed the helmet into his stomach and marched away from him to wait on the pavement.

Lewis locked the helmets away, grabbed my clutch, and then handed it to me before he walked past with a careful expression. He gestured to stairs that led down to a basement flat.

"Why did you bring me here?" I asked as we walked into the small apartment. It had an open-plan living and kitchen area that was smaller than my parents' living room. A hallway at the side of the kitchen clearly led to the bedroom and bathroom. The space was stylish but cold. He had no photos on the walls. Just generic artwork. The lack of light was depressing too. I hated this flat for him.

It was like it was a stopping point.

"How long have you been here?" I asked before he could answer my last question.

"This flat? Two years. And I brought you here because I wanted to be able to talk and actually hear you."

In the glaring artificial light, I could see now that his sleeve tattoo was blackwork, where larger areas of black ink made for dramatic effect. Whoever his artist was, they were talented. The art was amazing.

I took a step forward, peering at it.

The short sleeve of his T-shirt hid part on his shoulder, but I could make out what looked like the bottom of a woman's face. The branches of a graphic-style tree touched her chin as it blossomed across his biceps. The roots of the tree morphed below it into stunning roses and thistles, and embedded in the petals was half the face of a clock with roman numerals. I couldn't make out what time it was at.

Curiosity plagued me.

Knowing Lewis, every inch of his sleeve of tattoos held meaning.

Lewis lifted his arm, seeing my perusal. "It took five three-hour sessions."

"It's beautiful," I answered honestly. "Do you have more?"

He nodded. "Got my first tattoo a few months after ... well, after I left. It's a take on the Adair coat of arms."

"*Loyal Au Mort,*" I said, remembering their clan motto meant Faithful unto Death. The thought made me snort. "Guess some things are hard to live up to."

His expression clouded as he crossed his arms over his chest, defensively. "Is that a dig?"

Pretending to be unaffected by his indignation, I shook my head, glancing casually around his personality-less apartment. "Merely the truth."

"You wouldn't know what the truth was if it bit you on the arse, Callie Ironside."

"Rewriting history, Lewis?" I kept my tone casual as I wandered around the small space, my heels clicking on his hardwood floor. My calm indifference seemed to bother him, and I could admit I took a sadistic pleasure in pissing him off.

In the early days of our friendship, we'd actually fought a lot. We were super competitive with each other. However, I always thought that was because we instinctually trusted we could be that way with each other and not have it break us. I never thought *anything* could break us. That was our problem in the end. I'd thought that, while Lewis had known better.

I'd loved him more than he'd ever loved me, and I hadn't wanted to stand in his way of making the life he wanted for himself.

"Nope." He watched me as I trailed my hands over a sideboard where he kept a record player—the only thing in the room so far that really spoke to this being Lewis's home. He'd been a huge music lover and had introduced me to so many artists from all eras. "I remember exactly how we ended."

"Is that why you brought me here? So we could rehash what doesn't need to be rehashed?"

"If it didn't, you wouldn't have fled the club, fled me."

I stopped to face him. "I didn't flee you. I'm not a clubber. You know that." Give me a quiet pub and a live band over a nightclub any day of the week.

"Was he?"

I scowled. "Who?"

"The French bloke you left back in Paris."

Discomfort shifted through me. "You don't really want to talk about our exes, do you?"

"Did you love him?" Lewis asked hoarsely.

The vulnerability in his question gave me pause. I stared at him, trying desperately to understand why his expression was so tight, so pained. "Why would you care if I did or didn't?"

Lewis huffed, turning away from me in frustration. "I'm not the one rewriting history, apparently."

"Can we not do this?"

He whirled around, his blue eyes flashing. "I thought you went to Paris and weren't coming back. After everything ... I thought you'd left Ardnoch after all. For *him*."

Oh.

He thought after our breakup, I'd become a hypocrite. That I'd done something for someone else that I couldn't do for him.

In a way, I had. "I left Ardnoch for me. But it was never permanent. I didn't lie when I said it would always be my home, where I wanted to live my life. But I'm glad I spent those years in Paris and traveled a bit. I never *didn't* want to travel, Lewis. I just didn't want to leave everything behind that meant something to me. You can't say the same."

Lewis stepped toward me. "That's not what I did."

"Really." I shrugged. "Because it sure felt like it at the time."

EIGHT
CALLIE

SEVEN YEARS AGO

Excitement buzzed through me as I strolled to Fyfe's small house. It was only a five-minute walk from mine, and I knew Lewis was there this afternoon. I couldn't wait to tell him about Ina Urwin's flat. It was a small studio off Castle Street, but it would be perfect for us as a starter place. We had discussed finding somewhere between Ardnoch and Inverness to simplify Lewis's commute, and we could still do that. But Ina's flat was so cute and just a hop, skip, and a jump from the bakery.

It would make those early mornings so much easier for me. And Lewis would be closer to his family this way. Our parents might not like the idea of us moving in together after graduation, but I'm sure they loved the idea of us staying in Ardnoch. Lewis could attend Inverness University while I worked full time at the bakery.

Our own place.

Giddiness filled me at the thought of curling up together to watch movies every night, cooking together, talking to each other about our days. And, of course, not having to figure out when and where we'd have sex. We could have sex anytime we wanted.

The thought made me grin.

After our bust-up a few weeks ago, things had been so much better. Lewis had started talking about our future again, planning it with me, and making sure he was spending time with me. His earlier distance was forgotten. I mean, he was a bit broody still, but I think that's because he was nervous about starting university.

As I approached Fyfe's small house that he'd shared with his very absentee mum until she disappeared a year ago, I felt a pang of melancholy that I wouldn't be doing this for much longer. Fyfe's elderly neighbor, Deirdra, had lied for him and told the school that his mum had left him in her care. They even produced a fake letter with her signature. Truth was we all knew that even before Fyfe's mum disappeared, he'd been looking after himself.

Luckily, the house had been an inheritance, left to his mum by his grandmother, so all he had to do was scrape together money for bills and food. We'd offered to help, but he was adamant he could do it himself. I didn't know exactly how he got his money, but it had something to do with computers. Now that he was eighteen, it didn't matter. Genius that he was, he'd gotten into one of the best computer science programs in the UK and was leaving us for the University of Edinburgh after the summer.

He was the friend I'd miss most.

Fyfe's had also become the place we hung out most since there was no parental supervision. With that in mind, I let myself into the house without knocking. A quick glance into the living room produced no boyfriend and no Fyfe, and then

I heard the rumble of their deep voices coming from the kitchen.

The door to the kitchen was open and though I couldn't see them, I could hear them out in the garden.

"You need to tell her," Fyfe said.

I took a step into the room, excited to share my news with Lewis.

"Callie will never understand. I'm fucked."

Lewis's tone, his words, drew me to a halt. My pulse suddenly throbbed, and I found myself scooting back into the doorway between the kitchen and living room, out of sight.

"We graduate in a few weeks, and your girlfriend doesn't know you haven't accepted Inverness's offer. And she definitely doesn't know you applied to UCL and got in."

Last summer, I'd been working out with Lewis's Aunt Robyn who boxed. The boxing bag had swung back and caught me just right, knocking the wind out of me. I felt that sensation now at the realization that Lewis had applied to a university in London. That he hadn't accepted Inverness like he said he had.

Had he said?

Or had I assumed?

"It doesn't matter. I'm going to Inverness."

"So why haven't you accepted it? Lew ... you can't stay here for someone else and you need to accept London before the acceptance deadline expires."

"It's not someone else though. It's Callie."

I held my breath, feeling utterly sick.

"Look, there's nothing stopping you guys from doing the long-distance thing."

"It's not just ... Callie never wants to leave here, so there's no point going to London because I'll end up back here, anyway."

"Is that what you want, though? To live in Ardnoch for the rest of your life?"

I think I stopped breathing altogether as I waited for his response.

"You know it isn't. But it's what she wants."

Oh my God. Tears blurred my vision.

"And—don't bite my head off for this—are you absolutely positive you want to build your entire future around your high school girlfriend?"

"Fyfe—"

"I know you love her. Callie is lovable. But ... this is your life we're talking about. One day you might wake up and resent her for keeping you here. That's not fair to *her*, man."

"I don't know." His voice was thick with emotion. "The thought of hurting her fucking kills me ... That night at your party made me feel like shit. Knowing I'd hurt her. Anytime I think about it, it eats me up."

"But?"

"We're eighteen. It has to cross her mind, too, that maybe ... realistically ... There's no guarantee that who we'll be in ten years will be someone that either of us still wants to be with."

I covered my mouth to muffle a sob. This couldn't be Lewis who was saying these things. Not *my* Lewis.

"I mean, people grow up, people change. Right?"

"Right," Fyfe agreed. "You've only ever been with Callie. Maybe you need to experience other things, other places ... even other girls."

"I don't know. I love her. I do love her."

"Just admit it out loud, Lew. It's only us here. Who am I going to tell?"

There was a moment of silence in which my heart ached.

"Callie says she's one hundred percent certain that our future is together. She's got it all figured out. I become an architect at Dad's firm, she runs the bakery with her mum, we get married, we have kids, and they grow up here in Ardnoch ... That scares the fuck out of me. Like, how can she be so certain that that's what our future should be? Doesn't she want to go out into the world and see and experience it? I'm ... I'm not sure in the way she's sure that *that's* our future. Together." I heard his shaky exhale as the fissures in my heart turned into a giant crack. "Fuck. I don't know what to do. The thought of losing her scares the shit out of me. Maybe that means I am sure."

"You wouldn't be having these thoughts if you were sure. Just because you love someone doesn't mean you're meant to be with them."

The pain in my chest was almost unbearable, and I could feel the sob welling up inside me. I didn't want him to see me break down. I didn't want to give him that. Instead, I slunk out of the house as quietly as possible. There was woodland not far from my parents' bungalow, behind Lewis's Aunt Arro's and Uncle Mac's house.

I hurried through the streets toward the woods, and I kept walking into them until there was no one else around.

Then my knees gave out and I fell to the forest floor, finally releasing the pain cracking my chest in half in hard, wracking sobs.

———

I lay on the ground until the soil beneath the bracken and leaves started to chill my bones. Then I scolded myself for falling apart and I pushed to my feet.

I would be stronger than this.

To survive, I needed to take control of the situation.

There could be no doubt between us.

I couldn't live like that.

Whether it was right or wrong, I needed absolute certainty. I needed to know I was loved beyond any measure of doubt.

Back at home, I numbly asked Mum that if Lewis called, she should tell him I wasn't feeling well. For the next few days, I avoided him until I finally felt ready to face him. Mum was so worried, but I couldn't even voice what I'd overheard Lewis confess. After switching off my phone to avoid his calls, I turned it on the day I'd decided to confront him and found so many missed calls and texts from him, my resolve wavered.

> You ok? Your mum says you're sick? Do you need anything?

> I love you. Feel better.

> How are you feelin this morning?

> Hey, you feeling any better? Your mum says you're still in bed.

> Cal, you there? I'm worried.

> Seriously, txt me back.

> This isn't like you. Pls call me.

> I love you.

He loved me. Just not enough to want to stay. And worse, not enough to admit that to me. Was he really going to spend his life here in Ardnoch with me when it wasn't what he wanted? He'd put that on me?

Screw that!

My fingers trembled as I texted back.

> Meet me at the woods behind your Aunt
> Arro's in 30 mins.

Dots appeared almost instantly.

> R you ok?

> Just meet me.

> OK. See you in thirty. Love you.

I didn't reply.

———

I felt brittle and empty as I waited for Lewis.

The truth was I was grieving more than my relationship with him. I was grieving the future I thought I'd have. I was grieving that feeling of safety he'd given me. Because I thought he was one of four people on the planet who loved me unconditionally and without limit.

It was shattering to realize he wasn't.

I heard the crunch of his feet on the woodland floor and reluctantly faced him. Lewis was striding right for me, his expression harsh with concern. Before he reached me, he finally seemed to register the "stay back" vibes I was giving off.

He halted abruptly. "Callie, what's going on? I've been worried sick."

"Have you?" I glared disbelievingly at him.

Lewis scowled. "What does that mean?"

Spit it out. Get it over with.

"I overheard your conversation with Fyfe the other day. You were in his garden."

I swear all color leached from Lewis's face. "What—"

"When were you going to tell me about UCL? About any of it?" My anger started to rise and with it the volume of my voice. "Or were you really going to stay here with me, even though you don't know if that's what you want?"

Panic flared in his eyes, and he took a step toward me.

I stepped back.

"Fuck. Callie ..." His tone was pleading. "I was only thinking out loud. It didn't mean anything. I want to be with you. Of course I want to be with you."

I couldn't believe him now, though. He'd confessed his deep inner thoughts to *Fyfe*. Not me! Not only that, he'd made me feel like shit for weeks while he grew brooding and distant. And now I knew why. "Do you want Ardnoch? Or do you want a future elsewhere? Be honest. I deserve that, Lewis."

His expression tight, he took a shuddering breath as he raked his hands through his hair. The soft strands fell back around his jawline as he released them to shrug helplessly. "I don't know."

"You don't know or you don't want to admit how you feel?"

"I love you," Lewis whispered hoarsely.

"That's not what I asked."

"Fine." He shrugged again. "I ... I admit that the thought of studying architecture at one of the best unis in the country appeals to me. Living in London appeals to me. I've spent my whole life here, Callie. I want to experience other places. I don't want my life to be this narrow."

I flinched like he'd hit me.

Lewis winced. "I didn't mean it like ... I didn't mean you. I'd love for you to come with me."

His words to Fyfe rang through my head. They'd been ringing in my head for two days. "I don't want to leave Ardnoch. Everything and everyone I care about is here. The thought of leaving them, missing out on their lives, scares me.

Because I know how easily people go away. A lesson I thought you'd learned too."

"Callie—"

"'I'm not sure in the way she's sure that that's our future. Together.' That's what you said to Fyfe."

"I was just thinking out loud. It didn't mean anything."

"What about the weeks you spent pushing me away? I've felt rejected all this time. I've felt like I was losing you for months. Do you know how painful that has been? And I was, wasn't I? Losing you. The last few weeks of you being more present were merely you trying harder because you felt bad about the truth. So it does mean something. It means a lot to me." Tears blurred my vision and frustration thickened my throat because I wanted to be calm and adult through this. I didn't want to fall apart. "You know, you're right. I was a hundred percent certain of our future together. That I wanted *you* forever. Not once, not *once*, have I ever contemplated wanting anyone else. And I thought that's how you felt about me." My tears slipped free. "But it's not. You're not certain, are you?"

Renewed panic etched Lewis's features as he moved toward me. This time he didn't stop, even as I waved him off. He took me by the biceps, bending his head to mine. "It was just a thought, Callie. A stupid sliver of uncertainty. But it didn't mean anything. I might not be certain that I want to go to Inverness, but I'm certain of you. Of course, I am. I don't want to lose you." His grip turned almost bruising. "Please."

I shook my head, the tears falling fast and free. "I don't believe you. You kept UCL from me. You kept everything you've really been feeling and thinking from me. Maybe if you'd just been fucking honest, Lewis!" I shoved out of his grasp, stumbling away. "Instead I overhear you telling someone else all the things you should have told me. Making a fool out of me! Pushing me away, flirting with other girls.

How many other people know about this, Lewis? Only Fyfe? Or your family, our friends? Have you humiliated me?"

"No." He shook his head, his expression distraught, eyes shimmering with tears. "Callie, I'm sorry. It was only Fyfe. But I won't ever do that again. I promise."

"It's too late!" I cried, throwing my arms up as the last word came out on a sob. "I can't keep you here when I know it's not what you want. And the whole time you're in London, I'll be thinking about those words you said to Fyfe, about you and me, and I'll constantly be worrying 'Has he met someone else?' 'Has he found someone he *is* sure he wants to spend the rest of his life with?' Or maybe you're bored and want to fuck other girls, which is even worse!"

"No," he repeated, stumbling toward me, eyes wide and frantic. "Callie, I didn't mean it like that. That will never happen."

"I don't believe you!" I shrieked.

Lewis halted, staring at me in crushing disbelief. "Are ... are you breaking up with me?"

I sobbed, pulling the sleeves of my shirt over my hands before wrapping my arms around my stomach as if to hold in this violent emotion that was shuddering to break free. "I ... I'd always be unsure of you now." I swiped at the tears as they kept falling. "And I won't be the person who stands in the way of what you want."

"I want you!" he yelled, his own tears brimming over. "I want you. I love you."

We stared at each other in abject grief as we cried together in the woods. Seconds felt like minutes as time suspended.

Until finally I could speak. "I think you want something more and you're too afraid to admit it to me. And I want someone who wants to be here with me. You can't, hand on heart, say that, Lewis."

"I can," he pleaded again. "I can. Don't ..."

I knew we could stand here for hours going around in circles, but the truth was, two days ago I had utter faith and belief in his love for me. And all it took was a few weeks of uncertainty and a few words to tear enough holes in that belief to make it impossible to hold on to. I let the cold sharpness of reality settle in as I swiped the tears from my face.

Voice brittle but calm, I stared him directly in the eyes. "We're over, Lewis. Go to London."

"You don't mean that," he whispered.

"I always mean what I say," I said pointedly. "*I* always know my own mind. And it's made up. We can't go back. I won't go back. You want something more beyond Ardnoch. I want something more from the person I plan to spend the rest of my life with. Here."

"I can't believe this is happening." Lewis wiped his nose, suddenly looking like a lost wee boy. "I can't believe you're breaking up with me. After everything we've been through, and you're throwing me away like this?"

"I can't see any other way."

Anger darkened his expression. "Well, fuck you, Callie. Fuck you for giving up at the first fucking speed bump." He marched past me, bristling with rage. "Enjoy your sad fucking life in Ardnoch."

Renewed pain sliced through me, but I waited until I could no longer hear his footsteps before I let myself burst into tears again.

NINE

LEWIS

PRESENT DAY

I didn't want this conversation to devolve into a bitter argument, even though it frustrated me beyond measure how she perceived our breakup. One of the reasons I'd decided to leave, not to stay and fight for her, was because I was pissed off that she didn't even try to understand. She cut me out of her life. No mistakes, no errors, no wavering allowed.

That was her failure in our breakup.

Mine was walking away instead of fighting for her. But I was a kid, and I could give myself grace for that decision.

However, I was a man now.

"Drink?" I changed the subject.

"You got any whisky?" She surprised me by asking.

I raised a brow. "I have a bottle of Ardnoch."

"My favorite. With ginger ale, if you have it."

That made me smile. "I don't."

"Straight it is, then."

As I poured us both a dram of my uncles' whisky, I was aware of Callie looking around the flat as if in search of something. Finally, she took a seat on the couch and pulled her phone out of her clutch. I hated that my immediate concern was that she was texting some bloke. I despised being a jealous guy, and I felt like I'd been playing that role for seven years now.

"Just texting Eilidh to let her know we left."

Shit. Though my sister had plenty of friends to keep her occupied, I hadn't even thought to let her know I was leaving. I'd been concerned with chasing Callie. "Good shout, thanks."

I handed her the whisky and sat down on the other end of the sofa, turning my back to the armrest so I could face her. Raising the glass, I said, "To reunions."

She gave me a droll smile that didn't reach her eyes but raised her glass too. "To reunions."

We stared at each other as we sipped.

"Mmm. Your uncles don't know how to be bad at anything, do they?" Callie murmured.

"Since when do you drink whisky?"

"I had a glass on my eighteenth. Took a liking to it, much to Mum's surprise."

Her eighteenth. Her birthday is August 2. Mine's in March, so I'm only a few months older than her. We'd celebrated my eighteenth with an unsupervised party at Fyfe's, and Callie and I had gotten drunk and had sex in Fyfe's mum's old room while everyone partied beyond the doors. For Callie's eighteenth, my uncle Arran, the youngest of my uncles, had taken me to Inverness so I could get obliterated. We'd had a lot of whisky that night too. Dad had been furious when we returned the next morning with the worst hangover, but Uncle Arran must have talked to him because he got over his snit quickly.

It was the worst summer of my life, avoiding Callie before
I left for London. Wondering if she was kissing someone else
on her eighteenth birthday. But she'd asked Fyfe to her party,
and everyone else in our class who was still in Ardnoch that
summer. Fyfe said she didn't kiss anyone else, and that she was
sad, though she pretended she wasn't.

"Where did you go just now?" Callie asked, brows
pinched.

I shook my head. "Nowhere."

She frowned but shrugged, taking another sip of her
whisky. Her lips plumped over the rim of the glass and glistened with the amber liquid after her sip. I found myself
licking my own lips at the memory of how soft her mouth felt
beneath mine, on my skin, around my—

"So …" She gestured around the room. "This seems like a
nice part of London."

Small talk. I could do small talk if that's what she needed.

"Aye. Lucky to be blessed with a wealthy family," I
answered dryly. "Hopefully I'll start earning enough to cover
my own bills now, though."

The corner of her mouth kicked up. "I hear that. Mum
paid for me to go to school in Paris. There was no way I could
afford it otherwise. But I'm hoping that what I've learned will
benefit her, too, by benefiting the bakery."

"Sometimes it makes me feel guilty. The money. The
advantages. I have a friend. Sean. Really nice bloke. From
Dublin. He was brought up in care, moved from foster
home to foster home. Worked his arse off to go to UCL to
study architecture and then had to work harder than any of
us to stay here. The guy barely slept he had so many side
jobs, just so he could afford the shitty flat he had to share
with two other blokes, who were not good human beings." I
scrubbed a hand over my beard. "I asked him in third year to
move in with me, that my rent was covered, so he could

focus on class and the internships. He got so pissed off, saying he didn't need the handout. It made me feel like a privileged arsehole."

"I think it was a kind offer."

"But do you say that as someone who comes from money?"

"No." Callie shook her head. "You forget that before Mum and I came here, back when I still called her Mom"— she slipped into her American accent with ease—"we had nothing. We lived in a studio apartment and instead of a living room we had two twin beds. Mum tried to hide how hard things were, but I could always sense her worry and stress. Any help we got was so appreciated. Our neighbors were this amazing couple, Juanita and Eli, and even though they didn't have much themselves, they helped us out when they could." Callie gave me a reassuring smile. "Your offer to your friend was generous. I'm sure deep down he was grateful for it. But sometimes we must do things for ourselves. Especially if that's all we're used to."

"I've never had to do anything for myself. I've always known that if shit hit the fan, I had my family's money to bail me out. Doesn't say much for me, does it?" I didn't know why I was telling her this stuff. It was so easy to fall back into real conversation with Callie. And for the most part, our relationship had been strong because we could tell each other anything. The one thing I hadn't been able to voice had been the very reason we broke up.

I believed now if I'd been honest with her, we'd have worked things out.

"I'd agree if you didn't work your arse off. You didn't get into UCL because of your family, Lewis. You didn't graduate with job offers to several top architect firms because of your family. That was all you. You've never been lazy, and it would be so easy to be lazy in your position."

Pleasure rippled through me. "How do you know about the offers from the firms?"

Callie rolled her eyes. "Don't get a big head. Eilidh told me. Your sister likes to tell me things about you all the time that I don't ask to know."

I didn't want to believe her. I wanted to believe that she ate up whatever bit of information about me she was fed. Like I did with her. "So ... why Paris?"

If she was surprised by the change of subject, she didn't say so. "What do you mean?"

"I mean, when we were together, you never mentioned it. How did it come about?"

"I actually was going to talk to you about it before we broke up," she said tonelessly, like our breakup no longer bothered her. "Thought we could come up with a plan. Maybe for you to do a transfer to a French uni for a couple of years while I trained at the pastry school. Or we'd wait until you'd graduated and then go. I knew you wanted to travel, so I thought you'd have liked the idea." That's when I saw it, the crack in her facade. Her smile was pained.

As for me, I felt like my chest was splitting down the middle. "I would have loved it." It wasn't a lie. It would have been the perfect balance for both of us. A chance for me to live elsewhere for a time, to see a bit of the world, until we came home to Ardnoch. Knowing what I knew now, missing my home like I never imagined I would, I would have been more than happy with that plan.

Instead, I came to a city that made me lonelier than ever and Callie went to Paris and thrived there.

Life was ironic that way.

"It took me a while to get up the courage to go alone, but a few years ago I decided it was now or never."

"And you're glad you went?"

"I loved living there and learning and experiencing another

culture ... but I think I loved it because I knew I'd return home to my family at the end of the adventure."

"To Ardnoch."

She nodded.

"I'm proud of you," I said quietly. "Am I allowed to say that?"

A strange expression crossed her face for a moment. Then she nodded. "Of course. I'm proud of you too. You set out to do exactly what you wanted. And here you are in London, about to start your career at a prestigious design firm." Callie's gaze dropped and she shook her glass at me. "Got any more?"

I nodded and stood up. When I reached for her glass, our fingers brushed. Callie snapped her hand back like she'd been burned.

This time, it didn't hurt. This time her reaction gave me hope.

———

An hour later, my skin was flushed from my fourth whisky, and I could tell by the slight glassiness of Callie's eyes she was feeling the effects too.

"Don't you worry about her?" Callie had kicked off her shoes and was curled up on the end of the sofa. Her elbow rested on the back, while she leaned her head on her palm. "Sometimes when we talk, I feel like she's got this wall up. And I don't remember Eilidh ever having a wall up."

I nodded, because I knew exactly what she meant. For the past hour, we'd talked about everything and nothing, skirting the tension between us and catching each other up on our families. Currently, we were discussing Eilidh's career and her sudden overnight fame. "She says she can handle it, but I wonder if she's too proud to admit that maybe she wasn't quite as ready for this life as she thought. Probably because my uncles tried to warn her, and she was so adamant that she could deal with it all."

"Have you tried talking to her?"

"Of course. She tells me she's great. Never better. And then she changes the subject."

"Yup. That's exactly what she does to me."

My tongue a wee bit loose from the whisky, I said, "I'm glad you and she remained friends after our breakup."

Callie stared at me, cheeks flushed, eyes narrowed. "It wasn't Eilidh's fault."

Her tone suggested she thought it was mine. I sighed. Heavily.

"You're like a different person," she whispered sadly.

That made me frown because I didn't think I'd changed that much.

"Not a different person." She waved off that thought. "Just older and a little changed for being older. I didn't see you become who you are now and ... it's weird."

"How so?"

"The tattoos." She gestured to my arm. "The bike. The beard. The man bun."

My lips twitched at how angry she sounded on the words *man bun.* "You don't like it?"

She rolled her eyes on a huff. "You know you look good, Adair. Don't fish for compliments."

I grinned. "You look good too. Better than good. You look sexy as fuck."

Her eyes flared. "Don't flirt with me."

"I'm not. I'm merely observing and speaking a truth. You grew up sexy, Callie Ironside."

Callie's cheeks flushed a deeper shade of red at the hoarseness in my voice. "That's something else that's different about you. You never used to be so flirtatious."

"I used to compliment you all the time."

"That was different. You'd call me beautiful. But the Lewis I knew was reserved with that stuff."

"I'm not now," I promised.

She shook her head, sitting up. "No doubt you've had plenty of practice flirting with a smorgasbord of women over the last seven years."

If only she knew. "As opposed to all the practice you had with Remy and Gabriel and whatever other French bastard you let taste you."

Her eyes flashed. "Taste me? Really? And how do you know their names?"

"Eilidh," I lied. "She's a wealth of information about how easily you got over me, sweetheart. How many guys have there been?"

"None of your business. Just like it's none of my business how many women you've slept with."

Jealousy was a tight ball of heat in my chest. Possessiveness made my brain foggy. Or maybe it was the whisky. Or both. But right then, all I wanted to do was throw this woman—*my* woman—over my shoulder and then on my bed so I could erase every single man she'd ever been with. "Funny how it still feels like my business."

TEN
CALLIE

I gaped at Lewis in disbelief. Who was this guy? Anticipation and indignation coursed through me, and I found I couldn't stay sitting. Slowly, I got to my feet and then shook my head. "You did not just say that."

Lewis stood too. "We both know it's true." He took a step toward me, and my skin, already warm from the whisky, suddenly caught fire at the heat in his eyes. It was predatory and sexual and thrilling, and a look he'd never bestowed on me before. "Sex with other people will never be what it was between us."

This was no longer the *boy* who'd left me behind.

And I would be lying if there wasn't a traitorous part of me that wondered what it would be like to have sex with this version of him.

Fear of the repercussions of that triggered me, and I was speaking before I could stop myself, my words an effort to put him off. "Neither of us knew what we were doing. We were kids. And frankly, I've had better sex since then."

I regretted the words. Mostly because of the hurt that

flashed across Lewis's face before he could hide it. Determination (and anger) masked the emotion.

He took another step toward me. "I doubt it."

My pulse raced the closer he got. I had to tilt my head to keep hold of his eyes, and I couldn't see past his broad shoulders. Suddenly, I was picturing him naked and above me, my hands coasting across those hard muscles as he thrust between my legs.

I wanted that. There would be no first-time awkwardness or fumbling with him either. It would be as easy as breathing with Lewis.

I wanted it so badly, it was wiping all rational thought from my head. I had to fight it. "It's true." My words came out weak and hoarse and I hated him for that too. "You're too much of a gentleman for me, Lewis. I like my sex more adventurous now. A little rougher. I like ..." I sucked in a breath as he closed the distance between us, his body touching mine.

"You like what?" His expression was fierce with fury. And desire.

My lower belly squeezed deep and wet heat licked between my thighs.

Fuck.

Fuck. It.

I'd pay for it in the morning.

"In ... in bed ... I like a guy to take control."

Surprise lit Lewis's eyes and then something darkened them. "Noted," he growled. Then his hand was on my nape, bringing my mouth to his as he bent his head to take it.

ELEVEN
LEWIS

Her lips were as soft and as familiar as I remembered, and I groaned, needing a deeper taste. She'd tried to skewer me with her words, tried to stop this thing between us by pricking my pride. All she'd done was fire my blood. Callie wanted me to take control? I was very happy to do that, as long as the end result was watching her come around me.

She was kissing me back like that's all she wanted too.

With no other thought but having her after all these years of fucking pining, I hauled Callie up into my arms. She was curvier and softer in my embrace, and I couldn't wait to kiss every inch of those curves. With a moan that vibrated down my throat, Callie wrapped her long legs around my waist and clung to me as we devoured each other's mouths on the way to the bedroom.

Following her down to the bed, I broke the kiss, but only to shove her dress up to her waist and pull her simple black cotton underwear down her legs. She panted beneath my body, staring up at me, eyes still a bit glassy with alcohol, skin flushed with desire. For a moment, her words about having had better sex pierced through my bubble, renewed hurt making me resentful and determined in equal measure.

"Do you want me to fuck you?" I asked, unbuckling the belt on my jeans. "Because we're not doing this until you tell me yes."

Callie's eyes flared with surprise. "Aye," she whispered breathlessly.

"Hard?" I growled.

Her gaze dipped to where my erection strained against my jeans zipper. "So hard," she moaned, squirming a little.

Years of pent-up longing obliterated all rational thought. I yanked my wallet out of my back pocket of my jeans. There were only two condoms inside, and they had been in there a good long while, but they would do. I threw my wallet onto the floor and pushed my jeans and boxers down low enough to free me. Once I rolled on protection, I pinned Callie's wrists at either side of her head, enjoying her breathy moan of excitement. It also reminded me she wasn't lying about the new things she'd discovered about herself while in bed with *other men*.

I wanted to erase every single one of them.

Without taking a moment, my only focus on being inside her, I guided my cock to her entrance and thrust inside.

Hard.

"Lewis!" Callie gasped, as her wet tight heat hugged my cock.

For a moment, I gritted my teeth, the pleasure so intense I was afraid I'd come and embarrass myself. Opening my eyes, I stared down at Callie, and seeing that pleasure matched on her face was too much.

I was inside Callie. After all these years, she was here with me.

I started to fuck her, like I'd never fucked her. She grasped at my arse, as she tilted her hips frantically to meet my thrusts. Her undulations made me slide in deeper. Shivery heat sparked down my spine and tightened in my groin.

"Fuck," I huffed. "You feel so amazing, so right. So good, tight, hot, so perfect," I muttered incoherently as I moved over her.

Her lips parted on her pants of excitement; her thighs pressed to my sides as I drove into her body. I moved to grip her wrists again, pinning them back down on either side of her head as my drives increased in speed and strength. The whole bed shook as I growled Callie's name over and over.

"Nothing's better than this, than us," I panted hard. "Say it."

Callie moaned, shaking her head.

"Say it, Callie. Say you need this. My cock, me, fucking you."

I felt her inner muscles ripple around me as surprise flared again in her eyes.

"Do you know how many times I've thought about this?" I groaned as ecstasy built inside me. "You in my bed, that look on your face as I pump into this sweet pussy."

"Lewis!" Suddenly she was coming around my cock on a gasp of shock. It felt so amazing, her tight inner muscles squeezing me, that I couldn't hold back my release any longer.

"Callie!" I tensed between her legs seconds before I came, my cock pulsing inside her. Bliss shuddered through me as I poured myself into her.

It felt never-ending.

I couldn't remember the last time I'd come that hard.

Never.

I'd never come that hard.

My muscles turned to liquid as I slumped over her,

pressing my face into her throat as I tried to catch my breath. She smelled so good. Even now, I wanted her all over again. But then I felt Callie tense beneath me. Panic flared.

Not wanting to give her time to run away—to ruin this—I lifted my head, stared deep into her eyes, and saw the confusion and sadness in them. I wanted to erase all of it. So I kissed her. Hungry, wanting, devouring her so she didn't have a chance to overthink. I broke the connection only to pull my T-shirt over my head and throw it away.

Then her hands were on me as our mouths crashed together again. Soft strokes across my pecs and around my back, fingernails biting into me as our hips began to undulate against each other. I was growing hard inside her.

Shit.

I pulled out, and she gasped with the sensation. Eyes hot on her, I dealt with the used condom, throwing it into the rubbish bin by my bed, before grabbing the second condom out of my wallet and moving over her body. "Last one," I told her as I ripped it open. "Better make it good. Take your dress off."

"Only because you asked so nicely." She smirked, pulling her dress up, revealing every inch of her. Her abs were defined, her thighs lean and strong, which suggested she still did martial arts or at least worked out, but her hips were slightly softer, her waist curving with more definition.

And Callie's breasts.

Fuck, I'd be dreaming of them for years to come.

Larger than I remembered, and still perfect, with dark pink nipples that made my mouth water. "You are a walking wet dream." I drew one of her nipples between my lips and sucked.

"Oh!" Callie arched into me, her legs wrapped around my waist as she caressed my back.

I licked and laved and sucked at her until she was crying out in pleasure, then I moved onto the other nipple until it was just as swollen and flushed from my attention. Trailing my lips down her stomach, taking my time, I touched every inch of her, memorizing her slopes and curves until she was imprinted on my palms.

Looking up at her as I lay with my head between her thighs, memories washed over me. "Do you remember the first time I licked your pussy?"

Her lower belly rippled as her nostrils flared and cheeks flushed.

Callie liked dirty talk.

Also noted.

"I remember," she whispered.

"I remember how you came on my tongue," I whispered hoarsely. "How it felt to know I gave you that."

"Lewis ..."

Afraid to let thoughts of her other men intrude, I bowed my head and thrust my tongue into her. Her familiar taste cascaded over me.

"Lewis!" she cried out. Her hands clutched at my head as her thighs tightened around my shoulders.

Satisfaction thrummed through me. Taking her clit between my tongue and teeth, I sucked and licked until Callie's cries of pleasure filled my bedroom. And I didn't stop. Holding her hips tight in my grip, I held her captive while I tormented her clit until it was swollen and she was soaked. I kept going. I wanted her to remember this for the rest of her life.

A glance at Callie revealed tears rolling down her cheeks as she came for a third time, her hands now limp at either side of her head.

Her breasts heaving and trembling.

Mine. The fierce possessive thought came over me as I watched her shudder through her fourth orgasm of the night.

And before I could think, I was moving over her, tilting her hips, pulling them off the bed so I could plunge into her.

"Lewis!"

"Hold onto the headboard," I commanded.

She did, and I pulled back only to drive so hard into her the bed shifted beneath us. Her desperate moans and cries spurred me on. I *fucked* her. I fucked her with such intensity, I hoped I imprinted on her goddamn soul.

The bed slammed against the wall as I powered into her. Her inner muscles were swollen from her climaxes and if she felt sensational before, the experience was on another level now.

"Is this what you need?" I growled.

"Yes! Yes, yes!"

"Take me, mo chridhe." I bared my teeth, her inner muscles clasping hotly to my cock as I thrust in and out of her wet channel. "Take my cock. It's yours. Only yours, mo chridhe."

"I'm coming, I'm coming!" Callie cried like she was almost panicked. And then she screamed, her eyes rolling back in her head. And I felt it. I felt how fucking hard she came. Her inner muscles throbbed in fierce clenches around my cock, like a tight hand jerking me into my own climax.

I bellowed her name as my balls drew up and I exploded. My hips juddered in what felt like the longest orgasm anyone had ever experienced.

"Fuck, fuck." The muscles in my arms trembled as I held myself over her. She still throbbed around me, little aftershocks of pleasure trembling through my whole body. Sweat dampened my skin, my heart pounding so fiercely in my chest and ears, I could barely hear anything over it.

We caught our breath and finally, Callie seemed to return

to the reality of the moment. Our gazes held, a sense of awe passing between us.

She was right.

Back when we were kids, the sex had been good, sweet. The sex between two kids who loved each other.

But this ... this was something else. Something hungrier and more powerful ... and I wanted to do it over and over again. With only her. For the rest of my life.

Callie's eyelashes fluttered as her whole body seemed to melt into my bed. "Phenomenal," she murmured sleepily. "I feel like butter on hot toast."

I smiled as an overwhelming ache filled my chest, threatening to crack it. There were only a few times when we were younger that we'd had the opportunity in which I could give my girl multiple orgasms before I needed to get her home. But on those occasions, she'd wanted to fall asleep after, and I'd had to keep her awake until we arrived at her place.

Considering tonight was the best sex we'd ever had, it wasn't surprising to see her lashes flutter close. Especially after the four whiskies and however many cocktails she'd had at the bar.

Reluctantly, I eased out of her, and her eyes opened briefly as she moaned. The sound unbelievably sent renewed blood rushing to my cock. With a sigh, I got off the bed and watched as she fell back asleep, her chest rising and falling slowly.

After I cleaned up, I returned to pull the duvet beneath her out, knowing that wouldn't wake her either. She hadn't changed as much as I'd feared. All the wee things were still the same.

Shoving the duvet in the cupboard to be laundered later, I pulled out a fresh one, and eased it over my unexpected companion. Then I got in beside her and drew Callie into my arms, relishing the way she snuggled against my chest like we'd never been apart.

I kissed her temple. "I've missed you so much, mo chridhe."

Her light breathing was the only answer.

"But I won't need to miss you anymore," I promised, determination filling me. Settled and at peace with my plan—more at peace than I'd felt in years—I coasted my hand over Callie's waist, comforted by her warmth.

Sleep claimed me easier than it had since the last time she belonged me.

———

The sound of a whining engine and the familiar shouts between the blokes that cleaned mine and my neighbor's windows woke me.

And even though I'd been sleeping alone for a long time, I remembered Callie should be in my bed. My eyes flew open, and I turned my head on the pillow to find the space beside me empty.

Disappointment and something worse crept in, fully pushing me out of sleep state. I pushed to sitting, rubbing a hand over my beard. "Callie?" I called.

Nothing.

Knowing what I'd inevitably find, but not wanting to discover it, I reluctantly got out of bed and checked the bathroom.

No Callie.

Padding down the hall, naked as the day I was born, I entered the living space.

No Callie.

With a huff of anger and hurt, I turned around and headed back to the bedroom to pull on pajama bottoms, only to return to the living space in search of a note.

There was none.

None in the bedroom either.

Her clothes and purse were gone.

Callie was gone.

Without a word.

Like a one-night stand desperate to be rid of me.

For a moment, I wanted to dwell on the fact that she'd treated me that way. However, if I let my hurt and anger win, then we'd be right back where we started. And I didn't want that. I wanted to get past this.

Hands shaking, I found my phone in the kitchen. There were a couple of texts from friends and one from Eilidh this morning.

> Callie already on her way back to Ardnoch.
> What did you do?

Irritation made my skin hot, but I didn't reply to my sister. Instead, I scrolled through my contacts and hit the call button.

After a few rings, he picked up. "Morning, son. You all right?"

The sound of my dad's voice eased the franticness that threatened to consume me. "No. I need to know something."

"Okay?" he replied slowly, his concern evident in his voice.

"Does your offer for me to come work with you still stand?"

There was a moment of hesitation, then, "Are you serious?"

"Completely."

"Then, aye." Dad's delight was obvious. "Of course. The job is yours as soon as you're ready."

"I'll need to find a place to stay."

"Stay with us." He was so eager, I felt guilty for staying away for so long. "Until you find a place. You can have the annex."

"Really?"

"Absolutely."

"Thanks, Dad."

"Your mum is going to be so happy, Lew."

"Good. I'm looking forward to being home." I only had to hope that Callie Ironside would be as happy about the news.

TWELVE
CALLIE

TWO WEEKS LATER

"And what are those?" Mrs. Rankin asked, pointing with a look of distaste at my signature Saint Honorés.

I explained patiently what they were, even though I wanted to scream at her that they were the same pastries she'd asked about every day the bakery was open for the last two weeks.

Morag from Morag's Grocery stood behind Mrs. Rankin and rolled her eyes.

We both knew Mrs. Rankin knew exactly what all the new pastries in Callie's Wee Cakery were. She was merely making a passive-aggressive point that she didn't like the new changes. And she didn't like that I'd left Ardnoch for three years and thought I could waltz back into my mother's bakery and village life like I'd never left.

"Hmm." She sniffed and shot Mum a look, but she was

too busy helping another villager out with her order. As were our customer service assistants, Angie and Cathy. "All of these fancy French things ... There was nothing wrong with what your mother used to sell, you know."

"There *was* nothing wrong with them, Aisla," Morag said from behind her, "as there's nothing wrong with Callie's pastries. In fact, they're divine, and I'd quite like to sample one before the end of time."

I pinched my lips to smother a smile as Aisla Rankin shot Morag a displeased look over her shoulder. "Perhaps you should reconsider sampling any sweet treats, Morag."

Morag raised a brow. "And what does that mean?"

"Nothing. Just that you might have been sampling a few too many lately."

Oh, no she didn't.

The customers crowded into the store sucked in their breath, appalled.

"Mrs. Rankin," Mum called.

She turned her glower on Mum. "Yes?"

"I don't take kindly to you insulting my customers, and since you're clearly displeased with our new array of baked goods, I don't think you'll be too put out when I tell you I must ask you to leave."

Gaping at Mum, I wanted the floor to open up and swallow me.

This was what I was afraid of.

Since my return to the bakery, there had been some hiccups with the new menu. People were a bit disgruntled at first that some of the cakes Mum had been baking for years were no longer on offer, to make room for my new recipes. I was gutted on day one when local customers left in a huff without buying anything, and I was so sure I was going to cost Mum her business if we didn't return it to the status quo. However, Mum remained calm and assured me that in a tiny place like Ardnoch, sometimes people weren't eager for change. It took time.

As for tourists, they snapped photos of my pastries, oohing and aahing over them. That only made me feel slightly better because I wanted to win over the people who lived here.

Our kind friends and family heard about the terrible day and dropped in throughout the next week to buy the pastries and make a big show around the village about how delicious they were. When we opened on Saturday, customers returned and decided to give my inventions a try.

We'd stayed busy, but there was always at least one customer who bemoaned the lack of the old treats. I told Mum maybe we should put some of the old cakes back and take away some of the new, but she'd flat out refused.

"Yours are better," she'd told me with blunt pride. "And only the best is served at Callie's Wee Cakery."

But now this ...

It had come to Mum booting one of her regular, long-standing customers off the premises.

Mum had complained about Mrs. Rankin almost every day. The older lady was really getting on our nerves ... but in my absence, I'd forgotten something. No one messed with me and Harry while Mum was around to see it. People always thought they should be intimidated and afraid of Dad ... but Mum was the biggest Mamma Bear around.

"What a way to treat a loyal customer!" Mrs. Rankin spat.

"It is." Mum gestured to Morag. "Morag has been patronizing my bakery since the first day it opened, and I won't see her insulted beneath its roof."

"Wait until the rest of the village hears of this insult to *me*!" Mrs. Rankin fumed as she sneered at Morag.

Morag tilted her chin. "Don't you be looking at me like that, Aisla Rankin. And you can forget about coming into the store for your Friday sandwich, too, until you apologize."

"Huh! Keep your sandwich. It's too vinegary, anyway." She sniffed haughtily and started to push past the congregated and very entertained customers.

"That's not the sandwich, it's your sour tongue!" Morag called after her, getting the last word in.

As soon as the door closed on Mrs. Rankin, despite my concerns about the business, I tried but failed to smother a snort of laughter.

Morag stepped up to the counter, her eyes dancing with amusement. "She had that coming."

"That sour tongue comment was perfect." I bit my lip against more laughter. "But what if she tells everyone not to come to the bakery?"

I could feel Mum studying me, but I kept my attention on Morag.

"No one pays a lick of attention to Aisla Rankin. Or Ursula." Morag referred to Mrs. Rankin's daughter, who was in her forties but according to gossip still thought she was a high school mean girl. Morag tucked a loose strand of teal-colored hair behind her ear. "Now, just to spite the auld witch, I'll take an Ardnoch Saint Honoré *and* an apple candy rose puff."

I boxed up her cakes with a smile and slipped a wee salted caramel macaron in as a thank-you.

The rest of the morning, as all mornings at the bakery since that fateful first day back, flew by and we were out of products before noon. Angie and Cathy immediately began to clean out front.

Phil no longer worked at the bakery.

Another reason I felt guilty and worried about my effect on the business.

Mum's assistant had been working and learning from her for over two years. He'd never made it known he was upset about my impending return, but two mornings after my trip to London, he texted Mum to let her know he wouldn't be back. He said he didn't feel there would be much room for him at the bakery now, nor the attention he needed from her to become a professional baker. That he couldn't stay where nepotism flourished! He was moving to Inverness to attend catering college.

Dad called him a spoiled man-child and told me not to worry about it.

Mum was upset by his defection, but also told me not to worry about it.

I worried about it.

For the most part, being back in Ardnoch was easy. Our friends and family welcomed me back like I'd never left. Yet there were some, not even as mean as Aisla and Ursula Rankin, who were a bit standoffish with me. Like I was new to the village all over again.

The worst was my own brother. I couldn't tell if Harry was a moody, prepubescent almost-twelve-year-old who didn't want to hang out with me or if he was pissed off at me for being away for so long. Whatever it was, anytime I tried to chat or hang out with him, he either disappeared out the door and got on his bike or locked himself in his room to play on the computer.

Part of me wondered if leaving had been a huge mistake. Feeling unsettled and concerned about my effect on the business, on my brother, was an excellent distraction from the thing that plagued me more than any other part of my life.

My unforgettable night with Lewis.

Now and then, out of nowhere, I'd see Lewis moving over my body. I could hear my moans mingling with his groans. Feel his hands, smell his aftershave, remember his mouth ...

I shook my head of the memories and pulled off my apron. Mum disappeared into the kitchen to start work on a commissioned wedding cake, and I crossed the bakery to lock up. As I was pulling the blind down, a tall figure appeared on the other side, accompanied by a familiar but not so familiar face.

Delight and shock shot through me. "Fyfe?"

He grinned and I quickly unlocked the door, stepping outside to embrace my old friend. Fyfe hugged me, giving me a hard squeeze. As I pulled back, I stared at him in wonder. He looked so grown up ... and manly. When we were kids, he was always shoving a pair of spectacles back up his nose. There were no glasses to be seen. His face, while handsome, had been long and narrow, and despite the fact Lewis trained him in tae kwon do (because he couldn't afford to take the classes with us), Fyfe had always been slim and wiry.

The same warm, dark eyes I'd always remembered stared back at me, but otherwise, I almost didn't recognize him. Fyfe had filled out. His jaw was now wide and strong and peppered with a short brown beard. Thick brown hair was cut and styled to perfection and so obviously soft. And broad, broad shoulders stretched out a navy silk cotton shirt that was rolled at the sleeves, revealing strong forearms. The shirt was paired with suit trousers and black dress shoes.

Fyfe Moray was a *hot* grown-up.

When did that happen?

And what was he doing here? I blurted out the latter.

"What am I doing here? What are *you* doing here?" Fyfe teased with a flash of straight, perfect white teeth.

"I'm back from school in France ... but what are you doing here?" I repeated.

"Didn't your mum tell you?"

I shook my head.

"I've been back for about eighteen months. Got my own cybersecurity company. We do work for the estate, the distillery, private customers ..."

I couldn't believe Mum hadn't mentioned it. Then again, where there was Fyfe, there was Lewis, and I'd made it clear I didn't want to hear about the latter. Impressed but in no way surprised by his success, I squeezed Fyfe's arm and felt the hard muscle beneath. "That's amazing. I'm so happy for you." It was on the tip of my tongue to ask him if Lewis knew he was back in Ardnoch, but I was afraid to say his name.

"I never thought I'd return, but it kind of lures you back, right?" Fyfe said, glancing down the quaint main street of the village, with its cobbled roads and Victorian-style lampposts.

"I never intended to not return," I reminded him. "But I didn't think you'd come back."

"Aye, there are some memories here I'd rather forget." Fyfe sighed. "But some I never want to forget. Like all of us together. We had fun, didn't we?"

"We did." Until we didn't. "Where are you staying now?"

"McCulloch Farm. I bought one of the houses on your aunt Allegra's development."

Of course. Before I left Ardnoch, my aunt Ally (she wasn't technically my aunt, but I'd always treated her as such) and her husband, Jared, were about to break ground on a small development of contemporary eco homes on a parcel of their farmland.

"Fancy." I knew from Aunt Ally they were only building five houses, each with a generous plot of land, and sustainably developed so they were inexpensive to run. I also knew they were worth a pretty penny. "Do you like it?"

"I do. I'd love to have you over for dinner sometime."

"Sounds great. I can't wait to catch up."

"Is there room for one more?" a deep, familiar voice said at Fyfe's back.

Fyfe whirled, revealing his old best friend and my ex.

The man I'd disappeared on two weeks ago, when I awoke to find myself in his bed. After a night of whisky-fueled sex that had blown my mind.

Lewis Adair had grown up in more ways than one and had surprised the heck out of me.

He'd also scared the utter bejesus out of me because when I saw him lying there, asleep at my side, I'd felt nothing but crushing grief. Aye, I'd given the appearance of moving on and dating other men. Yet, I'd never truly let them get close to me. And I didn't know if it was because I'd given that part of myself to Lewis and there was no way to get it back, or if I was just afraid to try to give it to someone new in case I got hurt all over again. Because the truth was, while I'd done a valiant job of pretending like I was okay after our breakup, I felt a physical hurt in my chest every day for months.

Months and months.

Then one day, long after he'd left Ardnoch, I realized it didn't hurt every day anymore. It only hurt sometimes. Mostly whenever someone mentioned him, or something happened to remind me of him. Moving to Paris meant I experienced that hurt less and less until eventually, I went weeks without thinking about him. And even then, it was a flicker of a shadow of a ghost of pain.

But lying in bed next to him two weeks ago, it felt like the first day after we'd broken up.

It hurt so badly.

I couldn't give him that kind of power over me again, so I'd slunk off without waking him, thinking worst-case scenario I might see him at Christmas if he deigned to visit his family.

Yet, somehow, he was here.

Standing outside the bakery, staring at me as if he hadn't seen me in years.

"You're here." Fyfe reached out to pull his friend into a hug and they made quite the picture, two big, handsome guys giving each other a manly thump on the back. "Are you all unpacked?"

Unpacked?

What?

Lewis looked at me. "Aye, the annex is mine until I can find somewhere, so I'll be inviting myself to dinner whenever the chance arises."

"Happy for the company, mate."

"Wait." I swallowed hard, my mouth dry. "Unpacked? Annex?"

What on God's green earth was happening?

Lewis's gaze was intense and searching. "I'm home, Callie. I took a job at my dad's firm."

At my gaping nonanswer, Lewis spoke again, this time over the rushing blood in my ears. "I've moved back to Ardnoch. Permanently."

THIRTEEN
LEWIS

W ell, that could have gone better. I didn't know what I was expecting. But Callie spluttering "Nice to see you both" before hurrying back inside the bakery and locking the door behind her wasn't it.

Was it foolish of me to hope that our night had meant something to her, too, and she was just scared to admit it?

Maybe I needed to give her time to adjust to the idea of me being back, but I was afraid if I left it too long, she'd fail to understand that she was the main reason I'd come home.

"Go and see her."

I looked up from my coffee. Mum stood on the opposite side of the island, sipping tea, watching me carefully. I'd come across from the annex for my morning coffee only to discover Dad was already up and out buying groceries. Mum was dressed especially nice for the day. I would have said as much, but she was studying me with a look I knew well. Ever since she came into our lives, she'd always seemed to understand what Eilidh and I were thinking.

"She ran away," I reminded her.

"It's big news for her." Mum leaned on her elbows, expression sympathetic. "Before she left for Paris, Callie did a good impression of being fine on the surface, but I know from Sloane that it was far from the truth. Now, we've tried not to bug you two about what happened all those years ago—as much as it kills us not to know—but Sloane said Callie lost something that day. The sparkle in her eyes. And you did too." She reached over to touch my hand. "You didn't come back only to be with us ... so don't overthink things. Go after what you came home for."

"What did you come home for?"

The question came from behind. We both turned to watch my wee sister Morwenna descend the stairs. Our home hadn't changed much over the years. Designed by my father, it was a timeless piece of architecture that I'd only begun to appreciate as I got older. What a privilege it was to grow up in a house that had been built to capture the ocean views while withstanding life on the coast. It was open-plan living so that light spilled in from the glass walls facing out toward the water.

Morwenna was the spitting image of our mum with her copper-red hair, chestnut-brown eyes, and dimples. Her coloring was so different from mine and Eilidh's it was the only giveaway we had different birth mothers. Sometimes it was difficult for me to reconcile the tall teenager in front of me with the wee girl who'd asked for constant piggyback rides when *I* was a teenager.

"All of you," I answered her question.

Sliding onto the stool next to me, she gave me a far-too-knowing smirk. "So not Callie, then?"

"What do you know about it?"

"I was seven when you left for uni, Lew, not a fetus." She shrugged. "Callie stopped coming around after you left. Suddenly, she's back from Paris and now you're here. It doesn't take a genius to work out." After that dry and correct supposition, she turned to Mum. "Do I have to go today?"

Mum pursed her lips. "Yes, you do."

"But it's a baby's birthday party."

"What's this?"

Morwenna sighed. "Mum is making me go to Rose's fourth birthday party, even though I'm in the middle of the best book ever."

"All your cousins will be there."

"Under duress. Like me."

"Actually, unlike you, they enjoy spending time with their family."

"Forgive me if I prefer the company of faeries."

At that, I looked at Mum and mouthed *Faeries*?

But she was too busy glowering at my sister. "What is so wrong with your family, young lady? You have a wonderful family, and you should not take them for granted."

"I see them all the time!" Morwenna slipped off the stool. "I don't want to go."

"You're going and you're wearing the dress I put out for you."

"I don't want to wear a dress!"

My eyebrows shot up. Somehow, I'd missed Morwenna hitting the crabby teenager age. Eilidh went through hers around the same time, whereas I was a year or two older before it hit. Dating Callie had pulled my broody head out of my arse, though.

As it would again.

Hopefully.

Mum sighed heavily. "I'm asking you to attend this party because Sarah would do it for you."

"Sarah?" I asked.

"Cavendish," Mum explained. She was a famous local author who married an English film writer and producer.

They were in my parents' friend circle and close to Callie's family because Sarah was Callie's Aunt Ally's cousin-in-law. "Their daughter Rose is four. They bought one of the houses Allegra built so they could spend their summers here instead of in London. We're going there today if you'd like to join us."

I thought of Callie. "Will she be there?"

Mum knew whom I meant. "Sloane said no."

"Perfect opportunity to go see her, then, while everyone is out."

She gave me a knowing smile. "Very true."

"Oh, so Lewis doesn't have to go but I do?" Morwenna threw her arms up before crossing them over her chest. "That's so unfair."

"Lewis is a grown-up, but when he was your age, he attended all our family events without complaint because he understands the importance of family."

Morwenna scoffed. "Then why has he been gone for seven years! Eilidh too! They left and now I have to put up with you smothering me because of it!"

"Morwenna," I clipped out, sounding so much like my father, I pinched my lips shut in surprise.

My sister's face crumpled at my angry tone. "I'm not going!" She turned and hurried upstairs.

I looked wide-eyed back at Mum. "What was that?"

She heaved a beleaguered sigh. "I'm hoping just hormones. She says it's nothing else. We've checked in at school and she seems fine there. She has friends. So I've attempted to reassure your father that it is stupid, horrible, teenage hormones. I'd forgotten what it was like to be thirteen and a girl."

I'd only been home a few days, but since my return, Mor had been fairly quiet and spent a lot of time in her room reading. "You said she has friends?"

Mum nodded. "Sometimes she's happy to spend time with them, but other times she wants to be alone to read. I'm worried about her, but Ery and the others have assured me it's a phase. And when I give her a gentle prod to be social when she's not in the mood ..." She gestured toward the stairs. "This happens. So I don't know."

"Want me to talk to her?" I blanched, remembering her gripe about my absence. "Or maybe not."

"She's not angry at you." Mum rounded the island. "She's mad at the world because all these hormones are flying around in her body, confusing her, but she doesn't understand why she's mad at the world, which is incredibly scary and lonely, and I hate it, but all she can do is go through it. All we can do is remind her we're here. And while I understand that reading is an escape from it, I don't want her to shut everyone out. Family or friends. So I need to push a bit, I think."

I stared upstairs, hating that my sister was feeling that way. "I've thought over the years that being a girl is shit sometimes, but never more so than now."

"Wait until you have a daughter of your own. They're so cute for the first eleven years." She teased and patted my shoulder. "Now, off you go. Go see the girl you came here for."

At the weariness in the back of Mum's eyes, I took her hand from my shoulder and pressed a kiss to the top of it. "Always remember, you are the best mother a child could ask for. Mor is lucky to have you. We're all lucky to have you."

Tears brightened her eyes. "I'm so glad you're home, sweetie."

"Me too."

As I drew my motorbike to a stop outside Callie's front door, my stomach dropped. The Volvo SUV in the driveway was her stepfather's. There was no sign of any other vehicle.

But he'd have heard me pull up because now that I was

back in the Highlands, I was riding my Harley-Davidson Fat Boy. It was my pride and joy with its sharkskin blue and chrome detailing, and its 114 engine that rumbled like only a Harley could.

That rumble, however, was my undoing as I saw Walker appear in the large front window of their bungalow.

Switching off the engine, I removed my helmet and left it on the bike. Very few people would dare to steal from me, especially outside Walker Ironside's house.

Feeling like a boy of sixteen all over again, I ignored the sudden nervous gut churning and strode up the front walk. The door opened before I even reached it and Walker stepped out.

It shocked me to realize he didn't seem so big and broad as I remembered, now that I'd caught up to him in height. Back in London, I'd taught tae kwon do classes and worked out every week at the gym. I'd filled out since Walker had last seen me.

But he was still an inch or so taller and the most intimidating bastard I'd ever met in my life.

And you want this guy to be your father-in-law one day?

Walker did not look like he wanted *me* to be his son-in-law. He looked like he wanted me anywhere but on his front stoop.

"She's not here," he said without preamble, slowly crossing his arms over his chest. His biceps flexed with the move, reminding me of his physical prowess. And I was certain it was deliberate.

"Nice to see you, too, Walker," I dared.

His expression never changed. "I think that's still Mr. Ironside to you."

Right.

Trying to cover my agitation, I asked, "Do you know where Callie is?"

"I'm sure if she wanted you to know, you'd know."

"Right. Well, thanks, anyway." *For nothing*. I turned to go, but he spoke again.

"I don't know what happened between you two all those years ago."

I looked back over my shoulder.

Walker scowled. "I do know that if you've come back to Ardnoch to hurt my daughter again, I will end your life slowly and painfully. I don't care who your family is, Adair." Walker took a step toward me. "They can't protect you from me if you hurt *my* family."

Sensing the absolute honesty in his threat, I faced him again.

Fuck it.

"I love Callie. I loved her then and I love her now. And I came back for her. To stay. To win her back. And you can hate me and mistrust me all you want. You can threaten me with bodily harm and attempt to stand in my way. But it won't stop me from trying to remind Callie that she and I belong together. And if by some miracle she decides to give me another chance, I will *never* leave her again."

Callie's stepdad studied me with that intimidating blank expression.

Then after what felt like an age of inspection, he merely nodded. "She's at Fyfe's this morning. He invited her over for breakfast."

Fyfe's?

Why didn't my friend tell me?

Jealousy I knew I shouldn't feel, but couldn't help, coursed through me at this information.

"Thanks."

Walker nodded again. "Oh, and if by some miracle you do convince Callie ... if I see her on the back of that bike going at anything above forty ... I'll kill you. Make that a blanket statement—if you hurt her physically or emotionally or put her in harm's way physically or emotionally, I will end you." With that, he stepped inside, closing the door on me without another word.

His threat wasn't unexpected, and he'd said similar on multiple occasions when I was a teenager. It had terrified me then, just not enough to stop dating Callie. Now? Well, since he hadn't killed me yet, I wasn't too concerned.

I did feel dejected, and a bit pissed off at Fyfe (which I knew wasn't fair), as I strode toward my bike. However, as I was throwing my leg over it, my phone buzzed in my pocket. Slipping it out, I relaxed at the name on the text.

Fyfe:

> She'll probably kill me for this, but Callie's here with Carianne. You should stop by.

Grinning, all resentment disappeared. Everyone should have a friend like Fyfe Moray. The mention of Carianne, Callie's old friend and Fyfe's ex from when we were kids, barely registered. All I could think about was seeing Callie. Since our night together, the memory of it had tortured me. The thought of never being able to experience being with her again was an agony I couldn't shake. I was determined that this year would end with Callie Ironside in my bed for the rest of fucking eternity.

FOURTEEN
CALLIE

T he houses on the development were spaced out across the large parcel of land so if Fyfe wanted to, he never had to talk to his neighbors. One of his new neighbors, I'd discovered, was Aunt Ally's cousin-in-law, Sarah, and her husband. My mum was heading over there to help set up for their daughter Rose's fourth birthday, so she'd dropped me off at Fyfe's. I knew Sarah and Theo split their time between Gairloch and London, but it looked like they were putting more permanent roots down in Ardnoch too.

When we were younger, I used to tease Lewis that I had a crush on Sarah's husband. He was outrageously good-looking with a sexy, plummy English accent, and it used to make Lewis adorably jealous whenever I waxed lyrical about him. When we were really young, Lewis used to blush around Allegra, so it was only fair. Not that it wasn't understandable. Aunt Ally was beautiful and sweet and had an undeniable charisma. She was also married to the love of her life, Jared (Sarah's cousin), who owned the farm Fyfe's home sat on.

Aunt Ally and Uncle Jared had started off with building glamping pods to rent out. Those had become so successful that they'd expanded the business into holiday lodges. And then instead of selling off some more of their extensive land to a housing developer, they'd decided to develop the plot themselves. On top of their businesses, Allegra was a successful artist and ran an art gallery in the village called Skies Over Caledonia.

When I was younger, I envied Aunt Ally so much. She'd claimed Ardnoch as her own and made a home here with the love of her life. I thought I'd follow in her footsteps, and we'd maybe even raise children together. But Lewis had left, and Aunt Ally and Uncle Jared had decided to enjoy a few years of just each other before starting a family. She fell pregnant as I departed for Paris and as her sister, Aunt Aria, and her husband North adopted a wee boy called Maddox who was three at the time, now six years old. And Aunt Ally had a two-year-old called Collum. I was his pseudo aunt, and he barely knew me. But I intended to change that.

"You're off in dreamland."

I turned from staring out of Fyfe's floor-to-ceiling glass window overlooking nothing but rolling fields and trees to meet Carianne's eyes.

Carianne and I had stayed in touch after I left for Paris, and we always caught up whenever I visited home. She worked as a stylist in a hair salon in Thurso and lived in a small upstairs flat a few streets behind Castle Street. When we were younger, she'd wanted to get out of Ardnoch but had no money. So she'd stayed and trained at the salon. After Fyfe invited me over to breakfast this morning, I'd discovered Carianne here and that she and Fyfe had struck up a friendship again when he'd returned to Ardnoch. They'd only dated for a year when we were kids, and it had ended amiably, so we'd all remained friends.

Her pretty blue eyes held mine. We shared a similar coloring with dark blond hair, blue eyes, and olive skin, but that was where the similarities ended. She had delicate features, whereas I had big eyes and full lips. I was also outgoing and laid-back about most things. Carianne used to be a huffy child. She'd wanted everyone to be her best friend but no one to be anyone else's best friend. She easily felt neglected even when you were giving her your full attention, and if something happened—anything—her first thought was always for herself.

However, after her first thought, she'd take some time to process and then she was sympathetic and loyal and caring. She was one of the first to call if you were sick or sad or if something had gone wrong in your day. Her gifts were always considerate, and she was a good listener when a person needed her to be. No one was perfect. I certainly wasn't. And so I'd put up with the annoying huffy side of Carianne so I could still have all the other lovely qualities she brought to a friendship.

We hadn't spent much time together in the last three years, but I wanted that to change and to see all the ways she'd grown up in my absence.

"It's strange to be back here with you and Fyfe," I finally answered. "In a good way."

"How can we compete with Paris and French lovers, though?" Carianne teased, throwing her arm around me to give me a squeeze.

"Let's not talk about French lovers," Fyfe said from the kitchen where he was making breakfast.

"Look at him." Carianne nodded to Fyfe as he cooked. "All grown up and cooking breaky in his swanky house. Wee Fyfe Moray has come a long way."

Fyfe rolled his eyes at her comment.

"He has. And we couldn't be prouder."

"Bursting with it," Carianne assured.

"Stop it," Fyfe grumbled, "or you'll make my head swell. Just get over here and eat up."

We sat down at the midcentury-style dining table as Fyfe served us fluffy homemade pancakes, bacon, and scrambled eggs.

"This looks delicious." My belly grumbled. "Marry me, Fyfe."

Fyfe raised an eyebrow as his doorbell rang. "I think that might piss off the person at my door."

"What?" Carianne and I asked in confusion.

Instead of answering, Fyfe strode from the room and down the steps that led to his front entrance.

"Is there someone else coming?" I asked Carianne.

She shrugged. "Not that I was aware of."

A male voice met Fyfe's and I stiffened in my chair. My pulse sped up as realization hit.

After Lewis showed up outside the bakery yesterday afternoon to announce his return, I'd fled.

Aye. Like a coward, I'd hurried back into the bakery and refused to leave until I was certain he was gone. Fyfe had called me last night to apologize for not warning me of Lewis's return and to invite me to breakfast to make up for it.

I wasn't mad at Fyfe. I hadn't even known he was back in Ardnoch, let alone expect him to update me on Lewis's comings and goings.

But I was mad at Lewis for not giving me any warning.

Why was he back?

Disturbing my peace and blissful denial!

And now he was here ... again.

Fyfe gave me an apologetic smile as he led Lewis into the open-plan living room. "Take a seat, Lew. I'll plate you up some breakfast."

"Thanks, smells great." Lewis zoomed in on me. "Morning, Callie."

"Lewis!" Carianne jumped from her chair and crossed the room to throw her arms around him. Her head barely reached his shoulders.

Lewis grinned and returned her embrace. "Hi, Carianne."

"Oh my God." Carianne pulled back to stare up at him. "Look at you all MC hot."

"What?" He chuckled.

"Motorcycle Club. I heard you're riding around the village on a Harley looking like a proper biker with all these tattoos." She slapped his biceps where said tattoos were. "I gotta tell you, you're looking good, Adair."

I tried not to scowl at the flirtatious note in her voice and decided she was merely being funny with an old friend.

Lewis's attention turned to me. "How are you?"

Carianne stepped away from him, her expression falling. I tried not to overanalyze that as I shrugged at my ex. "I *was* fine."

His lips pinched together at the implication I was no longer fine. "Do you mind if I join you?"

"Of course she doesn't." Carianne gently shoved him toward a seat. "It's been seven years and she's shagged half of Paris. I think she's over it."

What the actual hell? "Carianne!"

She blanched at my expression. "Oh, Callie, it was a joke. Everyone knows that was a joke, right?"

Lewis folded his large body into the chair but didn't look at anyone while Fyfe brought over plates for his friend and himself.

"Aren't jokes supposed to be funny?" Fyfe gently chided Carianne as he took his seat.

"You're right." Carianne gave me an apologetic, pleading look. "I'm sorry, Callie."

"It's fine." Embarrassed and now wondering if that's what everyone was saying behind my back (that I was sleeping my way around France!), I felt my appetite dissipate. If I did want to shag half of Paris, that was my prerogative, but I hated the idea of people gossiping about me, *shaming* me.

I loved Ardnoch, but the small-town life had kind of worn on my nerves this week.

"Anyway ..." Carianne glanced between Fyfe and Lewis for help. "How are things? Lewis, when do you start working at your dad's firm?"

"Tomorrow." He gave her a toothless smile. "I heard you're a hairdresser now. How's that going?"

"It's good, it's good. I keep busy. I just started doing hair extensions too."

"Good."

"Are you staying at your parents'?"

"The annex, aye. Until I find somewhere."

"The flat next to mine is up for rent. It was a holiday let, but they've decided they want a permanent tenant." Carianne practically fluttered her freaking lashes at him. "It would be nice to be neighbors. I could bring you sugar anytime you ran out."

Feeling Fyfe's gaze, I shot him a disbelieving look.

He grimaced in sympathy.

So I wasn't losing my mind.

Carianne was flirting with Lewis!

Breakfast turned sour for me. Out of politeness, I ate what I could of Fyfe's delicious cooking and tried to catch up with my friend while trying to ignore the fact that my other friend was flirting with my ex. To Lewis's credit, he valiantly attempted to deflect the flirting and kept shooting me worried looks.

Carianne was oblivious.

And as hurt and irritated by her as I was, I had to remind myself that I'd never told her I still harbored feelings toward Lewis or that I'd had sex with him a mere two weeks ago. As far as she was aware, we broke up when we were kids like she and Fyfe broke up, and so Lewis was fair game.

But it wasn't the same.

She and Fyfe dated for a year and were never that serious.

Lewis and I dated for three years and made everyone sick with how in love we were.

You just ... you just didn't come on to your friend's ex-boyfriend and certainly not in front of said friend!

Finally, unable to take much more, I pushed away from the table. "Sorry to love and leave you, but I have some prep to do this afternoon for opening tomorrow."

Fyfe frowned. "Your mum gave you a lift here, right? I'll take you home."

Lewis shot to his feet, his chair scraping back so hard it almost toppled. "No, I'll do it."

I gave Fyfe a pleading look, but it went ignored as he cleared his throat. "Aye, that's a better idea."

"I can give you a lift," Carianne offered instead.

I was about to pounce on that when Lewis glowered at her. "No, you can't."

Carianne's lips smacked shut in shock at his tone.

He winced. "Sorry. Sorry." He turned to me, emotion swarming in his eyes. "Let me take you home. Please. I'd like to talk."

Recognizing the determined expression, I knew I could run away from Lewis only for him to approach me another day until he got what he wanted, or I could get this awkward encounter over with now. "Fine."

Relief eased the tension in his shoulders. He nodded and then turned to Fyfe. "Thanks, bud."

Fyfe smirked. "No problem."

Suddenly, I had the sneaking suspicion that Fyfe had told Lewis I was here. I cut him a dirty look that only made our friend grin unrepentantly. "Thanks for breakfast," I half seethed.

"You're very welcome," Fyfe replied dryly.

I looked at Carianne. "Talk to you soon."

"Aye." She nibbled on her lower lip, not quite looking at either me or Lewis.

Lewis was so focused on me that he didn't even say goodbye to her as we walked out. In fact, as soon as the door closed behind us, he rested his hand on my lower back to lead me toward the sexy bloody motorbike parked on Fyfe's driveway.

Chrome pipes gleamed in the late-morning sunlight.

I tried to ignore the shiver of awareness that skated up my spine at his possessive touch. Unable to ignore it, I stepped away from him. Which was pointless since I was about to be pressed up against him.

Lewis frowned down at me. "You okay?"

I nodded.

He opened the locked box on the back of the bike and pulled out two helmets. Lewis handed one to me. "Your dad warned me if he caught you on the back of my bike and I was doing anything more than forty, he'd kill me. I felt like a teenager all over again."

My lips twitched with laughter. "When did he say that?"

"I stopped by your place this morning."

Oh. "Did he tell you I was here?"

"Eventually. But so did Fyfe."

"So I can be pissed off at both of them."

"Are you?" Lewis looked adorably uncertain, a stark contrast to his tattooed biker facade.

I sighed. "I don't know. Honestly, I've been trying not to think about you or why you're back."

He glanced away, squinting against the sun. Then without another word he popped on his helmet and swung his long leg over his bike. Arousal flushed through me at the sight, and I cursed my physical attraction to him. Why, oh why couldn't we have grown apart in every way possible? Instead, I was more drawn to the arsehole than ever.

With an angry grunt, I slipped on the helmet and got on behind him. He waited until I'd scooted close and wrapped my arms around his waist. My breasts pressed against his back as I turned my head to the side. Then we were off.

Lewis definitely didn't stick to forty.

He didn't ride like a maniac either, but we sped down the coastal road and it took everything within me not to spread my arms wide and throw my head back. This was different to riding in London. We zoomed around the bends and turns, heading into Ardnoch. And it felt like flying. Plus the Harley growled, and that purring vibration felt good. Too good.

To my surprise, Lewis took a turnoff just outside Ardnoch. I recognized it—it led to a small car park where a path cut through the dunes and down onto the beach.

There were a few cars parked because summer was officially only a week away, and the weather was lovely. As soon as the Harley's engine stopped rumbling, I hopped off the bike and removed my helmet. "What are we doing here?"

Lewis tugged off his helmet and smoothed a hand over his hair. Those chunky silver rings on his manly fingers that weirdly turned me on glinted in the sunlight. "You said we could talk."

I had, hadn't I? I thought it would be outside my parents' bungalow where my dad would be watching with such an intimidating presence it would put Lewis off, and he'd leave.

And I'd escape the temptation of him once more.

"I really do need to get back, though."

Lewis swung off the bike and stood to face me. We could

hear the ocean waves lapping beyond the dunes, the sound of a dog barking, seagulls mewing in the clear sky above. Barricaded from the coastal wind, we stood in a soothing warmth that was opposite to the storm roiling inside of me as we stared at each other.

Flashes of that night kept flickering in my mind.

Clear as day, I could hear his groans, feel the way his body tensed and shuddered, how he throbbed thick and hot inside me.

Flushing with need, I retreated from him.

Lewis scowled. "Fine. Then I'll get straight to the point. I came back for you, Callie. I moved back to Ardnoch to be with you. After that night, you can't deny what's still between us."

At once I wanted to throw myself in his arms and sob with relief, while the other half of me wanted to run away from him. To jog all the way down the beach back to the village, so he couldn't see how bloody terrified I was to have him back and saying these things. Because what if in a year or five or ten, he decided he was bored with Ardnoch all over again? That he needed a city like London to inspire him? To keep him satisfied.

The last time I'd been this torn in two was seven years ago, lying on a forest floor in an angsty mess.

I couldn't go back there. I couldn't endure it. The uncertainty would taint our relationship.

Taking a shuddering breath, I released it before replying, "First, I'm sorry for walking out on you two weeks ago without a word. It was cowardly, and I would have been hurt if you'd done that to me."

Lewis gave me a nod. "Thank you for saying that. Apology accepted."

"But, Lewis ..." I held up a hand as he took a step toward me. He halted. "It was a mistake. A drunken mistake. I'm sorry if I led you on, or made you feel like it was more than it was, but I don't want to be with you." My hands shook so much, I fisted them at my sides. "So if you came back here for me, like you said, you should really take time to think about that. Because you should only stay in Ardnoch if it's what *you* want. Not for me. I'm no longer part of the equation."

I couldn't read his expression. The sun hit behind his head, casting his face in shadow so all I could see were his features and not the look in his eyes. He watched me, though. For a good few seconds. Then he nodded. Calm. Accepting. Strangely not full of fight for someone who'd upended his entire life to follow me to the Highlands.

He pulled his helmet on without another word and got back on the bike.

Confused, disappointed, hurt, and feeling like a brat for feeling any of those things, I put the helmet back on and gingerly returned to my seat behind him.

As we rode into the village, I tried not to worry about the villagers who witnessed us together on his bike. Instead, I enjoyed the ride, knowing it was probably my last with Lewis Adair.

FIFTEEN
CALLIE

The day after Lewis dropped his bombshell, Mum and I arrived home from the bakery at the same time Harry returned from school. The end of term was quickly approaching, and after the summer holidays, Harry and his friends would be going into first year at high school. He was twelve in July. And I realized that I'd missed a huge chunk of his childhood.

It was never clearer than when we pulled into the driveway as he walked up the stoop.

"Look how tall he is." I sighed, sad that he'd grown up while I was gone and that it had affected my relationship with him.

When Harry was little, he could be deliberately annoying, like any wee brother, but because of our age gap, we mostly had a good relationship. He was just as likely to come running to me for a hug and reassurance as he was to Mum or Dad.

"Your dad says Harry has to get paired up with the older teens at jujitsu."

I nodded, because that made sense. While I'd gotten into tae kwon do with Lewis when we were kids, Harry had decided he wanted to learn jujitsu because that's the martial art Dad studied. He now led a class in Thurso. And if Dad did it, Harry wanted to do it. While he had Mum's coloring—blond hair, brown eyes—he looked like Dad. When we were younger, there was a part of me that envied Harry. And I worried that Dad would love him more than he loved me because Harry was his blood, and I wasn't. But it was like Dad knew and when Harry came along, he made certain that I never felt left out or like I was loved less.

If anything, in a slightly sexist way he didn't intend, he was more protective of me than he was of Harry. Yet, I knew that came from Dad's own trauma. He didn't mean anything by it. His sister was killed, and he couldn't save her, and now Dad was overprotective of the women in his life. I could understand that.

Harry turned and gave us a wave before heading into the house.

"I'd say that's an improvement, but he was probably waving at you."

"What are you talking about?" Mum asked, unclipping her belt.

I gave her a look. "Harry is avoiding me."

Mum scoffed. "Callie, he's a preteen boy whose only interests are martial arts, video games, and soccer."

"Football," I corrected her, getting out of the car. "You've been here fifteen years, so that's inexcusable."

She chuckled at my teasing as she followed me out. "Fine, fine, football. My point remains. Your brother isn't avoiding you—he's just being a boy."

I harrumphed at that because I wasn't so sure.

Inside, we found Harry at the dining table with his backpack open. Our parents had a rule that our homework had to be completed as soon as we got home, so it was done and out of the way. It seemed Dad was still at work. He tended to do early-morning to early-afternoon shifts at Ardnoch Castle where he worked security, so I could only guess he was running late or on overtime.

Mum bent down to kiss Harry's head. "Hi, baby boy. How was school?"

"It was fine. I wish they'd stop giving us homework now. School's nearly ending and then we're not even going back there after summer. Why do we still have homework?" Harry complained.

"Just humor your teacher and do it. Like you said, it'll be vacation time soon. Do you want a snack?"

"Aye, please." He tapped on his iPad to start whatever exercise his teacher had given. I did think it a bit cruel he was still getting homework this close to the end of term. I couldn't remember our teacher doing that at the end of primary school. Truthfully, I couldn't remember much about primary seven. I'd gone from anticipating the jump to middle school back in the US to suddenly still being in primary school here in the UK and then immediately going into high school at twelve, per the way the Scottish school system worked.

"Got any grand plans for the holidays?" I asked, leaning on an empty dining table chair, attempting conversation.

Harry looked up at me. Except for his eyes and hair, he really was the spitting image of Dad. He could pass for fourteen, he was so tall and broad for his age. "This is Ardnoch, not Paris," he said with attitude. "Not much to do around here."

Mum turned from making Harry a sandwich in the kitchen and met my gaze. She frowned, having heard his tone. *"I told you so,"* my expression said. Sighing inwardly, I tried again. "Maybe we could go for a run in the car this summer. Just you and me."

"You don't have a car," he said to his iPad.

"I'm getting one."

"Mum and Dad buying that for you too?"

"Harry," Mum scolded. "That's unfair."

He shrugged. "It's the truth. Everyone says it."

My stomach dropped. "Says what?"

"That you're mooching off Mum and Dad. That they paid for Paris only so you could come back and take the bakery from Mum because you're too lazy to build something for yourself. That you think you're something special because you stayed in Paris, even though you're mooching off Mum and Dad again by moving back in with us. Everyone thinks you're pathetic."

I gaped at him, stunned, not only by his words but the contempt with which he said it. So much contempt for an eleven-year-old. Was that really what he thought? What everyone apparently thought? I mean, they had to be saying it a lot for it to get back to a kid.

"Harry Ironside, don't you ever speak to your sister like that again," Mum warned, approaching the dining table. "Apologize, now."

He shoved away from the table, grabbing his things. "I'll do this in my room."

"Harry—"

"And she's not my sister. She's my half sister. Her dad is a psychopath, which is probably why everyone hates her. You should go back to Paris. No one wants you here." He marched out of the room, ignoring Mum calling his name in fury.

I knew he was only a kid and probably unaware of how deeply his words cut, but I felt shattered by them. Not merely the words themselves—hitting right at my greatest fear about myself—but that Harry seemed to hate me so much. Maybe going to Paris really had been a mistake.

"Callie ..."

"I'm going for a walk."

"Callie, he didn't mean it."

"No, he meant it. And people are clearly gossiping about me."

"Your brother should not be one of them. And there will be consequences for what he said to you."

"What did he say?"

We turned to find Dad standing in the doorway. So engrossed in the horrible moment with Harry, I hadn't even heard his car pull into the drive. I glanced at Mum and gave a slight shake of my head. If Dad found out, Harry would be in for it.

Mum ignored me. "Our son said terrible things to his sister and I'm frankly baffled and too upset to even ..." She threw her hands up, tears gleaming in her eyes. "I can't believe one of my kids could be that cruel."

"Mum." I shook my head at her. "He's just a kid."

"And you would never have said anything so nasty to anyone when you were his age."

"Because I wasn't a coddled eleven-year-old who's never had a hard day in his life. Harry has grown up with *two* loving parents in a financially secure home. You can't compare us. Circumstances made me more empathetic."

"Are you really defending what he said?"

"Wee yin?"

I turned at that. Even after all these years, Dad still called me *wee yin*.

"What did he say?" Dad repeated, striding into the room. He bristled with tension and even though he'd cut me to the quick, I suddenly felt a bit sorry for Harry. I couldn't bring myself to tell Dad.

Mum repeated his words verbatim.

Dad's expression darkened and he marched toward the hallway.

"Dad, don't."

He looked back at me. "He's twelve in July. He wants to

start spewing nasty shit like that as if he's a man, then he can take a telling like a man."

I looked at Mum in worry.

She shook her head at me, fully trusting Dad to deal with it in the correct way.

Too concerned I'd caused a rift between my parents and Harry, I followed Dad against my mother's whispered wishes for me to stop. He was already in Harry's room, the door ajar. I held my breath, listening as I watched Dad tower over Harry's bed where my brother sat with his iPad on his lap.

"... Is that what you said?" Dad growled.

"So what if it was?" Harry whined. "It's the truth."

"Do you even realize how much you hurt your sister? Does it even compute? Do you even care, Harry? Because we've got big problems if you don't care that your sister is out there looking like you punched her in the gut."

Harry flinched and looked away. "I didn't think it would bother her that much."

"That you said she wasn't your sister? Or that you referred to her as the daughter of a psychopath? Or that everyone hates her? None of that was supposed to bother her?"

Silence from my brother.

"If you choose to wield words like weapons, you have to deal with the consequences. And if you're grown up enough to say terrible things to people, you're grown up enough to handle the truth."

I frowned, wondering where Dad was going with this.

Dad lowered himself onto Harry's bed, elbows on his knees, hands clasped. "Harry, look at me."

My little brother didn't bother attempting to deny the order. He turned his head, and I watched as he struggled to meet my dad's gaze.

"There are two reasons I never, ever want to hear you tell your sister she's not your sister or hear you throw her birth father in her face. One—when your sister was only a year younger than you are now, she was terrorized by that man. *Terrorized*, Harry. He kidnapped Callie and held her at gunpoint before he tried to kill your mother. You have no idea how traumatic that was for them. I never want you to be in a position to ever fully understand that. Ever. So I won't go into the details. I will say if you did know what your sister has been through, you would be disgusted with yourself for using that man as a weapon against her."

I heard an inhale of breath and turned to see Mum standing, eyes wide with sadness at the reminder of all we'd been through. And concern that Harry was too young to even know this much. But I'd experienced the trauma as a ten-year-old, and I'd come out all right. Harry was almost twelve, and I did agree with Dad to an extent. If he could use those words against me, he was old enough to understand what he was talking about.

I reached for Mum's hand and squeezed it in reassurance.

Turning back, I watched Harry lower his eyes, his expression tight. I realized why when a tear slipped down his cheek. Damn.

"Can you possibly imagine what that was like for Callie? That her own father could do that to her and to your mum? Do you understand now why you should never throw that in your sister's face?"

"Aye." His voice was quiet and young. "I'm sorry."

Dad reached for him, and Harry bent his head forward, pressing it against Dad's chest. Dad squeezed the nape of his neck, his voice softer, but still gruff as he comforted him. "And two, I legally adopted your sister, and in every way that matters, she is my daughter. Callie is just as much my daughter as you are my son. She is your sister in every way that matters. And if I hear you ever say differently again, I'll take away every electronic device in this house that you love and you won't get them back for six months."

"I'm sorry," Harry whispered again, his voice cracking. "I ... Axel Beaton and Greg Anderson and his mates have been hassling me at school ever since Callie got back."

I flicked a shocked look at Mum.

"Hassling you how?" Dad asked.

Harry pulled back, wiping at the snot under his nose. "They made a comment about Callie being a slut. They'd been on her social media and saw her with a couple of guys. I took a swing at Axel and because I reacted, they're at me every day, saying stuff about her."

"What stuff?"

"That she's taking the piss out of you and Mum, taking your money, taking Mum's business, shagging loads of guys, that her dad is a murderer and she's tainted, that we're sick for keeping her in the house in case she murders us in our sleep. It's constant, nonstop!"

Tears blurred my vision as I turned away. Mum tried to pull me into her arms, but I slipped out of her grasp.

Kids didn't just have that information readily at hand. They were overhearing adults talking about me. Gossiping about me. And they were using it to torment my wee brother.

No wonder he hated me.

Needing air, I trusted Mum and Dad would find a way to help Harry. I was probably the last person he wanted to deal with, so I grabbed Mum's car keys and hurried out of the house.

I found myself driving into Ardnoch. In Paris, the shower in my apartment was so rubbish, I'd started a ritual of having a glass of wine while sitting in a bubble bath instead. I felt like taking the world's longest bubble bath and drinking a mammoth glass of wine.

Parking outside of the Gloaming, I kept my head down to

avoid meeting anyone's eyes as I wandered down the cobbled lane that led to William's Wine Cellar. It wasn't even five o'clock yet, but I didn't care. Let the arseholes gossip and call me a drunk along with everything else.

As soon as I walked into the wine shop, I spotted Carianne at the wine wall and wanted to turn around and walk right back out. We hadn't spoken since yesterday and now her joke about me shagging half of Paris came back to me. It was too similar to what Harry said. I wasn't surprised by his language. There were kids in my class at that age who tried to emulate the adults around them and swore all the time. And worse.

Staring at Carianne, I suddenly wanted to know who was saying those things about me and how it had gotten back to a group of primary school kids.

I gave William a nod of hello before approaching Carianne.

She glanced toward me at the sound of my footsteps and her face burst into a friendly smile of recognition. "Callie, how are you?"

Without preamble, I asked, "Who's gossiping about me, Carianne?"

Her eyes widened. "What do you mean?"

"People are spreading rumors about me. Please tell me who."

Whatever she saw on my face made her sigh heavily. "Yesterday ... I should never have said what I said, even as a joke. Especially ... while you were gone, nosy bastards were following your social media. The more conservative types gossiped a bit, like dating two men in two years meant you were giving it to anyone."

Indignation flushed through me. "Even if I was, whose business is it? If I was a man, would they even care?"

"Exactly!" Carianne nodded in vehement agreement. "I've

said as much to a couple of women who've tried to talk about it in the salon."

"What women? Do they have kids?"

She bit her lip and nodded. "Jana Anderson was one of them."

I scoffed, looking away. Harry had mentioned a boy with the surname of Anderson. What was wrong with people? "Do I even know her?"

"She used to be Jana Bailey. She was a few years older than us."

"I don't remember her."

"It's not personal, Callie. She's the biggest gossip from here to John O'Groats. You're just gossip fodder to her. Plus, she's friends with Ursula Rankin, and we both know her and her mother like to have a target for their bile." Carianne took a step toward me. "But yesterday *was* personal. I'm so angry I said that. It slipped out because I wanted ... look ... I ... I was going to talk to you about this ..." She licked her lips nervously and suddenly, I felt sick with anticipation. "You're my friend, so I would never have done anything about it then, but the truth is, I've always liked Lewis. Always. Even when I was dating Fyfe. And it's been years since you and Lewis broke up. Now that he's home, I'd like to ask him out on a date. I want to be honest about that with you. I mean, you don't want him back, do you?"

The idea of Carianne and Lewis nauseated me.

Yet only yesterday, I'd told Lewis I didn't want to be with him. I shook my head, barely hearing anything over the rush of blood in my ears. "I don't ... but ... Carianne, it would be weird for me for you to date him. I'm not going to lie about that."

My friend slowly exhaled, searching my face. "I get that. I do. But I really like him, Callie."

"You don't know him anymore," I argued.

"He can't have changed that much. He was always the kindest, loveliest guy, and *I* appreciate that about him."

What? Like I didn't?!

"And I think it would be unfair to say you don't want him but you don't want anyone else to have him." She reached out to squeeze my arm to gentle her words.

And I wanted to burst into a sobbing mess.

What a bloody day.

I nodded numbly, because she was right about that. It would be childish to mark Lewis as off-limits to Carianne. We lived in a small village. Our romantic options were few. Lewis Adair was a catch, and if it wasn't Carianne, it would be someone else.

She bent her head, expression sympathetic. "And if I hear anyone talking shit about you, their ears will be ringing by the time I'm done with them."

I nodded again.

"It'll blow over, Callie. You're the latest gossip because you've just come home. But once you're here a while, they'll find someone new to talk about. You know what they're like."

I did. I'd just never taken the brunt of it before. When there was gossip about me and Mum all those years ago, I imagined she protected me from the worst of it.

Being home seemed to have caused nothing but trouble so far. If I left, maybe the bullies would leave Harry alone.

And if Carianne and Lewis began dating, I wouldn't want to see that.

How ironic would it be if Lewis ended up staying in Ardnoch, and I ended up leaving?

"I have to run. Promised some girls from the salon I'd bring wine to a potluck." Carianne grinned and then kissed my cheek. "Thanks for being the best. Love you."

I don't know how long I stood there in that shop before I

finally got up the strength to grab a bottle of wine, pay for it, and get back in the car.

There were missed calls from my mum, but I couldn't talk to anyone right now. Instead of going back to my parents' house for a bubble bath, I drove to the car park where only yesterday I'd told Lewis I didn't want him, where he'd taken the news like he barely cared. His reaction made little sense since he'd apparently returned to Ardnoch for me.

Kicking off my shoes and dumping them in the car, I grabbed the wine bottle and stomped through the dunes.

The coastal wind hit me, fluttering through my light shirt and whipping my hair back off my face. I barely felt it. This part of the beach, as I hoped, was empty at this time of day, even though it was low tide. The sand was soft and golden, resistant to my footfall until I neared the shore where it was compacted by the water's continual caress. The cold sand squeezed pleasantly between my toes as I walked along the edge, letting the water kiss my feet before falling back again. Miles of it stretched on ahead, and dark green hills loomed in the distance where the earth jutted out into the sea. Sunbeams cut through the white clouds, and light bounced and glittered across the gentle waves.

I sucked in a breath, trying to pull myself together.

It shouldn't bother me feeling rejected by my brother, by my village, and in a way, by Carianne who was choosing her attraction to Lewis over me ... but it hurt so badly, I wanted to disappear.

After what my real father did to us, Mum asked if I wanted to see a therapist and I'd said no. It didn't take a therapist to tell me that the kind of traumatic rejection and lack of love I'd experienced at my real father's hands had scarred me deeply. I handled rejection like it was the end of the fucking world.

Having chosen a twist-cap wine bottle, I moved to take the

cap off and guzzle it down. But my hand hovered over it. The last time I got drunk I had sex with Lewis, and it messed with my head.

More than that, I could hear Aunt Ally's voice in my head. When she was younger and going through something traumatic, she escaped into drugs and alcohol and ended up in rehab.

I didn't want to turn my weekly ritual of a wee glass of wine and a bubble bath into downing a bottle by the ocean. It changed it from a simple pleasure to a tool to numb my feelings.

Stopping, I hugged the bottle to my chest and stared out at the vastness of the water before me. Sometimes I wondered what it would be like if a body never tired and you could dive into the ocean and swim for eternity, free of troubles, heartache, and responsibilities.

I let its rhythm soothe me, lull me, calm me.

Until I felt ready to return home to face my family.

Sixteen
Lewis

The best thing that could've happened after Callie's rejection was starting the new job at my dad's firm. I was already familiar with most of the staff and other architects because I'd worked part time for two summers at the firm before leaving for uni.

If anyone was bothered that my dad was a partner and I'd been hired out of nepotism, I didn't get that impression. Hopefully, it was because my reputation preceded me. I'd worked on a couple of projects during my degree that had received national recognition.

Dad, as was his way, threw me right in and set me up with a new private residential client. The couple, Jack and Ross, had bought a plot of land between Inverness and Tain that overlooked the Cromarty Firth. It was a great plot in a superb location, but it was a very small bit of land. The challenge was a welcome one, and even though we were still in the early stages, I'd gone out with Jack and Ross to physically assess the plot. My mind already whirred with possibilities. At this stage, it was research—what the client wanted to see in the design, what the plot offered in size, and how the sun moved throughout the day in that location.

As well as working on this individual design, I was assisting on a larger project Dad was heading up for a small housing developer looking to build luxury homes in Aberdeenshire. Dad's firm was recognized as a leading sustainable, coastal property designer. We used glazing technology that allowed a building to become a part of its surroundings. In simple terms, we incorporated a lot of glass into our designs while maintaining structural integrity and homes that could withstand high winds, salt water, and sunlight.

All that to say, I was extremely busy my first week back in Ardnoch. I joined my family in the evenings for dinner and was relieved to discover that Morwenna was still the funny, sweet girl she'd always been—but with mood swings. At night, I sometimes rode my bike out on the open road, much to my parents' dismay, or I retreated to the annex to watch TV or read. As much as I liked being around them, I needed to find a place of my own soon.

A place I could brood about Callie without infecting anyone else with my mood. I did try to be present, but my parents kept asking me if I was all right, so I knew I wasn't doing a very good job.

It wasn't that I'd given up on Callie. It might have seemed like it to her last week when I took her home without another word, but I was processing. All week I'd been racking my brain, trying to think of what I could do to prove to her I wasn't going anywhere.

Then I'd remembered all the emails and texts I'd saved from her.

After we'd broken up, I'd reread our past texts thinking I might die from how much I missed her. Then almost a year later, after having not looked at them in a while, I accidentally called her. Thankfully, I hit end call before it even rung out.

But it had shaken me enough to decide to delete her from my phone. Before I did, I exported all our texts to my computer and saved the file.

Remembering that, last night I pulled out my laptop and spent the evening reading through our old conversations. Some of them seemed childish and silly now, but most of it served to remind me how much Callie and I understood each other. How easy it had been between us. And how extraordinary it was that a relationship that was so easy and comfortable had also been full of excitement and youthful passion.

We discovered we still had the latter. In fact, more so than ever.

But I truly believed we could have the former again.

And then, I'd come across a string of texts that Callie had sent about a year after we'd started dating. She'd just read a book where the guy did all sorts of romantic things and I'd joked that we were beyond that now. Comfortable as old shoes. I'd done it to wind her up, and she'd fallen for it. Callie had responded:

> Now I wish I'd made you work harder to get me last year. All you had to do was say you loved me and I gave in. *blows raspberry* BOO to that. Last year's Callie was an idiot.

> I think she's awesome. I'd have had heart failure if you'd dragged it out.

> Askin you to take me out on special dates wouldn't have been draggin it out. It would have been fun for both of us.

> What kind of special dates?

> Srsly?

Seriously. I want to know the hoops I was supposed to jump through. 😉

Really wishin I'd done it now. I think you're takin me for granted. 😊

Never. I know how lucky I am.

😳

So. Dates?

OK, you asked for it. Date 1: Picnic on the beach @ twilight, with all my fav snacks. If u don't know what they are by now, I give up.

LOL. Walkers' pickled onion crisps, peanut M&Ms, and your mum's homemade chocolate truffles. Oh and a bottle of Irn-Bru.

I love you.

You really need to eat healthier snacks.

Shut up. Like your fav snack is carrots & hummus. Anyhoo, date 2: Zip-lining. Date 3. Night at theatre. 4. Trip to National Museum in Edinburgh. 5. Weekend in Skye to see Fairy Pools. 6. Night alone with you in the annex 😉

Flirt.

Only ever with you, though. Love you.

Love you too, mo chridhe.

Oh you know that does things to me.

Ha. Go to sleep, you flirt.

Night, baby.

Night x

The text string had caused an ache of nostalgia and longing. All the conversations I found between us did. But I also realized in reading them that I never flirted back with her. I told her I loved her, but she was right when she'd said I was reserved. Maybe it was just being a kid and not having the kind of confidence Callie did, or maybe I hadn't put in the effort. I didn't flirt with her, and I'd never taken her anywhere special.

Looking back, I had taken Callie for granted.

In more ways than one.

Well, no more.

It clearly was going to take more than *I love you* this time to get her back. And I was ready. I was buckled in for the long haul.

————

The following Saturday, I woke up with plans to pop into the bakery and try one of Callie's pastries that everyone was talking about. Mum had brought a few home and unsurprisingly, Callie's desserts looked phenomenal and tasted even more so. I thought maybe starting small by supporting her business might be the thing to do by dropping in personally.

And it was also an excuse to see her since I hadn't seen her all week.

I said as much to Mum when I stopped into the house for a coffee before I left.

"I think that's a good idea." She stared at me before she continued, "There was talk that you and Callie were seen on your bike last weekend."

Of course there was. "Aye, I gave her a lift home from Fyfe's." I exhaled slowly and confessed, "After telling her I still loved her and wanted her back and being resoundingly rejected."

Mum's expression fell. "Is that what's been bothering you all week?"

I nodded. "But I'm not giving up."

"Good." She considered me again. "I wasn't going to say anything because I wasn't sure if Callie was a subject I'm allowed to mention ...?"

"She is," I assured her. "Please don't walk on eggshells around me. I don't want that."

"Well ... she's having a bit of a tough time at the moment. I was talking to Sloane, and Harry's being bullied at school by the kids of some of the nastier parents who are gossiping about Callie. Apparently, they've been harassing Harry with the gossip."

My skin heated with anger. "What gossip?"

Mum suddenly looked wary. "That ... she's taking advantage of Sloane and trying to take over the business ... and that she was ... promiscuous in Paris."

"What the fuck?" I snarled. "What fucking century are these people living in?"

She rounded the island to press a soothing hand to my arm. "They are a small minority in Ardnoch, but they do enough yammering to ruffle a few feathers. Sloane and Walker have spoken to the school, and with the school year ending, everyone is hopeful that it'll blow over for Harry. But she said Callie is having a hard time dealing with it."

"Aye, you know why?" Fury at these fucking people turned my voice hoarse. "Because this place is her safe place. It has been ever since she and her mum arrived here. How dare they?" I pushed away from the island. "I want to know who's spreading gossip about her."

"So you can do what, Lewis?"

"Tell them that I'll make their lives a misery if they don't quit it."

Mum shook her head. "You'll only make it worse for her. Trust me. Your father and I put up with our fair share of gossip. I was the young nanny who seduced an older man who should know better."

I blanched, because I remembered. And I remembered the kids at school who teased me mercilessly about it because they were picking everything up from their gossiping fucking parents.

"The gossip died down. And it will for Callie too."

"I just ... I just wish that I was there for her. That she'd let me be there for her."

"That will take time too." She reached up to cup my face and smiled tenderly. "But she won't be able to resist you for long. Who could, my sweet boy?"

I chuckled as I took one of her hands to press a kiss to her palm. "Only you could get away with still calling me that."

Her smile widened and she stepped back to gesture toward the door. "Go stop in and see how Callie is. And maybe grab me a pastry if there's anything left."

———

I never made it to the bakery.

I'd been walking toward it after parking behind Castle Street when I heard someone calling my name and saw Cari-anne waving across the street from Flora's Café.

When she waved me over to her, I cast an impatient glance toward the bakery. The manners my parents had instilled in me, however, forced me across the street once there was a break in the busy traffic. The tourists had already started to descend for the summer season.

"Come have a coffee with me in Flora's," Carianne said without preamble. "I've got a table. C'mon." She was heading inside before I could say no.

With another wistful look at Callie's Wee Cakery, I followed Carianne into Flora's.

"Lewis!" Flora waved past her crowd of customers at the farthest end of the small café. "Look at you! How are you?"

Everyone stared at me, only half of them locals, and I grimaced at being the center of attention. "Good, Flora. You?"

"All the better for seeing you, son. Have a seat. I'll have Effie bring you a coffee. What do you want?"

The customers waiting to be served glowered. I smiled apologetically. "Cappuccino, Flora, thanks."

"Coming right up."

Carianne grinned from ear to ear as I took the seat at the small bistro table. I bumped it with my knees because my legs were too long for the furniture. Carianne reached out to stop her coffee from spilling. "Preferential treatment from Flora, huh?"

I shrugged. Flora had always been nice to me. Trying not to come off as impatient, I shot the bakery another look through the window.

"They're closed."

I looked back at Carianne. "What?"

She gestured to the bakery. "They sold out ten minutes ago."

"Already?"

She nodded. "Tourists are loving Callie's new pastries."

"That's impressive." Though disappointing for me.

"I'm glad I saw you, Lewis, because I wanted to ask you something."

"Here you go." A young girl I didn't recognize placed a cappuccino in front of me.

"Thanks."

Her cheeks bloomed bright red when I smiled at her, and she muttered something under her breath before practically skittering away.

Carianne snorted. "My god, how does it feel to make women turn to mush around you?"

I stared at her, bemused. "Excuse me?"

She laughed. "I think your cluelessness makes you even hotter."

Last Sunday, I hadn't known what to do with Carianne's flirting. I thought she was joking around, but maybe I was wrong.

"I've always liked you, Lewis," Carianne confessed abruptly. "Like, really liked you. Would you fancy going out on a date?"

Stunned, it took me a second to muster up a response. And then first I glanced around to make sure no one had heard her. I didn't want it getting back to Callie. There was no sign anyone was listening in, thank fuck. I'd never really paid much attention to Carianne before. She'd always just been Callie's friend and then Fyfe's girlfriend for a while. But she had similar coloring to Callie. Blond, blue-eyed. She was a bonny girl. Or woman, now. Yet, I hadn't even recognized that about her because ... she wasn't Callie.

And Callie would forever be the most beautiful woman I'd ever seen.

Deciding not to beat around the bush, I answered honestly, "As flattered as I am, Carianne, I'm still in love with Callie, and I came home to win her back."

Her lips parted in surprise. "After all this time?"

"After all this time."

"After she dumped you like a moron?"

Irritated, I gave a slight shake of my head. "You don't know what you're talking about. No one knows what happened between me and Callie but me and Callie."

Carianne flushed and looked down at her coffee. "I'm sorry. I didn't ... I love Callie. I just have always thought she was silly to let you go."

"Like I said, there's more to the story than that. I fucked up back then too."

"Did you hurt her?"

It was none of her business, so I didn't respond.

Carianne sighed. "Well, now I feel like shit for even asking you out. I always assumed Callie broke up with you and was over you." Guilt crossed her features. "She did tell me it would be weird for her if I asked you out. I thought she was being petty. Ugh. I'm an awful friend."

Hope lashed through me and in my self-absorption, I blurted, "She said that?"

"She said that." Carianne shook her head. "All this time ... you know, last Sunday I thought she was acting kind of jealous when I was flirting with you, but I assumed I was being paranoid. I mean, she had that gorgeous French boyfriend. I really thought she was over you."

Aye, she didn't have to keep reminding me of that. "She was jealous? Do you think?"

"Oh my God." Carianne rolled her eyes. "I hadn't a hope in hell, did I? You are so gone for her."

I gave her a sheepish shrug.

"Fine. Even though I'm slightly heartbroken because I've been harboring a crush on you forever," she admitted without embarrassment, "I am going to help you because you're both my friends and you deserve happiness."

"Help how?"

She leaned forward. "When I was dating Fyfe, I was ready to break up with him because I fancied my best friend's boyfriend more than I fancied my own boyfriend."

"Harsh." I felt the need to say on Fyfe's behalf.

"Aye, but true. Anyway, I then heard that Olivia Smith fancied Fyfe and was waiting for me to dump him."

I kept my mouth shut because I knew Fyfe had slept with Olivia after he and Carianne broke up.

"So, that made him more attractive to me and I didn't dump him. We stayed together another two months."

"That's childish, Carianne."

"Very," she agreed. "But I'm telling you ... if you pretend to date me, Callie will get so jealous, she'll have to admit how she feels about you."

It had worked on me when we were kids when Callie dated Michael. It had made me realize I didn't want to lose her.

But we were kids.

Surely, we'd evolved past those kinds of games.

"I don't think so."

"I do." She threw back the last of her coffee. "Think about it. I'm happy to help give her a nudge. She's stubborn, you know. It'll be for her own good."

I sighed, picking up the cappuccino to sip and consider.

The impatient part of me that wanted Callie now was seriously tempted by the offer.

SEVENTEEN
LEWIS

"**N**o. Absolutely not. Worst idea ever." Fyfe shook his head at me, as if he was disappointed I'd even contemplated Carianne's plan.

My gut told me it was a stupid idea, and would most likely push Callie further away. Yet, Carianne's conviction that Callie would be jealous tempted my devil. I wanted to do whatever I could to make Callie see that she wanted me too. That our night together three weeks ago wasn't a drunken mistake. It was fate correcting a *prior* mistake.

I opened my mouth to tell Fyfe what Carianne had said, but my mobile rang, cutting me off. Seeing it was Eilidh video-calling, I answered. "Perfect timing."

Eilidh wore not a scrap of makeup, which was unusual. She was usually fully done up because she was either coming from the studio or an event. She looked young and baby-faced on my screen. "What's perfect timing?"

"What are you up to?" I asked instead.

"Who is it?" Fyfe asked from the opposite sofa. We were hanging out at his place since *he* actually had his own house.

"Who is that?" Eilidh's eyes widened slightly.

"Fyfe." I looked at my friend. "It's Eilidh."

"I haven't seen Fyfe in ages. Turn me around."

"I'll come over," my friend suggested instead, pushing up off the opposite couch to come sit beside me. He leaned his head in toward the phone. "Eils."

"Eils?" Eilidh grinned at him. "It's been years and all you've got is Eils?"

"Hey, I've been here for almost two years, so that's not my fault," he teased.

"Holy crap, let me look at you." She comically peered closer as if that would make her view any clearer. "Fyfe Moray, I always knew you were a smoke show."

Fyfe groaned and got up to return to the other sofa. "And you haven't changed a bit."

He missed the way Eilidh's smile fell, but I didn't. As soon as she realized I was paying attention, she pasted on a bright smile. "So, what's perfect timing?"

"Are you okay?" I asked.

"I'm fantastic. For the first time in ages, I have a few weeks off before the next project."

"Is that the film you're shooting in Romania?"

"The very one. I've been lounging around my flat, doing bugger all for a few days. It's nice, but I'll get bored soon enough, I suppose."

Something about that didn't ring true at all. And there were dark circles under her eyes that I only just noticed. "Eilidh—"

"Perfect timing for what?" she repeated.

Deciding she'd probably hang up on me if I pushed her, I relented. "I was telling Fyfe that Callie said she doesn't want me back. And then I ran into Carianne and she proposed we pretend to date to make Callie jealous."

"After asking him out!" Fyfe called before getting up to come sit next to me again. He looked into the camera at

Eilidh. "He forgot to mention Carianne asked him out for real first."

"Not surprising." Eilidh shrugged. "I always knew she fancied Lewis."

"Aye, apparently even when she was dating me." Fyfe appeared mildly affronted.

"I remember telling you she wasn't good enough for you," Eilidh pointed out before giving me a sharp look. "And you're an idiot if you trust a woman who has admitted to secretly harboring feelings for her friend's boyfriend and boyfriend's friend for years. Let me tell you, Carianne is hoping that by pretending to date her, you'll fall in love with *her* instead, like some fucking stupid rom-com."

"That sounds like Carianne," Fyfe agreed.

Confused, I huffed, "Carianne's nice, no? I mean, she loves Callie."

"Maybe." Eilidh grimaced. "But she's also always been jealous of Callie. When we were kids, it didn't matter what Callie had, Carianne had to have it too."

"I remember that." Fyfe nodded. "When we were dating, if Callie got something, Carianne wouldn't shut up about it until she got it too. I just thought it was what girls did."

"No." Eilidh screwed her face up at him. "Way to generalize us."

They bickered back and forth while I considered what they'd said. Maybe I was letting my impatience get the better of my rational thinking. Eilidh was right. Carianne had confessed to having feelings for me for a while, and I didn't want to lead her on.

And Callie ... my gut screamed that it would only reinforce Callie's idea that I wasn't constant in my love.

It was, in fact, the stupidest fucking plan I'd ever considered.

"You're both right," I cut my sister and friend off from whatever they were bantering about.

"We are?" Eilidh wrinkled her nose. "About what again? Fyfe befuddled me with his mild misogynism."

"Uh!" Fyfe made a noise at a pitch I didn't know was possible for him. "How dare you?"

My wee sister grinned mischievously. "You're so easy to wind up."

He rolled his eyes and turned to me. "What are we right about?"

"That pretending to date Carianne to make Callie jealous is a bad idea. Not only is it childish, but I think it would push Callie further away."

"Agreed," they said in unison and then shot each other a mock scowl.

"So ..." I sighed heavily. "Any ideas on what I should do next?"

"Well." Eilidh smirked. "I know this might not make you happy, Mr. Impatient, but I think you should try a different tactic. It'll take longer, but it's more likely to work."

"And what's that?"

"Ask her if you can try to be just friends."

"Just friends?"

"Just friends. Then you can spend time together without all the pressure and you can remind Callie that you're a loyal, good person she can trust."

I looked at Fyfe.

My friend nodded. "She's right."

"Did it hurt you to admit that?" Eilidh teased.

Fyfe shot her a look. "Why? Because I'm mildly misogynistic?"

"Did I say mildly? I meant wildly."

"Friends," I interrupted them. "You both think I should propose friendship?"

"If you want to prove that your first thoughts are to Callie, then aye," my sister insisted. "She needs trust to build between you again."

I realized with some chagrin that Eilidh was correct. I'd returned to Ardnoch so hell-bent on getting Callie back, I'd come at it from the perspective of what I wanted, not what Callie needed. If I really was determined to play the long game, then I had to court Callie stealthily.

Friends first.

EIGHTEEN
CALLIE

The following Monday, a postcard arrived at my parents' house for me. It was from an old friend. The postcard had the words "Greetings from London" along with an image of Big Ben on it. On the back was a hand-written message:

Taking some time to see the world. Being here makes me think of you. Maybe I'll come to Scotland to say hello to ma belle amie. Gabriel.

It was out of the blue. After the way things fizzled out between us, I hadn't expected to ever hear from Gabriel again. Yet I was glad. It was nice to know he still thought of me and I was relieved to hear he was taking some time for himself. There were many things he didn't tell me and I think one of them was how stressed his work made him. I didn't really expect him to travel all the way to Ardnoch to see me, but I appreciated the sentiment and the postcard put a smile on my face. As did the fact Mum and I sold out at the bakery by eleven o'clock that morning. Now that tourists had fully descended on Ardnoch, we were busier than ever. It had been a good morning so far.

I'd been there to see a bride's face when she saw the wedding cake Mum had made for her. She'd burst into tears of happiness, and I was so freaking proud of Mum for creating such special moments for people.

Then Arro Adair, Lewis's aunt, had stopped by the bakery before work. Apparently, Mum had told her I was looking for a place to rent. It was true. Although Harry had apologized and I knew he meant it, I still sensed a slight resentment from him that I'd inadvertently made his life so difficult these past few weeks. I thought maybe if I got my own place, it might help ease things between us. And maybe it would shut up all the folks who were saying I was mooching off my parents. My salary from the bakery was decent, enough to get a small flat.

"Our cottage, the one you used to stay in when you first moved here with your mum, is back on the market for rent," Arro had explained as she bought a couple of pastries. "It's yours if you want it."

The two-bedroom cottage Mum and I had lived in before moving into Dad's bungalow was a quaint period property on Castle Street. Honestly, I loved the cottage. But ... "I'm not sure I can afford it."

Arro had suggested a rental figure that made me gape. "Surely, you can get more than that?"

"Maybe. But I'd rather have you living there because I know you'll take care of it."

"Aunt Arro, are you sure?" The aunt part had slipped out because it's what I started calling her years ago when I was with Lewis.

She'd beamed, her beautiful pale blue eyes lit with delight. "Absolutely. It's yours."

I almost burst into tears, but I had too many customers to see to, to indulge in that reaction. Promising to call her later, I shot my mum a giddy smile. She returned it, but I saw a twinge of sadness in hers. I assumed it was because I'd only just returned home and now, I was moving out. And I was sad to do it. Scared, even. But I was twenty-five and I'd lived in Paris on my own for a few years. It was time.

As the ladies cleaned up, I moved across the floor to lock the door just as Carianne waltzed in. She saw the empty counters and sighed. "Darn. I wanted to take some cakes into the salon. Late start this morning." She tucked a strand of her own perfectly coiffed hair behind her ear.

In comparison to how well put together my friend looked, I had to be a fright. My nape and forehead were damp with sweat and tendrils of my hair escaping my hair tie stuck to my skin. "Sorry." I gestured around. "Today we were cleaned out by eleven."

"I'll keep that in mind." Carianne shot Angie and Cathy a look before lowering her voice. "Do you have a minute?"

"Uh, sure." I gestured for her to follow me behind the counter and into the kitchen.

Mum and Carianne greeted each other.

"We're just nipping outside for a minute," I told Mum before leading my friend out back into our private parking area. There was no one about out here, compared to the busy main street on the opposite side of the building. "What's up?"

Carianne drew her shoulders back. "I want to keep things open and honest between us ... so you should know that I asked Lewis out on a date. And he said yes."

A sudden bout of nausea overwhelmed me, and I turned, in a panic, afraid I was going to be sick. Leaning on the wall, I swallowed frantically, trying to stop the sensation from turning into reality.

"Oh my God, Callie, are you okay?"

Rage thrummed through me, but I stuffed it down, like I always did. I wasn't afraid of anger, but I'd always been afraid the rare times in my life when I'd felt *hateful* anger. Because I didn't want to be like him. Like my real father.

And right now, I fucking hated Carianne.

And Lewis.

He'd come back for me, my arse! It didn't take him long to change his mind about that.

I waved off my so-called friend, gulping in a lungful of air. "I'm fine. I ... uh ... I've just been feeling a bit sick lately. Maybe coming down with something."

"Oh." Carianne stepped back like I might be contagious. "Okay. Well ... are ... are we okay?"

Everything that had happened in the last few weeks crashed down on me.

The villagers, people I'd grown up around, talking shit, trying to make me feel bad for going off and experiencing life and the world. Gossiping in front of their kids and saying things they shouldn't overhear, only for it to be repeated with the sole purpose of tormenting my wee brother.

And me just smiling and bearing it because I wanted everyone to like me, to accept me, to love me.

Look where that had gotten me! Stressed out of my mind trying to make the bakery work, leaving my parents' house out of necessity rather than want, and agreeing that it would be wrong of me to be pissed off if my friend dated my ex-boyfriend.

I pushed off the wall and glowered at her. "No, Carianne, we're not okay. Don't come around me anymore. I don't want to see you."

"Callie!" Carianne called after me, audaciously sounding shocked. "Callie, don't be like that."

"Fuck you," I replied without heat. "And fuck Lewis Adair too."

I let the bakery door slam shut behind me.

Mum gaped, clearly having heard my last words.

I shrugged, like I wasn't in incredible emotional pain. "Carianne asked Lewis out, and he said yes."

Anger darkened Mum's face. "Are you kidding me?"

"Nope." I tugged hurriedly at the knotted tie on my apron. "Do you mind if I leave early? I could do with a walk."

"Of course. Can ... can I do anything?"

"Nope."

"Callie—"

"I feel like I can only trust you and Dad right now," I choked out. "I was supposed to come back here and be happy. Safe and happy. Like always. And right now, I would give anything to be back in Paris. Anything." Maybe the postcard from Gabriel this morning just made me long for a simpler place. A place where the connections I made had been shallow, easy, uncomplicated. No one had wormed their way into my heart, friends or lovers. Right now, that seemed like the answer. Because if you only cared on a superficial level, no one could hurt you.

———

That evening, I dragged myself to Thurso for my first tae kwon do class since returning to Ardnoch. I was feeling a bit out of shape and ready to get back to it. When we were kids, we had to drive all the way to Inverness for a class, but Dad had told me there were two guys running classes in the same sports center where he held his jujitsu school. One of them was one of his security guards at the estate.

I'd signed up online a few nights before Carianne's revelation. I considered not going to the class tonight, but in all honesty, I needed the physical exertion and somewhere to focus my hurt and fury.

The last thing I wanted or expected was to walk into the class and find Fyfe at the head of it, chatting with Lewis.

No.

They couldn't possibly be the guys who ran the class.

Dad would have told me.

I turned as if to bolt, but Fyfe caught sight of me. He wore his white dobok. It had the World Taekwondo badge on the chest.

"Callie." He patted Lewis on the shoulder and headed over to me, his black belt knotted around his waist. Five gold stripes on the end of it told me Fyfe was now a fifth dan black belt. Wow. From the bloke who couldn't afford lessons, to a fifth dan black belt. He'd surpassed even me. "I saw your name on the list. Glad to have you in the class."

I tried not to look beyond him at Lewis. "You're the instructor?"

Fyfe nodded. "Me and Evan Willis. He's a security guard at Ardnoch Estate. He runs the Tuesday and Saturday classes."

"Callie." Lewis approached. He also wore his whites. His black belt had four gold stripes on one end and three on the other. He'd advanced to seventh degree.

My own belt still only had three because I'd stopped going to gradings while I was in Paris. And gradings were where you were tested to advance to the next level. Now seeing the gold stripes on both Fyfe's and Lewis's belts, I felt an old familiar competitiveness rise in the wake of my anger.

"You're taking this class now too?" I practically spat at Lewis.

His eyebrows rose in surprise. "Is that a problem?"

"No." I shrugged with an ambivalence I didn't feel. "Just looking forward to kicking your arse."

He smirked, assuming this was banter, and pointed at my belt. "You need a few more stripes before that happens."

Oh, I was so ready to pulverize him.

———

Fyfe, as it turned out, was a hard taskmaster. He'd split the group up by age and then levels. We were a small class of twenty, with the kids at the front, teens in the middle, and adults at the back.

In the row in front of me were two guys and a woman. One guy wore a white belt, so he was a newbie, the other a green belt, and the woman a blue belt with red tape on the ends, which meant she was close to advancing to red.

Lewis and I, the only other two black belts other than Fyfe, stood at the back. The first half of the session, it was easier to ignore his presence. If only because Fyfe's style of warm-up was utterly exhausting, and I was feeling those three weeks I'd missed training. The stretching was nice. Or it would have been if I hadn't felt Lewis watching me. I tried to focus on how much I enjoyed stretching and decided I really needed to get back into Pilates too. Once I had my routine at the bakery down, I could start incorporating some home sessions.

After stretching, however, Fyfe hammered us. My thighs burned from tuck jumps, my core from the multiple variations he had us do for the plank, and I was out of breath at one point from running back and forth across the hall.

Finally, once he was assured we were warmed up (and frankly ready to kill him), Fyfe began splitting us up so we could practice patterns.

Lewis tried to talk to me in those moments, and I told him to be quiet.

He had the audacity to appear hurt.

Then, with twenty minutes of class left, we broke into sparring.

Fyfe approached Lewis and I once the kids and teens were started. "I'm thinking, Callie, I could introduce you to Sharon." He gestured to the woman who wore the blue belt. "And you could spar with her."

"I want to spar with Lewis," I insisted. "The two black belts against each other. It's only fair."

Fyfe cut Lewis a look.

Lewis nodded, though he glanced at me warily when he did.

A few seconds later, everyone was paired up. No one wore sparring gear, so we weren't supposed to hit hard. Usually sparring gear was only worn at competition and grading. Or at least, that's how it had always been at the classes I'd taken previously.

Reluctantly, I bowed to Lewis as he bowed to me.

He'd barely straightened when I struck out, but Lewis was fast and blocked the straight punch. His eyes widened slightly as I struck again and we were suddenly a blur of jabs, strikes, and blocks. Lewis didn't back down, though I saw the slight confusion in his expression at my fierceness. He kept coming at me, and I had to turn to avoid hitting the wall. I used the moment to pivot on my heel and strike out with my other leg in a back kick. It almost hit him, but he darted out of the way, yet too close to my zone. I threw an elbow strike that brushed his ear.

"What the fuck, Callie?" he muttered, using his palms to block my incoming hook punch, his feet to block my front kicks, sidekicks. And then he went on the offense, though he held himself back, merely trying to hold me off with his longer legs and greater power. Muted power. I knew in the back of my mind that if Lewis let go, he could really injure me, if I allowed him past my defenses.

The tank beneath my dobok was drenched in sweat, my suit coming loose from my belt, my breathing hard and fast. I was vaguely aware the rest of the class had stopped to watch us.

"What is going on?" Lewis asked quietly, his own breathing a little fast, shallow, but unfortunately nowhere near as labored as my own.

"You really want to know?" I asked, letting all my hurt and fury blaze from my eyes.

Lewis lowered his arms. "I really want to know."

In answer, I dropped to the floor and kicked out at the side of his ankles, hitting his weak spot. It was a move my dad taught me years ago. And it was forbidden in tae kwon do. You were not allowed to hit below the waist.

Lewis's back slammed onto the mat. He was uninjured but stunned.

"Foul! Unsportsmanlike conduct!" Fyfe yelled from across the room, storming toward me, anger darkening his expression. And disbelief. "What are you doing, Callie?"

A smidgen of guilt flickered through me.

But then I remembered Carianne's little visit to the bakery this morning.

I knew the rules. As a black belt who knew better, my deliberate attack on Lewis was grounds for removal from a class.

But I ignored the guilt, choosing not to care. I swept past Fyfe. "Don't worry, I'll see myself out. Wasn't coming back here, anyway."

The class gaped, but there was freedom in suddenly not caring if everyone loved or hated, accepted or rejected me.

"Callie!" I heard Lewis call.

But he'd hurt my feelings. Abandoned me. Engaged in a

drunken one-night stand with me. Returned to Ardnoch claiming to want me back, but when I said no because I mistrusted his love, he proved my mistrust was warranted by agreeing to date my friend.

I didn't know him anymore. And honestly, I found myself asking all over again if I'd ever really known Lewis.

So, fuck him.

I was done.

NINETEEN
CALLIE

B y the time I'd gotten home after the class, my phone was practically on fire with missed calls and texts from Lewis. Obviously, Eilidh had given him my number. I immediately blocked him. Then Eilidh tried calling. When I didn't answer, she'd texted:

> What's going on? Lewis says you're mad at him for some reason.

I'd texted back I didn't want to talk about it, and not because I was being huffy or melodramatic. But because I was done, and I had no more energy or headspace to deal with my ex. I wished he'd stayed the hell in London.

As the bakery was closed the next day, I got up to have breakfast with my parents and Harry before Dad left for work and Harry for school.

"Are you okay?" Dad asked. I could feel his penetrating stare as I sat down at the table with a cup of coffee and a plate of scrambled eggs he'd cooked for us all.

"Fine." I shrugged. "Actually, I'm going to call Arro about

the cottage. I was hoping I could move in there as quickly as possible."

"You're leaving?" Harry's spoon fell into his bowl of cereal.

Surprised by the dismayed expression on his face, I nodded. "It's about time I had my own place, don't you think?"

My wee brother swallowed, glancing nervously from Mum to Dad and then back to me. "You're not going because I was a dick to you?"

"Harry," Mum scolded. "Language, please."

He grimaced but repeated with some modification, "You're not going because I was mean to you?"

"No, of course not," I semi-lied.

Harry seemed to sense the lie because he stared guiltily at his bowl. "I am sorry."

"Harry, I know that."

Still not looking at us, he continued, "I, uh, I googled it. There are a lot of newspaper articles about what Mum's stepmum tried to do and about your real dad and stuff."

Shifting uncomfortably, I tried to unclench my fist from around my fork. Never, not once, had I been inclined to google it. Mum's stepmum hiring Nathan Andros to kill Mum for her inheritance wasn't ordinary news. Especially because my maternal grandfather had been a wealthy attorney to Hollywood stars. The trauma we'd experienced was played out as entertainment in the news, and I remembered the paparazzi arriving in Ardnoch to hound us.

Thankfully, the furor around the family drama had died down. It flared up again a year or so later when Mum's step-mum's and Nathan's trials started. They were both sentenced to life in prison, the former for conspiracy to commit murder, the latter for kidnap, assault, and attempted murder.

Once all that circus died down, I'd never wanted to deal

with it again. I hadn't googled it ever. In fact, I liked to imagine that our story didn't exist for strangers to read.

Harry reminded me that it *was* out there. Anyone who was anyone could read my story. One saving grace was that most of the articles had our names as Sloane and Callie Harrow. Anyone who'd entered our lives in the last fourteen years wouldn't think to google that name.

Harry finally looked up, and tears gleamed in his eyes. "The articles on the trial talked about what he did to you and Mum."

"What happened to the parental controls?" Mum asked Dad.

He grimaced. "They're not set for stuff like that."

"It's fine. I can handle it." Harry jutted his chin defiantly. "And now I know how bad I messed up. Okay? I shouldn't have said what I said. I shouldn't have taken what Greg and Axel were doing to me out on you. I'm sorry."

I knew how much it must have taken for him to say that. Reaching across the table, I smoothed a hand down his arm. "Harry, I really appreciate that. And I forgive you."

"So you'll stay?"

I gave him an affectionate smile. "I'm twenty-five, kiddo. I really do need a place of my own. But I'll still be around all the time. So much, you'll be sick of me."

Before Harry could respond to that, our doorbell rang.

Dad excused himself, saying he'd get it.

"It was nice of Arro to offer," Mum said.

I nodded. "Can you imagine me back at the cottage? Full circle, eh?"

Mum smiled, a lingering sadness in it. "Without me, though."

"Mum."

"I'm sorry. I know it's time for you to get your own place.

You were in Paris for three years alone, for goodness' sake. It's just ... strange that you'll be here but not *here*."

"Does that mean I can have your room?" Harry suddenly inquired, head cocked in thought. "It *is* bigger than mine."

Laughing, I replied, "You got over me moving out quickly enough."

"Wee yin ..."

Turning in my chair toward Dad, I froze in shock at the person who stood beside him in our living room.

"Gabriel?"

———

It was so weird seeing Gabriel in my childhood bedroom.

Gabriel may have been shorter than some men who shall remain nameless, but he had a magnetism that made him seem larger than life. He was very masculine in my girlish room. It was still decorated in the pink wallpaper I'd chosen as a teen. Gabriel rested his arms behind him on my bed, seeming at ease as he took in his surroundings.

Handsome as hell, with light brown hair, sea-green eyes, a cut jawline, and a brooding mouth, it stunned me that at that moment, he didn't do anything for me. We'd had great sex and I'd found him attractive (obviously), but I realized that I was completely shut down when it came to the opposite sex. I didn't want to contemplate why.

It would make me angry and hurt all over again.

Gabriel's attention returned to where I sat in my armchair in the corner of the room. "You look beautiful," he said in his gorgeous accent, his smile tender.

"You too," I replied.

"Merci. I think."

I smiled, but I was certain it didn't reach my eyes.

He frowned. "Something is wrong. Is it me? Are you angry I showed up?"

"No. I mean, you said you might in your postcard, but I hadn't really expected you to. Why come all this way?" Considering how relieved he'd seemed when I ended things, I never thought I'd see him again.

Gabriel nodded and sat forward, resting his elbows on his knees. "Like I said on the card, I took a break. I needed it. I'm traveling for a few months so I can decide if I want to remain in la police."

My suspicions about his job might have been correct then. "Too stressful?"

"Something like that."

"Where are you traveling?"

"Here." He grinned. "And London, of course. Perhaps America. I am seeing how it goes. Unplanned."

"Exciting."

"Oui. It would be very exciting if you came with me, but I know you will not."

I was surprised he'd even want me along for the ride. As tempting as running away was, despite how shitty I'd felt in Ardnoch these past few weeks, I wouldn't be chased from my family. "I'm where I'm supposed to be."

"Je sais." He pushed up off the bed and crossed the room. I watched him a little warily as he lowered to his knees in front of me and took my hands. "Callie, I ... I came here to apologize for how I treated you. I was not a good boyfriend to you in those last few months. And I am sorry if I made you feel like I did not care for you."

Shocked by the apology, I reassured him, "Gabriel, I never ... we were never very serious. I didn't take it to heart. There's no need to apologize."

"There is." He was grim-faced. "Because I have feelings for

you, and we could have had more if I had been better." His eyes darkened. "If I had been a better man."

There was something about the look in his eyes, his tone, that set my teeth on edge. Something ominous. And it reminded me of those moments I'd felt the same shivery spark of warning back in Paris when he was brooding or extra evasive.

"You really don't have to apologize," I insisted, feeling my emotional walls climb higher.

It was maybe selfish and unkind, but I didn't want a heart-to-heart with Gabriel. For me he was a French fling, and for the most part, we'd had a good time together. He'd made living in Paris less lonely. As brutal as it might sound, I didn't want him to exist outside of those memories for me.

Gabriel seemed to sense what I didn't say. He gave me a melancholy smile and released my hands. "You are so beautiful. I forgot how beautiful you are."

"Thank you." I didn't know what else to say.

"I do not ... I do not think we shall see each other again."

I didn't think so either.

"May I ... May I give you something? Something to remember me?"

"Gabriel, I'm not likely to forget you," I promised him.

He grinned that cocky, self-assured smile that had lured me into his bed in the first place. "Perhaps not, but I brought it with me specifically to give to you." He lifted off one knee to pull a jewelry box out of his back pocket. Thankfully, it was too long to be a ring box. He snapped it open. Inside was a pendant on a chain. It was an unusual long, rectangle-shaped pendant molded out of silver and liberally engraved with flowers and vines in the Gothic style. "It belonged to my grand-mère," he explained. "She was Scottish."

My eyes widened. "Really?" He'd never spoken about his family while we were dating.

"Oui. She had passion and was strong. As you would say, she was fierce." He smiled fondly. "I cannot explain it, but even though we will likely not see each other again, I feel this belongs to you."

A family heirloom? "No, Gabriel, I couldn't."

"Please," he insisted. "It feels right to give it to you, my way of thanking you for our beautiful time together. And hopefully, a way for you to always remember what we shared."

The pleading look in his gorgeous eyes undid me. I found I couldn't say no. I reached out for the necklace. It wasn't my style and looked a bit heavy, but it was a lovely thought and keepsake. "Thank you. I'll take good care of it."

"And perhaps pass along to your daughter so you can tell her about the handsome French man you knew before you knew her father."

I laughed at his mischievous grin as he closed the box and placed it in my waiting hand. Then he pressed a soft kiss to my knuckles. "Do you have time this morning to show me around your village before I leave? My bus arrives at two."

"I can drive you wherever you need to go."

"No." He shook his head adamantly and stood. "Just take me for a coffee so whenever I want, I can picture you here in your little village, safe and happy."

TWENTY
LEWIS

Callie's fury last night all made sense now.

At first, I was bemused by the fierceness with which she attacked me. Callie had always been competitive (we both had), but this was different. I sensed from the moment she walked into the class that she was raging at me. I just had no idea what I'd done now. Then to swipe me with a move that wasn't even allowed in tae kwon do and walk out like she didn't care? It was out of character. As was not answering my calls or texts, or even responding to my sister once I enlisted Eilidh's help.

I assumed turning up at her house was a bad idea too.

Then Carianne called me as I was attempting and failing to fall asleep.

Apparently, she'd taken it upon herself to begin the "ruse" without my go-ahead. And Callie had basically told her to get the fuck out of her life. Now that might have reassured me Callie still had feelings for me, except Carianne was in a panic and wanted "to end the ruse" because she hadn't expected Callie to be so cold or unforgiving.

It was then I understood what had happened in class.

I couldn't believe Carianne. I would never hurt a woman, but I wanted to wring her bloody neck.

Because as I'd feared would happen, Callie hated me.

I'd felt it in her fight.

And seen it in her eyes.

I just hadn't understood it until now.

Suffice it to say, Carianne and I had words about her taking it upon herself to tell Callie we were dating when we weren't. She then acted affronted, as if this was all my fault, when I'd never once agreed to the pretense. I'd hung up on her.

Now I was skulking around Ardnoch, hoping to bump into Callie so I could explain. I was supposed to be working from home on my client's Tain project, but I'd decided to grab lunch in town. I knew the bakery wasn't open on a Tuesday, but Eilidh had mentioned Callie could still be found there practicing new recipes.

To make myself feel less like a stalker, I stopped in at the Gloaming to say hello to my uncle Arran. We chatted a bit about business and the twins, and then I made my excuses to leave. Deciding the best vantage point for the bakery was Flora's (and aye, I was aware this made me seem *more* like a stalker and I was not proud of myself), I strode toward it, stopping across the road as cars drove down Castle Street.

As the way cleared, Flora's door opened and there she was.

Callie stepped out of the café, laughing. Looking so far from the vengeful woman she was last night. Then my heart fucking stopped as some bloke followed her out and took her hand.

Recognition hit.

I'd seen him in photos with Callie. It was the French ex-boyfriend.

What the fuck?

They strolled down the street and I found myself following, my heart thumping wildly. I felt sick. Panicked. Outraged.

When they stopped at the bus stop, I didn't even care if Callie saw me. She was too busy, though, engrossed in the Frenchman. He turned and rested his hands on her hips, pulling her to him. Possessive fury burned like hellfire in my chest.

It boiled over as he bent his head and pressed a kiss to her lips.

It wasn't a passionate kiss.

But it might as well have been.

I knew if I stayed around and watched any longer, I'd do something I'd regret. That we'd all regret. In all likelihood, I'd lose any chance of winning Callie back if I did what I wanted at that moment.

Nah. The appearance of Gabriel was merely a setback.

It didn't mean I'd lost her.

I refused to believe that.

Even as anger at her roiled inside me.

Striding back to my bike, I got on it and waited. The bus to Inverness passed, most likely halted at the bus stop. Sure enough, Callie appeared a minute or so later in the distance, strolling alone toward the bakery.

Gabriel was gone.

Good riddance.

She didn't look my way. Instead, she disappeared through the front entrance of Callie's Wee Cakery.

The Harley rumbled to life as I switched on the ignition and then I rode it down the side street and into the car park of the bakery. Hoping she didn't lock me out, I quickly crossed to the back door and thudded on it.

TWENTY-ONE
CALLIE

The day had thrown me for such a loop that I didn't even think when I heard the thudding on the bakery's back door.

I reduced the volume on the music on my phone and crossed the kitchen to see who was here.

The sight of Lewis looming in the entrance made my heart leap into my throat and I moved to close the door.

He barged right in.

"Uh, excuse you!" I snapped.

"Unless you want Morag to hear this conversation, I'd close the door," he bit out in an uncharacteristic growl of anger.

What the hell did he have to be angry for? "I don't want to have a conversation with you, Lewis. I am done with you."

"Because Carianne's an idiot who asked me out and when I said no because I'm still in love with you she suggested that we pretend to date to make you jealous? To which I did not agree because it's fucking stupid."

What? I gaped at him, stunned. Because it was surely so silly he'd made it up. "Eh ... can you repeat that?"

"You tried to kill me last night for no reason." Lewis tugged a hand through his long hair. "And if that French fucker thinks I'm going to allow him to steal you from me, he's sadly mistaken."

Whoa. There was way too much in that to digest. "Don't you dare go all caveman on me, Lewis Adair. I am not some *thing* to be stolen. I belong only to me."

"And me." He pounded his fist passionately against his chest.

I'd never seen him so agitated. Not even when we'd broken up.

A shiver skated down my spine at the blazing look in his eyes.

"As I belong to you."

"Lewis ..."

"I did not say yes to dating Carianne. And I did not agree to pretend to date her to make you jealous."

"Then why did she say so?"

"Why do you care?" His question was quiet, desperate.

Honestly, I wanted to throw a bloody rolling pin at his head. "Because you walked out of my life seven years ago, never looked back, then drunkenly slept with me three weeks ago, returned to Ardnoch supposedly for me, only to ride off into the sunset like my rejection didn't bother you, and then you said yes to dating my old friend."

"I didn't!"

"How can I believe you? You lied about what you wanted when we were kids and you have given no indication that you hadn't moved on until three weeks ago. And even then, your actual commitment to the idea of us has been shaky at best."

"Me?" Lewis spat. "What about you?"

"Don't even," I seethed. "I was the one who wanted a life together. You weren't."

"I was a kid!" Lewis exploded.

It was so unexpected, so loud, so aggressive, I flinched.

Lewis saw and remorse tightened his features. His voice was quieter as he continued, "I was a kid who was scared about his future, like most kids who are asked to make decisions at seventeen years old that will affect the rest of their lives. Most of us have a wobble or two about that, Callie. But you wouldn't allow me that. I had to be perfect, or I was fucking cut out of your life like I was nothing."

Aghast that he saw our past like that, I shook my head, tears threatening when all I wanted was to be strong and collected. "Not true."

"Not true?" Lewis took a step toward me. "Who actually moved on, Callie? Between the two of us?"

"We both did. You moved to London and left all of us behind."

"I moved to a different city. That doesn't equate to leaving everyone behind."

"That's how it felt." I curled my lip in jealousy and disgust. "And God knows how many girls you shagged. By how different you were when we slept together, I'd say you'd learned a *lot* in the seven years we were apart."

He gave a bitter laugh and didn't say anything for a second. Then ... "I'm fucking pathetic."

"Excuse me?"

"I'm pathetic," Lewis repeated with a sneer of self-directed contempt. "I came here to clear up the mistake Carianne made. To offer my friendship. To try to get to know each other again and build trust. And all I can think is why? You don't see me."

"Don't turn this around—"

"How many men have you slept with?"

Fury made my throat so thick, I couldn't speak past it.

"Do you know how many women I've slept with?"

I didn't want to know.

I hated him.

His gaze was unflinching. "I couldn't sleep around. The thought of it made me feel sick. The guys at uni gave me a hard time. But it's the way I'm wired. I can't do casual sex. I tried first year of uni with a girl in our halls. I got so drunk in the attempt, I vomited on her lap instead."

Though he was talking about other girls, I couldn't help but wince in sympathy, even as my heart rate escalated.

"Then because I knew I couldn't do hookups, I tried to date a girl in second year. Roisin. We dated for two months before I slept with her. But I couldn't love her. Six months into the relationship, I ended it. There was no one after that. And I watched you move on in Paris. First Remy and then Gabriel. I despised the idea of you with them. It ate me up inside."

At his confession, his haunted tone, I felt guilty, even though I knew I shouldn't.

"So I tried to sleep with this woman at the firm I worked at. Charlotte. Took her out on my bike, went for drinks, went back to hers ..." Anger and love and resentment flickered across his face. "And I couldn't. I couldn't sleep with her, like I couldn't sleep with anyone else and like I couldn't tell my girl-friend I loved her ... because I'd already given myself to you."

His jaw trembled as his eyes turned glassy with emotion. "I fell in love with you a long time ago, and I never got that part of me back. The thought of anyone else feels fucking wrong. But then I see you out there. On the street, kissing that French guy, and I think what a goddamn moron I am for holding on to something that you clearly let go of a long time ago. Because I realized that's what I've been waiting for. Why I can't be with anyone else. I've been holding on to hope that you and I would find our way back to each other. Told you. Pathetic."

At my shocked silence, his jaw clenched, and he looked away. Then with a little huff of disbelief, he marched past me toward the door.

Reeling from his revelation, I was almost too late. Just in time, I snapped out of my stupor and I whirled. "Lewis."

He'd pushed open the back door, but now he paused.

"I honestly don't know if I can give you what you came here for," I told him tearfully, "but never think that I moved on easily from you. I was ... I was broken when you left." Tears escaped before I could stop them. "I promised myself I would never love again like that. With everything. With all that I was. And I never have. There were only three men after you. The first a mistake. The second Remy and the third Gabriel. Mere distractions. Nothing more."

"Callie—"

"I promised I'd never love anyone the way I loved you," I reiterated through gritted teeth. "Not even you again."

His expression fell. "Callie—"

"I'm not ..." Confused and heartsore, I shrugged helplessly. "Give me a few weeks. Some space to process everything you've told me." Something like hope lit his eyes, and I didn't want to hurt him. "I can't promise anything. Friendship or otherwise."

Lewis nodded slowly. "Okay."

"Thank you for being so honest with me." It took a lot for someone to admit what he had. It had also torn me up. Because as much as I hated the idea of Lewis with anyone else, I also hated the thought of him lonely and waiting for me, watching me with Gabriel and how that must have been for him.

I was so damn confused.

"You're welcome." His expression softened. "So, Gabriel isn't part of the equation?"

Rolling my eyes, I huffed. "No, he was just stopping by during his travels. For the last time."

His reply was gruff. "Good."

I smirked and shook my head.

"So ... you'll reach out when you're ready?"

"I'll reach out," I promised.

TWENTY-TWO
CALLIE

TWO WEEKS LATER

I was going to be sick.

Which wasn't unusual these days.

"Perhaps you're coming down with a stomach bug," Mum had suggested when I was sick at the bakery yesterday.

I'd thought maybe she was right when the next morning I'd upchucked my breakfast into the toilet in my cottage. Last week, I'd signed the rental agreement, and my family helped me move in. A few days after I'd settled into the home that brought with it some cozy nostalgia, I'd gotten a new car, so I didn't have to rely on other people for lifts everywhere.

Thankfully, that morning the bakery was closed, because as I'd sat back on my heels, exhausted, my eyes alighting on the tampons peeking out of my bathroom cupboard, a cold dawning slid through me. Mum had unpacked the boxes for the bathroom. Maybe if I had, realization would have hit me sooner.

My period was late ... and I'd missed my last period.

I'd been so busy settling back into the business and the village and dealing with the emotional turmoil of Lewis's return, and then revelations, it hadn't even occurred to me that I'd missed my period.

I'd missed my period after sleeping with Lewis.

Unable to think or talk to anyone until I knew, I cleaned myself up and grabbed my purse and car keys. Knowing that if I bought the pregnancy test in town, or nearby, it would be all over the village in hours, I drove to Inverness.

By the time I arrived in the city and purchased a pregnancy test from a large pharmacy, I hadn't been able to wait the hour to know. I slipped into the pharmacy's customer restroom and peed on the stick.

Nausea rolled through my stomach as I stood there. Sequestered in the stall of the loos, I listened to people come and go as I watched the test stick like a hawk. I'd paid extra for one of the digital tests.

A few minutes later, the word *Pregnant* appeared on the screen. And below it: *5–6 weeks.*

"Oh my fucking, arsing, bloody, shitty, fucking, fuck, fuck!"

Awful silence rang in the wake of my outburst.

Then I heard a female voice joke, "Want to bet she's either just got her period or she's pregnant."

Another woman chuckled.

Sometimes I really hated Scottish people. And I said that as one of them.

I burst out of the stall and marched over to the sink to wash my hands. Glaring at the two women in the mirror, I shook from head to toe. "Oh, it's all fun and jokes out here, eh? If you must know, nosy parkers, I'm pregnant. Happy?" I threw the pregnancy test into the bin and promptly burst into tears.

A few seconds later, I was enveloped in a stranger's arms, her perfume making me even more nauseated. But I clung to her as she soothed a motherly hand over my back. "There, there, sweetheart. It's going to be all right."

Was it?

Because right now, a tumultuous mix of thrill and absolute terror overwhelmed me.

———

The strangers were called Ellen and Shirley. Ellen was the person who hugged me through my tears. She told me she had a daughter around my age and would hope someone would comfort her if she wasn't around to do so. They'd insisted on walking me back to my car, and chatted to me about nonsense everyday things, like the weather, in an effort to calm me down. It worked, and I was in a fitter state to drive home than I had been in the restroom. I thanked them and they wished me luck before waving me off as I left the car park.

Nearing home, I called Mum to ask her where she was. She told me she was with Aunt Ally and Collum at the art gallery. I'd seen Aunt Ally as much as possible since I'd been home, and I even babysat Collum last week so she and Jared could have a night out at the Gloaming together. It seemed only fitting that she was there when I found Mum. I told her to stay put, that I was on my way. Mum sounded curious and a bit worried.

After we hung up, I called the doctor's office to make an appointment. The receptionist asked what it was pertaining to, and I told her I'd rather discuss it with the doctor. She tried to insist, and I insisted she mind her own business. She harrumphed, but I got an appointment for two days' time.

Skies Over Caledonia Art Gallery was situated around the corner from Flora's, just off Castle Street on Sutherland Way, the street opposite the Gloaming and home to the village hall. Aunt Ally's art gallery was two doors down from the village hall and next to one of three stores that sold overpriced Scottish-themed gifts to tourists.

I parked outside the Gloaming, praying I saw no one who would make it impossible not to stop and say hello to. My prayers were heard, and I hurried across the street and straight down toward the gallery. As I approached, I could see past the lovely pieces of glasswork, paintings, and jewelry displayed in the window to the main floor of the gallery. Aunt Ally had Collum in her arms. He was big for two, his legs dangling as he slept with his head on her chest, his arms tight around her neck. Aunt Ally held him like he weighed nothing as she and Mum chatted quietly. Strangely, there was no one else in the gallery. Then I noticed the closed sign hung on the door. Nevertheless, I let myself in, my gut churning like crazy.

The entire drive home, I'd tried to think of the right words to say to my mum. The perfect words.

And I had them ready on the tip of my tongue when Aunt Ally whirled around, and I saw Collum's sleepy but teary face resting on her upper chest. Suddenly, I saw my future in vivid color.

I was going to be a mum.

An actual mum.

Responsible for a small human being.

The room started to shift beneath my feet.

"Look who's come to see us," Aunt Ally crooned gently in her American accent. "Aunt Callie. Aunt Callie"—she whispered to me now—"we had to close the gallery because our little boy is teething again and he's understandably making quite the ruckus."

How the hell am I going to do this? I suddenly wondered in a panic.

Allegra had Jared. And aye, they were both busy, but they

had each other to share the exhausting, terrifying job of parenting.

"Baby girl." Mum suddenly moved past Allegra, a deep frown furling her brows. "What's happened?"

At that moment, the perfect words deserted me. I shrugged, tearfully, my hands coming to rest on my still-flat belly. "Well, I did as promised. It didn't happen to me at sixteen."

Confusion gave way to realization as Mum looked down at my hands on my belly. "Oh, Callie." She reached for me and pulled me into her arms, her embrace tight. "Oh my sweet, sweet girl. It's okay. It's all going to be okay." Her loving support and acceptance were my undoing.

I burst into tears and clung onto her like I was a child again.

———

Keeping it from Dad was the worst, even more so for Mum. But I didn't want anyone to know until the doctor confirmed my pregnancy. There would be no fear that it would be leaked from the doctor's surgery either, because the last time that happened, Mrs. McKay found out her husband had cancer before he had the chance to tell her. The person caught gossiping was fired because there was such an uproar in the village about it. Therefore, I could rest assured that while the people working in the surgery might know before Dad ... and Lewis ... they wouldn't tell them.

I asked Mum to accompany me, and I think I must have left crescent shapes in her skin from where my nails dug into her while she was holding my hand.

Dr. Mulligan confirmed it.

I was just over five weeks' pregnant. How hadn't I realized sooner?

"It's still too early to be showing, generally," he'd replied. "And you've been under some stress, returning home and settling into the business. Sometimes when we have a lot on our plates, it's easy to lose track." He'd cleared his throat. "Now to a somewhat delicate subject. During your first antenatal appointment, you'll be offered a blood test for STIs. But if you feel it's important, I could run those now."

Embarrassment made my cheeks hot. This was what came of living in a small village. Everyone knew I was single, including Dr. Mulligan, so everyone would also know I was pregnant from a hookup.

But with Lewis.

Who'd told me he'd only ever slept with one girl in the whole seven years we'd been apart.

Still, my last health check had been after I broke up with Gabriel.

"I don't think there's any hurry for that," I replied quietly. "I'll do it at the antenatal appointment."

Dr. Mulligan nodded and set out the schedule of what was to come. I trusted that Mum was listening intently because I was lost in my confused and aching emotions.

Since I was a kid, I'd dreamed of having my own family. I'd even dreamed that Lewis would be my children's father. Yet never in those dreams were we separated and co-parenting.

I barely remembered leaving the doctor's office with Mum. Instead, I remained in brooding silence while Mum drove us home. Except we didn't return home. She drove us to An Sealladh, a restaurant fifteen minutes outside of Ardnoch, that sat on the coastline.

I looked at her questioningly, but she patted my hand and got out of the car. Following her out, we walked into the restaurant together. Since it was brunch time, it wasn't rush hour inside and was fairly quiet. Thank goodness. I couldn't deal with crowds right then. We snagged a table at the back beside the glass wall that overlooked the North Sea. There was an outdoor balcony, but today it was too overcast to sit outside.

"What can I get you ladies?" A younger girl appeared to take our order.

"A pot of English breakfast tea to share and two plain scones," Mum ordered for us.

Hopefully, I'd keep it down. I had actual morning sickness. I was fine during the day and evening but upchucking in those first few hours after waking. Mum said she'd been exactly the same when she was pregnant with me.

"So..." Mum gave me a wobbly smile. "I'm going to be a grandmother."

"The youngest grandmother ever."

"Not really. But young."

Afraid she was disappointed in me, I asked quietly, "How does that make you feel?"

"Callie ... ever since you came into my life, I had a purpose. Moreover, I raised a child who is my best friend, and I know how lucky I am to say that."

Tears burned in my eyes.

"And as your mom and best friend, you must know that I am always here for you. I will love my grandchild so fiercely, and they will know that I am always there for them too."

A tear slipped free, and I dashed it away, embarrassed to be crying in public. Turning my head, I stared out at the water, hoping no one would see my tears.

"Baby girl, I have to ask ... is it Gabriel's? I just ... I can't seem to make that math work. Right?"

We hadn't had this discussion. In the two days we'd waited anxiously to see the doctor, she hadn't asked. And I hadn't told her. I couldn't bring myself to tell her because I couldn't deal with the unraveling of messy emotions all that would bring. Aunt Ally hadn't asked either. She'd texted me every day to check in, but she hadn't pressed for information.

I looked back at my mum, sure my heartbreak and confusion roiled in my eyes. "It's Lewis's." I turned away as my face crumpled.

"Oh, Callie." Mum sucked in a breath, fighting tears too. She'd always gotten upset anytime I was upset.

The young girl serving us returned quickly with our tea and scones, and I felt so rude because I couldn't look at her as Mum whispered a quiet thank you.

Sucking in a shuddering breath as we left the tea to steep in the pot, I finally felt in control enough to look at my mum again. "It happened in London. When I went there for Eilidh's wrap party."

Mum made an *O* shape with her mouth.

"We were drunk. Catching up. Trying not to get angry at each other. Trying to be civil. The attempt got out of hand. I don't even know how it happened or how I let it happen."

"I do."

I raised an eyebrow.

"Callie Ironside, you have loved that boy since the moment you set eyes on him. And he has loved you back all these years too. I remember the way Lewis watched you after what happened with Nathan, and I remember thinking how I'd never seen a little boy look so ready to jump in front of a moving bus for someone. And that's how it's always been between you. When you moved, he moved, and vice versa. Like two halves of a whole. Neither complete without the other. Even though you were kids, I always assumed you two would be forever. I don't know what happened when you were eighteen. I wish I did."

Her words made my chest ache even harder.

And so I told her.

Everything.

About how I'd felt him growing distant, pulling away, how I'd tried pathetically hard to keep him close, only to over-hear his conversation with Fyfe.

As I spoke, Mum poured our tea and made up a scone for me. She pushed the tea and plate toward me as I relayed my last conversation with Lewis. "Am I to feel guilty that I attempted a relationship when he couldn't?"

Mum gave me a chiding look. "I love you, Callie, but let's be honest. You've never, not once, attempted a relationship with anyone else."

I sighed. "You know what I mean. I at least attempted companionship. It's not my fault he couldn't." Though I felt wretched about it. "He was the one who left."

That was when she pursed her lips so hard, they bled of all color. My stomach knotted. "What? I know that look. You don't agree?"

"Can you handle some blunt honesty right now?"

Indignation made my skin hot. "From you, always."

She nodded, her warm brown eyes sympathetic. "I think that technically Lewis left ... but that you didn't give him much of a choice."

Renewed guilt flushed through me.

"I think that understandably, you were deeply scarred by Nathan. That a father could do that to his kid ..." Her mouth wobbled, as it always did when she spoke about my birth father. "And I think that a consequence of everything you went through is that you demand absolute love, loyalty, and certainty from the people you give your heart to. And so far, it's been easy. Your dad and I adore you, and you've never doubted it."

"Is it wrong to want that kind of certainty?" I shrugged helplessly.

"You should always demand love and loyalty, my sweet girl. But truly giving that back to the people who give it to us means being able to recognize when their mistakes or weaknesses are not malicious. To understand and to remember they're human, and humans are not perfect. To love them on their worst day. Now, if someone is constantly making those mistakes or hurting you, then, of course, I would want you to rid yourself of that person."

"But Lewis ...?"

Mum reached over to take my hand. "Was a boy. A boy who grew up in a tiny village where everyone knows him ... and I don't think questioning whether this was the place he wanted to be was a capital offense. I think most kids at that age would have concerns, thoughts, curiosities, a desire to explore. And I don't think having a brief uncertainty about whether a teenage romance had a future is a capital offense either. He was steadfast and loyal, and he made you feel loved. And I think the very first time he messed up, you weren't very forgiving. I'm sorry, but that's what it sounds like to me, baby girl."

It was everything Lewis said to me in the bakery two weeks ago. And it was everything I'd said to myself over the years but refused to deal with because then it would mean that losing Lewis was my own fault.

A sob threatened to burst out of me, and I was almost choking trying to keep it in. I let my hair fall over my face as I turned to look out the window and silently cried.

"Oh, baby girl, I'm sorry."

I waved Mum off, trying to pull myself together.

For the past two weeks, Lewis had done as promised and given me space. Maybe in that time, he'd decided I wasn't worth the trouble. I'd broken up with him in what amounted to a teenage temper tantrum because I'd needed more than anyone our age could have given, all because my real father was a sociopath who'd messed me up. Then I'd spent the next seven years dodging truly meaningful relationships because I reckoned if Lewis Adair wasn't capable of loving me the way I needed, then no one else had a snowball's chance in hell.

As it turned out, he had every right to be angry with me. And yet he was still ready to forgive me because he loved me.

Once I calmed, I looked back at Mum. "I know you're right. I just ... I don't know where I go from here. Lewis said he came back for me ... but I doubt very much an instant family was on his mind."

"It doesn't matter," Mum replied sternly. "You didn't ask to get pregnant either, Callie, but a child *is* coming. So Lewis will have to man up and deal with it, just as you're having to deal with it."

I took a shaky sip of my now lukewarm tea.

"Will you tell Lewis first before you tell your dad?"

I gave a huff of laughter. "I think I should, if only to warn him to put a bloody ocean between him and Dad."

"Your father won't kill him. I'll make sure of it."

Looking into Mum's eyes, I felt nothing but gratitude for her. "I'm scared."

"I know." And I knew she did. Now more than ever, I was in awe of her.

"But I'm also not. Because I have you. I used to think that Ardnoch was my safe place." I reached over and curled my hands around Mum's. "But you're it. You're my safe place, Mum. Always and forever."

She blinked, and her tears fell unashamedly down her cheeks as she tightened her grip around mine.

TWENTY-THREE

LEWIS

"It's architect designed," the estate agent informed me as we walked through the brand-new home. "Award-winning architect Thane Adair was behind this beauty." She frowned as she glanced down at the note in front of her and looked back up at me. "Any relation?"

"Aye." I nodded, standing in the middle of the living space and feeling already at home. It had my dad's style stamped all over it. "He's my father. We work together."

"Oh, you're an architect too?"

I nodded again. Dad was the one who gave me the heads-up that a house he'd designed, one that was among his favorites, had come on the market. It was situated on a small piece of private land, nestled in woodland, between Ardnoch and Golspie. The home was designed so that the living space was upstairs and the bedrooms downstairs. The first floor was a modern midcentury dream with two walls made entirely of glass. With woodland at the back of the home, the living space emulated the experience of being in a tree-house. The stairs brought you up into the kitchen and island, and beyond that was a living and dining area. Off the dining area, Dad had designed an oversized square window box.

I stepped into it and sat down on the plush window seat. There were windows on all three sides and it literally felt like you were hanging in the trees. Below I could see the twinkle of water from the man-made moat around the house. Water was taken from a downhill stream on the back of the property through underground pipes and pumped into the moat, where propeller turbines attached to a hydropower system created hydroelectricity to power the home. There was also a bank of solar panels out front where there were no trees to block the sunlight.

The nook Dad had created off the dining room was a bit of magic.

Callie would love it.

The estate agent prattled on about details I already knew because Dad had told me everything. The client was an Australian businessman who wanted a holiday home in the Highlands. However, recent financial troubles meant that he was selling the home and for less than it was worth so he could sell it quickly. It was still expensive. But as the home was run on the latest eco-first technologies, the next owner would save big on utility bills.

I followed the agent down to the ground floor to the four bedrooms. The primary suite had a floor-to-ceiling window that abutted the moat so while lying in bed, it was like being on a boat. Dad had outdone himself with design experiences in this house. I could see why it was one of his favorites.

But was it too much for only me? A four-bedroom home in the woods. It wasn't a massive home, but four bedrooms for a single guy ...

I hadn't heard from Callie in over two weeks. Not a word. I'd gotten on with getting settled back into Ardnoch, enjoying distracting family dinners that had gotten so unruly we needed two tables to accommodate everyone. But it was nice being surrounded by my aunts and uncles and cousins. Between family and work, I didn't have much time during the day to contemplate Callie or the future.

Nighttime was hardest. Lying in bed, wondering if I'd wasted seven years of my life secretly believing that Callie and I would find our way back to each other.

"What do you think?" the estate agent asked as we stepped outside. The front of the home, the driveway that led into the property, still needed a bit of work.

Yet it was a spectacular house and knowing how much Dad loved it, it would be nice to keep this particular creation in the family.

I just ... it was a lot for a twenty-five-year-old bachelor.

Still, I couldn't help but imagine Callie here. I knew, like I knew myself, that she'd fall head over heels in love with this place.

"I'll have my solicitor reach out with an offer." I found myself saying.

Apparently, I was still a hopeless fool for Callie Ironside.

———

Since I'd taken time out of a working morning to view the house, my intention was to return home and get stuck into projects. It was great not having to be in the office often since the commute was a bugger. I didn't know how my dad had done it every day, back when working from home wasn't as popular.

I knew Dad was out with a client, so I could use his office. The other good thing about having my own place was I could use one of the bedrooms as an office, and Dad would get his space back.

Truthfully, I was feeling a bit jittery, which was normal

considering I'd called my solicitor ten minutes ago to ask him to put an offer on the house. Without discussing it with anyone. I'd talk to my family later. For now, Mum was working at the preschool and had roped Morwenna into helping there during the summer holidays for extra pocket money.

My parents' home was one of five built on a parcel of land along the coastline of Caelmore, just outside Ardnoch. It was land owned by my family, and each house was lived in by my aunts and uncles and cousins. There was no excuse for missing Sunday dinners in this family. Some folks might have hated living that close, but I liked it. Whatever the situation called for, I always had an aunt or uncle I could turn to growing up.

As I rode down the country road that led to the homes, I spotted a vehicle in the driveway of my parents'.

One I didn't recognize.

But as I approached the house, a figure came into view. A person sitting on the front porch.

It didn't take me long to recognize her, and my pulse quickened as I pulled in beside the white car and watched Callie push up to her feet. I wasted no time getting off the Harley and removing my helmet.

Callie walked down the steps slowly, looking a bit peaky and a lot nervous.

Worry overrode my relief at seeing her. "Callie, what's wrong?"

She gave me a wan smile. "We ... we need to talk."

———

My concern was growing by the second. I couldn't stop glancing over at Callie as she sat on the sofa, twisting her fingers nervously. I'd never seen her so antsy, and the fact that she didn't look well was freaking me the fuck out.

I brought over the glass of water she'd asked for and sat on the sofa opposite. There were dark circles under her eyes. "Are you sick?" I blurted out, palms sweaty at the thought of something being seriously wrong with Callie.

"I ... I did go to the doctor this morning."

No.

Fear rose up inside me. She *was* sick.

The Adair men were cursed after all.

Hadn't Uncle Lachlan thought that for years before he met Aunt Robyn? The Adair men were cursed to lose the women we loved. There was a long line of evidence to support the theory, leading all the way to my birth mother, Francine, dying in her sleep from an aneurysm. Anytime I thought of what it must have been like for Dad waking up to find her gone, I couldn't ... the idea of Callie ...

"Lewis, no." She leaned toward me, suddenly recognizing the terror on my face. "I'm not sick. Sorry. I ... Lewis, I'm pregnant. I'm just over five weeks pregnant. And since you're the only person I've had sex with in the last three months ..."

The baby was mine.

Holy fuck.

First, I experienced a wave of relief that Callie wasn't ill.

Then terror.

Then more relief that the baby was mine.

Then more terror.

And finally, an overwhelming mix of terror, relief, hope, and more terror.

Callie's anxiety registered through all of that. "Fuck." I pushed up off the couch and sat down next to her, taking her hands in mine. "Don't look like that. You must know I'm going to be there for you and our baby."

"You're not angry."

I frowned. "Callie, you didn't make the baby alone. And

...," I winced, "I used two really old condoms that night, so it's probably my fault."

She burst into laughter, and I couldn't help but grin in relief as she full-body cackled at my confession. As her amusement tapered off, a tenderness and sorrow crossed her face. Then she was throwing her arms around me, and I melted into her, breathing her in and holding her close.

"Thank you," she whispered tearfully.

"For what?" My voice was gruff.

"For being you." Callie eased out of my arms and I reluctantly let her go.

"So ..." I exhaled heavily as the reality of the situation weighed down on me. In less than eight months, I'd be a father. To a tiny human. That wasn't terrifyingly daunting or anything. "What's the plan? What do we do?"

"Well, I have my first antenatal appointment in three weeks, and we'll go from there. For right now, the doctor says I'm healthy. I've got some morning sickness and I'm a bit tired, but otherwise I'm fine."

Which explained her peaky pallor. I reached for her hand and folded it into mine. "That's great. I want to be there for everything. But what I really meant was ... what do we do? My mind hasn't changed, Callie. I want you. This hasn't changed my mind about that. Has it changed yours?"

She nervously licked her lips. "We have a lot to talk about."

Hope filled me because she hadn't said a flat-out no. "Could we talk about it on a date? Would you go on a date with me?"

Callie stared at me in awe for a second, and after the past few weeks of rejection, I honestly didn't understand her current expression. But I was relieved as any man could be when she whispered, "Aye, Lewis. I'll go on a date with you."

TWENTY-FOUR
LEWIS

S uffice it to say I couldn't concentrate on work for shit after Callie left. She promised she was fine to drive, but I insisted she text me to let me know she'd arrived home. I was gratified when she did. I replied that I'd drop by her cottage at three o'clock in the morning for our first date.

Did you mean to type 3AM?

I did. At this time of year, it's twilight.

What the hell are we doing at 3AM?

You're used to 3AM starts, no?

Aye, but that doesn't answer my question.

You'll just need to wait and see.

Honestly, I was glad for the distraction of my family returning to the house in late afternoon. I'd spent all my work time instead planning our three a.m. date and buying baby books. I was clueless about babies, and I hated that feeling of incompetence. By the time Callie gave birth, I'd know everything I needed to know. It was easier to deal with practical stuff like knowledge than to really think about the reality of having a baby in our lives that we had to feed and clothe and keep alive. Or how this would turn our lives upside down. Or how we had so little time left for just the two of us to reconnect.

I wanted to make the most of it.

By the time I got up the nerve to leave the office to give my parents the news (Callie's mum and Aunt Ally already knew, and she was returning home to tell her Dad and brother), my wee sister had disappeared.

"Where's Mor?" I asked my parents as I wandered into the open-plan living space. They were working together—Dad put away groceries while Mum prepped to cook dinner.

Mum flicked me a harried look. "A toddler puked all over her today at preschool and she says she's traumatized and doesn't want to talk to anyone."

I flinched, realizing that very situation was in my foreseeable future. "So ... she's in a mood?"

"Pretty much. Just leave her be."

I really wanted to tell everyone at the same time, but ... "I have to tell you something."

They both stopped what they were doing because my voice was shaking.

Clenching my hands into fists, I attempted to get myself together, but reality was kind of sinking in now and my knees were definitely trembling. Adrenaline had to be coursing through my body, understandable considering my entire life had changed in an instant. "Well ... first, I put an offer in on the house."

Dad beamed. "Was it accepted?"

I held up a hand to ward him off. "I haven't heard back,

but that's not really the main news. When I was coming back from the viewing, Callie showed up. And, uh, well, for a bit of context—and I'm sorry if this is TMI—she and I slept together in London almost six weeks ago, and she is very much pregnant as a consequence of ... that ... event. Pregnant. With my baby. Callie."

Mum's mouth dropped open like a cartoon, the corn cob she clutched in one hand and the knife in the other frozen in midair as her entire body ceased movement.

Dad took a tentative step around the island. "Are you ... are you ... you're going to be involved?"

I scowled. "Of course I fucking am." It hadn't even occurred to me I wouldn't be.

My father deflated with relief. "Thank God."

Frankly, I was insulted. "You thought I wouldn't?"

"I thought she might not want you to be," Dad assured me. "I know things are difficult there."

"I'm going to be a grandmother?" Mum asked, looking a bit spaced out, hands still hovering.

Dad approached her and gently took the knife from her grip. "Yes, Regan, our son is going to be a father, and you are going to be a very beautiful, very young grandmother. That's happy news. Right?"

I sagged, like air deflating out of a balloon at my dad's words.

Mum stared into his eyes. "Our son is going to be a father."

Dad nodded patiently.

"We're going to be grandparents."

"We are."

She blinked rapidly, coming out of her stupor. Then suddenly, she dropped the corn and flew around the island at me. I braced as she threw herself into my arms. "Congratulations, sweetheart. I know how scared you must be, but never forget your dad and I are always here, and we will help you and Callie through this."

With a shaky grin, I returned her fierce hug. "Thank you."

Dad joined us, placing a hand on my nape to give me an affectionate squeeze. "Congrats, son."

"Thanks."

Mum released me but kept one arm around my waist. "So, does this mean you and Callie are back together?"

"I don't know. But she's letting me take her out on a date tomorrow."

Mum's dimples appeared as she let out a girlish squeal of delight. I chuckled, suddenly exhausted. Mum then started cataloguing everything we'd need and how she'd call Sloane in the morning so she, Callie, and Sloane could get together to organize a baby shower.

"Uh, that's great, Mum, but Callie gave me the impression that she wants this to remain among family until she's a bit further along."

"Oh, of course. We can make plans without telling anyone yet."

Deciding to take her reaction as a win, I let her be and turned to Dad. "How bad is Mor's mood? I really want to be the one to tell her."

"She's fine. Go tell her." He clapped me on the shoulder. "And if you want to chat about anything, I'm here. I was only a few years older than you when you came along, you know."

"I know. Thanks, Dad."

He gave me a warm look. "You make me proud, son. Best accomplishment of my life ... raising a good man like you."

"Fuck, Dad," I huffed out gruffly. "I'm already an emotional wreck."

Chuckling, he patted me on the shoulder again. "Go tell your wee sister she's going to be an aunt."

When Eilidh moved out, Morwenna had asked for her

bedroom because it was bigger. After Mor grumpily granted me entrance, I realized I hadn't been in it in ages because in that time it had been transformed into a bedroom/library.

I raised an eyebrow. My parents had hired someone to paint a mural of a misty forest on the wall where Mor's bed was placed. The largest wall in the room was filled with floor-to-ceiling custom shelves, stacked to the brim with books. There was even a ladder on a rail so she could reach the top shelves.

"This is amazing." I gestured around the room. "The mural is beautiful."

"Allegra McCulloch helped me paint it."

My eyes widened. "You painted this?"

Morwenna was huddled against her pillows, knees drawn to her chest, reading a book. She lowered her eyelids and nodded shyly. "Allegra helped."

Shit.

I really had been a terrible brother. I didn't even know my kid sister was a talented artist. Or that she even liked art. What else didn't I know about her? "May I?" I gestured to the end of her bed.

She shrugged and I decided to take that as a yes. Sitting down, I stared around her room again, suddenly regretting all those years I'd stayed away. Half of Mor's childhood. "I have to tell you something and I haven't told Eilidh yet, so I need you to keep it to yourself until I do."

"You're telling me first?" Mor dropped her book, expression stupefied.

I frowned. "Aye, why?"

"Because you never tell me anything. Especially not before you tell Eilidh."

Hearing the hurt in her tone, I studied her carefully. "Have I been an awful big brother?"

She shrugged again. "No. It's just ... I've always felt a bit left out. You and Eilidh are so close in age, and I don't have ... you guys are close. I don't have that with you both."

It was true that the age gap between us made for a different dynamic. I suppose it had never occurred to me that it might bother Mor. But suddenly, I wondered if she felt like an only child half the time. Was she lonely? I hoped not. She had our parents and a huge gang of cousins a mere few hundred yards away.

"I'm sorry you've felt left out."

Mor seemed to grow some confidence at my apology and finally looked at me. Frustration gleamed in her chestnut eyes. "People at school either tease me for being Eilidh Adair's wee sister or they just want to be friends with me because of her. They're so fake. And they all ask me questions about her, and I couldn't even answer if I wanted to because Eilidh never bothers to talk to me. I haven't heard from her in weeks. She texted me to ask how I was, and I didn't reply, and she didn't even bother sending another text to see if I was okay."

Damn it, Eilidh.

Not that I could come down on my sister, since I hadn't been much better. But I would have texted Mor again or called.

I made a mental note to talk to Eilidh about making more of an effort.

"I'm sorry." I found myself apologizing again. "I'm sorry we've been so wrapped up in ourselves."

Morwenna's eyes gleamed, and I felt even worse as she blinked rapidly as if fighting back tears. Her lips pursed and she shrugged again before gritting out, "It's fine. I'll be leaving when I'm eighteen and I probably won't talk to any of you for months."

"That won't be happening," I said gruffly. "No way is my wee sister taking off into the world without checking in. In fact, I'll probably send an armed bodyguard with you."

The corner of her mouth pulled up, as if she was secretly pleased by the thought. "Whatever," she muttered, but there was a lightness in her tone that hadn't been there before.

"So ... I came to tell you that you're going to be an aunt."

She frowned, processing this information. Then she gaped. "Oh my God, who did you get pregnant?"

I chuckled at her bluntness. "Callie."

Her eyes widened and then she snorted. "Well, that's one way to get her back."

"Cheeky wee shite." I laughed, and my sister burst into giggles. I hadn't heard her laugh like that in ages.

Mor's amusement petered out and we shared an affectionate smile. Then she sobered. "Are you scared?"

I nodded.

Mor considered this and then she offered quietly, "You'll be okay, Lewis. I think you'll be a good dad."

Emotion clogged my throat. "Thank you."

TWENTY-FIVE
CALLIE

I was fully awake when Lewis knocked on the cottage door at three in the morning the next day. The nausea hadn't kicked in yet either, which was great. Last night, I'd stayed at my parents' house until eleven in the evening. Dad had been stunned by the news and angry at Lewis, and I had to talk him down from challenging him to a duel.

No, really. I think if we lived in the days of dueling, Lewis would be at the other end of my dad's pistol.

Yet, to protect Lewis, I found myself explaining everything that had ever happened between us to Dad. Apparently, the truth did the trick. I think Dad had been imagining the worst all this time—that Lewis had cheated on me.

Still, I got the impression that my parents needed me close for as long as possible. Mum had wanted me to stay over, but I knew I had to get used to living on my own at the cottage. Even more so now. Harry was quiet about the whole thing, and I worried that he was anxious the news would make him a target at school again. Hopefully, it would all blow over by the time school started up after summer.

Growing up in a village came with pros and cons. There was always someone there to give you a helping hand, and no one banded together to protect a villager from an outsider faster or more ferociously than those in Ardnoch. We were all so used to the estate's celebrity members that we didn't bother them—Ardnoch was a safe space. So much of our economy depended on the estate that no one would dare talk to the press about the members-only club and the people who frequented it.

But bloody hell, did we like to gossip among ourselves. Everybody was in everybody else's business, and news traveled faster than the speed of light. So I couldn't allow myself to feel guilty for what was happening to Harry because we'd all dealt with that kind of stuff. Yet I couldn't help but worry about him on top of everything else.

That night, I'd lain in bed, my alarm set for two o'clock. I didn't sleep. I lay there worrying about how I was going to manage running the bakery with a newborn in tow. And I worried about this date with Lewis and all the things I needed to say to him. It was a relief when my alarm went off and I could get up to prepare for our date.

"This is the strangest hour for a date ever." I answered the door as soon as Lewis knocked. I kept my voice low so as not to disturb my neighbors.

Lewis stood on the pavement, the streetlights glowing against the hazy dusk of twilight. His sexy smirk still made me weak at the knees. "You look beautiful."

I was dressed in jeans, a T-shirt, and a cardigan, and my hair was pulled back in a ponytail. I wore only a touch of mascara and blush. This was the most boring outfit I'd ever worn on a date, but I didn't know where we were going, only that it was still chilly at this time of the morning, even if it was early July. "I've looked better." Grabbing my keys, I stepped out of the cottage and stared up at my handsome date. He wore his hair loose for once and looked like a rock star more than a biker this morning.

"You're always beautiful to me." Lewis leaned down and whispered in my ear, "And always sexy as fuck."

I shivered at the words and the way his breath puffed against my skin. Oh boy. Swallowing hard, I pulled back to peer up at him. "Seriously, where is Lewis and what have you done with him?"

He chuckled and gestured to a Range Rover parked at the curb. "Ready?"

I immediately pouted. "Where's the bike?"

"Eh, you're pregnant." He placed a hand on my lower back, leading me toward the 4x4. "There is no way I'm putting you on the back of my bike."

Damn it. I knew he was right. Disappointed but also appreciative of his forethought, I got into the passenger side. "Is this yours?" I asked as he climbed in behind the wheel.

Lewis shook his head. "Borrowed it from Dad. But I'm going car hunting this weekend. We'll need something big enough for a baby's car seat."

"I have a car."

"I know. But I want to be able to drive you to your doctor's appointments and whatever else you need."

As we drove down Castle Street, I found myself staring at his profile in awe. He was buying a car just so he could drive me around. "You ... you seem calm about the whole thing."

He shot me a quick, patient look. "A baby is on its way, Callie. Aye, it's scary, and we wouldn't be human if we weren't terrified, but there's no point wallowing in that. Because ... it's also exciting. And we have lots to talk about and prepare for."

At that moment, I felt so ashamed.

I fell quiet as Lewis drove toward the main beach parking.

The car park was almost empty, except for a couple of motorhomes. There was nothing but the sound of the surf beyond the dunes.

"Are you okay?" he asked.

"What are we doing here?" I asked instead.

Lewis didn't respond with words. He got out of the car and rounded it to open my door. As I stepped out, he pulled a picnic basket and blanket from the back seat.

With his free hand, he clasped mine tightly and led me toward the beach. A sand-covered boardwalk guided us down through the dunes and out onto the stretch of smooth, perfect beach.

In the twilight, there was not another soul in sight, and a summer morning mist hung in the air.

"Callie ... are you okay?"

I squeezed Lewis's hand. "I have so much to say ... and yet ... I'm not sure I can."

Instead of answering, he tugged on my hand, and I followed him down the beach. He chose a random spot to spread the blanket and gestured for me to take a seat. I kicked off my trainers and sat down, pulling my knees to my chest. I was glad for my cardy because there was a cool breeze blowing up from the water. The gentle tide and quiet rhythm of the sea lapping against the shore calmed my racing heartbeat as Lewis sat down and began unpacking the picnic basket.

I watched as he pulled out a bottle of water, sparkling fruit water, and ... a bottle of Irn-Bru. Thinking it was a strange choice for an early-morning picnic, but thinking this whole thing was strange, I let it go. There were scones and mini jars of jam and clotted cream. Croissants that looked an awful lot like my mum's. I *hmmed* at that and he grinned.

Lastly, he pulled out a bag of peanut M&Ms, Walkers' pickled onion crisps, and ... my mum's homemade truffles in a

Tupperware box. "Where did you get those?" I asked, reaching out to steal one. Mum hadn't made those in ages!

"The same place I got the croissant and scones."

"Mum?"

Lewis nodded. "She might have grabbed the pastries from the bakery and made me the truffles last night."

"But I was there last night."

"She made them when you left and placed the box outside for me to collect before coming to get you."

My brows furrowed as I stared at the picnic. When we were kids, the crisps, the truffles, and the M&Ms were all my favorite unhealthy snacks. As was the Irn-Bru, something I hadn't drunk in years. "What is all this?"

"It's your perfect first date." Lewis drew his knees up to his chest, too, his arms dangling over them. Then he gestured to the beach. "A picnic on the beach at twilight with all of your favorite snacks."

A memory prodded at me. "Why does that ... I said that?"

He nodded, meeting my probing stare. "You texted me a list of your perfect dates and this was date one."

Awed, shocked, emotional, I choked out, "And you remember that?"

Lewis stared at me as if I was the most extraordinary thing he'd ever seen. "I kept all of our texts. I'd read them over and over until I realized I was driving myself crazy. So I saved them to my computer before I deleted them from my phone. When I came back to Ardnoch, I remembered I had them and started reading through our old conversations. There was one where you told me the kind of dates you wanted to be taken on." His teeth flashed in the dusk. "I had planned to take you on all of them, but date two is zip-lining, so that'll have to wait until after the baby comes."

I suddenly felt a clawing panic as self-loathing filled me.

All this time he'd been holding on so tight to us. "I don't deserve you, Lewis."

At my cold pronouncement, he glowered. "Don't. Don't make that decision for me. Not like before."

I winced and turned away, letting out a shuddering breath. "I ... I did this to us."

"*We* did this to us."

I shook my head. "No, I let it end like this. You would've fought if I'd given you the chance."

"We were kids, Callie. We have to let it go."

"Can you?" I asked incredulously. "How can you trust me, Lewis? I've spent the last seven years hating you because it was easier to do that than listen to the voice in my head screaming at me that I was the one who fucked up. That I punished you for being human, that I was rigid and unkind and selfish."

"Callie ... fuck." Lewis slid across the blanket and wrapped an arm around me, trying to pull me into his side.

But I was stiff. Because I didn't deserve his comfort.

He let out a puff of air. "I understand why you were hurt back then. I was distant, and you did hear me tell Fyfe I wasn't as sure as you were that we had a future together. If I'd heard you say those things, I would have been hurt too."

"The difference is, Lewis, you would have forgiven me, and we wouldn't have lost seven years of our lives together. And now ..." My fears bubbled to the surface. "I'll never know if we would have made our way back to each other naturally. This baby has forced us back together."

"No, it hasn't." He gripped my chin gently and turned me to face him, to look in his eyes. His expression was fierce as he entreated, "We can raise this baby without being together. If that's what you want. But it's not what *I* want. I wouldn't have gotten up at two a.m. to bring you to the beach for a picnic if I didn't want you. I wanted to come home years ago, and I didn't because I couldn't live in the same town as you and watch you have a life with someone else. As soon as you left me in London, though, I knew that I *had* to come home. For me and for you. And that was before I knew you were pregnant."

"Why?" I begged, eyes filled with tears. "I pushed you away. I didn't trust you. I didn't give back to you all that loyalty I was asking from you. I snuck out after we had sex."

"The latter I get because it was intense. So, I forgive you for leaving that morning. As for the rest ... you were a kid," he whispered gruffly. "Callie, you were a kid. And you'd been through more than most kids. I won't hold that moment against you. Not when there are a million other moments that prove how loving and sweet and funny and kind *my* Callie is." His thumb swiped over my cheek in a caress.

I wrapped my hand around his wrist but didn't push him away. "What ... what if you don't like who I am now?"

"I do," he said without taking a beat. "You're still Callie. And I'm still me, but I've grown up too. I missed Ardnoch, Cal. I missed it more than I ever thought possible. And I kicked myself because I thought I wanted out ... and I lost you over that. But I know what I want now. I want you, here, for the rest of my life."

I was humbled by his conviction, and my heart suddenly felt too big in my chest. "I still think we need time. To take it slowly. To date. To make sure ... this is what you want."

Lewis frowned and pulled his arm from my grasp. "You're not sure?"

He deserved my honesty. "I would give anything to spend the rest of my life proving to you I can be who you deserve ... but I'm afraid I don't deserve you. Everything's a mess, Lewis." Tears slipped down my cheeks. "People are gossiping about me, Harry was getting bullied at school because of me ... and now everyone's going to think I trapped you."

"Callie, stop." Lewis took me by the shoulders, his expression determined, passionate. "Who gives a fuck what anyone else thinks? All that matters is what *you* think, what *I* think, and that our families support us. And we have that from them. Everyone else can go fuck themselves."

I let out a huff of laughter.

"I mean it." He cupped my face in his palms. "I hate that they've made you feel bad about yourself. You are so impressive, Callie. You lived in a foreign country for three years by yourself. You trained at a top pastry school in Paris and instead of taking that experience to some fancy, pretentious restaurant in a city, you brought it home to your mum's bakery. Because family is the most important thing to you. And I was your family, so I get that our past will have fucked you up. But I don't want to hear another word about whether you deserve me. We both made mistakes. But we're both here now."

"How can you trust me?" I begged to understand his openness because it put me to shame. "I want you to believe that you can make mistakes, that you can be human and weak with me, that you don't have to be perfect all the time. But can you?"

"Aye, I can." Lewis nodded. "I believe you won't do that to me again because I can see how much it's hurting you right now. But more than that, Callie ... I love you so much, but I am not a man who will walk on eggshells or become someone else to suit you. I am who I am, and you'll either love me or you won't. Knowing that, I wouldn't take a chance on you if I didn't think you could handle me being myself with you."

Love, so much love it was overwhelming, crashed over me.

I was still *in* love with Lewis Adair.

And it was terrifying because now I knew what it felt like to lose him.

I leaned my cheek against his shoulder. "I'm scared."

He pulled me in tight, resting his cheek on the top of my

head. "I know. And if you want, we can take this slow. We'll ... date."

Amusement trembled on my lips. "While I'm pregnant with your baby?"

"Aye." He chuckled. "Christ, Callie ... we're having a baby."

"I know." I slid my arm around his stomach and held on while we watched the sun rise into the sky. "Everything is going to change."

"Not everything," he promised. "Not the way I love you."

I let out a shuddering breath. "I have always loved you too. Always only ever you."

In answer, Lewis pulled back. When I raised my head to look at him, he brushed a gentle kiss across my mouth. A sudden desperate hunger rose in me, and I curled my fist into his shirt and pulled him in deeper.

Reluctantly, we broke the kiss, panting against each other's mouths.

"Slow," Lewis said gruffly. "We'll take it slow."

Knowing he was right, I eased back and glanced down at the picnic. "We should eat some of this."

———

The rest of our picnic was less intense. Some of the awful thoughts and feelings I'd been suffering through these last few days were dulled by Lewis's acceptance and determination. I knew he was right. That I had to stop worrying about what everyone thought of me. The only people who mattered were those who had proven they loved me and were proud of me.

We packed up the picnic to head back after a couple hours of chatting about everything and nothing. We talked about Harry and Morwenna, our parents, our jobs, and, of course, about the baby. Lewis wanted to be at every appointment, which I was grateful for. Yesterday morning I'd felt alone, despite my mum's comforting support. Now, I felt like—even with things still new again between us—I had a partner in Lewis.

"Oh, and I should probably mention I put an offer on a house yesterday."

I straightened from putting my trainers back on as Lewis picked up the picnic basket and blanket. "A house?"

He watched me carefully. "That's where I was coming from before you told me you were pregnant."

"Oh."

"I know we said slow, and we'll take it slow ... but it's a four-bedroom house in the woodlands between here and Golspie. I put an offer on it because I think you'd love it."

Oh. I gaped at him, feeling that surge of overwhelming emotion again.

And with it, nausea.

I gagged, covering my mouth as I bolted toward the sea. I made it just in time to upchuck into the water.

A few seconds later, I felt a tug on my ponytail as Lewis pulled it away from my face. He soothed a hand over my back as I retched over and over, throwing up everything I'd eaten.

Finally, I sagged back into his broad chest, and he tucked his chin between my shoulder and neck. "Better?"

I nodded, shaking. "I should head back, though. The morning sickness can last a few hours."

"Shit. Really?"

"Aye."

"Let me stay with you, then."

"Don't you have work?"

"I can fob it off for a few hours."

I turned in his arms. "Thank you, but I'll be fine. And if you're buying a house, you should really go to work."

At my pointed comment, he tugged me closer so my breasts were flush with his chest. "Did that freak you out?"

I chuckled. "Surprisingly, no."

"If they accept my offer, I'd like you to come see it."

I nodded, my stomach somersaulting again at the thought of Lewis buying a house he thought I might like. He was so wonderful; it was hard to take in after all these years of unfairly resenting him.

He leaned in as if to kiss me, and I backed up. "Uh, no." I covered my mouth.

Lewis chuckled. "Damn, I forgot. That's what you do to me. I forget one second from the next, and all I can think about is your mouth." This time when he leaned in, it was to murmur in my ear, "When we're done taking it slow, *my* mouth is going to know every fucking inch of you again."

This flirtatious side of Lewis was new, but I couldn't say I didn't like it. I shivered as he pulled back, a cocky smirk on his face. He knew exactly what affect he had on me.

I playfully slapped his chest and pushed him away. "Big flirt."

He grinned and tugged on my hand, leading me back up the beach. It was like he couldn't help himself and needed to touch me all the time. I couldn't say I didn't like that either. In fact, I was feeling extremely needy, and his affection was soothing that neediness.

Back at the cottage, however, I convinced him to go to work.

Minutes after he'd left, I slumped over the toilet, exhausted from retching into it again. I wished I hadn't told Lewis to go to work.

Realizing I wanted him there, needed him, that those few hours on the beach were the calmest I'd felt in weeks, I knew that it didn't matter if we took things slow.

The moment Lewis Adair walked back into my life, a

missing piece of me clicked back into place. And I'd always need him now. Taking it slow, in reality, meant nothing.

Because I was already as deep in it with Lewis as a person could be.

TWENTY-SIX
CALLIE

Most mornings Callie's Wee Cakery was open, there was already a queue at the front door, waiting for us to unlock it. I'd spotted Aisla Rankin at the head of that queue, and I somehow knew right away why she'd made the effort this morning.

I shot Mum a concerned look. "I only told Lewis two days ago. Surely, not everyone knows?"

"Who did Lewis tell, other than his family?" Mum and Regan had been calling each other constantly since the news broke. And we were all set to have a family dinner next weekend. I was a bit nervous of that because I was still so early in the pregnancy. In a perfect world, I wouldn't have told anyone until much later, but the cat was out of the bag, so to speak.

"No one else, as far as I'm aware. Not even the rest of the Adairs." Lewis had phoned Eilidh yesterday to relay the news, and I knew he'd sworn her to secrecy. She then video called me to squeal hysterically in excitement before dissolving into blubbering sobs about how we were finally going to be real sisters, and she couldn't wait to be an aunty. I didn't want to tell her she was jumping the gun a bit with the sister stuff because ... well, I didn't want to voice that, even if maybe it was technically true.

"Morwenna?"

I nodded. Once Eilidh calmed down, she also told me Lewis mentioned that Morwenna had been feeling neglected by her older siblings and confessed as much when Lewis told her about the pregnancy. "I've got a few days before I ship out to Romania, so I'm stopping off at Ardnoch to see you and to check in with my baby sister," Eilidh said, guilt etched on her expression. "I'll see you tomorrow afternoon."

I was so looking forward to my friend's visit home.

The thought that everyone somehow knew about my pregnancy and Aisla Rankin was here to insult me made me want to run and hide in the kitchen. But I wouldn't give her the satisfaction of seeing my anxiety. "Mor wouldn't have said anything."

Mum shrugged. "She's a kid. She maybe told a friend without thinking. Maybe even Harry did."

"No, we swore him to secrecy." But we hadn't sworn Mor to secrecy.

"Don't worry." Mum squeezed my shoulders. "I'll ban her for good if she starts any nonsense."

"Are we missing something?" Angie asked as she and Cathy exchanged a look.

"Nothing." Mum covered for me. "Let's open the doors."

And I knew the moment that door swung open that Aisla Rankin *knew*.

She had her nose in the air, sneering down at me as she approached the counter.

My stomach churned. I'd had no sickness this morning, and I'd resent Mrs. Rankin for more reasons than one if she provoked it to make a return. "Good morning, Mrs. Rankin," I choked out. "What can I get for you?" I made no comment about how last time we'd seen each other, she'd announced she was never setting foot in our establishment again.

"Well, the truth might be nice."

I felt Mum pass off a customer to Angie and move to my side.

"May we help you?" Mum's tone held a warning.

Mrs. Rankin raised her voice. "It has been brought to my attention that your promiscuous daughter has seduced Lewis Adair and trapped him with a pregnancy."

Oh my God, she did not just say that.

Everyone in the bakery went utterly silent.

"Get out," Mum seethed.

"I assure you I have no wish to be here, but it is encumbered upon me as an upstanding member of this village and a woman of good morals to warn my neighbors against spending their hard-earned money in an establishment run by a girl who would allow *multiple* men to use her body and then trap one with a pregnancy. Who's to say it's even Lewis's and here you are ... you've ruined that boy's future and forced him back to Ardnoch. I see it as my job to make sure everyone knows who you are, so they can be more particular with their money and where they choose to spend it."

I knew it.

I knew vile people like Aisla Rankin would spread the rumor that I'd deliberately gotten pregnant to trap Lewis. I'd never considered they'd question whether he was the father!

"How dare you, you vicious hag." Mum's voice rose to meet Mrs. Rankin's. "You tried to pull this crap when I first opened my bakery, your daughter tries to pull this crap on anyone she takes a dislike to, and now you're both trying to do it to my daughter. Well, not this time! Not with my kid."

"Well, it is clear where she's learned her sins from!"

"Don't you dare!" I yelled. She could talk shit about me all she wanted, but she would not say a word against my mother.

My mum pressed a soothing hand to my arm before rounding the counter to face Mrs. Rankin. "I know you like to think that you have some authority in this village, but the truth is, everyone thinks you're a bitter woman with nothing better to do than sit on your sanctimonious throne of thorns, judging everybody else. So you can spread your little rumors all you want, Mrs. Rankin, because the people in this village who know better, know I have one of the best kids in the world and she's going to make a great mom ... and they also know that Lewis Adair has loved my daughter since he was a kid, and he'd be the first one to boot you out on your ass for talking to her like that. Since he's not here, that's gonna be my job." She leaned into Mrs. Rankin, who gaped comically. "That's your cue to get the hell out of my bakery and keep my daughter's name out of your mouth!"

And proving that bullies are just cowards, Mrs. Rankin bolted from the bakery as if the hounds of hell were nipping at her heels.

I gawked at my mum in utter hero worship until clapping broke through my stupor, and I glanced over to find Flora from the café clapping like she'd watched the best show ever. The rest of our customers burst into applause too, some whistling, others laughing, and Mum's cheeks bloomed a rosy-red as she groaned abashedly.

Chuckling, I rounded the counter and threw my arms around my mum. "You are my hero."

"No one talks to my kid like that."

When we pulled apart, it was to find Flora at our side. She beamed in delight. "Let me be the first to say congratulations."

Now I was blushing. "Thanks."

"You and Lewis have always made a beautiful couple. I'm very happy for you."

The cat was well and truly out of the bag.

For the rest of the morning, I was congratulated by

villagers who stopped by, and I knew that outside our door the whole place must be buzzing, not only about my pregnancy, but about Mum booting Aisla Rankin from the premises in spectacular fashion.

Sure enough, at noon, as we were nearing the end of today's inventory, Dad strode in with my little brother. The estate was super flexible with his schedule and allowed him to take the mornings Mum and I were working off so he could be at home for Harry during the summer holidays. He usually dropped Harry off at a friend's house in the afternoons or here at the bakery.

Dad strode through the store, filling up the space with his large presence as he always did. He rounded the counter, Harry trailing at his back. He cupped my nape and bent his head to search my face. "You okay?" and I knew by his concern that he'd heard.

I nodded in reassurance.

Dad gave my nape a squeeze and released me. I watched him as he strode past me to where Mum stood.

"Hullo, what are—" Her words were cut off as Dad swept an arm around her waist and pulled her up onto her toes into a passionate kiss.

Grinning, I looked away as Mum wound her arms around his neck and kissed him back.

I could tell by the disgusted look on Harry's face the kiss lasted a while.

Then I heard Mum ask breathlessly, "What was that for?"

"Mamma bear" was Dad's succinct reply.

The news that Dad found Mum's fighting spirit hot disturbed Harry. He grimaced at me. "Gross."

"How do you think you're here?" I teased. "Some girl was bullying me at school, Mum got in her mum's face, Dad witnessed it, and bam, suddenly, she's pregnant with you."

Harry looked sick. "That's not true, is it?"

I laughed. It wasn't, but I was taking too much pleasure in his disgust.

My wee brother rolled his eyes. Then he considered me. "You okay? Obviously, we heard. Mrs. Rankin is an auld witch."

"You missed Mum verbally drop-kicking her, though. It was worth it for that."

We shared a grin, and I wrapped an arm around his shoulders. "Want a yumnut?"

"What's a yumnut?"

"A doughnut yum-yum. I made them this morning and kept a few aside for you and Dad."

"What's this?" Dad's ears perked up as he turned from murmuring in quiet conversation with Mum.

I laughed because Mum always said she was pretty sure she won Dad through his sweet tooth. He always said he had to double his daily workouts to burn off all the baked goods she'd tempted him with.

As Angie and Cathy promised to watch the front, I huddled in the kitchen with my family, eating yumnuts and laughing, the ugly confrontation from earlier completely forgotten.

It was a shame, then, when my mobile phone rang in my purse. Seeing an unknown number flash on the screen, I thought about not answering because it was most likely spam.

Yet for some reason, I answered. Stupidly.

"Good morning, may I speak with a Ms. Callie Ironside?" a woman with an American accent asked.

"Uh, speaking."

"Ms. Ironside, my name is Eva Holland. I'm your father Nathan Andros's attorney."

I froze, my heart rate suddenly escalating. "What do you want?"

Hearing my tone, Dad hushed my mum and Harry, scowling in concern at me.

"Ms. Ironside, your father—"

"Don't call him that," I cut her off.

"All right." She sighed heavily, as if I was inconveniencing her. "Mr. Andros is eligible for parole. His parole hearing is in a few weeks. Were you aware?"

"No." I suddenly felt cold. The thought of my birth father out in the world ...

"He's demonstrated remorse and is determined to show the parole board he has been rehabilitated. He does feel, however, that he cannot truly demonstrate that without a possibility of reconciliation with his only daughter."

Oh, this really had been the day from hell. "Are you kidding me? How did you get my number?"

"Ms. Ironside—"

"How can my scumbag of a birth father afford an attorney? You're not a public defender, right?"

"No—"

"In other words, dear old psychopath Nathan has made some connections in the clink and was hooked up with an attorney. Aye, that sounds legit rehabilitated to me—"

"Ms. Iron—"

"You tell Nathan I hope he rots in prison forever and as soon as I get off the phone, I'm going to make it my mission to ensure that board denies him parole. Oh, and fuck you, thank you very much." I hung up the phone and immediately blocked the number.

Mum's cheeks had lost all color. "Nathan's up for parole?"

I glowered, my heart pumping wildly. "Something I think we should have known about, no?"

Mum turned to Dad. "I need to call my lawyer."

Dad nodded. "What did his attorney want?"

"Nathan asked her to reach out," I sneered. "So he could reconcile with me."

"Over my dead body," Dad warned.

"And mine," I assured him.

Mum rushed to my side. "I will take care of this. I don't want you thinking about it ever again. It's too much stress on the pregnancy."

Knowing she was right, I closed my eyes and sucked in a deep breath.

"Just forget about it," Mum insisted. "I'll take care of it."

When I opened my eyes and stared into hers, I knew she would. I trusted her implicitly. After all, she'd saved us from Nathan before.

I nodded and drew her into my arms, more thankful for her than I could ever put into words.

TWENTY-SEVEN
LEWIS

I t was a typical summer day in the Highlands. Five minutes ago, my window wipers were going a mile a minute to keep up with the rain lashing the windscreen. Now I had to pull my visor down as the sunshine blared through the break in the clouds. My SUV rolled forward in slow-moving traffic, and I kept glancing at the digital clock on the dash. Our appointment time was creeping worryingly closer.

"We'll get there," I reassured Callie.

"We're fine." She sounded much more laid-back than I was feeling.

The past few weeks had been a mixed bag of emotions. First and foremost, I was relieved and over the bloody moon that Callie was giving us a real shot again. We'd been on several more dates, none of which were on the list she'd sent me, but I planned to make those happen in the future. I'd already booked us tickets to see a play in Edinburgh in a few weeks' time so I could take her on date three and four in the same weekend. I hadn't told her yet.

My offer on the house was accepted, and I'd invited Callie

to see it before I finalized the offer. I wanted to make sure she loved it. Of course, she more than loved it. She thought it was spectacular and had already named it *An Caisteal Beag*. The Wee Castle. Because of the moat. I finalized my offer, and the house would be mine in two weeks. I was already looking into having its registered address name changed to An Caisteal Beag. And I was very much already imagining Callie and I raising our child there. I could picture sitting in the window box with our son or daughter, reading to them or watching the wildlife in the surrounding forest.

Slow, I reminded myself as I pulled into the car park at the hospital in Inverness. Everything else was going so fast, I had to resist the urge to pick up the pace on the rest.

The last few weeks had been rough for my Callie, and I wanted her to feel safe with me. When I'd heard what Mrs. Rankin (a woman I barely even remembered but who seemed to think she was some kind of mouthpiece for the village) said at the bakery, I'd wanted to rail at her. Her viciousness did catch and there were some others who turned their noses up at Callie if she entered their establishment or passed them on the street.

They were saying she'd trapped me and that's why I'd come home.

Fucking misogynists.

I couldn't stand for that. Our family and friends had rallied. The Adairs had influence, and Mum had said loudly and clearly in Flora's one day, "Well, Flora, if we thought Callie had 'trapped' Lewis, do you really think there would be such love and friendship between our families? We love Callie, and if I hear anyone say a bad word against her, they can expect a piece of my mind."

It tempered some of the gossip. As did the fact that my family was attentive, and Callie couldn't seem to go anywhere without one of them at her side. Mum, Eilidh when she visited a few weeks back, Aunt Arro, Robyn, Ery, and Monroe. Every single one of them made sure they were seen at Callie's side.

Then an actor accused of breaking up the marriage of the director on her latest movie fled to Ardnoch and the paparazzi arrived in town. As per usual, they were shut down by its residents and being here was pointless for them, but it got everyone talking about something else. Things seemed to normalize for us, as much as they could.

Except Callie told me about her birth father's lawyer calling and how her mum was dealing with it all. She couldn't help but worry about the possibility of Nathan getting parole. The lawyer had tried calling again, but Sloane's lawyer sent a cease and desist. We were waiting to see what happened next, and I hated her birth father for polluting this time for us.

As terrified as I was to be a dad, I got through it by focusing on the day-to-day. Big-picture thinking was still a bit overwhelming.

Once I'd parked and we paid the fee, I took Callie's hand in mine, and we strolled toward the hospital entrance. Glancing down at her, I experienced a sense of rightness that calmed my nerves.

Sensing my stare, Callie looked up at me. "Are you okay?"

"Never better," I promised her.

As we made our way through the hospital corridors to the antenatal clinic, a possessive thrill stirred in me. Some latent caveman part of my DNA was illogically proud Callie was mine, and I'd shown it to the world by getting her pregnant. Fucking idiot. Lost in my amusing (and never to be shared with Callie) thoughts, I barely noticed an older woman coming toward us. But I definitely observed when she visibly startled at the sight of me and hunched in on herself, hurrying past us.

Callie glanced over her shoulder with a frown. "What the heck was that?"

"It happens," I answered with a shrug that belied my true feelings.

See, it never occurred to me when I grew my hair out and got tattoos that a small contingency of the public would find me intimidating. I was taller than my dad, as tall as my uncles Lachlan and Brodan. They'd never complained of that kind of reaction, especially from women, but then they hadn't grown out their hair, gotten a bunch of tattoos, or looked more suited to a motorcycle club than an architect's firm.

I didn't perceive it so much in London, but here in Inverness, I noticed some folks—men and women—crossing the street as I walked down it. Even in Ardnoch, a tourist or two had crossed the street to avoid walking past me. And while women, in general, didn't seem to mind my appearance, there were a few, like the one we just passed, who were visibly intimidated.

That stung because I'd cut off my own fucking arm before I'd ever hurt a woman.

"Why?" Callie was pissed. "Because you're tall and have tattoos?"

"Callie." I squeezed her hand, not wanting to upset her, ever, but especially not while pregnant. "It's fine."

"It's not fine," she huffed. "I'm so sick of people and their judgmental nonsense."

I tightened my grip, gently pulling her into me as I lowered my voice. "You don't know why she reacted that way."

"What do you mean?"

"Maybe something happened to make her afraid. If so, I feel bad for her, not angry."

Callie halted in the middle of the corridor. The morning sickness seemed to be over, and Callie had some energy back. Her skin glowed healthily, and there were no dark circles under her eyes. She was beautiful either way, but right now she was so stunning, my self-control was on a tightrope. "You are the sweetest man I've ever known."

I smirked, abashed. Leaning down, I murmured, "How about the sexiest?"

Her blue eyes glittered with laughter and flirt. "That too."

There had been a lot of flirting these past three weeks. Some kissing, hand-holding, hugging. But nothing else because we were taking it slow. And fuck, was it killing me slowly.

We checked in for our appointment and as soon as we sat down in the waiting area, Callie grumbled, "From avoiding you in the corridor to practically panting all over you."

I asked her what she meant as I rested our clasped hands on my thigh.

"The receptionist," she murmured under her breath. "She was undressing you with her eyes. Totally inappropriate. You're here with your pregnant girlfriend."

I didn't hear anything else but "pregnant girlfriend." I grinned.

Callie glowered. "Oh, you like that?"

"The pregnant girlfriend part, aye. Didn't know we were calling each other *boyfriend* and *girlfriend*."

Her eyes widened as she realized what she'd let slip. "Well, I mean, we're d-dating—"

I cut her off with a quick kiss. "I'm your boyfriend."

"Aye?"

"Aye."

A smile tugged at her lips, giving her away even as she shrugged casually. "Cool."

I chuckled. "Cool."

Our appointment slot came and went as we waited, so we passed the time chatting quietly about the new house. It came partially furnished, but Callie reckoned I needed to switch some pieces for softer, plusher furnishings to add coziness. She was right. As it was, the house was very masculine, and I loved it, but I hadn't only bought it for me. Even if it took me the entire pregnancy to convince Callie to move in with me, I wanted the place as inviting as possible to her. So I was subtly trying to get her to put her stamp on it.

"Maybe we could go sofa shopping," I suggested. "I need your help to pick something."

"Sure." She shrugged happily.

"And mattress shopping." The bed in the primary suite was built into the design, but I didn't like the current mattress. "Something sturdy so I can give it to you how you like it."

Callie's eyes practically popped out of her head as she smacked my arm with her free hand and glanced quickly around to make sure no one was listening. "Lewis!" she hissed.

My shoulders shook with quiet laughter as our eyes met. I'm sure mine were reminding her of how hard she wanted it the last time we had sex because her cheeks bloomed an uncharacteristic shade of pink.

Fuck, she was adorable. I stole another quick kiss.

"Callie Ironside," a voice called from our right, and we turned to see a woman in a dark blue smock.

We stood up, and her eyes fell on us.

Callie's hand tightened around mine in a way I knew she wasn't even aware of, and I pulled her into my side.

The woman moved toward us, a friendly smile on her face. "Hi, Callie, I'm Verity. I'll be your midwife."

"Nice to meet you. This is my ... boyfriend. Lewis."

Boyfriend. That hurt in a really good way. "Nice to meet you."

"You too. Come this way."

She settled us into a private room. I saw the midwife note Callie's tight grip on my hand, and she gave her an understanding smile. Verity was warm and kind, and I was relieved to observe Callie relax. The first few questions were easy. Where Callie lived and who she lived with. I was hoping the latter answer would change sooner rather than later.

"Do you have friends and family nearby?"

Callie nodded. "I'm hardly ever alone."

Her gaze flicked between us. "And I do have to ask if Lewis is the father?"

"He is."

"I am."

Verity gave me a smile. "Congrats to you, too, then."

"Thanks."

She asked me for my full name, date of birth, and all that stuff, and then asked Callie if she'd ever been pregnant before, if she smoked, how much alcohol she drank, about her mental and physical health.

"And do you have a job, Callie?"

"I run a bakery with my mum."

The midwife paused and looked up from her iPad. "Not Callie's Wee Cakery?"

Callie smiled. "That's the one."

"Oh my goodness." Verity beamed. "I am in love with your bakery. My wife and I make a trip into Ardnoch once a month just so I can get my fix. The new pastries are to die for. I could swim in a vat of those Ardnoch Saint Honorés."

"Thank you so much. That means a lot."

"I knew you looked familiar and now I know why. I'm sorry if I'm fangirling, but I always tell my wife how lucky we are to have a bakery like the cakery so close when you could be working in a top restaurant."

Joy lit Callie's eyes and pride filled mine as I lifted her hand to kiss the back of it. I could have kissed Verity, too, because she had no idea how much my girlfriend needed to hear such kindness about her talent.

The appointment lasted an hour. Verity took Callie's measurements, measured her blood pressure, took some blood and urine, and explained exactly why she was doing all that. I tried not to let myself get anxious about all the bloody things that could go wrong with this pregnancy, even as Verity assured Callie that she was young and healthy.

We discussed how the baby would develop over the coming months, what kind of diet would be best and what foods to avoid, antenatal classes, breastfeeding, if she intended to have the baby at the hospital or at home, the tests and scans that needed to be scheduled. I hung on to every word because I wanted Callie to know that other than actually physically having the baby, she was not alone in any of this.

"Do you regularly exercise, Callie?"

"Pilates and tae kwon do."

"She's a black belt," I offered proudly.

Callie smirked. "We both are."

Verity nodded. "How long have you been training in tae kwon do?"

"Fifteen years."

"Okay. Well, Pilates is perfectly safe to continue while you're comfortable to do it, though you may have to avoid certain positions the further along you get. I encourage you to keep that up. However, I do think you should tell your martial arts instructor you're pregnant."

"He knows, and I'm already excluded from sparring and breaking." It was part of the rules that Fyfe had to enforce as an instructor.

"That's good. I think since you've been training for years, it's safe to continue classes as long as you're avoiding physical combat with your peers."

We'd talked about tae kwon do after Fyfe agreed to let

Callie back into his class. He was nervous of her being there while pregnant, and Callie was frustrated by the limitations set on her but willing to oblige. Though I knew she already missed sparring. I'd reminded her it was only for the next six and a half months, and then she could try to kick my arse any time she pleased after that.

Not long later, Callie and I were walking back to the car.

"Verity was really lovely," she said with relief.

"She was. How are you feeling?"

"Like reality is kicking in a bit. You?"

"Same." I held open the car door for her and hurried around to the other side. It had been a few days since I'd been out on the Harley and while I missed it, I had more hope than ever that once the baby was here, I'd have Callie back on my bike.

"Did you take everything in that she said?"

"I did," I promised. Then as we started driving out of the car park, I forced myself to say, "I've been checked. I know she's running tests for STIs, but I want you to know that I had a health check after Roisin. And you were the last person I slept with."

"I know. You don't have to worry about that. I had a health check after Gabriel. So I'm pretty certain all is good there."

Gabriel.

I'd avoided bringing him up since seeing him in the village that day because I didn't want to ruin anything between me and Callie. In fact, both of us seemed to be avoiding discussing the seven years we'd been apart, which I wasn't sure was healthy and knew we'd need to broach soon. There hadn't been an opportunity to approach the subject of Gabriel. Until now. "So ... what was he doing in Ardnoch?"

"Gabriel?"

"Aye." I tried to keep my hands loose around the steering

wheel. The truth was I despised how jealous that bloke made me feel. I was the one in a car with Callie, being called her boyfriend while she was pregnant with my child. That's all that mattered. At least I wanted it to be all that mattered.

Callie released a slow breath. "He was honestly just stopping by on his travels. And he wanted to apologize."

"For what?" I frowned. "Shit. You don't need to tell me. It's none of my business."

"No, it's fine. He ... look, I told you before, what he and I had wasn't serious. We never shared anything too personal with each other. Especially Gabriel. In fact, he could be downright evasive. But the last few weeks we were together, he was really distant, and I ended things weeks before I left Paris because of it. He acted like he didn't care. So he was apologizing for being a bit shitty in the final weeks of our relationship."

I nodded, trying to stop myself ... but I couldn't. "So, the kiss at the bus stop?"

"You saw that?"

"How else do you think I knew he was in town?"

"I'm sorry." Callie reached over to caress my knee in apology. "Really. It was only a goodbye kiss."

I nodded again.

She patted my knee and sat back. "You want the truth?"

My stomach churned. "Always."

"It was awkward. Gabriel being in Ardnoch. Selfishly, I didn't want him there. I wanted him to remain in Paris as a memory. He was only a distraction, Lewis. Everything that came after you ... it was all just a distraction. Life ... life feels real again. And I don't know if that's particularly healthy for either of us." She let out a huff. "But I can't help but feel that way. It's like ... like we really are two halves of one whole."

Relief and joy and overwhelming fucking love choked me, and I couldn't speak. I wanted nothing more than to kiss her so hard, she'd never forget it. I could feel her waiting nervously for my response and slumping in disappointment when it didn't come.

Finally, after we crossed the Kessock Bridge, I pulled over onto a layby, switched off the engine, unhooked my seat belt, and cupped my hand around Callie's head. I swallowed her sound of surprise in the hungriest kiss I'd allowed myself in the last three weeks. I stroked her tongue with mine, inviting her to devour me right back. She moaned and looped her arms around my neck, pushing up off her seat and into me. Her tongue met mine and I shuddered, wishing we were anywhere but in the car.

A horn blasted, jolting us apart.

Breathless, we held onto each other for a few seconds more. Then I pressed another soft kiss to her swollen lips and whispered, "I feel the same, mo chridhe."

Her smile was slow and sweet as I released her so I could clip my belt back on.

As I merged into traffic, heading home, Callie suggested, "Maybe we could go sofa shopping in a few weeks?"

"And then mattress shopping after that?" I shot her a wicked grin.

"Hmm. But remember ... it'll need to be *sturdy*."

I burst out laughing, feeling lighter than I had in years.

TWENTY-EIGHT
CALLIE

Mum said my bout of morning sickness lasted exactly the same length of time hers did with both me and Harry, thus reinforcing the idea we were basically the same person. I was extremely glad to no longer be throwing up everything. There was still no bump to show for the pregnancy, but that was apparently totally normal when you were only ten weeks.

It had been another good week since our first appointment with our midwife. Mrs. Rankin's attempt to blacklist me (that sad lady needed to get a life of her own) never really got off the ground once the people who were ready to give me shit realized the rest of the village was ready to go to bat for me. The bakery had never been busier, and Mum was really impressed by how I was managing turnover with my fancy creations. I was even talking her into offering a delivery service from Inverness to John O'Groats after Verity said she'd do a two-hour round trip just to get one of my pastries.

And Lewis and I were almost perfect.

I say *almost* because other than the mind-blowing kiss he'd given me in the car coming home from the hospital last week, he'd been a total gentleman.

He was keeping his word about taking it slow.

I hadn't really realized we'd be taking it *this* slow with the physical stuff, considering I was already pregnant. Yet knowing how much emotion was attached to sex for Lewis, I understood. I still got pangs of guilt about sneaking out of his flat in London after learning just how much sex meant to him. The reminder that maybe I hadn't known him as well as I'd thought (that I had underestimated how much he loved me) made me want to make it up to him. I didn't know how to do that while we were taking it slow.

I was also very much aware I had been the one to suggest taking things slowly.

It seemed silly now in light of how easily we'd fallen back into our relationship. Much easier than I'd anticipated, considering all that had kept us apart.

Those were my musings as I wandered into the Gloaming Thursday afternoon. Lewis's uncle Arran wasn't bartending today. In fact, I didn't recognize the young woman behind the bar, so I assumed she was summer staff. The pub's main room was packed and a peek into the dining room told me it was busy too. The tourists had well and truly descended upon Ardnoch. Wondering how I'd ever hear Carianne over the din, I scoured the room for her and found her at a table near the very back of the old pub. She waved, and I wound around the tables toward her.

We hadn't spoken face-to-face since the mix-up. Lewis had explained fully Carianne's scheme and how she'd jumped the gun. We'd shared a few texts back and forth, and she'd texted to congratulate me when the news broke about the pregnancy. However, she'd done an excellent job of avoiding me so far. A part of me didn't mind her avoidance. The fact that she'd admitted to crushing on Lewis all this time and then asking him out made me wary of her. It was awkward knowing your friend coveted your partner.

It didn't help that Eilidh had flat-out decided Carianne couldn't be trusted. I wasn't sure about that. I still remembered the person who had been kind to me for most of our friendship, so when she asked if we could meet, I'd said yes.

"Hey." She gave me a tight smile as I slid into the chair opposite her. "How are you feeling?"

"I'm actually feeling really good."

"Nervous? I can't imagine having a baby at our age." Her tone suggested a hint of judgment.

"Twenty-five isn't that young."

"It's kind of young, but you always were so mature for your age. Lewis too."

I nodded. "How are you?"

"Busy. I've been so busy at the salon."

"Good."

An awkward pause hung in the air between us.

Carianne gave me a nervous smile. "Look, I feel like I've been avoiding you and I don't want to avoid you ... I just feel so bloody awkward that I asked Lewis out."

At her wince, I smiled kindly. "Carianne, it's okay."

"No, it's not. What was I thinking? I mean, like, I genuinely thought things were over between you and didn't even realize how badly you'd take it until I *pretended* to be going on a date with him. And now that you're pregnant and together again ... it's like ... how weird have I made it?" She threw up her hands in despair.

I laughed, instantly relaxing at her honesty. "Carianne, we can get past it."

She made a face. "Do you think?"

"Aye. I can. If you can."

"I don't want you to be constantly worried that I have a thing for your bloke, though."

Now I grimaced. "I mean ..."

"Oh, God, see!"

"But with time, I'll forget," I offered, hoping it was true.

"Really?" Carianne leaned forward, expression pleading. "Because I miss you and I don't want to not be there when you have the baby. I want to be Aunt Carianne, you know."

A pang lit my chest because I wanted that too. "Then it's done. We're on the road to forgetting all about it."

"Good." Carianne scooted even farther forward. "Because I've started seeing this guy from Inverness and I'm desperate to talk to someone who isn't going to tell everyone and their nan about it."

And just like that, me and Carianne were me and Carianne again.

———

"When does Lewis move into his new place?" Mum asked as we finished up dinner that evening. To be honest, I'd spent hardly any time at the cottage other than to sleep in it, and I think that suited my parents and Lewis just fine, considering I spent most of my time with them.

"He's in." I frowned. "Did I not tell you that?"

"No. My goodness. You mean, he's living there?"

"Moved in last night."

"Have you visited yet?"

I shook my head. "Haven't had the chance. He's working late tonight for that project in Tain, so we decided I'd go around tomorrow to see him."

"Have you bought him a housewarming gift?"

I patted my tummy. "Cooking one up as we speak."

Harry snorted, Dad smirked, and Mum rolled her eyes. "Be serious."

"I bought him a Sander Patelski framed poster."

"And what is a Sander Patelski?"

"An artist. He paints images of famous architecture."

"Very nice. I bought him something. We'll need to take it over." She looked at Dad. "Right?"

Dad was expressionless as he replied, "I've already given him his housewarming gift."

"You have?" Mum frowned. "When? What was it?"

"The gift of life when I didn't kill him for knocking up my only daughter."

I cackled, even though I knew he was being totally serious.

Later, Harry was in his bedroom, playing a video game before bed, and I was leaving to head back to the cottage. Mum and Dad were settling in to watch a movie while I grabbed my keys and shoes, but I heard the TV mute. Mum cleared her throat.

"Callie, I need to tell you something."

Her tone stopped me slipping on my other trainer.

When I looked over at her, I somehow knew this was about Nathan. I hadn't wanted to ask for any updates because I needed to bury my head in the sand about him. Now my heart was pounding a mile a minute.

"I didn't want to say anything until it was over, but this morning was Nathan's parole hearing."

I waited, barely able to hear anything over the rushing blood in my ears.

"I appeared before the board via video call to give a statement."

"Mum, you should have told me." I'd never have known she'd been through something so harrowing today. "Did you see him?"

She shook her head. "I only spoke to the board. I told them that Nathan had already used his lawyer to harass you into making him look good for the parole board, and how until that moment, when it only suited him, he'd never reached out or shown any remorse toward you. I shared my fears that he'd look for revenge against us. And I reminded them of everything he put us through and the lasting effects of his actions."

"Mum ... I wish you'd told me. Didn't they want a statement from me?"

"Yes, and I refused. I didn't want to dredge all that up again for you."

But she'd dredge it up for herself for me. "Mum." I got up and squeezed myself between her and Dad, wrapping my arms around her. As we hugged, Dad smoothed a comforting hand over my back.

"I'm okay," Mum promised. "Your dad was in the room with me the whole time."

Releasing her, I was almost afraid to ask, "When do we hear their decision?"

"We already know." Relief blazed in her eyes. "He was denied parole and he won't be eligible for another fifteen years. He's not getting out anytime soon, baby girl. And he never will if I have anything to do with it."

I hadn't realized how much the fear of Nathan out in the world, in *my* world, was weighing on me until the danger was no longer a possibility. I burst into tears, shaking with relief as first my mum held me and then my dad.

TWENTY-NINE
CALLIE

"You know, you really don't need to pick me up and drive me home," I'd teased Lewis as we walked outside to his SUV.

He'd insisted on collecting me after work that evening so I could visit his new house for the first time since he moved in. Lewis had even cooked us dinner—steamed salmon, potatoes, and a whole half plate of green veg. Someone had been paying attention to Verity's recommendations that I eat lots of veggies.

Lewis loved the poster I bought him as a housewarming gift, and my parents (well, Mum) had bought him a swanky set of pots and pans he was very grateful for.

Aye, it had been a good night. Especially when I told him the great news about Nathan. Lewis was so relieved for me, as I knew he would be.

However, there was an underlying tension between us. Or maybe it was just me. But I found myself gazing at my boyfriend like he was the most complicated, sinfully delicious entremets on the planet. The way his T-shirt stretched across his back as he moved. The way his sweats hung on his arse. An arse I knew was rock hard and bitable. When he was cooking with peppers, I'd cracked, "What does a nosy pepper do? It gets jalapeño business." Lewis had groaned at the dad joke, and I got an immediate flashback of him groaning as he came.

Seriously, everything he did turned me on. And not just like a wee bit. I was full-on horny, could-jump-him-and-ride-him-until-the-end-of-time *aroused*. I didn't know if it was the "taking it slow" that was making me want him all the more or if it was bloody pregnancy hormones or both.

All I knew was that I was *needy*. And if I wasn't so determined to give Lewis what *he* needed from our relationship, the taking it slow would be over by now.

It was almost a relief to go home. Though, even in the car, my gaze kept straying to his big man hands. He had great hands. Something about those silver rings on his long-fingered, big-knuckled man hands did something extra to me too.

As he drove from his stunning home toward Ardnoch, I ogled him. His strong jaw, handsome profile that was as familiar to me as my own face, the broad shoulders, thick biceps ...

My attention caught on his tattoos again.

Of course I'd studied them a lot over the last few weeks, but I hadn't seen him naked since our night together, and back then I hadn't been focused on his tattoos. His T-shirts nearly always hid the upper half of the woman's face on his upper biceps and shoulder. Now and then, I'd find myself looking at her, wondering ...

So I reached out and drew his T-shirt sleeve up.

"What are you doing?" Lewis asked, amused.

I swallowed hard, staring at the beautifully drawn face. "Lewis ... is that ... me?"

"Of course it's you," he said, as if it wasn't a huge deal he had my face tattooed on his arm.

"Oh my God."

He flicked me a look. "You didn't realize?"

"No." I traced my fingers over the tattoo. "What does it all mean?" I drew my hand down to the tree.

"The tree is my family," Lewis answered gruffly. "The roses and thistles are Ardnoch, and the clock ... it's set to the time and date I left you all."

A sharp ache flared across my chest. "Lewis ..."

"And if you look really closely, in amongst the thistles, you'll see two words in script."

Intrigued, I peered, searching. And then I saw it.

Callie Forever.

Tears filled my eyes.

Lewis glanced quickly at me again and saw them. "Shit. I didn't mean to upset you."

In answer, I pressed a tender kiss to his arm. How could I have ever doubted his love for me? It baffled me now that I could have been so young and impetuous and careless with his heart.

"I'll make it up to you," I whispered.

He frowned as he kept his eyes on the road. "Make what up to me?"

"Everything."

A heaviness fell between us, and I didn't know how to dispel it, so I asked, "Has anyone else seen the writing in the tattoo?"

Lewis drove onto Castle Street, heading toward the cottage. He grimaced. "Roisin saw it."

His ex. "Oh dear. How did you explain it?"

"Well, she was already pissed about the woman's face, and I lied to her and said it was from the artist's imagination, so I let her assume Callie Forever meant Caledonia Forever."

I snorted. "*Caley* for Caledonia is spelled differently."

"Did I mention Roisin wasn't Scottish?" He grinned

sheepishly as he parked outside the cottage. As soon as he turned off the engine, Lewis shifted to face me. "She found photos of you on my laptop and recognized you on my tattoo. It was the argument that led to the end."

I couldn't feel bad that Lewis was with me and not with her, but I did feel bad for her. The truth was I'd been jealous of any woman who had slept with him until I realized he still loved me. Now I didn't begrudge him his relationship with Roisin and the fact that he had sex with her. It would be hypocritical. And if my boyfriend had a tattoo of another woman on his arm and lied about it, that might mess with my head. "Poor Roisin."

Guilt flickered over Lewis's face. "Aye. I should have told her the truth, but I didn't want to hurt her. I ended up hurting her even worse, and though I did try to make it work, I think she knew then that you were the reason I couldn't tell her I loved her. And she was sick of waiting. I don't blame her." He considered. "You know, this is the first night since that night we've really talked about the time we were apart."

"I know. I think we have to find our way naturally with that stuff and not push it." My eyes drifted by him to my cottage. "I—" I halted, leaning past him as something caught my attention. "Is ... is my front door open?"

Lewis's head whipped around as he stared at the door. Then he let out a muttered curse. "Stay in the car." He demanded as he unclipped his seat belt and got out.

"Lewis!" No effing way was I staying in the car.

Lewis whirled around as he heard my door open and close. "Callie."

I gave him a look, and he gritted his teeth and waved me back. He approached the front door and then we both startled when a voice called out, "The police are on their way!"

We whirled to see one of the villagers who lived above the

outdoor clothing shop across the street, hanging out his window.

"Mr. Smith?"

His expression was grim. "I was drifting off to sleep when I thought I heard something. Looked out and saw two men leaving the cottage and getting into a black car. There was something off about it, so I called the police, worried about you."

My heart thundered in my chest. "Thanks, Mr. Smith."

A shared look with Lewis saw my worry reflected in his eyes. "We'll wait for the police."

———

My cottage was trashed.

Years ago, when I lived here with Mum, Nathan had broken in and destroyed the place.

I felt ten years old again.

Because my immediate thought was, somehow this was retaliation from Nathan.

Lewis and I waited for the police to arrive before we stepped inside with them. My books and ornaments had been knocked off shelves, my sofa cushions laid littered on the floor, anything that had a place was thrown about, some of it destroyed, some of it okay. The only thing that had survived was my TV.

The police asked me to tell them if anything was missing. Lewis walked around the cottage with me. Whoever had broken in upended my bedroom too. All my clothes were pulled from the closet, the drawers emptied of everything. My bed was stripped.

It looked like they were looking for something and the police officers said as much too.

In the end, the only things missing were my laptop and iPad.

Halfway through my statement, my parents and Lewis's parents showed up. Clearly, they'd been alerted by a nosy neighbor to the disturbance because we hadn't gotten around to calling anyone.

Dad took over. "No one touch anything," he'd commanded. "We need to dust the place for prints."

A bit perturbed by my dad's authoritative presence, the male police officer asked if I'd had any altercations with anyone or if there was anyone I could think of who might have an issue with me.

Mum and Regan hovered worriedly as the questions kept coming. I felt totally in a daze. Because whoever broke in didn't steal the diamond tennis bracelet Mum bought me for my eighteenth birthday, or the diamond earrings for my twenty-first. I had expensive costume jewelry, too, and a Miu Miu handbag I'd splurged on in Paris. Items that could be hocked for a sum.

But all they took was my laptop and iPad.

To make it look like a break-in?

I asked as much, and Mum's arm tensed around me. "Do you think it's Nathan?"

Dad cursed, looking ready to kill someone at the thought of my birth father tormenting me again after all this time, while the police exploded into a barrage of questions about who Nathan was.

Once the police had departed, after promising to pull any neighborhood CCTV and be in touch, Regan called Arro and Mac to let them know about the cottage.

"This place is cursed," Thane muttered, surveying the mess. "I can't tell you how many times something like this has happened here. Arro and Mac should just sell it."

"Aye, you're not staying here." Dad glowered around the

front room. "Once I get forensics done, we'll come back and pack up your stuff."

"Let's go home." Mum nudged me toward the door.

But Lewis stopped us. His expression was fierce with determination. "Stay with me."

I gaped up at him, shocked by the offer. What about taking it slow?

"She'll be better off at home with us," Dad insisted.

Lewis scowled, and I was impressed by the lack of fear in his eyes. "No offense, Walker, but Callie is my girlfriend and she's pregnant with my baby. She should be with me."

"I can protect—"

"I can protect her too." Lewis stared my dad down. "I'd die before I'd let anything happen to her."

Before Dad could protest, I reached out for Lewis's hand. "Okay."

Relief softened his expression. "Aye?"

"Aye."

Mum soothed a hand over my back. "You still have some things at ours. Why don't we go there first so you can pack a bag to take to Lewis's?"

"Fine." Dad bit out like he was still the final say. "Just promise me you'll get Fyfe out to install a system like the one at the bungalow."

Lewis released my hand to pull his phone out of his back pocket, his fingers tapping over the screen. "Done," he announced, with a respectful nod in my dad's direction. Then he turned to me and held out his hand. "Mo chridhe."

Standing there, in a crime scene, pregnant with a baby I'd never planned for, I should have been terrified. And part of me was. Yet, surrounded by my loving family, reaching out for the hand of the man who adored me, I couldn't help but feel weirdly grateful under the circumstances.

THIRTY

LEWIS

Last night we'd been so exhausted by the break-in, then grabbing stuff for Callie from her parents' house, that when we got to mine, I'd led her into the primary bedroom without discussing sleeping arrangements. All I knew was that we were both tired, and I didn't want her out of my sight now that there was a strong possibility the break-in wasn't a random burglary.

Sloane had wanted Callie to take the next day off work, but she was determined not to let whatever was going on interfere with her day-to-day life. It was a Saturday morning, so I didn't have work, but there was no way in hell I was letting Callie travel anywhere alone. She insisted I stay in bed, but I got up in the wee hours, both of us barely able to open our eyes from lack of sleep, and we got ready in silence. The only words we spoke were when I relayed I'd received a text from Eilidh that she'd heard what happened. She was upset she was out of the country with this going on. I already knew from previous conversations that Eilidh was worried she was missing Callie's pregnancy, and I'd had to remind her that Callie wasn't even showing yet.

I dropped Callie at the bakery, reassured to see Sloane waiting for her at the back door. After kissing her goodbye, I headed home to grab a quick nap and woke up to texts from friends and family who'd heard the news and were worried. There was also a text from Fyfe asking to meet for brunch. After replying with a request to meet me at the Gloaming, I tried to respond to everyone's messages. Mum asked me to come over for breakfast, but I told her I was headed into town to grab a late breakfast with Fyfe before I picked Callie up after her shift. I promised to check in with her later.

The village was heaving with tourists by the time I returned. I ended up parking in Callie's empty space behind the cottage before walking to the Gloaming to meet Fyfe. The late morning was already warm, and the sea breeze that would cool those on the beach was blocked here by all the buildings in its path. I passed strangers on the street, hearing accents that took me from America to China, and I had to wonder with how busy it was if we'd even get a table. Thankfully, Fyfe had already secured one in the dining area of the pub and hotel, and I settled into the booth across from him.

"Sounds like you guys had a night," Fyfe said without preamble.

"I'm knackered." I scrubbed a hand over my face. "I can't imagine how Callie's coping right now."

"I've got my top guy coming to the house tomorrow to draw up a security system option, if that's all right?"

"Sounds like a plan. Do I get the friend discount?" I cracked because I knew how bloody expensive Fyfe's services were. While he specialized in cybersecurity, he had a whole team at his disposal who did the full shebang.

"Callie does."

"Arsehole."

"Aye, you're welcome."

The server brought us menus and we looked them over as I filled Fyfe in on exactly what happened.

His expression was tight with concern. "You think it's her birth dad behind it? How? I thought he was in prison."

"Aye, with connections inside who bankrolled an expensive lawyer and tried to get Callie to reconcile with him for his upcoming parole hearing. Callie refused, Sloane went before the parole board with a damning statement, and Nathan was denied parole for another fifteen years."

"Revenge?" Fyfe asked grimly.

"Whoever did it bypassed diamonds, a TV, expensive kitchen equipment and handbags ... and only took the laptop and iPad. The place was trashed. It was more like a warning and a lazy attempt to make it look like a burglary."

"Fuck."

"Aye. Walker's looking into it, though. If it is Nathan, he'll figure it out and we'll put a stop to it."

"Not really what Callie needs right now."

Aye, worry had been gnawing at me all night and morning about that. "The stress on her. It can't be good for either of them."

"Aren't you taking her away next weekend as a surprise? Maybe you should tell her now, so she's got something to look forward to."

"Not a bad idea, mate," I agreed.

"Fyfe, Lewis!" Carianne suddenly appeared at our table. She made a shooing gesture toward me, and I slid along the booth to make room for her. Fyfe and I exchanged an awkward glance, and Carianne huffed as she slipped in beside me.

"Oh, please, don't be weird. Callie and I are all good." She nodded at me, wide-eyed. "I'm dating an older single dad from Inverness now." Carianne pointed across the room where a guy with graying ginger hair watched us warily. "You're long forgotten, Adair." She patted my arm. "No offense."

I raised an eyebrow. "None taken."

"Anyway, I wanted to pop over quickly and ask if the rumors are true. I tried texting Callie, but she's working. Did she really get broken into?"

"Aye."

"Oh my God, is she okay?"

"She will be."

Carianne sighed heavily. "Seriously, just when I thought things had quietened down around here for good. Anyway." She slapped my knee and scooted out. "Tell Callie to text me back. Her bestie is worried about her!"

Before I could respond, she'd returned to her own table, leaning in to talk to her date.

Fyfe turned from watching her. "Are things really okay there?"

"Awkward but fine." I shrugged. "Carianne means no harm. And as long as Callie's cool with her, I'm cool with her. She's moved on."

My friend sighed. "Eilidh doesn't trust her."

"Eilidh is getting cynical in her old age. And since when do you talk to Eils?"

He started scouring the menu. "She reached out after that video call. We text now and then."

I considered the way he wouldn't meet my eyes. "All above board, aye?"

Now his gaze flew to mine. "For fuck's sake, Lew, what kind of question is that? It's Eilidh. I wouldn't touch her if she was the last woman on earth."

"Good to know."

The familiar voice had me whipping my head up in surprise. Now Eilidh stood at our table, her arms crossed over her chest. She smirked at Fyfe but the smile didn't quite reach her eyes. "And for the record, I'd rather have a love affair with my right hand than repopulate the world with you, Fyfe Moray."

My friend gaped at her in shocked embarrassment, and I saved him from having to respond by sliding out of the booth to hug my wee sister. "What are you doing here?"

She melted into me, returning my embrace fiercely. "Weekend off. Thought I'd fly home to make sure you and Callie are okay."

I pulled back. "You came all the way from Romania for a weekend?"

"I was worried, and my production team is great. They chartered a private flight for me in the early hours of the morning. Uncle Lachlan let us use the private airfield on the estate." She rubbed my arm in comfort. "Are you okay?"

Grateful she'd made that effort, I smirked. "Weirdly wonderful and fucked at the same time."

Eilidh chuckled. "I'll bet. Mum knew I was coming and told me you'd be here, so I thought I'd stop in before I go home." If I wasn't mistaken, my sister was doing her best not to look at Fyfe. "I didn't mean to interrupt."

"Join us." I gestured to the booth.

"No, I should check in with Mum, Dad, and Mor." Ever since our talk about Morwenna, I knew Eilidh had been trying harder to be there for our sister. Even on the days Mor made it difficult.

"Are you sure?" Fyfe asked. "You're more than welcome to stay."

Eilidh flicked him a look but didn't meet his eyes. "Nah, I'm good." She leaned up to press a kiss to my cheek. "I'll stop by tonight so I can see the new house in person and check on Callie. That okay?"

"Of course."

A few seconds later she was striding out of the Gloaming,

only offering Carianne a wave of acknowledgment before she was gone. Eyes followed my sister, people whispering to one another in excitement, a few of the tourists' phones coming out to snap pics.

It was still so strange. I kept forgetting she was famous.

I sat back down across from Fyfe whose attention was on the door, looking lost in thought. He hadn't seemed to notice the flurry of excitement Eilidh had caused.

"She's fine," I promised him.

My friend looked back, wincing. "I didn't mean to insult her."

"It's Eilidh." I gestured around the room at the people who were still buzzing that she'd been in their presence. "She's got millions of people drooling over her on social media on a daily basis. She's not bothered if you don't fancy her."

Fyfe snapped his menu up to his face, the action a bit aggressive. "Of course not."

THIRTY-ONE
LEWIS

Instead of taking Callie home, we ended up at my parents' house, and Mum invited Callie's parents and Harry over for dinner. If it made them all feel better to have us with them, then we could do that, but I did want Callie alone so I could get a finger on the pulse of what she was feeling.

The chance never really came. Mum pulled out the board games after dinner and even Walker played, though, as per usual, he didn't say much. It was good for us. It brought out mine and Callie's competitive nature, and it was funny to watch Harry and Mor act like a younger version of us, bickering and egging the other on. Honestly, it was just really nice to see Mor come out of her shell a bit. For once she wasn't begging to leave so she could return to her book.

Callie was worn out by the end of the day, though, so much so we crashed in my parents' annex. The next morning, after breakfast with my family, Eilidh accompanied us back to my place so she could see it in person for the first time. I saw her pride in Dad as she walked around the home he'd designed, and perhaps a bit of longing. An emotion she was quick to hide. She stayed through lunch, and when Fyfe unexpectedly showed up with his security guy, Paul, I was relieved Eilidh was no longer acting strange around him.

Back to her usual self, she teased Fyfe mercilessly and flirted outrageously with Paul who was not immune to a famous actor's attentions.

Callie and I exchanged a grin. I didn't think Eilidh knew how to interact without flirting. Dad said she hadn't gotten it from him or our mother, Francine, but it was in the Adair blood because Uncle Arran and Uncle Brodan were the biggest flirts he'd ever known until Eilidh came along.

"You miss her," Callie observed once everyone left. Eilidh was off to catch a flight back to Romania.

I nodded. "I do. Sometimes I wish she'd chosen a normal career."

"She'll come back one day," Callie replied with sincere belief.

"How do you know that?"

"Because every Adair who's ever left this place has found their way home again."

———

The next morning, my body clock seemed to know Callie's early alarm was about to go off, and I woke up first. Only to discover I was spooning Callie, my morning wood digging into her arse. A plump breast filled my palm, and I realized I was also groping her in my sleep.

Fuck.

Slow.

She wanted to take it slow.

Hoping not to wake her, I released her, my thumb grazing a hard nipple. I had to stifle a groan as need tightened in my gut. Carefully, I withdrew, easing back silently from her.

I'd quietly taken care of myself in the bathroom and when

I'd come out, Callie was awake and stomping out of the bedroom with a grumbled "Morning." She didn't look in my direction and I felt confusion and guilt. Had she been awake after all, and I'd made her uncomfortable?

I found her upstairs making coffee, her back to me. She wore a strappy tank top, the hem rising to reveal her lower back and the way it sloped from her narrow waist to her curvy hips. The pajama shorts she wore were extremely short and cupped her perfect arse. Blood was traveling southward again, so I dragged my eyes off her. "You know, we never really discussed the sleeping arrangements?" I broached tentatively.

She whirled, her generous, unbound tits bouncing with the movement.

The woman was trying to kill me.

I looked past her to the coffee machine, thinking about cold showers and Walker Ironside to dull the throb of arousal.

"What do you mean?"

"I mean ... did you want your own bedroom?"

"Do you want me to have my own bedroom?"

At her smarting tone, I looked at her. "I want what you want."

"Fine. I'll move into the other bedroom." She abandoned her coffee and marched past me.

"Callie—"

"I have to get ready."

"Shit," I murmured under my breath, suspecting I'd fucked up but uncertain of how.

———

CALLIE

There was something therapeutic about making pastry. As I worked on the *détrempe* (the dough for making croissants), I tried to relax into the method, knowing it by heart. In fact, I was on autopilot as I took my last batch out of proofing and put the new batch in. Shaping the former batch into rectangles, I wrapped them and put them in the freezer where they'd stay until early the next morning. Then I worked on the butter blocks and put them in the freezer too.

Once all batches were in and everything else was prepped for me returning in the early hours, I stood in the bakery kitchen not knowing what to do. I'd dragged out prep for as long as possible.

With a sigh, I texted Lewis I was on my way home.

Home.

It didn't much feel like it with the two of us dancing around our attraction.

My phone pinged.

> Still at my parents. Been helping Dad with
> work project. Meet me here?

I should be grateful my boyfriend and Dad had eased up and were letting me go places by myself this week, considering everyone was on edge about the break-in. Especially as the police hadn't gotten in touch about the CCTV footage yet. Instead, I was agitated. Despite Lewis's weak protests, I'd moved into the guest bedroom.

Waking up to realize my boyfriend was taking care of himself in the bathroom instead of making love to me, I'd been hurt.

I knew we'd talked about taking it slow, but I was beginning to wonder if there wasn't more to it. Lewis was serious about sex. It was important to him. Not that it wasn't important to me, but it obviously wasn't good for him unless emotions were involved. And I got that. Sex with Lewis was explosive, and I think it was because of how we felt for each other.

But did that mean he didn't want to have sex because he still didn't trust me with his emotions?

That's not how he made me feel otherwise, and it was confusing the heck out of me. I mean, he got me pregnant, for goodness' sake, so it wasn't like he couldn't have sex when our emotions were up in the air!

Last night he'd gone and dropped the surprise that he was taking me on dates three and four from my teenage list of dream dates: We were going to Edinburgh to the theater (he wouldn't tell me what play) and to visit the National Museum. He'd booked us into the Scotsman Hotel and had planned this lush weekend getaway. I assumed he'd only booked one room, which was kind of a problem since I'd moved out of his bedroom to give him space.

The fact that I felt like I was coming out of my own skin didn't help. Every inch of me prickled with awareness when I was near him or even when just thinking about him. I had goose bumps, hard nipples, and slickness between my thighs on a regular basis. I'd eventually googled it and apparently, it was not unusual to be extremely horny late in the first trimester and during the second.

Last night, I'd taken care of myself in my lonely guest bedroom and was louder than I intended when I came. This morning, Lewis had watched me with a brooding intensity that made me want to jump him.

We needed to talk about it before I combusted all over him.

———

The plan was to broach the subject with maturity and calm.

However, after my decision to talk to Lewis about our non-sex life, he kept us so long at his parents' house, I had no option but to head straight to bed when we got home. Then I was up at three a.m., so there was no time then either.

Lewis was at work when I returned to the house in the afternoon. The security system hadn't been installed yet, and I'd promised not to be home alone without him, but I needed a nap.

An ache filled my chest as I wandered into the primary suite instead of the guest room. Lewis had made the bed, but I found myself kicking off my flats and getting in on his side. I wrapped my arms around his pillow, inhaling the scent of his aftershave and feeling a mix of desire and sadness.

The water from the moat around the house glimmered in the afternoon sun, and I let the peaceful magic of my surroundings lull me from my sadness into sleep.

I dreamed of Lewis. Of him slipping into the bed beside me and sliding his big man hand down my shorts, his thumb finding my clit.

I dreamed he fucked me until I was hoarse.

A sound jolted me out of sleep, and I blinked against the brightness of the room because I'd fallen asleep before I could lower the hidden blinds.

Footsteps on the staircase brought me out of my foggy, aroused state.

"Callie!"

Grumbling, I shoved out of the bed, hot and sweaty from the midday nap and the dreams.

"Coming!" I called and then winced at my poor choice of words. "Or not," I muttered.

Lewis was at the fridge, a glass pressed to the built-in cold-water dispenser. He scowled at me as I reached the top of the stairs and stepped into the living space. "You said you wouldn't come here alone."

I glowered right back. "I needed a nap."

Instantly, his face fell. "Why? Are you okay?"

Not in the mood for his mixed signals, I huffed impatiently and moved into the kitchen to grab my own glass of water. "I'm fine. I was up early so I needed a nap."

"Are you ... pissed off at me for some reason?"

"Nope."

"You sound pissed off."

"I'm fine," I gritted out.

Lewis sighed heavily. "Callie, let's not be one of those couples who bottle up their resentments and then treat each other like shit."

I whirled on him, anger flushing through me. "Oh, so it's okay to bottle up other feelings, though, until one of us wants to explode?"

His brows drew together, and he placed his glass down on the island. I watched him hungrily as he crossed his arms over his chest. His biceps flexed with the movement and I suddenly resented the hours he spent at the gym when he could be getting his exercise from having sex with me.

"What is going on?"

"Do you not trust me?" I blurted out.

Lewis studied me carefully. I stared back hungrily. Not only because he was a tall drink of sexy water with his messy man bun and tattoos and broad shoulders and six-pack hiding underneath his shirt ... but because that was all just very nice packaging for his steadfast and kind heart. It killed me that his good heart might not trust mine anymore. And we needed to talk that out because we had a child on the way, and I didn't want our kid getting caught up in the confused relationship of his parents.

"Why would you even ask that?" he inquired quietly, clearly confused.

Now I was even more confused. "Because ... because ... this

taking it slow is brutal, and I don't want to take it slow. And it's not only the pregnancy hormones, but my God, they are not helping. I feel like I could come if you just put your hand down my shorts—because I'm all in! I want this! All of it. But you clearly don't want to have sex and the only reason that could be is because you don't trust me fully yet."

His eyes had flared at my "come if you just put your hand down my shorts" comment, but now, he was gaping at me like I might be mad. "Are you kidding?" His question was hoarse.

"Nope." I threw my hands up. "Lewis, I think I might lose my mind if we take this any slower."

"And you think I want to take it slow?" There was an edge to his tone as he stepped toward me, almost predatorily. "Do you know what it's like for me watching you walk around in your wee shorts ... or listening to you make yourself come in the room next door?"

Oh. So he had heard that. "Maybe how it felt for me to know my boyfriend was taking care of himself with his hand instead of fucking me."

A grin prodded his mouth, even though his eyes gleamed with intensity as he crowded me against the island. My whole body at once softened with relief and grew hot at the feel of his erection digging into my midsection as he braced his hands on either side of me, caging me in. "I think we've got our wires crossed. If I don't want to take it slow and you don't want to take it slow ..."

My chest heaved as I flushed from head to toe with want. "Then why aren't you inside me already?"

THIRTY-TWO
CALLIE

One minute Lewis was kissing me like I was the goddamn air he needed to breathe, and I was trying to climb his body, and the next he lifted me gently into his arms to cross the room.

"What are you doing?" I panted as I looped my arms around his neck.

"As much as I'd like to fuck you like there's no tomorrow, we have to be careful." He set me tenderly on the couch.

I glared up at him in frustration. "Lewis, if I can still do tae kwon do patterns and run and jump and stretch ... we can have sex like there's no tomorrow. I'm not even showing."

"You sure?" He kneeled between my legs, spreading them.

"Aye!" I whined. "Lewis!"

"Fuck, you are horny," he teased as he reached for the zip on my shorts. "But I'm going to take care of you, mo chridhe. I always will."

Excitement made me speechless as I whipped off my T-shirt and bra. My boobs were a bit tender and my bra felt tight.

Lewis paused on shuffling my shorts and knickers down. "Jesus ... your tits ..."

"What?" I threw the shirt off the couch.

In answer, he cupped them in his hands and squeezed.

I moaned, arching into him as pleasure-pain scored down my belly. Lewis groaned, kneading my breasts, his thumbs rolling over my tight, hard nipples.

"You're so sexy, it's going to kill me," he said gruffly.

A glance down at his jeans revealed his cock straining against his zipper.

I wanted it in me. "Please," I pleaded.

He gave me one last knead before he coasted his hands down my stomach. "It's hard to believe there's a baby in there."

"Yup." I nodded frantically. "It happened because last time we were like this, you were fucking me into the next world."

"God, you've got a mouth on you when you're horny." He tugged my shorts down and stopped midthigh. The groan he let out was so guttural I almost thought he'd come. "Baby ..." He slid two fingers into me easily I was so drenched. "I didn't realize—" Lewis's eyes flared with heat. "I'm sorry. My poor girl, so fucking needy and where have I been?"

"You're here now," I gasped as he withdrew his fingers and plunged back in.

"You've never been so wet," he muttered, gritting his teeth as he pumped into me with his fingers. "God, you're the sexiest thing I've ever seen or felt."

"Hurry. I need ..."

Lewis quickly pulled my shorts and underwear completely off, throwing them over his shoulder.

"Take off your shirt. I want to see you."

He did, revealing his beautiful, strong, sculpted body. And the tattoo of me on his shoulder. The tattoo of the

Adair Family crest above his left pec. And another tattoo, script writing beneath his right rib that I hadn't paid much attention to last time we were like this. I reminded myself to take a closer look later as another flush of arousal moved through me. Lewis felt it as he pressed his fingers back inside.

I bent my knees, arching my hips into his touch. "Harder, faster."

"Like this?" He thrust into me.

My orgasm hit abruptly, and I came around his fingers.

"That's it, mo chridhe, take what you need."

As I shuddered and convulsed around him, he didn't stop. Instead, he pressed his thumb over my clit and began to rub. The tension started to build again instantly. "Lewis." I tried to reach for him, and he braced his other hand by my shoulder, leaning over me so I could. I smoothed my hands over his chest, his stomach. My fingers trailed over the script on his ribs.

Once he's gazed upon her, a man is forever changed.

I knew those words. They were from one of our favorite bands growing up. Lord Huron lyrics from one of *my* favorite songs.

"Lewis," I gasped, my eyes questioning.

He glanced down at my hand trailing over the lyrics. Then looked deep into my eyes. "Aye."

And I knew he meant they were about me.

I groaned, love and lust a powerful surge inside me. I wanted to feel all of him, to show him how much his love meant. Possessiveness thrummed through me as I slid my hand toward his cock. But he grabbed and pinned it before I could reach it.

I clenched around his fingers.

His nostrils flared. "I forgot how much you like that." His grip on me tightened as he held down my arm and started fucking me with his fingers. "Come for me again, Callie. Drench my fingers, baby, like I want you to drench my cock."

At his surprisingly filthy words, the climax hit me like a lightning bolt. I screamed, my eyes rolling back in my head as I came. And came.

I was still shaking, my inner muscles throbbing as Lewis took my right nipple in his mouth and sucked hard. It was all too much. My entire body, my nerve endings zinged with pleasure that was on the precipice of pain. I'd never felt anything like it. As he lavished attention on my breasts, I couldn't help but touch him wherever I could reach. My fingers in his hair, loosening the tie holding it off his face, on his neck, my nails scratching down his back as he played with my nipples until they were sore and swollen.

"Lewis, please," I begged.

He gave me some reprieve, kissing his way down my stomach, his touch tender, loving, and allowing me a moment to catch my breath.

But only a moment.

He gripped my thighs, spread me wide, and lowered his head between them. I was so hypersensitive that the mere touch of his beard against my inner thighs caused a mini convulsion to ripple through me.

"Fuck," Lewis groaned before he licked my clit.

"Uh!" My back bowed as unbelievably my lower belly clenched again.

"You are actually dripping," he murmured hoarsely, and I looked down to find him staring at me as if he'd like to eat me alive. "I'm so hard, I could pound a fucking brick in half." On that note, I watched as he pushed his tongue into me.

He didn't stop. He licked and sucked and devoured me with his mouth until I was crying out his name and shuddering around him.

As if he couldn't control himself any longer, Lewis

hopped off the couch and shucked out of his jeans and boxers. I gaped dazedly at his erection because it was straining toward his stomach, thick, angry, red, and the tip weeping with precum. "The best part of you being pregnant," he said gruffly as he came back down over me, "I can take you bare."

I chuckled, excitement making it breathy. "The best part?"

"It's a perk." He grinned wickedly and then his expression turned fierce and wanting as he pinned my hands to the couch and nudged inside me.

While I was soaked, I was also tight and swollen from multiple orgasms and I tilted my hips trying to ease his way. His thickness was such a relief, I moaned, muttering love and sex words as if I couldn't help myself.

"Fuuuuuuuck," Lewis groaned as he slid home. His arms trembled and he bowed his head, as if trying to gain control.

I smoothed a hand over his back, able to be patient now that he'd brought me to several climaxes.

"You feel so good and I want you so much." He raised his head to look at me, his features tight with strain as if he was struggling to hold back his orgasm.

"It's okay to come," I promised him.

In answer, he kissed me, hungry and deep and filled with so much longing. As his hips started to move, I felt that tension inside me catch, and I gasped in disbelief. Lewis broke the kiss. "Again?"

"It would seem so," I huffed out as each drive pushed me toward the edge.

"Then you're coming first." His grip on my wrists tightened, and he pulled out almost all the way and drove back in.

"Harder."

His lips twisted. "I'm trying to be careful."

"You don't need to be that careful. Fuck me harder."

"Jesus!" His hips snapped against mine. *Harder.*

I clutched his hips with my inner thighs, helpless beneath his grip and unable to do anything but take him.

"I love your pussy," Lewis confessed as if in awe. "Your taste, your heat. I could die while coming inside you and die a very happy fucking man."

"God, I love when you talk to me like that," I groaned, throwing my head back as he thrust into me, every glide a little harder.

"I want you on every surface of this house," he confessed. "We're going to fuck in every room so that every room I walk into, I'll have a memory of being buried inside you."

The tension in me exploded, and I came around him so hard, I felt my muscles clamp down on him and squeeze.

"*Fuck*!" he bellowed as I milked his orgasm from him.

Lewis grunted and groaned like an animal as he throbbed and released inside me. The sensation was so good. So unbelievably good.

He collapsed, still careful to hold most of his weight off me.

We both lay there, damp with sweat, our bodies humming with utter repletion.

Then Lewis pressed a kiss to my neck and proved me wrong with a murmured, "I'm going to be hard again in five minutes."

"Good." I wrapped my arms and legs around him. "Because I've probably got a few more orgasms still left in me."

THIRTY-THREE

LEWIS

Light streamed down from the domed roof of the museum as I followed Callie through the Grand Gallery.

Years ago, Dad brought me and Eilidh to the National Museum in Scotland, but I could barely remember the trip. Callie's grandparents on Walker's side were from the Edinburgh area, so I knew she'd visited a few times over the years, but this was her first time at the National, and it was the first time in days something other than me had her full attention.

The woman had been insatiable, and I wasn't complaining. Not in the least. Despite the lack of sleep these past few days, I was like a live wire. Callie had trained me to respond in seconds. As soon as she turned those hot eyes on me, I was ready to give her what she needed.

Right now, apparently that was learning about the twenty-thousand artefacts housed in the museum. And she wanted to see the Scottish gallery, to learn about Scotland through the ages.

"I may not have been born a Scot," she'd said, flipping through the museum's information leaflet, "but I might as well have been." Her smile had caused *feeling* to expand in my chest. "The Adairs go back how many centuries? And I have a wee Adair brewing in my belly. I've never felt more Scottish."

I kissed her at that, but she pulled away before I could deepen it. Now I was scowling as I followed her around like a lost pup.

We'd taken the train down to Edinburgh from Inverness yesterday afternoon, and Callie and I had flirted nonstop, so much so, by the time we got into our hotel room we dumped our luggage and started going at it on the bed without fully undressing.

The only time we stopped for a break was to grab dinner in the hotel, and the rest of the evening was spent relearning all the inches of skin we'd discovered of each other this past week. It had taken me very little time to figure out all of Callie's buttons and she mine. To be fair, mine was pretty much her saying "Let's have sex."

I was easy that way.

This morning, we made love, lazy, sweet, and slow. Overall, since we'd started sleeping together again, I'd felt what little distance had been left between us disappear. I hadn't realized how much Callie needed to believe I fully trusted her, and to know she thought my physical distance meant I didn't bothered me. I hated the idea of her ever feeling hurt. Now that she knew I was all in, too, things felt better than ever between us.

Yet, out of nowhere, since we'd walked into the museum, Callie had put up a physical wall. When I touched her, she eased away. And then there was the pulling away from my kiss.

Having no idea what I'd done to fuck up in the last fifteen minutes, I studied her, half hunger, half frustration.

July in Edinburgh was muggy, and Callie wore a white T-shirt with a rainbow cupcake and the words *In My Baking Era* on it. It was tucked into one of the many pairs of wee shorts she owned. The Converse on her feet might as well have been six-inch fuck-me heels for the way I reacted to her. Bracelets tangled together on her wrists as she tucked her long hair behind her ear to peer at Dolly the Sheep, the first-ever cloned mammal. She wrinkled her nose at the taxidermy and moved on, the ends of her hair brushing her lower back. Images of last night, of her hair swaying against her arse as she rode me reverse cowgirl, flashed across my vision.

Done with the distance, I marched over to her, took her by the biceps, and pulled her into a quiet corner of the gallery. "What's going on?"

Callie blinked up at me, confused. "We're ... in the museum. Looking at stuff."

Unamused, I scowled. "I mean, why are you keeping your distance all of a sudden and pulling away when I kiss you?"

"Eh, because if I don't, I'm going to get arrested for shagging you in public." She patted my chest reassuringly. "Don't take it personally, Lew. In fact, do take it personally because every time I look at your handsome bloody face or your shoulders or arse or hands or arms ..." Her gaze dropped to my arms, and I found myself struggling not to laugh as she licked her lips. "Mmm ... having a bit of an impulse control problem at the moment, so please keep your distance until we're back at the hotel. Mmmkay? Love you." She gave me a quick kiss on the lips and then hurried off to look at Toby the Whale.

And I stood there like an idiot, grinning. "Love you too," I murmured back.

———

For someone having impulse control issues, Callie certainly kept us busy doing the tourist thing all day. By the time we made it back to the hotel, we only had time to shower and change before our dinner reservation at a Michelin Star restaurant on George IV Bridge. It specialized in seafood, and Verity had said Callie could have fish as long as it wasn't high in mercury.

The food was amazing, and Callie couldn't stop gushing about how excited she was to eat in a Michelin Star restaurant. Her excitement level increased when I finally revealed I was taking her to see Shakespeare's *Romeo & Juliet*. It had been her favorite play in high school, and we'd argued about it at the time because I thought it was melodramatic piffle and Romeo was a creep for perving on a girl Juliet's age.

I saw the way Callie remembered our argument and how it ended with me kissing the anger right out of her. For the first time, the memory wasn't tinged with melancholy. I knew by the amused, nostalgic look on Callie's face she felt that too. We were healing from the pain of our past separation.

The museum, the dinner, the play, the sex ... it was my way of attempting to be a better boyfriend this time around. To give Callie everything she desired. But it also had the added benefit of distracting her from the break-in. The police were still reviewing the CCTV footage from a couple of businesses on Castle Street, and the team Walker had pulled in from his many contacts hadn't found any other fingerprints but Callie's, mine, and her family's.

Worry about who the perpetrators might have been, if it hadn't been a typical burglary, stirred in the back of my mind constantly. I couldn't contemplate the idea of Callie being in danger without my chest tightening like there was a vise winding and compressing it shut.

In a way, her insatiable appetite and this trip to Edinburgh was as much a distraction for me as it was for her.

Since I was late in buying tickets, our seats weren't spectacular, but we were at the end of the aisle in the stalls, and it wasn't a bad view of the stage.

Halfway through the first act, I was bored, my mind drifting to the list of things we needed to do in the house for the baby coming, excitement and trepidation for our first scan next week. We'd find out for sure Callie's due date, and we'd hopefully get reassurance that the baby was in good physical health. Verity had said we could ask at the twenty-week scan about the sex. Callie and I had discussed it, and we both wanted to know the sex of our baby.

A touch on my thigh brought my attention from my own thoughts to Callie's hand. I raised an eyebrow as she slowly caressed me, a bit too north of my knee. I cleared my throat and glanced at her.

She leaned into me, and I bent my head toward her. Her nose skated over my neck and she nuzzled her face against my jaw. "You smell so good." I barely heard her whisper.

Fuck.

Here?

My skin flushed as my heart started to speed up, hot blood traveling worryingly south. I shifted, covering her wandering hand with mine and placing hers on her own thigh.

She licked my neck and I stiffened. "Callie."

At my pleading tone, I heard her soft chuckle, and she relaxed back into her seat, attention fixed firmly on the stage.

Minx.

I waited until she was engrossed in the play again, and then I placed my hand on her bare knee.

She tensed, and I could practically hear her holding her breath. The audience suddenly tittered with laughter at something the actor on stage said, and I used that moment to slide my hand up her thigh, under her skirt.

Callie didn't stop me.

I kept my gaze on the stage, pretending to pay attention to the play while slipping my fingers beneath her knickers. She lifted her hips ever so slightly, and I pushed inside her wet heat. Always ready for me.

My cock was stiff against the zipper of my suit trousers,

but I honestly couldn't give a fuck. A red haze had crashed over me, and all I could think about was how she felt at my fingertips. Not wanting to make too much movement, I shifted my attention to her swollen clit and fondled her in the dark. It wasn't the most comfortable angle for me but it was worth it.

I heard her breath catch and glanced down at her. Her lips were parted, her chest moving up and down in quick, shallow breaths she was trying her best to conceal. She was so sexy, there was a wild, lost part of me that wanted to fuck her right there and then.

Instead, I forced myself to stare forward as I kept tormenting her. Her clit was swelling, and I knew she was close when she suddenly grabbed my wrist in a panic. At first, I thought she wanted me to stop, but she pulled me closer.

My insatiable, kinky Callie. That's what I'd call her from now on.

Unable to stop myself, I turned to watch her as she climaxed. It happened as the audience clapped in delight at something. Callie's nostrils flared, she bit her lip, and her body shuddered with keeping her climax quiet as she came on my fingers.

The woman next to me shot us a bemused look, as if she knew something was up.

And something definitely was. I was hard as a rock.

Leaning over, I brushed Callie's ear with my mouth and smirked as she shivered. "Can we leave?"

She nodded, and we quickly gathered our things. I was never so grateful for aisle seats. We pushed into the empty corridor outside the theater and Callie glanced at my crotch. Her eyes lit with delight. "I can't believe you did that."

"You liked it." I grabbed her hand, willing my erection to go away.

Walker and ice-cold showers.

Worked like a treat every time.

"I did." Her grip on my hand tightened. "We should have sex in public."

A man we passed in the lobby heard and raised his eyebrows. I chuckled. "Say that louder for the folks in the back."

Callie laughed. "Sorry. But we should."

"Where did you have in mind?"

She seemed to give this serious consideration. "When we get back to Ardnoch, let's drive to that wee beach car park and go at it in the car."

"You're so romantic. I feel so lucky," I teased dryly.

Giggling happily, she tugged on my hand, pulling me out of the theater. "Hurry up, because you're about to get luckier."

THIRTY-FOUR
LEWIS

Sunlight crept in through the cracks in the hotel curtains as Callie lay naked in my arms. Her head rested on my chest, her arm over my stomach as I rested mine on her hip over the duvet.

We were both awake after another enthusiastic night. Callie was a bit sore from all the attention, so we'd mostly taken care of each other with our hands and mouths. It had been one of the best nights of my life. Now, lying together, enjoying the quiet and the feel of her in my arms, I wished we could stay like this forever.

"We should enjoy this while we can," Callie said, breaking the silence, and as if reading my thoughts, she continued, "I doubt we'll have many peaceful moments like this together once the baby comes."

Of course, I wouldn't be human if I didn't feel a touch of trepidation at the thought, but I'd always wanted a family. And I felt lucky that this had happened with Callie and not with a woman I didn't love. For our child's sake as well as my own.

"Then we'll appreciate every moment." I caressed her

upper arm. "And remind ourselves that we have a shit ton of family who are more than happy to babysit when we need alone time."

I felt her smile against my chest. "That's true."

"You know ..." I tangled my fingers through her hair, playing with it. "Yesterday was the first time you've told me you loved me since we started dating." Shit. Did that make me sound like a needy bastard?

Callie pushed up to look at me. "No, it isn't."

"Aye, it is. You told me you loved me in the museum."

A deep frown marred her brow. "Is it really?"

I nodded, watching her carefully.

"I'm sorry if that's true." Callie cupped my face, her fingers scratching through my beard. "But you must know how much I love you. You do, don't you?"

"It's nice to hear it sometimes."

"I'll do better," she whispered. "I love you, Lewis. I love you so much."

"I love you too. Always have. Always will."

"Always only ever you," she repeated words she'd said to me weeks ago. "Once I have the baby, I'm going to get a tattoo. For you. For us."

The thought of me inked on Callie in some way made my cock twitch. "Aye? Where?"

"I don't know." She pulled the duvet away, revealing her beautiful naked body. "Where do you think?"

I joked, "I think you should get Property of Lewis Adair tattooed on your face."

Callie shook her head, laughing. "Arsehole."

"Do you want a boy or a girl?" I asked randomly as I reached out to slide my hand over her belly.

Callie covered my hand with hers. "I'll take either. I just want to have a relationship with them like the one I have with Mum. For them to know that I'm here for them, through everything, that I'm a place they can run to when the world seems too big and scary. That I'll never judge them, will always accept them, and will be the fiercest friend they've ever known. That's what I want." Her eyes gleamed with emotion. "When they grow up, I want them to consider me one of their best friends."

Gratitude crashed through me. How lucky was I that someone with Callie's good heart would be the mother of my child? Emotion thickened my voice as I replied, "Then that's the way it'll be."

She caressed my hand. "Do you want a boy or a girl? I won't judge you if it's one or the other."

"It's not," I answered honestly. "I'll love them no matter what."

Callie considered me. "This isn't the way I wanted to have a child. Accidentally. Do you know Sarah and Theo Cavendish?"

"Of course."

"She and Mum have gotten friendly through Aunt Ally. Anyway, she invited us to her baby shower and it was before Paris so I attended too. There was just us and Sarah's close friends so Aunt Ally didn't mean anything by it when she made a joke about how she thought Sarah and Theo never wanted to have kids. I didn't know anything about that. But Sarah got very emotional, and started telling us all how she *hadn't* planned for kids. That she and Theo had decided they just wanted each other. How terrified she was. How when she realized they'd gotten accidentally pregnant, she couldn't explain it, but she wanted their baby more than anything. She was so afraid to tell Theo."

"He wasn't shitty to her, was he?" I scowled.

"No. Not at all. Sarah said he was shocked but determined to reassure her that she had his support. Except, she could see he was struggling really badly with it. And she was scared that having a baby would change what they had together. Mum and Aunt Ally were so kind to her that day. I felt so awful for her and promised myself I'd never get pregnant accidentally." She snorted.

"Are they okay now?"

"Oh, Theo has turned out to be the biggest daddy's girl ever. He loves Rose more than he loves anything in this world."

"But you didn't want to have a baby this way?"

She looked up at me. "Like Sarah, I got lucky and fell accidentally pregnant to the man I love. But there's a part of me that's scared, concerned. I mean, I always thought you and I would have kids before we were thirty, but that we'd have the chance to live a little with each other. To travel. To soak in art and culture and food and music all over the world, to have sex in exotic places ... But we did this all backward."

"I know. But it doesn't mean we won't get to do all those things, Callie. I will make it my mission in life to give you all those things. And like I said, that's what family is for. Do you know how ecstatic my mum would be to have her grandkid for a week while we gallivant around Europe, soaking in the culture and having enough sex to give her another grandkid?"

"I doubt very much she'd be ecstatic to know you're sexually insatiable," she teased.

"Uh!" I made a very unmanly, high-pitched sound. "*I'm* insatiable?"

She quirked an eyebrow. "What does that mean?"

"It means that you've almost broken my fucking cock."

Callie laughed in delight and then rested a hand on my stomach, sliding it downward. "Fucking cock, eh? That sounds like a very useful piece of equipment."

My huff of laughter turned into a groan as she wrapped her hand around me.

The sound of my phone blaring beside us made me bite

out a curse. Callie, however, didn't stop her ministrations as I reached for it. "Let me go, mo chridhe. It's my dad and he wouldn't call for nothing."

With an adorably petulant twist of her lips, she released me and settled back against my chest as I answered the phone.

"Ah, Lew, I'm sorry, bud." Dad's voice was gruff. "Fyfe just called. He checked your CCTV ... the house has been ransacked. I think you and Callie should come home. Now."

———

It was even worse than what had happened at the cottage.

Rage shuddered through me as I walked through our home. "Well, now we really need to get new furniture," I offered with a dry amusement I did not feel. But guilt flashed on Callie's face like a neon sign, and I didn't want her taking that on. Therefore, I hid my fury as best I could.

The arseholes Fyfe had caught on camera were two men in black, wearing ball caps so we couldn't see their faces. They'd cut through the sofa cushions with a blade and ripped out all the stuffing. Drawers were torn from the kitchen, out of sideboards, parts smashed, broken. The mattress was sliced open on our bed and in the guest room. Clothing everywhere. Every shoebox upended.

"What the fuck are they looking for?" I turned to Walker, Dad, and Fyfe.

Fyfe winced and apologized for the fifteenth time. "Lewis, I'm so sorry about the delay."

The break-in happened in the wee hours of the morning and because the system wasn't fully set up yet, there wasn't an alarm trigger to my phone or to his company's system. He was checking in manually for me while I was gone. Fyfe had been asleep.

"Fyfe, mate, it's not your fault," I insisted.

"No, it's not." Callie patted him on the shoulder, expression wan with anxiety. "But I think we all recognize the common denominator."

We could, and it scared the shit out of me to think someone was after Callie.

"Do we think it's Nathan Andros?" Fyfe asked. "You definitely don't recognize the guys on the footage?"

We'd both looked at the footage before we walked inside so we were prepared for the mess we were about to encounter.

Callie shook her head. "Definitely not. But Lewis is right —what are they looking for? This isn't mere intimidation or stealing ... I mean, this time they left with nothing. They're looking for something."

"I don't like this." Walker glowered grimly at the wrecked living space. "And for that reason, I'm still leaning toward Andros. He likes to fuck with people. Maybe this is a mind game."

My dad let out a heavy sigh. "Is there anything you can do about that?"

Walker nodded, a coldness in his eyes that reminded me Ironside was not a man you crossed. And you definitely didn't mess with the people he loved. "I have a contact who can get a message to him on the inside."

Callie's eyes changed from bleak to angry. "I wish Mum had killed him. All those years ago when she shot him in self-defense. I wish he'd died. That's what he does to you. That's the kind of hate he instills in you."

Bridging the distance between us, I pulled her into my arms, and I felt her shake as she quietly cried. I met Walker's furious gaze and hoped he could read the words in my eyes, giving him instruction to put the fear of hell into Nathan Andros. Whatever that might take.

THIRTY-FIVE
CALLIE

SIX WEEKS LATER

Lewis's parents' home was a comforting cacophony of people talking over one another, asking to pass the food and drink, and calling back and forth between the adult and kids' table. The two tables weren't a deliberate attempt to separate the young from the older, but a necessity since the Adair family had grown exponentially in the last two decades.

There were twenty-four humans in Thane and Regan's living area, including the one in my belly. I'd counted. The five Adair siblings and their partners; my parents; me and Lewis (Eilidh was the only Adair not in attendance), plus Fyfe, who was an honorary member of the family.

Then there were the teens, Lewis's cousins—almost sixteen-year-old Vivien, who was the spitting image of her mother Robyn and had all the cocky confidence of her father. If I'd been half as confident and charismatic as Vivien at fifteen, I could have ruled the world. Viv was best buddies with her cousin, Skye, Mac and Arro's daughter. The cousins couldn't have been more opposite, but born in the same year, they'd grown up as close as sisters. Skye was reserved, artsy, and seemed to be one of the few people Morwenna gravitated toward, despite the two-year age gap.

Next in age to Skye and Vivien was Nox (Lennox), Brodan and Monroe's son. He was almost fifteen but thought he was forty, was as big a flirt as Eilidh, but was also the one keeping peace at their table as Vivien argued with her younger brother, Brechin, who was Mor's age. The siblings had been at each other's throats about everything and nothing, while Nox kept intervening in a laid-back manner that was a lot like his uncle Arran.

Arran and Ery's twin daughters, Keely and Kia, were next in age and kept calling over to me with questions about the baby. They were fascinated and excited to be aunts, which was a nice change of pace from Harry who thought it was weird he was going to be a twelve-year-old uncle.

His birthday was a few weeks ago, and he liked to remind everyone whenever he could that he was twelve, as if this was some kind of statement of manhood. The thought of high school had been a distant flag of beckoning teenagedom. That was before classes started, and now Harry wouldn't stop complaining about how much homework he had. Also, he didn't much like going from top of the school to the bottom. "The sixth years treat us like wee kids," he'd complained only five minutes ago, glowering at Vivien.

Vivien had shrugged insouciantly. "I'm not a sixth year. But you are a kid."

A brussels sprout had gone miraculously flying at her head a few seconds later and landed in Arran's glass of water with accidental precision. "What the fuck?"

"Language, for fuck's sake," Lachlan mock scolded,

making us laugh because seriously, it was an uphill battle to get the men in Lewis's family to watch their language now that the kids were all a bit older.

Arran had turned to the children's table. "Who did that?"

"Wasn't us, Daddy," Keely assured him.

Harry began to whistle, as if that weren't a dead giveaway.

Arran smirked and turned back around. "He's a wee comedian."

Dad threw a brussels sprout that hit Harry on the head with perfect aim.

"Oi!" Harry wrinkled his nose, rubbing his temple.

"Walker, really." Mum slapped a hand over her face in disbelief as the Adair men burst into a rumble of laughter.

Dad shrugged. "Now he won't throw another vegetable across the room because he knows his dad's got better aim than him."

I snorted, sharing a grin with Lewis as Arran got up, unbothered, to refresh his water.

Fyfe leaned over to us, chuckling. "I love your family."

Looking around, feeling the room filled with the buzz of life, I touched the now growing swell of my stomach. I couldn't be more grateful that my child would be raised among these wonderful people.

"Callie, is that a bump I see?" Regan asked from down the table, face bright with excitement.

"A small one." I nodded, smoothing my hand across the slight swell.

"How many weeks are you?" Lewis's Aunt Arro asked.

"Eighteen weeks. We had our fetal anomaly scan yesterday."

"All good." Lewis hurried to say. "Baby is in perfect health."

Robyn leaned past Lachlan. "Are you doing a gender scan?"

I nodded. "We want to know. We have an appointment at a clinic in the city in three weeks."

"Exciting." Ery smiled, genuine joy in her eyes. "Are you particular about what you get?"

"Just pray it's not twins." Arran winked.

Having heard that, Kia bounced out of her chair and looped her arms around her dad's neck. She pressed a loud kiss to his cheek and proclaimed, "You love us really, Daddy."

Arran's expression melted into utter tenderness as he leaned into her hug. "So much, Keekee."

"Wrapped around their little fingers." Ery shook her head, eyes bright with amusement. "I swear to God, they could come home and say they murdered someone but add 'But we love you, Daddy' onto the end of the confession, and he'd cover it up for them."

"Not wrong." He patted Kia's arm before she pressed another kiss to the top of his head and returned to the kids' table.

Lachlan turned to look at his daughter. "How come he gets that treatment and I get 'Dad, have you got twenty quid?' every five seconds?"

Vivien rested her chin on her palm. "You're too smart for that kind of manipulation, Dad. I'm completely transparent with you because I respect your intelligence."

Lachlan was just breaking into a smug grin when Vivien leaned forward. "But ... do you have twenty quid?"

Her father scowled and turned back to the table as Vivien shot Skye a devilish smirk.

Robyn leaned into Lachlan. "She loves you really. She's just fifteen."

"I do!" Vivien waved her fingers without looking back at our table. "For the record, if we need to get mushy, I do love you, Dad. Your movies are a bit meh, but you're great."

We all struggled to hold back our laughter.

"Children." Lachlan's lips twitched. "Great for the ego."

"What about my movies?" Brodan asked his niece.

"Oh, your movies were great, Uncle Bro. Why did you quit?"

"Note, she did not ask me that." Lachlan took a huge swig of his pint. His wife's mouth trembled with laughter while she soothed a comforting hand over his back.

Before Brodan could answer his niece, Regan interrupted. "You were saying about the sex of the baby?"

Lewis reached across the table to take my hand. "We're happy with either."

"I can't believe my nephew is going to be a father." Lachlan scrubbed a hand over his face. "I feel old. Or that might be because of my daughter. It's hard to tell these days."

"*I* love your movies, Dad!" Brechin yelled.

"You've never seen his movies," Vivien shot back.

"But I know I love them."

"Thanks, son." Lachlan raised his glass to him. "I'll give you twenty quid when we get home."

"Uh!" Vivien squeaked in indignation as Brechin did a victory dance in his chair.

"How do you think I feel?" Thane asked, taking a sip of whisky. "I'm going to be a grandfather, and I'm younger than you."

"Something you like to point out whenever you can." Lachlan shrugged. "But I understand. You need something to cling to since I'm so much better looking than you are."

Thane grinned. "Aye, you wish."

I noticed Fyfe taking everything in, thoroughly entertained, and I was reminded he hadn't had this growing up. These messy, chaotic, bantering, silly, loving scenes of a large family. Mum and I hadn't either until moving here. Then we'd become honorary Adairs, especially when Lewis and I were dating. This family had a magic about them. Orphaned siblings whose bond was so strong, they lived on the same patch of land here in Caelmore, and even though they'd been blessed with wealth in a material sense, they'd always understood their true wealth was in each other. Those who were lucky enough to be loved by them were forever fixed within that bond too.

Lewis had asked me to move in with him a few weeks ago. The house, which was now *our* house, had been cleared of the mess from the break-in. We'd ordered new furniture, some of which had arrived, some of which we had a few weeks to wait for.

Arro and Mac had been understanding when I broke the lease on the cottage, and they'd decided to sell it. It was snapped up in three days.

Now my home was with Lewis. I mean, it would always, always be with Mum too. But, aye, it was with Lewis. My attention turned to him as he laughed with Fyfe over a story they were telling about a new student in our tae kwon do class. I was still attending classes, so I'd witnessed the cocky wee shit who'd come in, total newbie, and challenged Lewis to a sparring match.

The kid was like a boxing bag. Every time Lewis defeated him (in two seconds, I might add), he bounced back, determined to take more. Lewis was being incredibly patient with him, but he was taking up class time, so Fyfe stepped in and floored the kid with a jump back kick. Like literally knocked him on his arse and the breath out of him.

I'd understood why Fyfe did what he did. People like that kid would get themselves or someone else hurt if they didn't learn from the get-go not to treat martial arts like a joke or worse, a weapon. But it didn't mean I didn't love the fact that Lewis had the patience of a saint. I kind of already knew that about him, though. My gaze swept lovingly over his face as he talked and laughed. Sometimes it took my breath away that he was mine.

As if he sensed me staring, he looked at me. He reached out casually and caressed my cheek before turning back to his conversation with his family. I smiled to myself and looked away, only to lock eyes with Regan.

Hers glistened with warmth and tenderness, and I'd know why later when we were leaving and she drew me into a hug and whispered, "Thank you for loving him the way he deserves to be loved."

Something about her words eased a bit of the guilt I still hung onto from our past.

Coming home to our beautiful house in the woods, it felt almost too quiet after our Sunday dinner with our families. I said as much to Lewis as we snuggled up on the sofa bed we'd borrowed from my parents until our new sofas arrived.

Lewis cuddled me into his side. "Wait until the baby is here. We'll be pleading for silence."

I chuckled, resting my head on his shoulder as he flicked through TV channels.

The last six weeks had been a mixed bag of emotions, but what was new? The police had reviewed CCTV but had no luck identifying the men who had broken into the cottage. We were pretty sure from their height and build it was the same men who broke into the house.

I might still be worried about a possible future burglary, but we were all pretty damn certain Nathan was behind it. Dad had reached out to his contact, and he'd been honest and up-front with me when he said that they'd paid someone on the inside to use force against Nathan. Despite my black belt, I wasn't an advocate for violence. I just wanted to know how to defend myself against it, since it had been perpetrated on me and my mother.

But I felt no remorse that Dad had someone beat up

Nathan as a warning. While that put me in a morally gray category, he was the one person in the world I had no compassion or sympathy for. He'd caused us too much pain.

Though he'd sworn to the "contact" that he had nothing to do with the break-ins, they coincidentally stopped after Nathan's attack. No more men in black, no more watching over our shoulders. Nathan was scum of the earth, and I wished it hadn't been him taking revenge for his parole hearing, but I wasn't surprised by it.

Intimidation was his favorite game.

Evil arsehole.

I shuddered anytime I contemplated the fact we shared DNA and that my blue eyes came from him. "The only good thing he ever gave you," Mum used to say.

Lewis loved my eyes too, but I was manifesting our kid inherited his shade of blue instead of mine.

"I missed Eilidh tonight," I said as we settled on an action movie that I probably wouldn't watch through to the end because I needed to be up early for work.

"She's finished filming in Romania," Lewis shared. I did not know that. "I think she's avoiding us."

"Why?" I sat up, frowning at him.

"I don't know. I'm worried about her."

"Like how you're always worried about her, or do you think there's something to be worried about?"

"I think there's something to be worried about."

"Then I'll call her tomorrow," I promised and cracked, "I'll guilt her into coming home by pulling the 'I'm pregnant with your niece or nephew' card."

"Aye?"

"Look at me already pulling the mum guilt card. How ready am I?"

He chuckled and tugged me back into his side. "Do what you have to do to bring her home."

I nodded, tracing a heart over his heart. "You know who else is avoiding us? Carianne. I've barely heard from her in weeks."

"Talk to her if it's bothering you."

"Hmm. I'm just ... She seemed cool about us last time we chatted, but maybe she's secretly upset about me and you. Or maybe she's no longer interested in a friendship because of the baby."

"If either of those are true, you're better off without her." He kissed my temple.

I melted into him. "I love you."

"I love you too."

"Let's switch off the movie and go have hot, sweaty sex."

His chest rumbled with amusement beneath my cheek. "One day, people will call you the romantic one in our relationship, but today is not that day."

Laughing, I got up, tugging him to his feet. "I promise I'll scream something really romantic when I come."

"I think we might have a different idea about what romantic actually means." He switched off the TV before I dragged him toward the staircase.

"Are you saying 'Lewis, you're making me come so good' isn't romantic?"

His laughter bounced off the walls as I hurried him downstairs. "No, nor is it grammatically correct."

"Ooh, I love it when you talk dirty to me."

I squealed as he suddenly lifted me into his arms, carrying me bridal style into our bedroom. "Never change, Callie Ironside." He lay me gently down on the bed and then braced himself over me, gazing deep into my eyes. "Well, maybe there's one thing I'd change about you."

I grimaced. "Oh?"

Lewis's voice was gruff. "Your name."

What?

I froze, wondering if he meant what I thought he meant.

"I know I gave you shit for not being romantic and, believe me, this wasn't how I planned to do this, but I can't wait any longer. I love you so fucking much, Callie. And I know this is the opposite of taking it slow ... but taking it slow would be a lie. I'm going to love you forever and I don't see any point in not telling you I want forever to start now."

"Lewis?" Blood rushed in my ears as I gaped up at him in abject joy.

He reached across the bed and pulled open his bedside drawer. I gasped at the ring box he pulled out. Sitting back on his heels, he popped it open, revealing a simple, elegant platinum engagement ring with a princess-cut diamond. It was perfect. "Callie Ironside ... will you marry me?"

Never in all the times I'd imagined Lewis Adair proposing did I burst into full-blown sobs. But that's exactly what I did.

"Fuck, fuck." Lewis's panicked voice cut through the painful cries I couldn't seem to control. "I'm sorry. I didn't—"

"Yes!" I sobbed, reaching for him through the blur of tears. "Yes, I'll m-marry y-y-you."

Bundling me into his arms, he rubbed a soothing hand down my back and pressed a hard kiss to my temple. "Why are you crying, then?" he whispered hoarsely.

I needed to get a hold of myself for his sake, so I took deep, shuddering breaths. After a minute, I had calmed, even though salty warm tears seemed to fall with a mind of their own down my cheeks. I pulled back to cup Lewis's face in my hands. "Because for so long I thought this dream was lost. These are tears of relief, Lewis. Of joy. I never wanted to admit, even to myself, how painful those years without you were. Now you're mine forever." I pressed a wet kiss to his lips, and he deepened it. When we broke apart, I leaned my forehead against his. "I have a notebook in my room, from high school. It has Mrs. Callie Adair scribbled all over it." I laughed softly. "I guess I manifested it."

Lewis laughed quietly and pulled back to raise my left hand. His eyes held mine as he slipped the beautiful ring onto my fourth finger. "Do you like it?"

"I love it." I kissed him again, smiling between kisses now. "Mrs. Callie Adair."

Lewis stiffened.

"What?"

He quirked an eyebrow and looked down at his crotch. "I think we just found my new kink."

I cackled with laughter, pressing my palms to his chest to force him onto his back. "Oh, you like the Mrs. thing, do you?"

"Say it again so I can check."

"I'm going to be Mrs. Callie Adair."

Heat flashed in his eyes. "Aye, definitely does it for me."

Without preamble, I straddled him, feeling the evidence of his newfound kink between my legs, and I whipped off my T-shirt and unclipped my bra. Lewis arched into me, caressing my waist and back with possessive tenderness as he focused on the slight swell of my stomach.

"Do you want me naked with nothing but the ring?" I teased.

His gaze flew to my glittering diamond. "I know you're joking, but I'd actually really love that."

I slipped off the bed to wriggle out of my jeans to do just that when I suddenly stopped. "I should really call my mum to let her know we're engaged."

Lewis raised an eyebrow and practically squawked, "Now?"

I pretended to take a step away from him. "I'll be five minutes."

I'd barely turned when I heard him hop off the bed. Then

I was swept up into his arms again before finding myself flat on my back.

Lewis pinned my hands to the bed, his thumb stroking over the engagement ring. "Your mum can wait. Your husband-to-be cannot."

My belly fluttered deliciously. "I think we just found *my* new kink."

"Aye?" Lewis grinned, leaning to brush shivery kisses down my neck and chest. "Do you want your husband to make love to you or fuck you, Mrs. Adair?"

Arousal flooded between my thighs. "Both," I answered breathlessly. "I think it can be both."

"Your wish, my command," he promised.

It was both.

It was very much, mind-blowingly, fucking fantastically both.

THIRTY-SIX
LEWIS

A knock sounded, and I turned to find my dad standing in my office doorway.

"Heard you got the plans submitted to the council for the Tain project?"

"Aye." I swung around in my chair to face him. "The clients are in love with the finalized plans, so let's hope the council doesn't knock it back."

"Unlikely," he assured me. "Not on a plot like that."

"Even with it being visible from the water?"

"Even then. I'll be surprised."

That reassured me since Dad had years of experience submitting plans to the local council. "Do you want to grab some lunch?"

"Aye, I was just coming to ask you that."

Fifteen minutes later, we'd grabbed a table in a restaurant in the middle of the city. "How's Callie?" Dad asked.

"Good." I nodded, scanning the menu. "She feels great, got lots of energy at the moment." I cleared my throat as my words immediately conjured images of how she was expending that energy upon me.

Dad snorted. "No need to say anymore. Second trimester. I remember it well. Good times."

I grimaced. "Dad, no. I don't even want to contemplate that between you and Mum."

"How do you think Mor got here?"

"Aye, aye." I might be a grown man, but my parents' sex life would never be a comfortable discussion. "Anyway, Callie is good. Marveling at Mum's ability to pull an engagement party together so quickly. Even after all these years, she hasn't quite grasped that Mum is Superwoman." Seriously, for as long as I could remember, Mum had always been able to juggle a million different tasks, pulling them off like it was easy.

"Regan enjoys the planning. She's ecstatic for you and Callie. We both are."

"Thanks." I looked up from the menu. "I've been thinking about my birth mum a lot lately."

Dad's gaze flew up and he waited silently for me to continue.

My parents had always made the subject of my birth mother a safe topic, approachable. "I've realized, now that I'm going to be a parent, I've never really asked about her. Francine. I don't remember her. And when Mum—Regan— came into our lives, after a while it just felt right to think of her as Mum."

"The first time you called her Mum she came into the bedroom sobbing with happiness," Dad said fondly. "You know she loves you and Eilidh as if you were her own."

"I know. I've always felt that. And I suppose ... I forgot to ask more about Francine because of it. Eilidh would try to talk to me about her, and I felt like I was betraying Regan, so I didn't want to. And now, I think about if something happened to me, and Callie moved on with someone else and our kid forgot about me ..." Guilt was a sharp ache in my chest. "I feel like shit. I feel like instead of betraying Regan, I betrayed Francine."

Dad's expression tightened but before he could respond, the server came over. We quietly gave our orders, and then once the server left, Dad leaned across the table. "Lewis, we all deal with loss in our own way. It was easier for you to fill the emptiness Francine left in our lives by accepting Regan fully as your mum. I never resented that. I was grateful for it. And it doesn't make you a bad son."

I nodded, releasing a heavy exhale. "You would talk to us about her if we asked ... but I'm a man now, and I want to know what my mother was really like. What your relationship was like. The truth is, I think you love Regan the way I love Callie, and so I can't imagine loving someone else that way. Did you? Love Francine that way?"

My dad shifted in his chair, a frown marring his brow as he contemplated my question. Finally, "I loved your mother. A lot. I wouldn't have married her otherwise. Francine was intelligent and funny and beautiful. Eilidh is her absolute spitting image."

I nodded because I knew that from photographs.

"But our marriage wasn't perfect."

Intrigued, I waited for him to tell me more.

"I ... I don't want this to change how you feel about her memory ... fuck, I don't even know ... I've never ..." Dad sat back in his chair, regret tightening his features. "Never mind."

"Dad ... I want to know who she really was."

He was quiet so long I didn't think he'd answer.

"Your mum cheated on me before Eilidh was born. With the man who tried to kidnap Eilidh from the school gates all those years ago."

Shock ricocheted through me. "Dad ..." My voice came out hoarse. "Is Eilidh ..."

"She's mine." He hurried to assure me. "I had a DNA test

done after Sean McClintock came out of the woodwork. He was grieving and he thought Eilidh was his."

I remembered it. I was just a wee boy, but I remember that man trying to steal Eilidh, how Regan had protected us with her body, refusing to let go of us. They'd told us he was a grieving, sad stranger whose wife and daughter had died, and that he'd mistaken Eilidh for his daughter.

"He was a teacher at your mother's school. I caught them together."

"Dad ... I'm sorry."

He nodded calmly, and I realized that he'd healed from it. Fully. Because of Regan. "I tried to forgive Fran because we had you, and she promised me it was a mistake. Then when she realized she was pregnant with Eilidh, I decided to let it go. To move on. For our family."

I was in awe of him because I wasn't sure I could have done the same.

"So, aye, Lew, I loved Fran. You have her sense of humor, you know."

I smiled. "Really?"

"Really."

"Was it hard to fall in love with Regan?"

"No." Dad expelled a breath. "I won't lie to you. As much as I loved your mother and will always love your mother, I have never loved a woman the way I love Regan. She healed me. And she healed the two people I love more than anything."

"Me and Eilidh," I said gruffly.

"Aye."

"But I could never forget Fran." He reached over and tapped my chest. "Because she's still here in you and Eilidh."

"It sounds like she had a bit of recklessness in her, though."

"Maybe. Aye."

"I worry that's where Eilidh gets it from."

Dad nodded grimly. "I worry too. Your sister throws herself at life, sometimes without thinking of what she's throwing herself at. She's all bravado, you know. Her heart's softer than anyone's, and I worry that industry will change her."

"Callie thinks she'll find her way home."

Concern creased Dad's brows. "Let's hope your fiancée is right."

Our food arrived and as we dug in, I offered, "Thanks for telling me about Fran."

"Anytime."

"I ... I'm not judging her. Just so you know. I don't feel it's my right since I never got to know her."

Dad contemplated me. "You're the best of men, Lewis. I am so proud to be your father. And Fran ... you were her entire world. You should know that."

Emotion clogged my throat and I nodded, unable to speak.

And so we ate in companionable silence while I contemplated everything he'd told me, promising myself that I owed Francine a visit. I hadn't been to her grave in a long time, and I had so much I needed to tell her.

THIRTY-SEVEN
CALLIE

Taylor Swift blared from the wireless speaker Bluetooth'd to my phone as Mum and I worked on the wedding cake she'd been commissioned to make for a wealthy client in Aberdeenshire. Usually, Mum only enlisted my help when the project was challenging. This was a six-tier wedding cake, each tier a different flavor, two types of sponge, and the fondant was to emulate rippling silk fabric. It would then be topped with a cascading arrangement of sugar flowers—peonies, roses, and lilies.

I was working on tier number three, a joconde sponge with Kirsch syrup and chocolate ganache. Basically, a wedding cake version of an opera cake. There was a skill to wrapping the fondant so it looked like draped fabric. Mum had shown me how and I'd practiced on rehearsal cakes before attempting the final thing. Mum was happy with my work, so now I was focused on the sugar flowers.

Although this wasn't my area of expertise per se—and I loved my pastry making—there was something therapeutic about cake decorating.

Mum and I were lost in the zone.

Until Taylor was cut off by my ringtone.

We both winced at how loud it boomed through the speaker, and I hurried over to disconnect it. The screen told me it was a friend from Paris. Stephanie. She was the one who had introduced me to Gabriel.

"Steph!" I answered, happy to hear from her. "How are you?"

"Callie." She pronounced my name like *Ca-Lee*. "I have sad news."

It was only then I heard the sorrow in her voice. "What's happened?"

"It is Gabriel. He's gone, Callie. His body was found in a hotel in Portugal. They are calling it suspicious circumstances. It's even made the news here in Paris. Something about corruption in the police department."

Abject shock and disbelief made me instantly light-headed.

"Callie?"

"I'm here," I choked out. "I ... I ... don't know what to say." The thought of Gabriel, beautiful, charismatic Gabriel, gone ... "How did he die?"

"It was a self-inflicted gunshot wound. But there's a journalist here in Paris who is calling it foul play. He said Gabriel was working with him to expose the corruption at his station. That he'd run away because he was in trouble and that he was killed for what he knows."

Oh my God. I stumbled back, grasping blindly for one of the stools we kept in the kitchen. I felt hands on my shoulders and turned to see my mum gently steadying me, her eyes wide with worry.

My tears slipped free. "Thank you for telling me," I said through them.

Stephanie sniffled. "He was a good person. He cared about you."

I nodded, my tears falling faster as a sob broke on my lips.

"I will let you go, but I will text you the funeral arrangements once I know." She hung up quietly.

"What's going on?" Mum asked in a panic as I lowered the phone.

"Gabriel."

"Your ex?"

I nodded, swiping at my tears. "He's dead."

———

A heavy cloud hung over me as I waited at the house for Lewis to return from work. I knew I'd have to tell him about Gabriel because I couldn't force myself to pretend I wasn't deeply saddened by the news. I might not have been in love with Gabriel, but I'd cared about him, and every time I thought of his special spirit gone from this world, I wanted to cry all over again.

Yet I was worried about Lewis, how he might misinterpret my sadness.

We'd come so far in such a short time. We'd offered each other trust so quickly, and I was proud of us for dealing with our past with such forgiveness and understanding. Still, I knew my relationship with Gabriel was a sore spot for Lewis.

I didn't want anything to ruin what we were building, but I also didn't want dishonesty between us.

When he strode upstairs into the living room that evening, I waited on our borrowed sofa, my hands twisted on my lap as I picked at a hangnail.

Lewis was already chatting about the lunch he'd had with his dad, but I couldn't process anything.

"Callie?"

Suddenly, he was in front of me, lowering his tall body

onto his haunches to take my hands. Worry creased his brow. "Callie?"

A tear slipped down my cheek before I could stop it.

Fear darkened Lewis's eyes. "The baby?"

Guilt flashed through me as I reached for his face, not having realized that would, of course, be his first thought. "No. God, no. The baby is fine. I'm fine."

He covered my hand and lifted it but only to press a kiss to my knuckles. "What's going on?"

Taking a deep breath, I told him about Gabriel, and I couldn't help the tears that freely fell down my cheeks.

Lewis muttered a hoarse curse and sat down beside me to pull me into his arms. "I'm so sorry, mo chridhe."

Surprised, I sniffled. "You're not upset that I'm upset?"

"Of course not." He kissed the side of my head. "Baby, I'd be upset if Roisin died. Of course you're upset. You dated him. He was a part of your life for a while. Plus, the circumstances are awful if that's true."

I sobbed suddenly, clinging to him. "I love you. You can never die, Lewis. Promise me."

He held me closer. "Mo chridhe, I wish I could promise you that, but no one can. I can promise you that I will love you long after I leave my body behind in this world."

That made me cry harder because the thought of him not being here was utterly terrifying. Suddenly, I needed him. I needed him to surround me and overwhelm me and make the rest of this sad world disappear.

I reached for his mouth, pressing a salty kiss to his lips.

Lewis kissed me back but then pulled away. "You're upset."

"I want to forget. Everything but you and me." I cupped his handsome face in my hands. "Make love to me, Lewis. Please."

He searched my face for a few seconds and then decision

made, he slipped his hands under and lifted me with ease as he stood. I looped my arms around his neck as he carried me downstairs, as if I was the most precious thing in the world.

Lewis lowered me to my feet by our bed and slowly, studying my expression, checking in with me, took my shirt and jeans off. He nudged me onto the bed and hooked his fingers into my underwear. My breath caught, excitement rippling through my belly as he slowly pulled them down my legs. He discarded them on the floor and stood gazing at me spread out on the bed. His eyes zeroed in on that gentle swell of my belly. Possessive wonder filled his expression.

He removed his clothes as slowly as he'd removed mine, taking his time, eyes moving over my body. His erection strained toward me, but Lew ignored it as he climbed onto the bed and bent his head to my stomach. My belly trembled against his touch as he planted soft kisses all over it.

"I love you," I whispered, a fresh tear spilling down my cheek.

Lewis looked up, his expression tightening at the sight of my tears. "Callie?"

"Don't stop. Never stop. Always only ever you," I promised.

He swallowed hard and eyes holding mine, he kissed his way down the swell until he reached the apex of my thighs. Then he gently opened my legs. I lost his eyes as he licked my clit.

"Oh my God," I whimpered, my back arching, hips lifting into his kiss.

He licked at me until my clit distended and then he sucked.

"Yes, Lewis, yes." My thighs fell open wider as the tension tightened and coiled. Lewis gripped my hips tight, keeping me right there, as he worshipped my body with his tongue.

I came on a cry of pure bliss, my hips shuddering against

him. I was still throbbing and pulsing as he pressed kisses all down my legs, around my ankles, which were surprisingly sensitive, before making his way back up my body. He stopped at the swell of my stomach and pressed a most tender kiss there.

"Lewis."

My breasts were next on his worship list, and I caressed and touched him as he laved at my nipples, groaning and grinding his hips against mine. My hands slid south, my fingers digging into his perfect, muscular arse, wanting him inside me.

Lewis grunted, lifted his head, but then crushed my mouth beneath his. It was hungry, but savoring. Like he was kissing me for the first time. I moaned and pulled at his hair tie. The silken strands fell free, and I wrapped my hands in his hair, holding his head to me, breathing in his kiss like it was everything I needed to survive.

Lewis slowed the kiss, nipping playfully at my lips, all the while he nudged his cock between my thighs. It was the quietest we'd ever been during sex. But it was perfect. We didn't need words at that moment as he slid slowly inside me, filling me. We continued to kiss as he thrust gently, but as the pleasure grew, it became harder to catch our breaths. Our lips parted, our eyes locked. My fingers bit into his waist, as I panted against his mouth and lifted my hips to meet his gentle thrusts.

"Mo chridhe." He glided in a little faster, a little harder as our orgasms started to build.

"Baby." I clung to him, my hands moving to his arse again so I could feel his thrusts. So thick. So beautiful. So deep. "No one has ever been so deep inside me."

His eyes flared with understanding and he slowed his glides again.

"Lewis?"

"Savoring it," he huffed out. "Savoring every second inside you."

It was torturous and beautiful, and I cupped his face in my hands as our hips moved in sync, not chasing climax this time, but enjoying the journey to it. Never in my life had I felt so connected to another person, and I could see that in Lewis's eyes too.

When my orgasm hit, it was so big, it took me by surprise. But I held Lewis's gaze as my inner muscles tightened around him and my body shuddered beneath his.

"Callie!" he gasped, tensing for a brief second before he groaned long and hard with his release.

He pulsed inside of me as he shivered through his orgasm, clutched in my tight heat as I continued to throb around him in little aftershocks.

"Fuck," Lewis panted, breathless.

I soothed a hand down his back, staring up at him, experiencing the awe I saw reflected back in his eyes.

"How lucky are we?" I whispered softly, grateful more than ever after the sadness of the day to have him in my arms.

Emotion gleamed in Lewis's eyes, and he bent his head to brush a soft kiss over my lips. "So lucky, mo chridhe. The luckiest."

THIRTY-EIGHT
CALLIE

TWO WEEKS LATER

I couldn't sleep.

Tomorrow Lewis and I were taking time off work to travel into Inverness for our gender scan. Knowing the sex of the wee peanut growing in my belly was going to make it even more real. My bump was still more of a swell, but Verity said that was perfectly normal at twenty-one weeks. Not everyone had an obvious bump at this stage and sometimes it took until the end of the second trimester for it to be noticeable.

Lewis had been working long hours on a project with his dad these past few weeks and between that and watching over me like a hawk, I knew he was exhausted emotionally too. I didn't want to wake him as I'd lain in bed, staring at the ceiling, stomach churning with anticipation. So, I quietly slipped out and left a note for him that I'd be at the bakery.

I had a couple of new creations in mind to try out.

There was one that was inspired by the Hungarian Esterházy torte, which was a cake made of layers of buttercream sandwiched between almond meringue. Mine consisted of hazelnut dacquoise and chocolate too. I wanted to recreate them into little miniature desserts topped with chocolate ribbons.

The Gloaming hadn't shut its doors yet, so there was still a hum of noise spilling out from the building into the village as I drove past. Cars were parked out front and a few people still strolled down Castle Street.

I let myself into the bakery and began working on my version of the Esterházy. First, I wrote down everything swirling in my head into a coherent list and drew a picture of the dessert. Then I started finessing the idea on paper. Of course, I wouldn't know for certain if the recipe worked until I baked it, but I had a good palate, so I had an idea of what would and would not work.

I was barely there twenty minutes when I heard the sound of rattling.

I jolted, pulse leaping as I turned and stared at the back door to the bakery. I locked it behind me, hadn't I? The blinds were drawn on the window that overlooked the car park, but a shadow flickered behind it.

"Lewis?" I called.

There was silence.

And then the door rattled more fiercely.

My stomach dropped.

I didn't even make it to my purse for my phone when the back door suddenly flew open and two strange men strode inside, closing it calmly behind them.

The men from the break-ins.

Had Nathan sent them?

Chest heaving, my eyes flew to my handbag. It was too far away.

There would be no option but to fight, if it came to it. I got into a defensive stance, holding my arms up.

One of the men raised an eyebrow.

The other sighed heavily. "No fight." He had an accent. "Où est-elle?"

He was French? "What?" I gestured with my fist. "This is private property. Get out."

"Où est-elle?" he insisted, menace flashing in his eyes.

"Get. Out," I repeated, chest heaving.

The other man gave a quick swipe of his head and pulled out a switchblade. "Où est-elle?" he repeated. "Easy way? Or hard way?"

Fear shuddered through me as I glanced down at my belly. I had more than me to protect now.

I threw myself across the room at the magnetic strip on the wall where we kept a large kitchen knife and turned in time to block the swipe of his blade. His companion started ransacking the bakery shelves as I fought off his clumsy swipes. I nicked him with my knife, and he dropped his switchblade, surprise flaring in his eyes as I abandoned the knife behind me and began punching out with force. Everything I'd been taught for the last fifteen years coalesced into this moment. My breathing centered as I used body hook punches to attack and then defend his blows, forcing him toward the door.

He had strength, but I had speed and skill he wasn't prepared for. When he kicked up with his leg, clipping my hip way too close to my belly, fury flooded through me. It fired me up, and I spun around on my left foot, launching into him with a jump-back kick that sent him flying into the rear entrance door and slumping to the ground, stunned.

I felt his friend come up behind me. I sidestepped the blow he threw to the back of my head, panting and grunting as I fought *him* off now. He was sprier, quicker, as he corralled me toward the front store. I kicked out, a front kick into his solar plexus, knocking the breath out of him. But suddenly, his companion was on his feet again, and I backed around the counter into the bakery store, my hands up, gauging how to fight them both off in such a tight space.

The sprier one jumped forward, rage contorting his features. I ducked his punch, swerving around the blow, only to grab his hair as I came up. Screaming with fury, I smashed his head into the counter, glass breaking beneath the strength of my adrenaline-fueled dunk.

"Fucking bitch!" The bigger guy rushed forward as I reversed, but he tripped over his downed companion and as he tried to stabilize himself, I twisted with my right side, throwing out a high side kick, snapping my knee back and then out. I felt the power of the blow to his head reverberate down my shin. It didn't knock him out, but it stunned him long enough for me to rush to the front entrance. My hands shook as I hurried to unlock the door, throwing it open, cool summer night air drawing me out.

"Help!" I screamed as soon as I ran onto the street.

However, Castle Street was quiet, not a soul in sight.

Except for the Gloaming. There was still light at the Gloaming. Still a few cars. Relief crashed over me as I moved to run toward it.

"Take another step, and you die."

Glancing over my shoulder, I found the bigger of the men (the one not smashed into my bakery counter) standing on the pavement, a gun in his hand.

"I did not want it to come to this."

In an instant, I was a child again and Nathan was waving a gun in my face.

Fear caused my knees to tremble, and I couldn't stop shaking as I began backing out onto the road. "P-please." I raised my hands defensively. "I don't know what you want."

"It. Where is it?" he asked in guttural French, walking onto the road to keep the gun pointed in my face.

Just out in the open. Where anyone could see. His recklessness terrified me even more than the gun.

Sweat dripped down his forehead. "Where is it?"

"Nathan didn't send you, did he?" I whispered in horrified realization.

The man frowned in confusion. "Where is it?" he repeated.

"I don't know what 'it' is," I replied with surprising calm. "Tell me what 'it' is."

"No. No games." He waved his gun. "Or I shoot you."

Tears burned in my eyes. "Please. Please. I'm pregnant."

"Don't care, bitch. You have five seconds."

"You're really going to shoot me in the middle of the street? There are cameras on this street."

"My employer will take care of that. Five. Four—"

Oh my God. Terror threatened to buckle my knees now, and I tried to think, think, think through it. Lewis.

Lewis.

I tried not to sob at the thought of what this would do to him.

"Two—"

A loud roar suddenly caught our attention, both of our heads whipping left. I winced against the glare of car headlights, heart jumping into my throat as those lights sped toward me, the sound of the tires squealing, the engine growls filling my ears.

Those lights swerved past me and straight into the Frenchman.

The impact threw him into the air as brakes shrieked on tarmac and the car skidded to a stop. My attacker crashed into the road a good thirty yards from us with a gross-sounding thud.

He didn't get back up.

The car door flew open, and a stilettoed foot appeared, followed by an ashen-faced Carianne.

I gaped at her as she wobbled out toward me on shaking legs. Her eyes were wide as they met mine. "Did I just bloody kill a man?"

My eyes flew to where he was still lifeless. "Well, let's hope so."

"I'm going to be sick." Carianne bent over and vomited onto the road.

I hurried to her, pulling her hair away from her face as my neighbors began poking their heads out of their doors and windows.

"I've called the police!" someone shouted.

"Are you two okay?" someone else asked.

I couldn't stop shaking, but I was alive.

Carianne stood up, wiping her mouth. "What ... I just saw ... I was coming out of the pub." She gestured toward the Gloaming, clearly in shock. "And he had a gun pointed in your face ... so ... I didn't know what else to do."

I grasped her cheeks in my hands. "Carianne, you saved my life and my baby's life."

"Did I really?" She wrapped her hands around my wrists, still wide-eyed, so much so I was genuinely concerned she was going into shock. "Well, that's quite something, isn't it."

I laughed tearfully. "Aye, my friend. That's quite something."

We embraced hard while our neighbors hurried over to us. I was vaguely aware of explaining the attack and informing them of the man still inside the bakery. So intent on Carianne, however, watching her for signs of shock ... I hadn't realized I was going through it myself.

I didn't even remember passing out.

THIRTY-NINE
LEWIS

Waking up to an empty bed and my phone ringing only to hear Carianne on the other end, hysterical and crying, telling me Callie had been rushed to the hospital, was the worst moment of my life.

As I'd hurried into clothes, she'd explained two men had invaded the bakery. Callie had fought them off. One had a gun. Carianne had knocked him down with her car, which didn't make sense at all unless the fight moved from the bakery to outside. Callie had passed out while they were waiting for the police and ambulance.

I called Callie's parents and my own on my way to the hospital, and Sloane, Walker, and I arrived at the same time.

"Where is she?" Sloane was frantic as we all rushed into the building.

"I don't know yet." We hurried over to the reception and our expressions must have been something else because the nurse behind the desk gawked at us for a second before she straightened her shoulders.

A minute or so later (though it felt like fifty), we were on our way to the maternity and neonatal ward, which had me in even more of a fucking panic. What if something had happened to the baby?

It was at that minute I realized how much I wanted our child. The thought had been a distant reality, a responsibility that scared the shit out of me, but one I'd face. Somewhere along the way, I'd started to imagine our baby in the real world. In my arms. Someone to love and protect as much as I loved and wanted to protect Callie. A wee human made up of me and her.

"It'll be okay." Sloane squeezed my arm as we made our way to the ward.

I couldn't speak.

We took a lift to the correct floor and when the doors opened onto a reception area, a familiar blond head popped up from a waiting room chair.

Carianne.

She rushed over to us as we stepped off the lift. "Oh, thank God."

"Where is she?" I asked quietly, afraid if I spoke any louder, I'd break down.

"She came to before the ambulance arrived, but they wanted to check her and the baby over." Carianne wrung her hands. Her eyes were wide, her cheeks wan. "They're checking her now."

"Have you been checked over?" Sloane cupped Carianne's cheek. "You look pale."

Carianne nodded. "I've been looked over. I'm still so jittery. The police had a lot of questions and they said they'll be back." Her lip trembled. "Do you think I'll go to jail?"

"Carianne."

She turned to Walker.

"Tell us everything you know."

At Walker's calm command, she explained what Callie had told her when she was conscious in the ambulance—two men had broken into the bakery, looking for something. They hadn't expected Callie's defense skills, and she fought them off.

"The police found one of them smashed into your bakery counter," Carianne told Sloane. "Callie just smashed his head right in there. Really bad arse of her. They took him away in an ambulance too. I don't know if he's alive."

Pride and rage mingled. That Callie had even been in that position ...

"Anyway, she got out and ran into the street. I was coming out of the Gloaming. I broke up with my single dad and was feeling sorry for myself, so I'd wasted the whole night looking for a hookup." She blanched. "Getting off track. Anyway, I glanced down the street and I thought I was seeing things because there was Callie backing onto the road with her hands up in the air. So, I was about to go to her when I saw this huge bloke with a gun pointed in her face. It was like a scene from a movie. Well, I didn't think." Tears blurred in her eyes. "I just hopped into my car and drove the bloody thing at him. What if I killed him?"

"Carianne." Walker bent his head to meet her eyes. "You saved my daughter's life. There is no way I'm letting anyone punish you for that."

"Really?" Her tears spilled over.

"Really."

"I second that." Sloane slid her arm around Carianne's shoulders. "Thank you so much."

"You're welcome." She sniffled and then looked at me.

I nodded in gratitude. "Anything you ever need, it's yours."

Carianne shook her head. "Callie's my friend, Lewis. I've always kind of hero-worshipped her, you know. I'd never let anyone hurt her if it was in my power to stop it."

"Thank you." I gave her a comforting pat on the arm

before striding toward the reception area where a nurse worked at a computer. "Hi, I'm looking for my fiancée, Callie Ironside."

She held up a finger before continuing to type.

I tried not to get agitated.

And just when I was on the cusp of barking at her, the nurse finally stopped typing and looked at me. "Can I help?"

Grinding my teeth, I took a second before I repeated my words.

She nodded and typed at her computer. "She's with the doctor now. I'll let you know when you can see her."

"Is she okay?"

Her expression softened. "I can't say."

Fuck.

I reluctantly returned to the waiting area and slumped down into a chair next to Walker, repeating what the nurse said.

A little while later a woman in a blue midwife's smock appeared. "Callie Ironside's family?"

We all popped up out of our chairs like we were in a game of Whac-A-Mole.

The midwife approached us. "Callie is asking for Lewis?"

"That's me." I was relieved to hear she was still conscious.

"This way."

I looked at Sloane. She gave me a strained smile. "Tell her I'm here."

I nodded, squeezing her hand before following the midwife out of reception and through the ward. She led us into a private room and the sight of Callie made my legs fucking tremble.

She was on a bed with her shirt pulled up, while a doctor stood at her side with an ultrasound machine.

"Callie." I crossed the room, reaching for her. I kissed her before she could say anything. She kissed me back and when I finally let her go, she gave me a tired smile.

"I'm okay. The baby is okay."

Tears clogged my throat. "Really?"

"Really." She caressed my face. "I'm sorry for scaring you."

I shook my head, clasping her hand to my cheek. "Not your fault. Your parents are here."

Callie nodded. "Good."

"Should we call them in?"

"Well." Callie looked at the doctor. "I wanted you here because Dr. Andrews checked me over, and all is well, but she kindly offered to share the gender of the baby. And I didn't want to do it without you."

Not having expected that, I curled her hand in both of mine, my gaze going from her belly to the ultrasound screen. "Oh. Aye. That would be good."

Callie smiled, and I marveled at her strength. That after everything she'd gone through tonight, she could still smile.

"You're sure you're okay?" I asked.

Dr. Andrews spoke, "Your fiancée is a fighter. Quite literally. I assume because of her extensive martial arts training, her body was able to absorb the shock of the physicality of the fight without endangering the baby."

"But she passed out."

"From dehydration." She nodded to something I hadn't noticed. A needle in Callie's other hand, hooked up to a bag of fluids.

Callie grimaced sheepishly. "I was so excited about finding out the gender that I barely ate or drank. I left you a note in case you woke up because I couldn't sleep and thought I'd do some work at the bakery. Sorry."

I kissed her free hand. "It's okay. You're okay, that's all that matters. We need to make sure you're drinking enough from now on, though."

"Ready then?" Dr. Andrews asked.

My pulse raced as we shared a look and then nodded at the doctor.

Callie jumped a bit at the coldness of the gel, and I felt her fingers bite into me as the doctor passed the probe over her stomach. The baby's heartbeat immediately sounded, a calm, whooshing noise that made me melt against the bed in relief.

"Lucky for us, Baby is in the perfect position ..." Dr. Andrews studied the screen for a second and then she turned to us with a smile. "And Baby is a girl."

Callie turned to me with a gasp of delight and then promptly burst into tears. I knew her well enough to know they were happy tears. I kissed them from her cheeks, murmuring my love, my chest so full of emotion it was painful. In the best way.

"Happy, mo chridhe?" I whispered against her lips as she pressed her forehead to mine.

"I didn't think I'd end this night saying so, but aye." She sobbed through the words. "I'm so happy." She curled her hand around my nape. "Are you happy?"

"My two best girls are safe and happy so I'm happy."

She lifted her head to look into my eyes. "Your two best girls. We're having a girl."

"We are."

"Can we get Mum in?" Tears still dripped down her cheeks. "I want to tell Mum."

"I'll go get her." I kissed her lips again, shot the doctor a grateful look, and hurried from the room to fetch Sloane.

I was going to be a father. I was going to have a daughter. That thought went around and around in my head, obliterating all the fear and concern about the attack and what it meant.

For the next ten minutes as Callie shared the news with her parents and Carianne, we let ourselves forget.

However, I watched Callie like a hawk and eventually, her expression fell. "I ... I think I know who those men are. I think I know what they're looking for."

It was her dad who gruffly asked her to explain.

"Gabriel ... my ex ... they're saying his death was suspicious in the French news. That he was working undercover to expose corruption in his police precinct."

"Why didn't you tell me that?" Walker asked, clearly irritated she'd kept such alarming information to herself.

"I honestly didn't think it mattered. I was wrong. Gabriel gave me a necklace when he visited. As a parting gift. Said it was a family heirloom."

"You're thinking it's not?"

She shook her head. "I'm thinking it's unusually shaped and there might be something inside it. They didn't find it at the cottage or our house because it's at yours. In my old bedroom."

"And no one can get past your dad's security system." Sloane shot Walker a grateful but slightly horrified look. "Do you think they tried?"

Walker was already pulling out his phone. "I'm sending a team to the house now. Where did you put the necklace, Callie?"

"It's in a Converse shoebox under my bed."

I retook her hand. "What are you thinking is in there?"

My smart fiancée contemplated this. "It's shaped like a USB stick."

"A flash drive?" her mum asked.

Callie nodded. "I never would've thought anything of it ... but the men kept asking *Where is it?* And they were French. In the ambulance on the way here, I thought of Gabriel. He never once introduced me to his work colleagues. I think he might have left evidence where he thought it was safe. Where they wouldn't think to look."

"But they *did* know about you ...," I trailed off, fury toward Gabriel brewing. "He put you in danger, Callie."

"We don't know that for sure yet." Sloane soothed a hand over my back.

"I don't think he would have meant to." Callie gave me a pleading look. "He wouldn't have left it with me if he thought the wrong people would come looking for it."

"Team is going in," Walker announced after ending his call. "Good thing Harry is with Regan and Thane."

"Shit." I shoved my hand into my pocket for my phone. "I better call them to let them know you're okay."

"No signal in here."

I frowned at Walker. "Then how come you just made a call?"

"I can get past signal blockers."

"Of course you can. Fancy calling my parents for me?"

"On it."

I looked at Callie only to find her sharing an amused chuckle with her mum. Despite my fears that Callie might be correct about Gabriel, I let some of the tension drain out of me. My fiancée and baby girl were safe. Not only that, but I was tying my life to a woman whose strength blew me away. There would never not be a time I didn't worry about her. I loved her too much not to. Yet it did reassure me somewhat to know how strong and brave she was.

She caught me staring. "What's that look for?"

"Just thinking ... what a badass my fiancée is."

Callie grinned. "I am kind of a badass, aren't I?" Her eyes flew to Sloane. "I get it from Mum."

Sloane chuckled and then put her arm around a wearied Carianne. "This one is a badass too."

Carianne gave an exhausted smile. "Didn't know I had it in me."

"Thank goodness you did, my friend." Callie's expression was tender and grateful. "I'll never forget it, Carianne."

"None of us will." Sloane pressed a motherly kiss to her temple.

A knock sounded at the door and the midwife appeared ... followed by a man and a woman, both wearing suits. "Callie, two detective constables are here to interview you about tonight's events. Are you able or shall they come back later?"

My stomach churned as I rounded the bed to stand by Callie's side.

She reached for me, threading her fingers through mine. "I can answer their questions, but only if my family stays."

And so we did, and I tried not to lose my mind again as I listened to Callie describe her ordeal. They asked Carianne questions, too, and when they were done, the female DC, DC Bridges announced, "We've identified the men. They're known by Interpol as expensive thugs for hire. If you find evidence to what you're suggesting, you'll need to turn it over. Especially as one of the men, Luc Barbier, the man Ms. West hit with her car, died thirty minutes ago from significant head trauma."

Carianne let out a whimper, and Sloane hugged her into her side.

"We're still reviewing all evidence," DC Bridges stated tonelessly. "So we're making no arrests tonight, but please don't leave the country, Ms. West, while the investigation is ongoing."

"Oh my God."

"We'll get any evidence to you as soon as possible." Walker stared the police officers down. "There's no one here guilty of anything but self-defense."

"That's what we'll determine," DC Bridges replied, impressively not intimidated by Walker. "We'll be in touch."

She held out her card. "Call us if you think of anything that might be helpful in the case."

Walker took the card with a grunt of disapproval. They'd frightened Carianne after she'd saved Callie's life. I wished I had the words to reassure Callie's friend that nothing would ever happen to her now if me or Walker had anything to say about it.

At Callie's tense expression, I looked her deep in the eyes so she could see that silent promise.

Her shoulders relaxed as she squeezed my hand in gratitude. "I love you," she mouthed.

"I love you, too."

EPILOGUE
CALLIE

TWO MONTHS LATER

"I'm surprised your savior isn't here."

I glanced at Eilidh as she sipped at a glass of champagne. A bubble of envy burst on my tongue along with the sparkling juice I'd sipped. I wasn't a big drinker, so I didn't mind the no-alcohol part of the pregnancy journey, but I did love a wee glass of champagne. "Savior?"

"Carianne." Eilidh sighed, tucking her dark hair behind her ear. She'd straightened her beautiful curls, so her hair fell in a sleek curtain around her face. "I can admit when I'm wrong about someone ... but I would've thought she'd be here."

Here was at my parents' bungalow where the living room was decorated for my baby shower. It clashed horrendously with the Christmas decorations, but that just made me laugh. The room was filled—Mum, Aunt Allegra, Aunt Aria, Sarah, the Adair women, including all their daughters, and Flora,

Morag, and a few other villagers Mum and I were friendly with. Carianne was the only friend missing from the celebrations. But I wasn't mad about it. In fact, I was really happy for her.

"One of the detective constables on our case ... Carianne's dating him."

"What?" Eilidh guffawed. "Isn't that, like, illegal?"

"They waited until after the charges against her were dismissed." It hadn't taken long. Dad had indeed recovered a USB stick from inside the necklace Gabriel gave me. I was quite proud of myself for sleuthing that one out. Fyfe had looked over its contents and there was a wealth of evidence on it against Gabriel's old precinct and the top brass in the police there. Bribery, racism, sexual assault, harassment, blackmail ... The list was endless. No wonder Gabriel had been so despondent and distant those last few months of our relationship.

Lewis went with me to Paris for Gabriel's funeral, and I learned more about Gabriel in that one day than in our entire relationship. His sister was there, a sister I didn't even know he had, though she'd known about me. It turned out that Gabriel's mother was killed in a home invasion and that was what had inspired him to go into policing. He wanted to help people, only to discover the people he was working for were abusing their power.

We now knew he and a colleague had gone to a journalist at a Parisian newspaper. His colleague was killed, and Gabriel had fled Paris. He'd left the evidence he'd stolen with me and told the journalist where he could find it. They'd tapped the journalist's phone, however, leading them to me.

At first, the *major de police* and the *brigadier-chef de police* responsible for Gabriel's unit and all the corruption didn't want to cause an international scene, so that's why they were careful with the break-ins. That's why they hadn't come directly for me at first. But as the journalist gathered more evidence against them, especially with Gabriel's death making national news, they'd gotten desperate—and that's when they'd sent those men after me.

It and the USB were the final death knell for them.

The men in question were awaiting trial. Paris was in an uproar about corruption within their police ranks. And Carianne and I had been cleared of any charges. While the man I'd slammed into the glass counter survived, I faced assault charges. But once the Highlands police reviewed all the CCTV footage, plus the evidence on the USB, they dropped the charges against me and Carianne.

And miraculously, Carianne had found love amidst it all.

"They're in Mexico for the holidays," I continued. "All loved up."

"Good for her."

I frowned, studying Eilidh. There were dark circles under her eyes but more worryingly, she'd lost that sparkle in them. "What's wrong, Eils?"

"Nothing." She forced a smile and then placed a hand on my bump. "My wee niece is growing in there, so I'm nothing but happy."

"I don't believe you."

Eilidh glanced at the others to make sure they weren't listening. They weren't. The living room was a cacophony of multiple conversations going on at once, while Halsey played in the background. My soon-to-be sister-in-law gave me a sharkish grin. "What do you want to hear, Callie? That I'm wildly fucking unhappy when I should be the happiest girl in the world?"

My stomach dropped. "Eilidh—"

"I'm kidding." She gulped down the rest of her champagne and wiped her mouth. "I'm going to be an aunt, two of my favorite people are getting married next year, I have five million followers on Instagram, a quarter of whom just come there to hate me because they think my uncles got me where I am, a quarter whom come to love on me, a quarter of them come to sexually harass me, and a quarter of them because they think I'm really the character I played on the show. I have offers for work coming out of my ears when most of my friends can't get an audition, so I am grateful, and I am happy. My life is what dreams are made of. Where is the champagne?" Eilidh marched into the kitchen, in search of more alcohol.

When I turned back from watching her, I met Aunt Allegra's gaze. She came over. "Everything okay with Eilidh?"

"Do you think she's drinking a bit too much?" I worried my lip.

"Is there a reason she would be?"

"I think she's miserable." I shrugged sadly. "And too proud to let anyone help."

"Maybe I can try." Allegra gave my shoulder a squeeze. "Go enjoy your party."

I tried, but the nagging worry over Eilidh wouldn't leave me.

I said as much when Lewis came to pick me up. At twenty-nine weeks pregnant, I still had a pretty neat bump, but there was a noticeable difference in the size of the bump from two weeks ago. The tight, full feeling in my stomach was weird, but the whooping sensation I felt anytime our baby girl moved was the strangest, most wonderful thing. When she kicked, I'd grab anybody in the vicinity to feel it, too, like no one else had ever experienced pregnancy before. Thankfully, everyone so far had been happy to indulge me.

Lewis had gotten more careful with me the bigger my bump grew.

Even as I explained my worries about Eilidh, I could see it took him a second to process it because he was making sure I was safe and comfortable in the car, the back of which was overflowing with gifts. We'd have to make a second trip to collect the rest because everyone had spoiled us.

As he started the engine, Lewis asked, "What makes you think Eilidh's unhappy?"

"She literally said 'I'm wildly fucking unhappy.'"

Her brother shot me an alarmed look.

"Then she went 'Just kidding' before downing her third glass of champagne."

Lewis sighed heavily. "I'll talk to Mum and Dad. Did it put a damper on your baby shower?"

I shrugged. "I'm always going to care more about Eilidh than a party."

"Which is why I love you." He reached over to smooth a hand over my knee. "Eilidh will be okay. I'll make sure of it."

At that, I relaxed. Because I knew Lewis meant it. We chatted about the party, the gifts, and what the guys had been up to at their version of a baby shower. Lewis got a bit evasive on that, and I pestered him for information.

"Will you stop?" He laughed as we pulled up to our house in the woods.

"You're not telling me what you got up to with the guys and it's weird," I huffed as I got out of the car before he could help me. Lewis rounded the bonnet, anyway, and I waved him off. "Not an invalid, sweetheart."

He grumbled under his breath but took my hand. "Fine. I'll show you what we were up to."

Instead of going upstairs, he led me to the downstairs bedroom we'd decided would be the nursery. We had grand plans to decorate it in the next few weeks.

My fiancé grinned over his shoulder at me before opening the nursery door.

I released his hand but only to cover my gasp of shock. Delighted surprise thrummed through me as I stepped into the now beautiful space.

Like the primary suite, this room had a floor-to-ceiling window so you could see the moat that surrounded the house. The low December sun gleamed on the water, bouncing its reflection off the opposite wall of the bedroom, a wall now papered in a mural that covered all four walls. Calm greens and teals painted a misty watercolor scene of a forest. Pops of purples and pinks drew my eye to the fairies and their little fairy wings dancing among the scenery. It was a fairy glen.

Against the main wall was the cot I'd told Lewis I liked best but thought was too expensive. On the other, a changing table, and in the corner, a beautiful rocking chair and stool, next to a matching chest of drawers and a wardrobe for all the baby clothes people had already gifted us. Lights shaped like stars had been strung along the top middle of two walls.

And a custom pink neon sign on the main wall above the cot spelled out the name *Harley*.

"You did all this in a day?" I whispered in disbelief.

Lewis nodded, wrapping his arms around me from behind, his hands cradling my bump as his chin rested on my shoulder. "Dad, Walker, Harry, Fyfe, and Uncle Arran helped. Do you like it?"

Tears of happiness blurred my vision. "Harley Adair is already the luckiest girl in the world with a dad like you to spoil her."

"And a badass mum like you to protect her." He kissed my cheek.

I leaned back into him, savoring the feel of his hard strength at my back. "Sometimes I'm so afraid, because I'm so happy."

"I understand." Lewis's voice was gruff as we both stared around the nursery. "You have so much to lose when you have everything."

"We do have everything, don't we?"

"Aye, we do."

"But ..." I turned my head to look up at him. "It hasn't been an easy road, Lewis. For either of us. We both had a shitty start. And we lost each other for a while. But ... maybe we're each other's reward."

"And Harley is the bonus?"

I grinned, nodding, as I turned back to stare in awe at the space Lewis had created with our family. "This is everything I ever dreamed of having back when we were kids."

"I know." His hold on me tightened. "I'm sorry I took a bit too long to give it to you."

I shook my head, still smiling. "I'm not. It means more now because of it."

"Aye?"

"Aye."

"Do you know how much I love you, Callie Ironside soon-to-be Adair?"

I smoothed my hands over his. "As much as I love you."

"Always only ever you." His voice was a gruff whisper in my ear before he brushed a kiss across my cheek.

I leaned into that kiss and whispered back a truth that had existed inside me since we met at ten years old. "Always only ever you."

Printed in the USA
CPSIA information can be obtained
at www.ICGtesting.com
CBHW011547110724
11466CB00006B/8